The Adventures of
Thérèse Arnaud
of the French Secret Service

also translated and introduced by Nina Cooper:

Emile Gaboriau: *Monsieur Lecoq*
Antonin Reschal: *The Adventures of Miss Boston, The First Female Detective*

The Adventures of
Thérèse Arnaud
of the French Secret Service

by
Pierre Yrondy

Translated and introduced by
Nina Cooper

A Black Coat Press Book

Edited by
Paul WESSELS

With the generous contribution of
Daniel AULIAC

ISBN 978-1-61227-181-1. First Printing. June 2013. Published by Black Coat Press, an imprint of Hollywood Comics.com, LLC, P.O. Box 17270, Encino, CA 91416. All rights reserved. Except for review purposes, no part of this book may be reproduced or transmitted in any form or by any means, electronic or mechanical, including photocopying, recording, or by any information storage and retrieval system, without permission in writing from the publisher. The stories and characters depicted in this novel are entirely fictional. Printed in the United States of America.

TABLE OF CONTENTS

LES AVENTURES DE
THÉRÈSE ARNAUD
ESPIONNE FRANÇAISE

N° 2

par Pierre YRONDY

Un drame dans le métro

Editions Baudinière

LES AVENTURES DE
THÉRÈSE ARNAUD
ESPIONNE FRANÇAISE

Introduction

Almost nothing is known about Pierre Yrondy. What is known and verifiable is that his major work was published in the mid-1930s. His two major creations were fascicules tracing the adventures of his regional hero, Marius Pégomas, and those of his female Secret Service agent, Thérèse Arnaud, both of which appeared in the mid- and late 1930s through the 1940s. An entry in the Italian *Center for Studies on Popular Culture*[1] website notes that Yrondy was active as a writer as early as 1924 and was still known to be alive in 1953.

Although no valid biographic data can be found, available information about his publications indicates he was an editor, publisher, novelist, dramatist and social activist. He edited and published a Paris journal, *Le Mont-Parnasse*, disseminating his political views via its pages.[2] The British National Archives conserves two letters to George Orwell from Yrondy as an editor.[3] The first of his two principal publications of social activism and criticism concerned the notorious political trial in the United States of two Italian emigrants initially accused of robbery, but later accused of anarchy and plotting against the American government. The trial lasted some seven years and was clearly politically motivated. Pierre Yrondy published *Le Martyre de Sacco et Vanzetti* (1927) using documentation he received from the trial. His second publication of social activism concerned the case of six French soldiers who were accused of desertion and shot during WWI as an example to other would-be deserters. He published *Les Fusillés de Vingré* (1924), a volume of letters from their wives and relatives revealing clearly that all six were innocent. Both these works were later

---

[1] CESPOC: Centro Studi sulla Popular Culture (http://www.popularculture.it/)
[2] The Bibliothèque Nationale of France holds all fascicules of *Les Aventures de Thérèse Arnaud, Espionne Francaise*. World Cat gives two alternate spellings for his surname: Pierre Irondi and Pierre Ironsi.
[3] http://www.nationalarchives.gov.uk/a2a/records.aspx?cat=103-orwell&cid=8-2#8-2

turned into dramas.[4]

Yrondy was convinced that modern warfare after WWI would not be waged with manpower on the ground, but with chemical weapons, bacilli, and gas. In the preface to his very contemporary *From Cocaine...To Gas!!!* (1934), he said, "The most important battles will be the work of espionage agents. They will be—and already are—charged with sowing death in the great centers and thus exterminating populations."

Although some are still available and still read in French, Yrondy's fascicules did not make it into English translation. He owes his classification as a regional writer to his male character, Marius Pégomas, the detective of Marseilles. Yrondy is, in fact, credited by some with being the creator of this genre.[5] His female character, Thérèse Arnaud, is one of the few long standing female characters to be the subject of popular French literature. There are 65 fascicules in all, published in two series, although some fascicules from the first series were re-published in the second series, making the total of original fascicules somewhat fewer than 65. The fascicules in this translation (1934-1936), except for "Thérèse Arnaud vs Mata Hari," were in both series, but given different numbers when published in the second.[6] Louis Claudel illustrated all of the fascicules.

Although Thérèse is a Secret Service agent and not a sleuth, she uses some of the techniques of the classical detective. She very much resembles the earlier French female detectives, Miss Boston and Miss Ethel King,[7] in that she is a modern woman, independent, intelligent, sure of herself and of her calling. She differs from them, however, in that she deploys and controls several sub-agents as assistants. Whereas Miss Boston worked occasionally with her friend and colleague, Chief Inspector Sokes of the New York Police Bureau, and Ethel King has only a housekeeper and an adolescent boy as assistants, Thérèse Arnaud has experienced agents, Friquet, Malabar, Languille, Marcel, and Loulou, who work for her. Even though they call her *the Boss* and report to her, some of

---

[4] The Sacco and Vanzetti trial was dramatized in five acts and seven tableaux written from documents furnished by "La Ligue des droits de l'homme," 1927-1929.

[5] "It is necessary to go back before the First World War to discover the pioneers of regional popular literature: Pierre Yrondy and Jean Toussaint Samat" (http://flicorse.kazeo.com/polar/du-neo-polar-au-roman-noir-regionaliste,a 558896.html)

[6] http://www.histoire-du-polar.com/editeurs/la-baudiniere-22741.html

[7] *The Adventures of Miss Boston* is available from Black Coat Press, ISBN 9781612271132. *The Adventures of Ethel King* will be published in 2014.

the fascicules begin either with one of her staff or with the Police[8] already in the middle of an investigation.

As a member of the Deuxième Bureau of the French Secret Service,[9] Thérèse Arnaud is known as Agent C.25 and as Mademoiselle Janine Félerat in Parisian high society. As C.25, she has almost unlimited authority and power. She reports to the head of the Deuxième Bureau, Captain Ladoux. Her agents, with various pseudonyms, have specific talents. The strong man, the muscle, is Malabar, a name meaning "the beefy fellow," called here, *the Colossus.* Firmin Friquet, also known as *Titi,* is the Paris urchin, the street-wise boy, and is also called, the Paris kid, handsome and always ready with a fast quip and an ironic laugh. He is, among other things, a talented make-up artist. Languille is called the Acrobat, and is used as a kind of second-story man, able to open almost any safe. Marcel, the Chemist, is in charge of specialized needs, such as acquiring certain chemicals, inventing new techniques for secret communication. He is also in charge of photographing and decoding enemy messages. A fourth agent, Loulou, is used when extra muscle is needed. With the help of these agents, Thérèse Arnaud, as Agent C.25, confronts the head of the German network of spies in Paris, Karl Himmelfeld, and in later fascicules a super-agent named Mademoiselle Doktor, head of all German agents in France. The other agent C.25 must face periodically for some time is the renowned dancer Mata Hari, beloved of Parisian government officials and Parisian society. The eight fascicules here trace Thérèse Arnaud's battle against Karl Himmelfeld, Mademoiselle Doktor, and Mata Hari.

As Agent C.25, Thérèse Arnaud works primarily from her home, where her house has an office, a chemical laboratory, a sliding bookshelf wall which hides a secret room and a fortified holding cell for interrogation of prisoners prior to handing them over to the civil or military authorities. When chasing enemy agents with her assistants, she occasionally uses a revolver, rides a motorcycle hundreds of miles, and drives a powerful, expensive, specially equipped touring car at speeds sufficient to destroy the engine. She also goes alone into spy hideouts as well as behind enemy lines. As a "New Woman" she smokes, swears and loses her temper. As C.25, she is pitiless toward German spies and the French who betray their country, even if she understands their motives for betrayal. The only sympathy she ever shows is toward Mata Hari, a rather dubious sympathy, not motivated, perhaps, by pity but by ego.

---

[8] For the sake of English readers, the specifically French form of Police in Thérèse Arnaud's day, the "Sûreté," has been replaced with the historically-neutral "Police." (Ed.)

[9] External Military French Intelligence Agency (1871-1940). Instead of translating this as "Second Bureau," *Deuxième Bureau* is retained as a superior nomenclature for this spooky division of the French Secret Service Thérèse Arnaud is a part of. (Ed.)

The first series of fascicules, dealing with events happening in 1917, was published in 1934-1936, on the eve of WWII. The second series was published in 1946 after the war. Yrondy frequently places C.25 in a physical world more resembling 1934 than 1917, and his style has more in common with the mid and late 20th century than with popular literature published from the 1860s to the next 90 or so years. Sexual activities are, if not explicit, at least alluded to in a way that no misunderstanding is possible. The fascicules are staccato. Incomplete sentences, duplicate adjectives, single strong verbs, exclamation points abound.

Nina Cooper

Editor's Preface

1934-1936 Editions

THE EXTRAORDINARY EXPLOITS OF THÉRÈSE ARNAUD, *the best agent in the French counter-espionage service.*

Spies are generally vile beings, disparaged individuals who practice the role of informant with the single goal of serving their appetites for money and debauchery. It's not the same for THÉRÈSE ARNAUD, whose conduct could serve as an example to many men, and those of the most courage. At the beginning of the war, having witnessed her father's murder by the Germans, she had, very naturally, as she said, "taken to the service."

Too valiant to take the self-effacing role of a nurse, her heart swollen with too deep a love of France, she consecrated her intelligence, her knowledge of languages, her beauty, her strength, her devotion, her courage, and, it must be said, her genius, to a more direct need.

THÉRÈSE ARNAUD CAN'T BE COMPARED TO ANY OTHER SECRET AGENTS.

Always on the go, always in full danger, her heart never weakened, even during the most dangerous interrogations. On the contrary, she never stopped throwing herself audaciously into the greatest peril. A hundred times she found herself in the middle of a battle; not in those battles where one returns covered with honor and glory, but in anonymous battles against invisible, unknown enemies, and just because of that, so much more to be feared.

THÉRÈSE ARNAUD is the noblest figure of the Great War. WE OWE TO HER BRAVERY, TO HER HEROISM, SEVERAL MILLIONS OF HUMAN LIVES.

With modesty as great as her courage, she did not wish her exploits to be published during her lifetime.

"Later," she said, "later, when I sleep my last sleep in my Land of France, it will be time enough."

THÉRÈSE ARNAUD reposes now in the cemetery of a tiny village in the East. All those for whom she sacrificed herself, without counting the cost, must henceforth know how and under what terrible conditions that great Frenchwoman fought magnificently for the Homeland.

May the EXPLOITS OF THÉRÈSE ARNAUD find a tender echo in the soul of this People of France to whom she had vowed her most fervent Love and her incomparable Loyalty.

Bibliography of Thérèse Arnaud

*: included in this volume.

1934

Deux Héros dans la nuit [Two Heroes in the Night]
Un Drame dans le métro [A Drama in the Metro] *
La Vengeance de Karl Himmelfeld [Karl Himmelfeld's Revenge] *
Le Secret de la villa [The Secret of the Villa] *
La Lumiere verte [The Green Light] *
La Vipère jaune [The Yellow Viper]
Du Sang sur les roses [Blood on the Roses]
Un Immonde chantage [An Abominable Blackmail]
Thérèse Arnaud contre Mata-Hari [Thérèse Arnaud vs Mata-Hari] *
L'Homme aux cent masques [The Man of 100 Masks]
Le Tango rouge [The Red Tango]
Le Château mystérieux [The Mysterious Castle]
L'Orgue de barbarie [The Barbary Organ]
L'As de coeur [The Ace of Hearts]
L'Assassinat de Thérèse Arnaud [The Assassination of Thérèse Arnaud]
Le Mort vivant [The Living Dead]
Le Sous-marin fantôme [The Ghost Sub-Marine]
L'Hôte de minuit [The Midnight Guest]
L'Homme aux tatouages [The Tattooed Man]
Une Dangereuse voisine [A Dangerous Neighbor]

1935

Le Danseur de la mort [The Deadly Dancer]
La Nuit du 16 [The Night of the 16th]
L'Evasion de Languille [Languille Escapes]
Une Arrestation mouvementée [A Troublesome Capture]
Un Ver dans le fruit [A Worm in the Fruit]
L'Etreinte mortelle [Deadly Embrace]
Un Prince étrange [A Strange Prince]
L'Exécution de Friquet [Friquet's Execution]
Mlle Doktor se trompe [Miss Doktor's Mistake]
Une Dangereuse machination [A Dangerous Scheme]
La Course à la mort [Race Toward Death] *
L'Empoisonneuse [The Poisoner]

La Machine Infernale [The Infernal Device]
La Main percée [The Pierced Hand]
La Femme au manchon [The Woman with the Muff] *
Un Héros de 15 ans [A 15-year-old Hero]
La Maison de l'effroi [The House of Fear]
Les Boules noires [The Black Balls]
Le Somnambule [The Sleep-Walker]
Le Club des vétérans [The Veterans' Club]

1936

Le Talisman du traître [The Trator's Talisman]
L'Homme aux trois doigts [The Man With Three Fingers]
Le Suicide du banquier [The Banker's Suicide]
Le Masque violet [The Violet Mask] *
Le Sourd-muet [The Deaf Mute]
L'Araignée de bronze [The Bronze Spider]
Le Criminel par ambition [The Ambitious Criminal]
L Enigme de la tour [The Tower Enigma]
La Rancune du Chinois [The Chinaman's Grudge]
Le Calvaire de Marcel [Marcel's Ordeal]
Un Attentat déjoué [An Attack Averted]
Un Repaire dans un cimetière [The Graveyard Lair]
Le Flacon d'encre [The Ink Well]
Le Triomphe de Malabar [Malabar's Triumph]
Le Bouton d'habit [The Uniform Button]
La Caisse vide [The Empty Crate]
Le Supplice de la vieille [The Old Woman's Torture]
L'Avion sanglant [The Bloody Plane]
Le Crime du mort [The Dead Man's Crime]
Une Nuit d'épouvante [Night of Terror]
Le Guet-apens [The Trap]
Le Plan No. 13 [Plan No. 13]
L'Enlèvement de Friquet [Friquet's Kidnapping]
Le Fauteuil truqué [The Trick Armchair]
Le Lévrier blanc [The White Greyhound]

A DRAMA IN THE METRO

I. At the Châtelet Metro

A terrible scraping of iron, a dull rumbling, a quavering whistle. A train came out of the tunnel and stopped at Châtelet Metro. A surge of the tightly packed crowd standing at the edge of the quay. At the same time an irresistible flow began in the overcrowded cars. People pushing, wanting to exit. Resistance of those going on and clinging together so as not to be drawn out of the car. And a confused brouhaha for a few seconds. Protests. Shouts. Obscenities. Then with the same whistle, the same dull rumbling, the same din of scraping iron, the metro train was again swallowed up into the tunnel.

Now in a long compact file, people were hurrying down the corridors to reach the connection to Line No. 4. The rush hour, 6:30 p.m. At that time, at the beginning of the war, the temporary disorganization of all methods of surface communication meant the number of metro travelers had multiplied. A whole nation of people worried, anxious, eyes made red by sad partings. Foreheads wrinkled with worry. Some of them, while automatically continuing their walk, tried to unfold an evening newspaper to find some hope in deliberately vague and imprecise information.

Suddenly there was a brusque halt which stopped short the progress of the crowd. A push backward. Some exclamations. Questions crossing each other. And a circle closed around a man stretched out on the ground.

"Get back a little. Give him some air!"

"He's fainted!"

"It's the heat!"

"He's some guy who's drunk too much…"

Contradictory guesses continued to circulate without anyone deciding to do anything helpful. A witness on the first row explained:

"I was walking behind him. There was pushing. A man passed by very fast. Then…I felt a shock, a body falling on me and sliding to the ground. And that was all…"

Suddenly a young man pushed aside the crowd with a quick, authoritative movement. A few protests very quickly quieted by the young man's determined behavior.

"Don't push!"

"What a savage!"

Paying no attention to the comments, the young man leaned over the unknown person. He kneeled down. They could see only a khaki raincoat, buckled at the waist, a soft hat pulled down over his forehead, hiding his eyes. And a silhouette, supple, svelte, young.

In the crowd which was continuing to grow, advice began to circulate again.

"He's a doctor!"

"Is it serious?"

"He needs to be picked up. He can't be left there!"

Indifferent, the young man methodically continued his examination.

With a rapid gesture he unbuttoned the overcoat and the jacket, placed his hand over the heart and massaged the unknown man. Now without waiting, he opened the vest. He quickly removed a large green leather portfolio bulging from the inside pocket. Then, seeming to have finished his examination, the young man stood up.

"So?"

The surprised witnesses began questioning again. With a new authoritative gesture, the young man stopped the murmurs. He declared firmly:

"The Station Master has to be told. I'll take care of it."

"Who is it?" a witness dared to ask. "The name of this unfortunate man is probably in the wallet with an address where he can be taken home."

"Yes…I'm going to do what's necessary."

The young man pushed aside the crowd and went down the corridor as a new wave of commuters descended from the next train. A few minutes later, a station employee, drawn by the assembly which now obstructed all circulation, alerted the Station Master.

The sick man was still stretched out. Not a movement, not a reflex. His eyes remained closed and his face began to take on a wax tint. The Station Master's arrival brought on another concert of exclamations, each person trying to explain the facts. Worried, he looked down at the man stretched out on the platform. Then, giving up trying to get the tidal wave of details, true, inexact, or contradictory, he grumbled:

"All right! All right! The main thing is to get a doctor first of all. Afterward we'll see…"

"A doctor…but the one who came immediately after the man fell…And who went to get you…"

"To get me? I haven't left my office during the last ten minutes and I haven't seen anyone. Neither a doctor nor anyone else, except the employee who came to get me."

Astonished murmurs rose. "Nevertheless, he said…" But a call came nearer and nearer: "A doctor! A doctor is needed! We're calling for a doctor!"

A little dry, thin, gray-headed man pushed his way through a passage with difficulty.

"A doctor? Here I am. What's wrong?"

Seeing the man on the ground, he didn't waste any more time; he was already kneeling. The pulse, a hand over the heart. The examination didn't take very long. The doctor soon stood up, making a face and in a few brief words to the Station Master he told him the results of his examination. There was a short discussion. Some orders were discreetly given for some employees to come quickly. The doctor again leaned over the man. He searched through his pockets. He removed several unusual objects that he gave to the Station Master: a microphone, a knife, but no identification, no address.

"As to the cause of death," he murmured, "only an autopsy will be able to tell us."

No exact information could be given to use as a basis for an official inquest. The facts remained mysterious. A man had died in the corridors of the Châtelet Metro. An unknown man, young, wearing a soft hat, and dressed in a raincoat, had stolen the identity papers of the cadaver.

"With such a situation, what can you do?" the Police Commissioner grumbled. How could the young man's presence be explained? How could the theft be explained? Was it a murder? Was the man in the raincoat both the murderer and the thief? Was there no connection between the man's death and the theft of the papers? And the objects found in the cadaver's pockets also weren't without surprises. And the audacity with which the theft had been committed, under the nose of numerous witnesses. The way the young man had disappeared. Many logical hypotheses were possible. But nothing permitted making a case for fear of going in a false direction.

II. The Contents of the Dead Man's Papers

The air of the cute little office was perfumed with the smoke of numerous cigarettes. And three men, each one following his own thoughts, with anxious looks toward a little clock, which, indifferent, continued to grind out the time. And sighs, heavy with worry, punctuated the thoughts of Thérèse Arnaud's assistants.

"Two o'clock, Malabar!"

The Colossus shook off his reverie.

"Eight o'clock, Friquet. I know that. What do you want me to do about it? If I knew where she was, I would go...despite the strict instructions we've received. I don't understand anything and I'm like you, I'm waiting. Your opinion, Languille?"

Languille made a very high, very wide gesture. "I don't know!"

"First catch your hare, says the Boss!" Friquet threw out. Even in serious circumstances, he didn't drop his good humor.

"Well," Malabar continued, "we've strictly followed the orders we were given. We immediately left the Châtelet Metro. And each taking a different way, we came here to her house. She should have been here a long time ago!"

"Her lateness means there's been something 'bad'..."

"Yes, and she was alone..." Languille worried.

"Where can she be?" Malabar worried.

"Oh! With her, it could be anywhere!"

The bookcase slowly slid back along the wall, showing an elevator cage. A soft hat, a raincoat, a tall supple, svelte form, and a voice saying gaily:

"Ah! You're all here. So much the better! I'm going to need you."

While the heavy piece of furniture mechanically slid back in place, the young man rapidly removed his raincoat and threw it across the room.

"Catch, Languille! Take a look inside. Study that while I go change. I've had enough playing young men."

Languille caught the raincoat on the fly. From the inside pocket he took a thick green leather portfolio and methodically began to examine the contents. He lit another cigarette before placing the papers in three stacks. Occasionally a wide smile lit up his face. Sometimes he frowned, emitting a strange growl which could be interpreted as a mark of great satisfaction or, on the contrary, a manifestation of contained fury. Friquet and Malabar, reassured now, but silent, watched without interrupting the work.

In a short time, the young man had changed into an elegant young woman wearing a dark gray suit.

"So? Languille?"

"Oh! There's enough to eat and drink inside that. We'll have enough to keep us busy, enough time to understand everything...if we can."

"We must!" Thérèse Arnaud answered firmly.

Languille held out the first stack of documents.

"Good. Identity papers…a passport. Everything is all right. Next?"

Languille handed over to C.25 a letter with seals carrying a first and last name, but without any address.

As a person very practiced in this type of work, Thérèse unsealed the envelope and read the letter inside.

"This is perfect," she murmured.

After a quick glance at a new stack of documents, C.25 remarked:

"Obviously what follows goes less well. That would be too simple! A great deal too simple! There's enough work for everyone this evening."

"This comes at a bad time! I was just getting sleepy!" Friquet joked.

"You'll be able to sleep," Thérèse said, sealing the envelope with the same cleverness. "You just have to take care of this letter."

"Take it to the Post Office?"

"No, it wouldn't arrive. There's no address. However, to be sure it reaches its destination, I'll take it myself."

"Where? Since…"

"Exactly, Friquet. That's elementary. You'll go find the address."

Friquet took the missive. He looked at the name and joked:

"At least that's clear. I like that Mr. Jean Durand! Just a simple glance at the telephone book and I'm certain to find the Jean Durand I'm looking for. I'll only have too great a choice!"

"You'll manage to verify it to find the Jean Durand I'm interested in."

"Then I won't catch sight of my bed in two weeks!"

"Oh! No, Friquet, the Jean Durand we're looking for is a perfume merchant, fragrance and cosmetics, maybe a hairdresser. It's a shop or a department store. So get going. Get to work and come back here immediately."

Having finished copying some notes, she held them out to Languille.

"You, you'll take this stack to Captain Ladoux. Urgently. And you come back here too."

Without further delay, her auxiliaries left. Malabar settled himself into an armchair and continued his meditations, waiting for a mission to be given him.

Thérèse Arnaud went over the notes spread out in front of her for a long time. She examined various codes with a worried look on her face. Entirely absorbed in her work, hours passed without her lifting her head. She finally made a gesture of rage and said:

"There's still a part of these texts that's escaping us. Always that key, that unknown number without which we can't do anything. We have the official German code. But what's missing is the code they use to communicate *between themselves*. So long as we don't have it, we risk going blindfolded into the simplest trap. Therefore, we have to have it!"

Languille had returned, mission accomplished.

"So…Boss. The briefcase?"

"The briefcase. Obviously the content is good, but, alas, the briefcase is too discreet. It's given up only a part of its secret. This, I've deciphered easily. It's confirmation of false information concerning the movements of armies that has been transmitted to the Deuxième Bureau from the Eastern region. As for the rest, the papers of the German spy murdered by the German espionage service in the metro, they're clear. He had false papers and a passport from Spain. And he was sent to meet someone called on the envelope Jean Durand, but in reality Karl Himmelfeld, according to the text of the letter."

"That Karl Himmelfeld would be…?"

"Chief of a German spy organization in Paris."

"Yes, yes," Languille, absorbed in his own thoughts, said, as C.25 once more, in vain, leaned over the indecipherable documents.

Friquet arrived, out of breath.

"Well?" C.25 asked.

Without a word he held out a list that Thérèse looked over rapidly. A smile appeared.

"Is that all right? Do you have enough Jean Durands to choose from?"

"Yes, but I've chosen the Jean Durand who is also Karl Himmelfeld. It would have been useless to give you that information. You wouldn't have found anything in the phone book. But this Jean Durand, fragrance and cosmetics store owner, Avenue de l'Opéra, seems to answer exactly what we're looking for. So much more so, since I've seen several times in the documents I've looked at, the word Opéra without at first knowing what it meant. So tomorrow I'm ready. I'll go see."

The three men stirred with the same movement. She noticed it, and just as calmly, she repeated:

"Yes, tomorrow I'll carry the letter to Karl Himmelfeld."

It was Languille who summed up his comrade's opinions.

"That's reckless folly! So long as we don't have the key, who knows if there isn't some sort of recognition signal or a secret word that the bearer of a letter must know to be identified. It's to go into the mouth of the wolf."

"Possible!" she replied. "I've thought the same things myself. Caution will have to be doubled. But to have this code that's indispensable to us, we have to go get it. And that means we have to go to Karl Himmelfeld's office. So…"

The silence of the three agents of C.25 approved this logic.

"Therefore, I'm going to explain your role to you and what I expect of you tomorrow. But, before that, Malabar, you must prepare the baggage. Be sure to put stickers from Swiss hotels on them. Then you'll have them taken to the Grand Hotel, where you'll rent a room for me. I'll arrive from Geneva this evening on the eleven o'clock train."

"Understood, Boss," Malabar confirmed.

20

"Me, I have the idea that there'll be a famous production before long, if not at the Opéra, but in the Avenue of the same name," smiled Friquet.

And well into the night, C.25 and her three faithful agents worked on their campaign plan.

III. The Spy Visits the Spy

At 8 a.m., an old woman, bent over by age, left the Grand Hotel. With short, tired steps she walked along the great boulevards. Some moments later, the bookshelf slid along the wall of Thérèse Arnaud's office and the old woman threw a morning newspaper on the table. Malabar, Friquet and Languille leaned over its pages. C.25 pointed out from among the many news items, the following:

At about 6 p.m. yesterday evening, an unknown man committed suicide with a strong dose of poison in the Châtelet Metro. The desperate man carried no documents that could identify his body.

"Case closed," Languille muttered.

"Nevertheless…," Malabar grumbled.

"Nevertheless," Thérèse finished the sentence, "we know he was murdered."

"And so?" Friquet asked.

"Yes, so?" Thérèse repeated.

"That's really what proves that it's dangerous to go like that, putting yourself at the mercy of Karl Himmelfeld," Malabar objected.

Thérèse Arnaud shrugged her shoulders slightly. Then she said:

"Quick! We don't have any time to lose."

They rapidly got busy preparing what was needed for the journey. Diverse information gathered from the beginning confirmed the hypothesis that Jean Durand, Avenue de l'Opéra, was really the person to whom the envelope found in the papers of the "suicide" was meant.

The old woman, with the same feeble steps, got back to the Grand Hotel at about 10 a.m. An hour later Thérèse Arnaud left again without a disguise and started toward the Avenue de l'Opéra. When she entered the store two of the employees were preoccupied. One of them was listening to the explanations of a very large and imposing servant from a fashionable residence who was going on about ways to restore the wig of "the Marquis." The other was in the hands of a salesman who, with the inimitable gift of the gab of the Parisian, was demonstrating the many advantages of a new palpably perfumed face powder. Thérèse Arnaud was attended by the owner himself.

She hesitated a few moments between two bottles of perfume before making her choice. Suddenly she decided. To pay, she opened a little purse stuffed with all kinds of small articles. She was looking for a 100 franc note. And to speed up the operation, she took out different objects from the purse, among them the letter carrying only the name of Jean Durand. Jean Durand gave his client a hard look that she took without flinching. Then he calmly picked up the letter.

"This way, please," he said, opening a little door that led into a dark corridor.

As soon as the door closed, the servant no longer insisted on giving suggestions about restoring the Marquis's wig and the powder salesman stopped promoting the advantages of his product.

Thérèse Arnaud followed Jean Durand. The corridor was dark and winding. It ended in a small dark courtyard which Jean Durand walked across silently. During the walk, she silently sized up the man she was going to confront: tall, big, heavy. About 40 years old. Dark complexion. High forehead, receding hairline. Quick and mobile eyes.

"This way," Jean Durand repeated, opening the door to a large laboratory with a skylight in the roof.

Everything was white, clean, well arranged: distillation tubes, test tubes, pans, flasks, everything that made up the work material of an honest Chemist. Separated by a thin partition, part of the laboratory had been made into an office with a rug on the floor, ordinary furniture, a cheap commercial wardrobe, a model of a series, an imposing, inelegant minister's desk, and three armchairs. This office was a small room lit by a narrow and high window. Jean Durand, who in this office became Karl Himmelfeld, pointed her to a large armchair, then sat down himself on the other side of the desk.

There was a short silence. She took advantage of this interval to commit to memory the smallest details. She instinctively envisioned methods of escape in case of necessity. There was only one way. The window was too high and too narrow to be reached. In addition, behind the glass the Sun cast the shadow of four solid bars, thick and close together. Therefore the only exit was the laboratory, the corridor and the small courtyard they crossed earlier. One other strange thing struck her. The laboratory and the office contained no safe or any heavy piece of furniture that could be used to hide documents of major importance. Even the arrangement of the laboratory might arouse some suspicion for it was too well arranged, too regular, suggesting that it was not used very often and was there for decoration only. The partition that separated the office and the laboratory was too thin to hide a secret safe or anything else. This examination, carried out by eyes habituated to seeing everything and discovering hidden things, hadn't taken but a few seconds.

"Then," Karl Himmelfeld asked, "you've come to enter my service?" Saying this, he opened the envelope given him. He read it rapidly, without stopping, taking down some numbers on a note pad which he later rolled into a ball and put in his vest pocket. Then he examined the packet of documents, a copy of which she had carried to Captain Ladoux. He opened a drawer of the desk and locked it again carefully. And very low to himself he murmured, "We'll look at that later."

A slight pause, and in the voice of a superior questioning an inferior, he continued.

"You've received no information about the mission I must confide to you?"

"None," she answered without hesitation. Almost repeating the text of the letter she had just handed over, she continued. "I was ordered to deliver this envelope to you. Here are my letters of introduction. That's all. I must learn the rest of my mission from you."

She held out to him the papers found in the briefcase of the man who committed suicide.

"Good. Here's what it's about. It's very simple, just another envelope to deliver."

She nodded that she understood.

"It's just child's play since you have there a passport perfectly in order to enter Spain. You'll make the delivery and nothing more."

With some insistence, Karl Himmelfeld concluded;

"The French mail functions rather badly. It's important that certain envelopes not go astray, and also that they arrive with the shortest delay…without raising any inopportune curiosity."

"Understood," Thérèse said.

"This envelope that I'm going to give you in a few minutes must be delivered as rapidly as possible to Von Krohn, our Naval Attaché in Madrid. In answer, he will give you a new envelope, addressed to me, probably."

"Excellent…"

There was another silence. Karl once more scrutinized Thérèse. The examination must have been favorable, since he finished with a gentler voice.

"When do you leave?"

"This very evening."

"Good."

Karl got up. He opened the door and gestured for her to enter the laboratory. "If you will please wait a few minutes, I'm going to prepare what's needed."

No sooner had Thérèse crossed the threshold when the door separating the office and the laboratory was closed. A moment of hesitation. Was this a trap closing on the Deuxième Bureau envoy? Had the fearless agent been unmasked because of some secret sign, because of some information contained in the correspondence that she hadn't been able to decipher? No, C.25 had managed without any trouble to deceive Karl Himmelfeld, who took her for a messenger of the German espionage service. But Karl was careful. And it's never helpful to let auxiliaries charged with more or less important missions know all the secrets. They need to know only what is strictly necessary for the success of the mission given them.

"There's something in that room that I'm not meant to see," she murmured to herself. "And that's just what I'm most interested in. Evidently the document safe is over there. But where? Fortunately, despite their care, these gentlemen don't think of everything and neglect the simplest things."

Looking through the keyhole, she followed all Karl Himmelfeld's movements. He had gone into a dark corner. He was probably searching for an electric button. The over-sized desk, slowly, noiselessly, pivoted around, using one of its small sides as an axis. In this way it uncovered in the floor without a rug at that spot a large rectangular plate about the size of a bathtub. Now Karl Himmelfeld leaned down. In the center of the plate, he lifted a metallic insert which held four buttons exactly like those of a safe. Then, probably because the secret word had been inserted, the plate separated in the middle and went back into the floor. Gently, without bumping, the safe came up and took the place of the desk. She saw him take out a dispatch case stuffed with documents. He chose some of them. Then he opened the drawer where he had, a short time before, hidden the envelope she had given him. He placed it in the safe. Then, he methodically did the same movements in reverse. The safe went back down through the floor. The metallic insert lowered, hiding the four buttons. The huge desk took its former place.

"Not a bad find," Thérèse said.

Jean Durand, alias Karl Himmelfeld, sat behind the desk. She saw him check the documents taken from the safe. He prepared an envelope. He took a big sheet of paper. He began to write rapidly.

"Nothing more to learn there," Thérèse thought, leaving her observation post. But in getting up, she held back a movement of surprise.

"The secrets must be important to be so well guarded."

She had just discovered, hidden in the door molding, two electric wires that ended at the copper button. It was obvious that after the store closed, a high voltage electric wire was activated that would inevitably kill the indiscreet person trying to open the office door.

"Good," she murmured. "We'll remember that when we have occasion to come back. And that will be soon."

Then she calmly sat down in a chair near the table loaded with flasks and test tubes.

"Yes, dust everywhere. No one works here very often."

She looked at the walls, trying to discover the presence of a cupboard, of a trapdoor. Nothing. Nothing but empty walls with no hiding places. And above, the narrow window.

"A good spy hideout," she thought.

Along a wall, the experienced eye of the intrepid Deuxième Bureau agent discovered in a corner a small pipe similar to a gas pipe. It went from the ceiling to the floor of the laboratory. At the top the glass window and the courtyard of the building; at the bottom a cellar actually transformed into a radio transmission post.

"We have to see that!"

The office door opened. Karl Himmelfeld held out to her a carefully sealed envelope.

"Addressed to: Von Krohn, Madrid," he repeated.

"Understood!"

His look, a glance unusually hard and cold, rested on Thérèse. Then the same look automatically made the rounds of the laboratory walls, as if trying to call to mind what Thérèse, seated in her chair, might have noticed, seen, discovered.

In reverse order, Karl and Thérèse made their way across the path previously used. She noticed that all the door handles were made of copper. No doubt that if she had leaned over a little, she would have discovered in the molding the two electric wires where the current, deadly to the indiscreet, circulated.

They went across the courtyard. She automatically was going to turn right.

"No, no reason to go through the shop," and he opened a door that led directly into the building's hallway. Then in a strange tone, without addressing Thérèse directly, he remarked:

"Curiosity is a vile fault…that's always punished."

He smiled a ferocious smile and repeated in the same tone: *"Always!"*

With a rapid step, C.25 went back down the Rue de l'Opéra.

"It's lucky I took the precaution of reserving a room at the Grand Hotel," she thought, noticing she was being followed. But she smiled when thinking that Languille's supple form was tacking along behind the person following her.

The old lady again left the Grand Hotel shortly after Thérèse herself had entered it, probably to pack her bags and prepare for her departure.

Arriving at her house, she found Friquet and Malabar waiting for her. They had taken off their disguises, one the flunkey of a fashionable house, the other of a powder salesman.

"What's new?" both agents asked at the same time.

"We'll have the code we're looking for in a few days. But until then, we won't be short of work. First of all, get word to Marcel. Tell him to come immediately. He has to photograph the documents contained in this envelope and get them to Captain Ladoux. Next we have to intercept the radio messages sent via Karl's post. And I have an idea that won't be easy."

"Well, I'm not ready to sleep," Friquet said.

"Oh, but you'll sleep very well tonight," Thérèse assured him.

"Oh, so much the better. My bed…"

"Don't worry about your bed. You'll sleep on the train. There's nothing like the rocking of an Express to give you good dreams."

"The train?"

"Yes. You'll have enough time. We aren't yet in Madrid. And from Paris to the border you'll have time to take a nice nap."

"Great! Spain! That's my dream! I used to know a woman there named Carmen. This will be a wonderful opportunity to get to know her again."

"That would be more difficult than to find the real Durand in Paris. He, by the way, is named Karl Himmelfeld," Malabar objected.

Just then, Languille arrived. He had stopped surveillance on the Avenue de l'Opéra when he saw Thérèse Arnaud leave Jean Durand's building.

"Boss! The guy's still waiting for you in front of the Grand Hotel."

"Perfect! He can go with me to the Orsay train station."

Then she distributed jobs to Malabar and Languille to accomplish whilst she traveled to Madrid. The documents she was to deliver to Von Krohn were photographed. Unfortunately, still because of the missing key, they could decipher only a part of them.

IV. A Successful Mission

The setting sun gave the illusion that the fields were ablaze, the trees appeared blood-red at the railroad crossings as the Express raced by. Standing in the corridor of a carriage, two travelers, immobile, eyes lost toward the rapidly disappearing horizon, looked at the oncoming shadows of evening. They were silent…at least in appearance.

"Is everything all right, Friquet?" Thérèse asked, almost without moving her lips.

He responded affirmatively by blinking. Then, always the joker, he added:

"Everything's all right, yes, but I've had enough of Spain! It's a country of châteaux, possibly, but not those of chateaubriands. Souvenirs of Spain: fleas in the railway carriages, fleas in the hotels. And meals of chick peas. Thank you! And to top off the luck, no dining car."

Thérèse smiled and then returned calmly to her compartment. And indifferent to the always changing scene unfolding through the window, her eyes closed, she reviewed the main episodes of her mission to Von Krohn. In fact, it was an easy mission that no remarkable incident had troubled. She was a great deal more preoccupied with the job she had decided to do in Paris. She judged the trip to Madrid was lost time. And the train that would drop her tomorrow morning at the Quai d'Orsay Station seemed slow to her.

She had reached Madrid without the least difficulty. She had delivered to the German Naval Attaché the envelope that Himmelfeld had entrusted to her. And in exchange she had been charged with taking back to Paris the mail of the German representative to Madrid. She produced the best possible impression on Von Krohn, who had warmly congratulated her on the speed with which she had accomplished her mission. On the other hand, she had been subjected to a multitude of questions. And the answers, clear, precise—and nevertheless perfectly false—that she had given, had attracted the sympathy of the Naval Attaché. He had even promised to recommend her to his superiors.

But from this trip, she had brought back the certainty that her hypotheses were correct. Karl Himmelfeld had a radio transmitter in his building. She had the proof of that when she talked with Von Krohn. The Naval Attaché had been given the text of a wireless transmission. He read it; he smiled and looked at Thérèse, saying:

"Here's some newly arrived information that hasn't been slowed down on the way…and it's about you. It's the order from Karl to return to Paris as soon as possible."

How much lost time! Nevertheless, she couldn't have done without the trip to Madrid. Without that she would have been tempted, from the first evening of her encounter with the famous Karl Himmelfeld, to break into his office on the Avenue de l'Opéra.

A dark night. A train whistling and kilometers adding to kilometers already traveled.

At Bordeaux, followed discreetly by Friquet, she left the train. She needed, in fact, to gain some time. Karl Himmelfeld had been told the time of her departure. It was simple therefore to know when she would arrive in Paris. But, the Secret Service agent didn't want to return the envelope Von Krohn had given her without photographing and trying to decipher the documents. C.25's plan for this was simple. Marcel and Malabar, contacted by Friquet would wait for her in Bordeaux. Marcel was ready to photograph the papers. Then, the envelope sealed again, she and her agents would leave by automobile. They should be at the Austerlitz Railway Station the next morning to meet the arrival of the Bordeaux Express. In that way, the German spy watching for her to get off the train would see her get off at the Orsay Station and go directly—without going to her room at the Grand Hotel—to Himmelfeld's office. That would remove all suspicion.

On the way! A powerful automobile roared through the night.

"We have enough time," said Malabar, who was driving. "The train currently takes 11 hours for the Bordeaux-Paris run."

During the journey Thérèse didn't think about taking the slightest rest. She needed a complete report on the work accomplished since her departure. Malabar and Marcel informed her as well as they could.

"First of all, the question of the wireless transmitter, Marcel?"

"Yes, it's true, a wireless post exists, but we don't know where. Some incomprehensible transmissions have already been intercepted. The interception showed the post was situated somewhere near the center of Paris. It wasn't possible to obtain any exact location."

"All right," she approved.

"It's possible," Marcel continued, "that the Germans always transmit in that code we don't know. At the present all the intercepted messages furnish no information, only words that don't make any sense."

She nodded as a sign of approval. While Marcel took Malabar's place at the wheel, Thérèse continued her questioning.

"And Himmelfeld, Malabar?"

"The information was accurate. Only the boutique and the hairdresser salon business on the Avenue de l'Opéra is used. Karl doesn't live there. He leaves the store every evening about eight o'clock."

"Yes, but the wireless transmitter functions at night…"

Malabar made a wide, incomprehensible gesture and continued.

"His private domicile is in Neuilly, a little house in a quiet suburb. He goes directly home and there are no comings and goings in the villa."

"Yes, but that's not enough," she objected.

"Patience, Boss! Languille has carefully checked out Karl's lodgings. Nothing to point out. It's the honest dwelling of Jean Durand, hairdresser and perfume merchant. A little safe that didn't resist contained only commercial correspondence and papers without the least importance. The cellars have no secret entrance."

"Yes…yes, all right," said Thérèse.

"Good. Now if there's nothing at Neuilly, everything is at the Avenue de l'Opéra. That confirms my hypotheses. In addition, here's the layout of the Neuilly house and also the map of Jean Durand's shop on the Avenue de l'Opéra." Malabar finished and handed C.25 two sheets of paper.

Suddenly, Marcel, who was at the wheel, seemed worried. He kept his foot on the accelerator pedal, but the speed of the automobile slowed progressively. For some time the speed indicator needle had been falling from 100, and having just passed 60, it continued to fall. Outside there was countryside, fields as far as you could see, and a cold and sinister night.

Two reflexes from C.25. A look at her watch—showing 4 p.m.—and another look at the map. Anticipating her question, Malabar pointed out on the map the approximate location of the automobile. C.25's mind rapidly calculated. They had to be in Paris at 9 p.m. and they still had 400 kilometers to go. In the middle of the night, there was no reason to expect help. A worried frown crossed her forehead. There was a short stop while Marcel and Malabar leaned over the open hood, an exchange of cabalistic words, guesses, verifications.

"Nothing!" Malabar raged. "That's incomprehensible. Nevertheless, I checked out the car this afternoon at Bordeaux, and I can guarantee…"

"The only thing that can be guaranteed," Marcel interrupted, "is that the car won't accelerate any longer. We're holding steady at 50, but for how much longer? From one minute to the next we must expect to stop along the road!"

Some more kilometers passed slowly! So slowly! C.25 considered the possibilities.

"Impossible to meet the Express at any station. Now it's ahead...It loses a half-hour at Tours...But useless to try to pick it up there. The slowness of the car is the problem, although the average speed seems to be maintained at 50. At 4:30 there's still 365 kilometers to go. A hope of picking up speed? That's very improbable."

An examination of train schedules confirmed that it was impossible to find a train at any point along the line that would arrive in Paris before the Bordeaux Express. And if the German spy posted at the Quai d'Orsay didn't see Thérèse Arnaud get out of that train, that would mean all the artful plans were ruined.

On the other hand, Marcel was also supposed to be in Paris at the same time as C.25. He had to develop his negatives and take the proofs to Captain Ladoux. And the Deuxième Bureau had to understand the documents at the same time as Karl Himmelfeld, so as to prevent the German spies from using the information furnished by Von Krohn. So?

As morning dawned, penetrating cold seemed to freeze energies and doubt seeped in. Her eyes closed, Thérèse felt for a moment discouraged. Despite her efforts no satisfactory solution came to mind. She had to be resigned...A burst of revolt!

"No! That would be too stupid!" she raged.

Malabar and Marcel remained silent, vanquished by the situation that destroyed all their hopes. And each passing moment confirmed the defeat.

V. Chasing the Express

At 6:00 a.m. 300 kilometers still separated them from their goal. And the car continued to roll along regularly, knocking off with difficulty its 50 kilometers an hour. Day had dawned sad and gloomy. Villages were awake. A cold, penetrating rain fell relentlessly, crashing down on the top of trees from a low, gray sky. Another stop at a garage, precious minutes lost. Malabar hurried to fill up with gasoline. Marcel took advantage of this short rest to again lean over the motor and try to discover the cause of the damage. In the car, Friquet was asleep. Thérèse got out. Pacing up and down, she tried to vent her fury against the road's paving stones. But in vain! The same silent anger, the same despair, was strangling the three agents.

A soldier appeared from a near street. He was moving toward the garage, rubbing his eyes, still heavy with sleep. The garage owner automatically asked:

"Did you have a good night?"

"Too short! But you always have to get over that. I slept well yesterday once my shift was over. I was up ahead. No point in going back to the barracks to sleep with the fleas...and the Captain closes his eyes so he can't see the time to come back."

Saying this, the soldier went into the garage. He soon came out pushing a motorcycle that he leaned against a wall. Once again he stretched lazily. He took a packet of tobacco out of his pocket and began to roll a cigarette. In no hurry, he searched for his lighter. He heard a woman's voice calling:

"Marcel!"

The noise of a motor, stifled by a cry of surprise: "Thief!"

And the motorcycle was already disappearing, driven by Thérèse Arnaud, carrying Marcel who had jumped on the baggage rack just as it started. Malabar stayed with Friquet, both arguing with the soldier who was still shouting: "Thief!"

The town was left behind. Now it was the open road slick with rain.

"A hundred...," she verified. She fixed her eyes on the speedometer. A calculation: 100 kilometers an hour—an average difficult to maintain as approaching Paris there would be speed limits when going through the suburbs.

"We need to gain some more time!" she shouted.

The trees were passed at a dizzying speed. The small towns and the hamlets together into the past. The wind and glacial rain planted sharp needles in the faces of the two motorcyclists. What did that matter!

"A hundred and ten!" Thérèse rejoiced.

And the motor continued to roar furiously. The kilometer signs flew by. It was a little more than 7 p.m. when a sign appeared carrying the information: Paris 200km. No obstacle stopped the rush forward. Villages crossed at high speed. Sharp turns taken without slowing down. Hills raced down, the motor at full speed. Settlements passed through without paying attention to the curses raised. Crossings traversed without taking into account the danger. Only one thing mattered: to be in Paris at the Austerlitz Station at 9 p.m.

Damn! Gasoline! A stop. A fill-up in feverish haste. Words exchanged.

"You have the negatives, Marcel?"

"Yes...on me!"

"Good! Let's go! Hold on tight...!"

The rest of the sentence was lost in a furious roar of the motor. The speedometer again moved in the dial. Before leaving the village the motorcycle had again reached the speed of 110km/h. Marcel too looked at the kilometer markers flying by.

"So...We have some chance of getting there....but only just...if nothing happens. But by that time, and with such a driver and under such conditions, we'll most certainly crash before long," he thought to himself.

Then a cry of triumph from C.25:

"One hundred and twenty!"

The rain picked up, spinning a curtain of fog which tied together the sky and earth. The horizon became lower, daylight faded. Sheets of wind threatened to unseat the motorcyclists. But Thérèse Arnaud ignored everything. Her eyes were fixed on the road. And she was distracted for only one minute, to look at the speedometer needle that was fixed at 120km/h.

"All hope isn't lost!" she shouted to Marcel, who, clinging to the luggage carrier, stoically took the shocks.

"Maybe we'll be lucky and the train will be late...and..."

The sentence wasn't finished. A more violent shock, a rapid slide over the wet pavement. The motorcycle slid out in a semi-circle and came to rest some centimeters from a huge tree.

"It wouldn't have taken much for our trip to have ended there," C.25 said. But she didn't stop any longer.

"The motorcycle's all right. So are we. Let's go!"

She stood the machine upright and headed it in the direction of Paris. A railway crossing barrier. A harsh puff of an approaching locomotive. A look to the right, a look to the left.

"Quick! Marcel!"

The gate open. The crossing barrier rose. The deafening sound of a passing train. But already on the other side of the crossing guard, Thérèse and Marcel had jumped on the motorcycle and the motor roared again. Trees, houses, villages, then only fields, fields wet with rain on both sides of the road. La Beauce, and 8 p.m. rang from a bell tower that the travelers scarcely had the leisure to admire.

"Ninety kilometers more!" she shouted. "We'll pick up speed. We'll get there!"

"I won't be sorry about that," thought Marcel, still clinging to the baggage rack.

Some minutes lost crossing Etampes.

"We'll have to make up that time," Thérèse announced.

"Yes!" Resigned, Marcel clung to the baggage rack. And the mad race started again.

But obstacles were multiplying. Traffic picked up on the road, heavy trucks, peasants' vehicles, a regiment of infantry. At another railway crossing that it was impossible to jump over in time a convoy of troops immobilized the motorcyclists. The time gained had again been lost.

At 8:30 a.m., Paris 40km. But 40km in suburban streets. Impossible to maintain an 80km/h average. And she looked at the speedometer needle which continued to pass the 100km/h mark...

A little beyond Juvisy the road ran beside the Paris-Orleans railroad for about three kilometers. The motorcycle kept abreast.

By way of the Grande Ceinture junction, a long train of material was slowly coming in. It was going to enter the main rails of the Paris-Bordeaux line, cross them and reach Villeneuve Saint-Georges, obstructing during its passage the main line. In the distance, behind the motorcyclists, the whistle of another train sounded. Repeated, impatient whistle of a convoy which demanded the right of way.

Thérèse Arnaud turned around. The motorcycle swerved. The brakes applied.

"Come on, Marcel, quick!"

Thérèse was already on the road. Marcel jumped. The motorcycle, riderless, ran into the ditch.

"Come on, Marcel. Hurry! No time to lose!" Thérèse explained, rapidly jumping through the hedges separating the road from the railroad tracks.

"Where are we going?"

"The train of materials which has just passed will oblige the express to slow down, maybe even to stop before going by the Juvisy Station. We have to take advantage of this pause. We just have to jump."

"Yes," Marcel answered. "Obviously! All we have to do is jump!"

C.25's calculations were accurate. The Bordeaux Express had slowed its speed, which was still sufficient to make the operation dangerous. They followed the rails. The train passed by. Locomotive. Freight car. Mail car. A turning disk now indicated that the way was free. A sound of the locomotive's whistle which was to continue its course.

"Hop! Marcel. Don't hesitate! It's leaving!"

Thérèse jumped. Marcel jumped, establishing a footing on reaching the slippery outside rail. The rest was only child's play. The doors to the big passenger trains open to the inside. Their entry passed unnoticed. The travelers, tired out by their night on the train, were still asleep in their compartments.

"Now let's separate to finish the trip, Marcel. As soon as we arrive you know what you have to do: develop the negatives and carry them to Captain Ladoux."

And calmly—still a little wet from the motorcycle ride—she took her seat in the Express she had left at Bordeaux.

There was still an empty case in the overhead rack. When she had settled in, she sighed:

"Yes. Now I have a half hour to take a rest!"

At the Orsay Railway Station, she hailed a taxi. A beggar came forward to open the door. She gave Jean Durand's address. When the taxi had left, the beggar couldn't hide his astonishment. There was an expression of stupor and incomprehension on his face. He mumbled several words which were lost in his unkempt beard. Then he disappeared into the crowd.

During this time Malabar and Friquet were attempting to take care of the theft of the motorcycle. It wasn't easy. While they stayed at the garage, the soldier left to report to the Police. Malabar saw a powerful automobile coming from the direction of Bordeaux. It stopped suddenly in front of the garage to fill up with gas. Malabar noticed that there was no reason for that automobile to stop. The gas tank was still three-quarters full. However, it seemed to him that one of the car's occupants carefully examined the automobile that had brought

Thérèse and her agents there. So Malabar leaned over the car's hood, which was still open. The driver of the car came up to him.

"What is it? A break-down?"

Malabar made a vague gesture. The other man continued:

"That's annoying when you're in a hurry."

"Yes...very..."

"Especially when the bosses aren't patient. We're going to Paris. And my bosses offer to take you if...it would be useful. Have to help out, right?"

Malabar looked at the chauffeur to memorize his features.

"No, thanks very much. I'm not in a hurry. I have enough time."

"You, yes...but..." and the chauffeur winked, motioning in the direction of the interior of the car.

"No...nobody...I'm going back alone...The bosses are far away!..."

The chauffeur didn't insist any longer. He quickly finished emptying a can of gasoline in the gutter pretending to fill the gas tank. Then he said some words to the car's occupants, who showed at least as much surprise as the old beggar had when he saw Thérèse get out of the train at the Orsay Station.

VI. First Skirmishes

She got out of the taxi in front of Jean Durand/Himmelfeld's shop. At first glance she could see that Karl was in a vile humor that morning. His eyes were steel gray. His voice was rough. His gestures were abrupt and authoritative. And two transversal lines across his forehead seemed to indicate, in addition to anger, an important preoccupation.

"I wasn't expecting you so early," he remarked without any friendliness.

Calmly, with a smile she explained:

"As Von Krohn was able to tell you, I was in his office when he got the message calling me back here. I left Madrid the same evening. The Spanish trains are slow and right now French trains are hardly any faster. From the border to Paris it takes..."

"Yes...Yes...all right," Karl Himmelfeld interrupted.

They had reached the laboratory. She noticed that a small table had been set up. There were still the remains of a hasty breakfast on it.

In the office, she gave Karl the envelope confided to her by the Naval Attaché at Madrid. Karl took it and examined it carefully. Then, probably temporarily, he placed it in a drawer. There was a long pause. She felt Karl's sharp, hard, cold glance resting on her. The impression of something wrong went away.

Then, at Karl's request, she began to relate the details of her interview with Von Krohn. She didn't leave out the questions he had asked her. And she faithfully repeated the answers she had given.

Karl listened without interrupting, without approving, without showing the least opinion, the least impression.

While she was making her report she noticed a piece of paper on the desk on which were pasted newspaper clippings. The paper was near enough to her and turned in a way that she could read without any trouble and without having to make any effort to bring it closer. All the newspaper clippings related to the suicide of an unknown man in the Châtelet Metro Station. When she had finished her report, the German stated:

"That's good." And he once again scrutinized C.25. Then he suddenly decided.

"Come back to see me here this afternoon. I'll have something to give you."

"Three o'clock...understood...I'm going to go rest until then."

He didn't seem to hear. In any case, he didn't answer. He conducted her back to the little courtyard. He opened the door which allowed her to pass directly into the vestibule. And there he repeated in the same enigmatic voice:

"Curiosity is a vile fault that's always punished...ALWAYS!"

Knowing she was being followed, she returned directly to the Grand Hotel. Her instinct made her feel important events had transpired and, despite all the precautions she had taken, suspicions were directed at her. So she was extra cautious. And despite her desire to communicate with Marcel and Languille, she didn't leave her room. At 3 p.m. she returned to Karl. She found him just as furious, just as worried. He gave her a mission of no great importance in Paris. She made an effort to accomplish that mission without raising any suspicion.

34

And for the third time in the same day, she returned to the Avenue de l'Opéra to find out the results of the mission she'd been given. There, she noticed that Karl, still as worried, was preparing to eat dinner in the laboratory.

"Tomorrow morning I'll need you again."

She nodded agreement. Karl was looking at her, and she thought she saw two meanings in his look. Karl was looking at her as you look at an enemy for whose bravado you can't help feeling a certain admiration.

She returned to the hotel only much later in the evening after having multiplied precautions and tricks to throw off anyone following her (if anyone was). She managed to rejoin Languille and Marcel, who were waiting for her at her house.

The Chemist immediately told her he had accomplished his mission to Captain Ladoux as rapidly as possible. A part of the documents that Thérèse Arnaud had brought from Spain and taken to Karl Himmelfeld had been immediately decoded. They were documents of the highest importance concerning the establishment of refueling bases for German submarines, an entire organization for allowing underwater crossings in the Mediterranean. Unfortunately, another part of the papers remained untranslatable. Always for the same reason: the details of the organization had been drawn up in secret language for which there was no key. It was urgent that they possess that key to give the papers brought back by C.25 their total value.

"That's good. I now have a number of reasons to hurry the events along. I have an idea that before long I'm going to be burned at Himmelfeld's. I have to have the key before that."

"A small burglary," Languille suggested, smiling. "I know about that…"

"My fine Languille, you're very nice, but your way is not enough and…most of all, it wouldn't work."

"To open a safe and take out what we need…not enough?" Languille said, astonished.

"Yes," she explained. "We must get that code. But, *it's absolutely necessary that Karl not be aware of the theft*. If he learns about it, he will immediately afterward change the code and we won't be any further along. We'll have to take them out, photograph them and…"

"That's my job," Marcel said.

But without noticing the interruption, she continued: "It's a question first of all of getting the code. And the second part of the plan, as important as the first: *put it back in place without any one being able to suspect for a single instant that it ever left Karl's safe.*"

There was a silence for several moments which everyone used to try to solve the proposed problem.

C.25 continued: "However, to attempt that I need everybody. Malabar and Friquet haven't yet returned. We must consider how to extract them from the situation in which I put them by stealing the motorcycle."

The bookcase slid back. The elevator appeared. Malabar and Friquet entered.

"Phew!" Friquet sighed. "Boss, you played some joke on us!"

But Thérèse was preoccupied. She interrupted him.

"That's over. You took care of it? That's the important thing. Let's not think any more about that story. It's over. I'm more worried about Karl's attitude. There's something wrong there, and it risks hampering our plans."

But Languille offered a likely explanation for Karl's worries.

"He isn't happy, this handsome Karl, Boss! That could be because his wireless isn't working well, or not working at all!"

C.25 paid attention, lifting her head.

"You didn't know that Jean Durand's building had been cleaned up."

"Yes? So?"

"So," Languille smiled. "It was child's play. I found the nice electric wires well wrapped in aluminum tubes going up the walls of the building. I cut the wires in three places and put the tubes back to make research easier. It was easy."

"That was nice work! Congratulations!" C.25 approved.

In fact, Karl's agents had prepared the following tracking system: to follow at some distance Thérèse's car, which, according to their estimations, ought to be broken down in the country in the middle of the night. Then following that, a helpful automobilist would offer two or three places in their own vehicle. Thérèse, short of time by the late hour, wouldn't refuse the offer. And then they would be able to steal the documents which she or her agents were going to steal or photograph. She would then fall into Karl's hands.

She would be unable to deny the facts. At the present, the situation was at that point. Suspicions were pointing to Thérèse. However, she was acting like the perfect German spy and no proofs against her could be raised.

"Since everyone is here, we'll take this up tomorrow," Thérèse decided. "We must take advantage of every occasion, and if need be, create one. We can't lose any more time in getting the code in our hands."

Then the roles were distributed.

"You, Marcel, have prepared what I told you to?" For answer, the Chemist put a small flat flask, hermetically sealed, in her hands.

"You'll stay here with everything necessary for photographing. My recommendation: work quickly. Languille will be the liaison. Malabar will be on surveillance available to exchange with Friquet."

"But…you'll still be alone, Boss," Malabar said, hesitatingly, "and after what I've seen…"

"What you have seen?…"

Malabar recounted the incident with the automobilists on the Bordeaux-Paris Road.

"Ah!" She said: "One more reason to act quickly."

"This time," Friquet growled, "that will be covered."

And what Thérèse couldn't understand was that Karl's anger had two causes, and two very different causes. First of all, obviously, the sabotage of the wireless transmitter, depriving him of direct communication with his superiors and his principal agents. Next the suspicions that he couldn't turn into certainty. Thérèse's arrival, presenting him with perfect regular documents—false but perfectly in order—and the name of a woman. Wasn't Thérèse Arnaud, wasn't she an agent in the French counter espionage service? Karl regretted having sent her on that very important mission to Madrid. He knew the importance of the documents that Von Krohn would give her. Then, those documents in the hands of the Deuxième Bureau...

So, Karl had again doubled caution. He had surrounded her with extra surveillance and not one of her actions or gestures had gone unnoticed since she had left the Grand Hotel to take the train to Spain from the Orsay station. On the return, he had a report on her trip. In fact, now Karl was torn between two absolutely contrary reports he had received. One indicated that she had gotten off the Irun-Paris train at Bordeaux. The report added that she had left Bordeaux shortly afterward to reach Paris by car...but that the car had had a breakdown, causing her not to reach Paris on time. Another report said that she had gotten off the Irun-Paris train at the Quai d'Orsay station. Next, a third message mentioned that the vehicle Thérèse had taken to return to Paris had been found in the area of Châtellerault...but left in charge of the chauffeur. Thus the proof that Karl searched for was missing. And the trap set for her had closed without getting the guilty one.

VII. A Juggling Act

The next day, Thérèse was on time for the appointment Karl had given her. Night had certainly not put an end to the German spy's worries. And his humor was even darker. Without a word he had her come into the office.

"Today this will become more serious," he began. "The satisfactory manner in which you accomplished your mission to Von Krohn shows me that I have in you an agent intelligent, active, and determined."

She murmured some polite words. Karl was watching her. Her correct impassive demeanor seemed to make Karl's fury boil over, but he contained himself. He groaned heavily and continued. "Here's what it's about. It's necessary to have precise information about the movements of troops and the effects that at present make up..."

One of Karl's employees entered. There was a short, private conversation. Two pairs of eyes again rested on the spy. Karl Himmelfeld became brick red.

"Good," he said. "I'll talk to him immediately."

Then, to Thérèse, after a moment's hesitation:

"Listen, what I have to lay out to you is rather long and detailed. I'll have to give you precise orders to allow you to arrive at a satisfying result. Right now it's impossible; we risk being disturbed at any moment."

"I'm at your service whenever you like," she replied docilely.

Karl seemed to make a decision.

"The shop is closed during the lunch hour. I myself don't leave. I take my meals here in the laboratory. If you wish, while eating lunch I can explain what I expect of you. Then! Until lunch!"

"Until lunch!"

The hours passed too slowly for her taste. She knew that the decisive moment had come and she was impatient to fight...and to win.

She went over mentally the dispositions she had taken. She went over the trumps she had in her hand. And she also tried to assess the strength of the adversary. Obviously, the situation was critical! She was at the mercy of the least incident that could unmask her. On the other hand, she knew that Marcel, Malabar and Friquet were at their posts.

At noon, Thérèse was facing Karl, who was beginning to eat with a robust appetite. No servant. No waiter. The courses placed on the table. A glance over the "field of battle." The laboratory: the door communicating with the office and the corridor was closed. She knew that Languille, not content with having sabotaged the wireless transmitter had taken advantage of a sweep of the office to saw the bars of the little window lighting the office.

"First of all," Karl began, "I must warn you that the mission I'm giving you isn't without risk."

"I'm not afraid!"

"I don't doubt that. Perhaps risk even pleases you," the German said in a more human tone. "They say there's a certain excitement in confronting danger, in playing with fire..."

He was waiting for an answer. Nothing. Not a word.

"Excellent. However, it's a question of a special kind of risk. It's not clearly danger but a sort of imprecise peril you'll have to run."

"I'll be on my guard," she answered. And then, "Oh! Pardon," and she kindly held out to Karl a dish on the table rather far from his hand that he was trying to reach.

He made an effort to smile. "Thank you."

Then there was a long silence only broken by the sounds of Karl's fork being put down on the dinner plate and the sounds of mastication.

"You are naturally absolutely free and will have all the resources to work with as you think proper to bring me the current positions of the Second Army and the areas where troops are concentrated, if you can. And in order to verify the information furnished me by an agent who, for some reason, does not entirely inspire me with confidence, the locations of artillery and munitions depots."

"Yes, yes, I see," she agreed.

"Therefore, in order to facilitate your task, I believe it would be good, for you, to put you in rapport with one of our agents, Fritz Ko…"

Karl didn't finish the name of the agent. His head fell down on his chest. A loud snore indicated his respiration. Thérèse looked at her watch and touched Karl's arm. He didn't budge. She pinched him. He didn't move.

"Good. Now, let's get going."

As a precaution she put on rubber gloves. A dash to open the door to the corridor. A bound to cross the little courtyard. A few steps to get to the end of the vestibule. A discreet signal to Malabar who returned with her. The same movements in reverse.

Thérèse and Malabar were beside Karl. Malabar went to open the door between the laboratory and the office. Languille and Friquet went to work. Their agility and their small stature had let them use the window to get into the building. The first minutes were well employed. The information Thérèse had furnished was precious and avoided loss of time. The desk pivoted; the safe was located; the four buttons were revealed.

"Now the word," murmured Languille.

"I know one very well," Friquet joked, "but it has five letters."

Thérèse watched her agents work; she directed the operations without participating directly. She watched Karl attentively, a very easy task. Karl had been put to sleep by a powerful soporific that the French agent had poured in his dinner when she passed the plate. He wasn't making the least movement. His breathing was harsh, whistling, but regular. His pulse was beating regularly.

"However, it wouldn't be any loss if he didn't come out of it," remarked Malabar, who was conscientiously going through the laboratory.

"Have you tried *Karl*," Thérèse suggested.

"That was the first idea we had, but it didn't yield anything."

New efforts, new failures. Time passing.

"Still nothing?"

"Nothing."

"For a good safe, it's obviously a good safe. But to open it is a devil of a job," Friquet signed.

"Try methodically," said Languille, "since, otherwise, by guesses we won't get any result."

Thérèse looked at her watch: 12:25 a.m.

"Until 2:00 p.m. we're all right, but a safe like that can resist longer than that, above all if we want to avoid violent means."

However," Languille raged, "that catches. It ought to be *Karl,* and nothing moves."

"K-A-R-L," Friquet repeated.

"C-a-r-l," Thérèse said.

A click and the plate went down into the floor and the safe came up to replace the desk. A quadruple sigh of relief was responded to by Karl's deeper, harsher snores.

"Friquet and Languille come watch him while I go look into the safe."

"Guarding him isn't difficult," Friquet remarked. "That pig doesn't want to skip out. He's having good dreams while we're wearing ourselves out."

At 12:50 p.m. Thérèse had finished her inspection.

"We have to hurry. We can't take everything, however," she said regretfully. "Come on, hurry up, Friquet! Carry that to Marcel."

"All right, Boss, speed and discretion, the motto of the house."

Languille remained the only one guarding Karl, who continued to snore peacefully.

C.25 examined the dossier in the safe. Not being able to communicate all of them to Captain Ladoux, she had to be satisfied with taking notes, looking for the most significant papers, the most important dossiers. And she was terrified by the powerful organization and the formidable espionage operation that she was discovering.

Malabar was walking around the laboratory. Suddenly he exclaimed: "Good Lord! It's the same system!"

In fact, the big table filled with flasks and test tubes had pivoted, revealing a metal plate. There was no security lock there, just an electric contact in a space between the boards. The iron plate went down through the floor. A stairway. An electric light. And a magnificent wireless station complete with the most up-to-date instruments for wireless transmissions, appeared to the eyes of Thérèse, Malabar and Languille.

"Oh! Those pigs!" Malabar growled. "In the middle of Paris!"

"Guard the man who has sleeping sickness for a little while," Languille said. "I'm going to make some slight changes to their wireless station that will work for me too. No sabotage, just first class work. After that I imagine it will work, even with the wires cut."

And he set to work rapidly.

"Eh! Eh! Be quiet old man, or..." Malabar threatened.

"Is he waking up?" Thérèse worried.

"Not yet, but he moved his arms."

She looked at her watch. 1:30 p.m. A decision. She rapidly opened her purse. She dipped a small cotton pad with the contents of a flask.

"No other way to prolong his sleep. I would have wished to avoid that."

A deep breath from Karl, who again avoided reality.

"He didn't regain consciousness," she said, "but with a man as strong as that you can't be too careful."

Minutes passed. Languille returned, satisfied with his work, saying,

"Nothing appears to have been touched, but, now, to make it work as well sending as well as receiving, these gentlemen will have something to keep them busy. Everything will have to be taken apart. However, it's very well installed in a superb concrete cellar."

But Thérèse was only half listening. 1:45 p.m. and Friquet had not returned.

"Malabar, don't leave any traces."

Everything was rapidly put back in place. The huge table returned to its place. 1:55 p.m. Friquet wasn't there. Karl's employees were going to come in. The shop would open.

"We have to get out, Languille. The safe. Close everything. That's all we can do with the safe now. We'll have to come back later with the code. Too bad!" decided Thérèse, who didn't try to hide her disappointment. Once again, the game that seemed easily won was lost. Everything was back in order in the office. It was almost 2 p.m.

"Leave," Thérèse ordered.

"But you, Boss!" Malabar anxiously asked.

"Me? I'm staying. I have to. Nothing happened. I was with Karl. He had a fainting spell. I brought him out of it. He must not notice anything. So long as he doesn't open the safe, nothing is discovered. When he regains consciousness he has to find me near him."

"But if he suspects, if he…"

She made a vague gesture and repeated without raising her voice, "I've told you, leave. I'm staying."

Doubly worried both for the Boss and for Friquet, Languille and Malabar regretfully obeyed. They knew their comrade too well not to know that if he hadn't returned that was because something had happened to him.

And Thérèse remaining alone with the still sleeping Karl produced the same thought. She was not thinking of her own danger. She was trying to guess what had happened since Friquet's departure.

VIII. Looking for Friquet

Back at Thérèse's house, Malabar and Languille found Marcel who was waiting, faithful to his orders, ready to photograph the documents and take them to Captain Ladoux.

"Friquet?" Languille and Malabar asked at the same time.

Marcel looked puzzled. "Friquet?"

"Yes, where is he? He brought you the secret code. When did he leave?"

"I haven't seen anyone."

"Nobody?" Languille and Malabar repeated.

There was a moment of silence.

"Has Friquet disappeared?" Marcel asked.

"Yes," Malabar answered hurriedly. "He left Jean Durand's shop. He carried the code. He was supposed to come straight here."

"And he hasn't arrived…"

Another pause for rapid thought. "That means that between the Avenue de l'Opéra and here he had an accident."

"An accident," Languille wondered.

Two telephone calls to commissariat offices that could furnish information about accidents happening between the Avenue de l'Opéra and Thérèse's residence confirmed the suspicion of Malabar and his friends.

No accident had been reported. So? Thérèse Arnaud's agents made a wide, vague gesture.

"We must go look for him," Languille proposed immediately.

"Where?" Malabar ironically asked. "Where do you want to look for him? Do you have an opinion? A clue? A basis from which to direct searches?"

It was Marcel who attempted to put together some hypotheses.

"Let's see. Let's go back over the chain of events. Friquet, carrying the secret code, left you on the Avenue de l'Opéra. At what time?"

"Twelve fifty exactly."

"It's two twenty-five. Too much time has gone by to expect Friquet to arrive, even granted that when he left, he felt that he was being followed and was obliged to break off communication."

"So?"

"So, logically, he's in the hands of Karl's auxiliaries."

"How's that? Friquet's not a child. He's not a man to let himself be kidnapped in the middle of Paris without saying a word, without attracting attention, without defending himself, if necessary. And in addition he knew the importance of his scheduled return. Nothing would have made him alter his direct route, not a trap, not an ambush."

"Maybe," Malabar objected.

"What's that? Explain yourself. What are you guessing?"

"I'm like you. I can suppose anything, but that's all. It seems to me that Friquet took a taxi as soon as he reached the Avenue de l'Opéra."

"Then no taxi accident, no…"

"Childishly easy. A taxi that seemed to be driving around without a fare that finds itself there by accident. And once in the car, on the way, locked doors that can't be opened, windows that can't be rolled down. Useless to cry out or to fight. A prisoner. They take Friquet away…"

"The villa at Neuilly?" Languille suggested.

"There or somewhere else, in just any hideout. Karl's agents don't lack places."

Another silence heavy with thought.

"However," Marcel, suggested, "for Friquet to have been taken prisoner by the German spies, you'd have to agree that the alarm had been given. They *knew* that Friquet was carrying documents. Therefore they were not ignorant of the fact that a burglary was attempted against Himmelfeld's safe. In that case it was easy to surprise *all* of you in the middle of your work. Instead of capturing one of Thérèse's agents, they would have gotten a nice net full."

"Precisely," Languille said.

"Yes," Marcel said, "and we got out of Karl's without any trouble."

"Therefore they don't know what happened at Karl's place. If they had known that, they would have laid the same trap for you that Friquet fell into. And that would have been even easier since you left separately. One man is easier caught than three!"

"Incomprehensible!" Marcel raged.

"It's useless to waste time arguing," Malabar decided. "We have to find Friquet. And me, I'm going back to the Avenue de l'Opéra. He obviously left Jean Durand's building. He might have even left by the coach door since the shop was closed."

"He must have left," Marcel noted. "None of you went with him. How did he leave you and where?"

"In the laboratory. He went down the corridor that's the only normal exit. We saw him open the door."

"And after that?"

"Afterward? That's all. He must have crossed the little courtyard."

"Yes, he must have, but no one knows anything about that. And what if the trap was between the laboratory and the door to the vestibule of the building?" Marcel wondered.

"Impossible. Languille and I left the same way at two o'clock."

"That means an hour and ten minutes later!"

"And we didn't notice anything. Absolutely nothing. Granting that there was a trap in the corridor, Friquet would have cried out, sounded the alarm. The door of the little courtyard isn't ten meters from the laboratory door…which stayed open. So we would have heard. And still, why did the trap that caught Friquet not take us too, since we went out of the laboratory the same way? What's more, if they were watching Friquet, they knew that we were there. So?"

"So," Languille reflected, "Malabar is right. We have to go back to the Avenue de l'Opéra. That's the point of departure for the business. We have to trace Friquet's passage, where he left from, if he left. And in that case, we have to establish the place from which he was abducted."

"I'm going there too," Malabar decided. "But be careful! They've certainly been alerted. So take precautions! However, I'm not sorry to go back to the Boss. She may need us. Marcel, are you staying here?"

"Yes! Alas! That's the order. There are cases where respect for orders is very painful. And I certainly would like to go with you."

IX. Two Tough Jousters

Immediately after Languille and Malabar's departure, Thérèse was actively busy with Karl. He had to be brought back to consciousness with the shortest delay, because the boutique was now open and he could be called at any moment. She did her best to wake him. Before that she had taken care to put her watch back a quarter of an hour. Then she did the same with that of Himmelfeld. Karl, deeply asleep, both because of the sleeping dosage he had absorbed and because of the chloroform she had made him breathe, continued to snore.

She emptied the contents of a third flask onto a handkerchief that she placed under Karl's nose. A reflex. An arm stretched out. The other arm raised and fell back inert. Then Karl's eyes began to blink. Finally his eyes opened trying to grasp some reality. The reality: Thérèse leaning over Karl attentively, asking softly,

"Are you feeling better?"

He answered with a deep groan. He slowly regained consciousness. It was obviously the effort of tense will power trying to escape the anesthetic's hold.

She said again: "Is your indisposition going away?"

Karl made a heavy, still clumsy gesture. He tried to speak but couldn't. His eyes rolled furiously. His nose pinched, smelling the odor floating in the laboratory. Finally, he regained the ability to speak. And he said in a commanding tone:

"Leave me!"

Thérèse stepped back a little. Karl followed her with his eyes.

"Stay there!" he commanded.

Then during long, silent moments he attempted to regain regular respiration.

"Are you better?" she repeated, obeying Karl's orders and sitting some steps from him.

He didn't answer. He surveyed the Secret Service agent coldly. Without letting it bother her, she calmly explained:

"That came on you suddenly. You were in the midst of giving me information, and suddenly....."

"I remember," Karl affirmed sharply. After thinking a moment, he asked:

"What time is it?"

"About two o'clock," she informed him.

"A good syncope," Karl murmured. "Let's see. When I lost consciousness it was...it was..."

"Almost a quarter to one o'clock," she lied. "I arrived at 12:15. We talked a long time and...

"Yes, almost," said the German in an expressionless voice. A short silence. "I remained unconscious for more than an hour! Yes, that's not the first time that's happened. And these days I've tired myself out."

44

Thérèse seemed to take a lively interest in the explanations Himmelfeld was giving her. Suddenly, after a pause, he posed the following question:

"And for an hour and a quarter you took care of me. It didn't occur to you to call someone?"

"Call?" she answered. "Who? The boutique was closed. I thought about it. But also I thought it was useless to tell the neighbors. You probably wouldn't care..."

"No. Obviously! You did the right thing! I thank you. But what did you do for me?"

"Oh! Just the obvious things. I loosened your collar. I stretched you out as well as I could..."

"Yes...don't you think there's a strange odor floating about here?"

She showed the third little flask.

"I remembered that I had a little flask of..."

"Let's see it!"

She held out the flask. Karl breathed it in deeply. Then he handed the flask back to her, murmuring: "Yes..."

Then for a long moment Karl observed Thérèse.

"Don't you find that it was strange?"

"Strange? Fainting...a syncope, due to overwork."

"No, not that!"

"Then what?"

"You know very well what I mean!"

"Me? Not at all."

Karl again groaned deeply. Then he rose. He took some steps around the laboratory. He stretched his stiff arms and legs. He seemed to be measuring their suppleness and elasticity. He pulled his chair near that of Thérèse.

"Really? You don't see the strangeness of certain facts?"

"Of certain facts?"

"That fainting spell that happened while we were alone, while the shop was closed. I would even say while we were sure of not being disturbed. Also, the duration of that syncope, this should have in any case bothered you. Your presence of mind in not calling anyone to help me. That bizarre absence of my memory that I know is excellent. It was only an hour later that you remembered that you had in your purse a vial that could help me regain consciousness. The truth may sometimes not seem real. Fortunately, it was you who were with me."

While Karl was calming down in giving these explanations, in an absolutely detached voice, Thérèse was trying to find where he was going with it. She was ready for anything. But in appearance she remained impassive, calm, smiling. Karl concluded:

"Yes, fortunately it was you who was with me. With anyone else I might have been suspicious. But you have given such proofs of devotion, from your mission in Spain, that I have every reason to be entirely reassured."

45

"I only did what my duty commanded me to do!"

"And I don't doubt for a moment that you're ready to continue! Besides, a very complimentary report from Von Krohn in your regard, confirms to me the excellent agent you are for us."

She made a vague gesture that could have been taken for confusion. Karl continued:

"That rapid return, such a rapid return from Spain, without even resting. Truly you are indefatigable! I regret that you hadn't been put at my disposition earlier. Nevertheless, you're not new to the service?"

"No, certainly, but I received orders that sent me abroad."

"Yes…Yes…"

Karl suddenly stood up. "Goodbye, then!"

Thérèse, somewhat surprised by this sudden dismissal, also rose. Karl explained more amiably:

"After this shock, I'm a little tired today. We wouldn't do any useful work. I'm going to take a little rest. And tomorrow morning…"

"Until tomorrow morning," she confirmed.

There were two small discreet taps on the laboratory door.

"Come in!" Himmelfeld shouted.

One of the employees entered and handed Karl a sealed envelope.

"It's urgent," he said.

"All right."

The employee left. Thérèse was going to follow him since Karl had dismissed her.

"Just a moment, please!"

Karl opened the message and read it rapidly. Only a few lines. It was obviously good news for him, because he couldn't keep from smiling. And he immediately lost that sullen look he'd had the last two days.

"I believe this message is of a nature to modify the rendezvous I gave you. It's nothing," he said. "But…strange even so."

Slowly, he accompanied her to the door. He opened the door and he stood back politely to let Thérèse, who was putting on her gloves, go through. She walked down the corridor, *followed by Karl*. She rapidly put on her rubber gloves over the other gloves. She had just noticed that, generally—and it had been that way every time she had left the laboratory—*Karl walked before her*. She walked very slowly, cautiously. She came to the door that led from the corridor to the little courtyard. She stopped, seeming to search for something.

"I don't see; I can't find the lock."

Karl directed the bright beam of an electric flashlight. "There it is; you have it under our hand."

Thérèse hesitated a moment. She gathered all her strength to jump and with a quick gesture she turned the door handle. The door resisted the push; it was locked. She jumped backward. She felt Karl rapidly fall back. A length of several meters of the corridor floor disappeared. Under her feet, the void. A fall.

Rather quick, rather supple, she hit the floor without being hurt. Darkness, and above the voice of the German spy, of Karl. Thérèse picked herself up.

"I always told you that curiosity is a vile fault! And a fault that's always punished!"

Then a gross laugh. "Really. There were too many strange things. And the first was enough. Before telling you goodbye, I'm going to let you in on some information that may surprise you. The real agent sent to me by the German Espionage Service was killed at the Châtelet Metro Station."

"I've known that a long time," Thérèse threw back at him in rage.

"And you didn't tell me," Karl ironically joked. A gross laugh and that was all. The floor had just closed again.

She was a prisoner. She remained a few moments immobile, trying to regain her calm.

"Fortunately I have my purse." She took out an electric flashlight. She threw the rays on the walls of her prison. It was a big, square room of about five meters with no visible doors.

"Reinforced concrete," she verified, tapping the walls. She began methodically to explore it. Then a voice she recognized:

"So Boss, they've sent you down to the metro too?"

"Friquet? Where are you?"

She saw Friquet in a corner of the cell. In a low voice she asked: "How did you get here?"

"Like you, Boss, by way of the air, directly! And without having had time to get a ticket."

"All right, tell me."

"Immediately after leaving you, Boss, I went down the corridor to exit. I was getting out quickly. I turned the door handle. Or, rather I tried to turn the door handle. I got a terrible shock. I felt the floor give way under my feet. And in a soaring flight, but with a somewhat hard landing, I arrived here. And I'm not unhappy to meet you here because I was beginning to get old down here!"

"The stupid trap! The usual mousetrap!" Thérèse raged. "But since Karl was asleep, since Malabar and I went down the same corridor in the other direction shortly before, who gave the alarm, who set the electric current? And what's become of Malabar and Languille, who also left the laboratory and went down the corridor?"

"Malabar and Languille? I haven't seen them. That's too bad, because with four of us we could play a game of *belote*. The more crazy people there are the more we can laugh! The room Jean Durand has furnished us free is really not very funny…It lacks comfort! And at the first opportunity I get, I'm going to be sure to take a walk downtown, if only to carry to good old Marcel the documents he may have to wait for a long time."

C.25 didn't answer. During Friquet's speech, she had inspected the walls. Reinforced concrete everywhere, no sign of a door.

"No other possible way out except the ceiling. A ray of light directed upward. At a glance the Secret Service agent murmured: "Four meters!"

"I went down them faster than we're going to go back up them. Besides, Boss, I was growing old down here and to distract myself I carefully examined all the walls. I didn't find the door leading to the metro."

Thérèse shut off the flashlight.

"Let's spare the batteries."

Then in the darkness, she began thinking. No use to delude themselves. The situation was serious. They didn't have the means to maneuver the metallic plate that covered the hole. To pierce the floor, they didn't have either the facility or the time. They hadn't any truly useful tool for such work. So? Condemned to die down there? And from what death? Hunger? Was it in Karl's plans to let his prisoners perish that way? Wasn't he going to try some way to get them to talk, to force—or try to force—some information out of them? Thérèse's mind remained clear. She could do nothing to get out of her prison. Only one hope remained: Malabar and Languille, who had gotten away safely. How to guide their searches? How to let them know the location of this prison? How would they be able to save the prisoners now that the alarm had been given. They couldn't get there except through the corridor. And the corridor was certainly watched by Himmelfeld's agents.

C.25 and Friquet were stretched out on the ground.

"Let's try to get some rest. We'll get back to it later," she had said. But for herself she scarcely had any illusions. See about it later? See about what? She had looked at her watch. It was 5:30 p.m.

"Good night, Boss!"

She hadn't answered.

"I'm going to try to sleep. That will be doubly useful," Friquet continued, "because *he who sleeps dines.* And things to eat here seem not to be very certain. That so much the worse, because this morning I ate very early."

Some time passed. Thérèse knew that Malabar and Languille wouldn't fail to go in search of the agents who had disappeared. But from all the evidence, they would have to work during the night. Wouldn't they be doing something rash by going into that house full of traps and fall themselves into Karl Himmelfeld's hands?

Thérèse suffered a passing attack of nerves. She didn't know how to reconcile herself to inactivity. She paced up and down while Friquet, calmer, was sleeping. Suddenly Friquet sat up.

"Boss," he exclaimed in a worried voice: "You don't smell anything?"

She smelled the humid air. "No, nothing. Why?"

"Then it was just a feeling I had. So much the better"

"What sort of impression?" she quickly asked.

"I thought it smelled like gas."

The Secret Service agent quickly stretched out on the ground. A few seconds of immobility, then she stood up.

"Get up! Friquet."

She looked at her watch. 6:15.

"There's no mistake. We have to find out where that came from!"

"Then I was right, Boss!"

"The pigs! To asphyxiate us like mongrel dogs not claimed at the pound."

Deep anguish seized Friquet and Thérèse. This time everything seemed over. The very trembling light of hope remaining to the prisoners, the intervention of Malabar and Languille, died out. Even admitting that the two auxiliaries would succeed in getting into Karl's shop and discovering the prison cell, it would be too late. Now, death was only a question of hours, of minutes. Everything depended on the output of the faucet which was filling the cell with deadly gas.

"If that's coming from above, there's nothing to be done about it," Thérèse thought. "The metallic plate is about four meters from the ground. I measure one meter sixty-five. Friquet measures one meter seventy. Me on his shoulders, or him on mine, with our arms extended we couldn't reach three meters sixty. A slight hope, if the faucet is placed in hand's reach. That's not impossible, seeing that the ceiling is moveable, which makes the installation difficult and easily thrown off the track."

Long, painful, agonizing searches. The odor of the gas was spreading more and more throughout the cellar, dangerously slowing down Thérèse and Friquet.

"Finally! I've found it," Friquet said triumphantly. "How nice it is to have talent!"

She directed the ray of the flashlight to the spot indicated. A little valve of weak diameter came into a corner of the prison at ground level.

"That's coming from underneath," she remarked. "There are two floors of cellars."

With the instruments in Thérèse's purse and a wad of cotton which could be used as gag or for chloroform, they succeeded not only in stopping the flow of the gas, but at least in blocking the pipe and, as a consequence, considerably limiting the output.

"That will let us hold out longer," C.25 thought. "But that's all. Unless Karl's agents find out that the gas is not escaping in sufficient quantities."

"And now we are definitely condemned not to sit down," Friquet groaned. "Decidedly this resembles the metro. It's underground. It smells bad, and you have to stand. But at least here you're less crowded. I'll wind up regretting Spain, the fleas, and the chick peas."

"If we were just condemned to remain standing," Thérèse thought, "that wouldn't be too serious. But unfortunately we have a great deal more to fear."

X. Help for the Lost Agents

Languille and Malabar saw their idea put into execution without delay: to return to the Avenue de l'Opéra to look for Friquet. The first results were absolutely nil. No trace. No information. No clues. The Marquis's domestic servant had gone to pick up his master's wig. He saw nothing suspicious in the shop. Communication with Marcel confirmed the continued absence of Friquet. Malabar and Languille soon became worried about the fate of the Boss. She hadn't left Jean Durand's building. The length of her stay was becoming unusual. Nevertheless, the two agents found no trace after their surveillance of the building.

"That's because all surveillance is useless," Languille deduced. "The interior is well enough defended to make outside precautions unnecessary."

Hours passed without anything that happened in the boutique being unknown to Malabar and Languille. They became impatient, finding the wait almost unbearable. They were in a hurry to go into action. And they already would have acted if caution had not dictated waiting, in order to avoid useless efforts ending in immediate failure.

"Something has happened to the Boss also," they concluded. "Has she fallen into the same trap that closed over Friquet? Should we look for her somewhere else?"

Malabar and Languille discussed the chances and possibilities of help. Should they separate and try, each on his own, to find a trace of one of the lost agents? They were at that point in their projects when they saw Jean Durand/Karl Himmelfeld leave. It was only 6 p.m.

"No point in waiting any longer," Malabar decided. "We're going to visit the whole building."

The plan was simple. The Acrobat would go in through the office window, as he had already done. As for the Colossus, he would enter by the little courtyard door. And they would go in, one ahead of the other.

Languille was the first to leave with great strides. Malabar put on his rubber gloves before touching the door. It was locked, a very natural precaution. To break it down would have been child's play for Malabar, but to work silently he used a burglar's tool. In addition, the lock was simple. It hardly resisted. The Colossus cautiously pulled back the door, which opened from the outside. He saw the rays from the electric light and Languille's silhouette coming toward him. He was going to enter, when suddenly the light went out, and Languille's voice shouted: "Be careful, Malabar! The floor!" Languille had disappeared.

Malabar saw the flooring continuing to open in a slow, regular movement. Then at the end of the track the mechanism began to reverse directions, starting to close the flooring.

At a glance, Malabar measured the length of the trap. The flooring was about to fall back in place. Two meters. One meter eighty. One meter fifty. The opening was getting smaller. A massive jump. His feet braced one side of the trap. The Colossus leaned forward and his arms reached the opposite side. A hole of about one meter remained open above a black space emitting an odor of gas. Malabar's muscles stretched. The trap was closing slower. A new effort, more tension. Malabar was using all his strength to prevent the trap from continuing to close. At last the mechanism stopped moving, held back just by the Herculean strength of C.25's auxiliary.

"Languille!"

"Yes, I'm here…with the Boss and Friquet. But we have to act quickly."

"No accident?"

"No!"

"Hurry up…I have a good grip…" Malabar gasped, "But…"

There were two vain attempts to throw up the rope Languille was carrying, then another attempt, a human pyramid, Languille supporting Friquet and Thérèse. C.25 came up first. She made fast the rope, then soon Languille and Friquet came up from the prison. Malabar released his hold and stood up.

"Phew! I was hot!"

The mechanism functioned once more.

"It's good to breath air!" Friquet smiled.

Thérèse had already recovered her calm. She decided:

"None of the instructions have been changed. You, Friquet, hurry and carry the documents to Marcel and come back immediately."

"This time I'll go with him," Languille suggested.

"All right! But be quick about it. Karl may not have noticed that the safe was opened while he was asleep. In that case, we've succeeded."

Nothing happened, but a somewhat anxious wait by Thérèse and Malabar on watch. Friquet and Languille returned without meeting any obstacle.

"Be careful! You never know what can happen in this satanic cabin," Friquet joked, as the little group went cautiously into the office.

The safe was once again opened. It gave no resistance. The secret code was put back in its place. Before leaving, C.25 glanced around to be sure that no detail would betray the fact that anyone had been there.

"No, everything is in place. Let's go!"

Very early the next morning, Thérèse Arnaud went to see Captain Ladoux.

"All my congratulations! That was a pretty piece of work."

"Congratulations!" she exclaimed, shocked.

"Yes, thanks to the information you brought me from Spain and that I immediately communicated, two submarines have been sunk before they even reached the Mediterranean. That's a victory already. As for the photographs of the code, they allowed us to decipher the documents we couldn't decode. And we have in our possession all the details of a well-established organization in case of a submarine war in the Atlantic Ocean and in the Mediterranean. We'll act accordingly."

C.25 remained silent a moment. Then she said:

"Mata Hari recently went to Spain. She stayed at the Palace Hotel in Madrid."

Smiling, Captain Ladoux looked at C.25. "Yes, she had an engagement there! She's a dancer! That's her profession! Where are you going with that? Believe me, we have many things more serious and more real to think about."

He gave an amused laugh. Then, with a slight shrug, he repeated: "Mata Hari!"

Thérèse Arnaud didn't answer and so he continued:

"Some things troubling in a different way are taking place in Greece. Would you like to go there?"

"What's it about?"

The agent on call announced the arrival of a visitor who had come through the secret passage. Captain Ladoux held out his hand to Thérèse.

"I'll tell you that in a few minutes. I think a new element of the problem is here." And he accompanied her to the door, repeating: "Congratulations on the Spanish business. But don't weigh yourself down about Mata Hari!"

"We'll see!" C.25 said with a smile.

KARL HIMMELFELD'S REVENGE

I. A Night in Montmartre

War had snuffed out the illuminated signs and the happy animation of Montmartre. Now gloomy, shadowy, silent streets showed a line of their shops closed by iron curtains. In the distance a clock struck midnight. A man, a soft hat pulled down over his eyes, the collar of his overcoat turned up, walked along rapidly. He glanced down the deserted Rue Mansart, where one lone door was partially open letting out a faint red light. The man hid in a corner and waited. Suddenly, a car with a powerful motor, coming up the Rue Blanche, let out in the silence a sinister, resonating blast of its horn. The man mentally counted the seconds: one, two, three, four, five. Then there was a second blast of the horn. Without leaving his hiding place, the man put his hand on his revolver holster. And, quietly, he again put his hand in the pocket of his overcoat. Some seconds passed. The silhouette of a woman appeared at the other end of the Rue Mansart, coming from the Rue Blanche, a tall, slim, and rapid shadow.

The man measured the distance that separated him from the silhouette: 100 meters, 50. His hand came out of the overcoat pocket. 30 meters. The hand, raised; the silhouette was still advancing. Suddenly a man jumped forward and with a rapid movement he immobilized the arm before the revolver had discharged its sharp bark. And an authoritative voice commanded:

"Stop that, you imbecile! You were about to pull off a nice job!"

Surprised, the man with the revolver stood immobile. His arm fell down beside his body. His face took on the astonished but respectful look of an uncomprehending inferior before a superior.

"Karl!" he whispered. And in spite of himself, he let his surprise spurt out.

"I was carrying out orders!"

"And you were also *executing* the woman. The orders have changed. That's all. Your mission is terminated this evening. You can go back!" Karl's sharp voice answered.

The man obeyed like a soldier. He left his shelter and rapidly disappeared into the night. Karl Himmelfeld watched him fade away into the shadows. Then, before leaving himself, he murmured with rage:

"Too bad! We would have been rid of that woman."

And with vague regret, himself deploring the orders received that he must carry out, he said: "But they want her alive!"

That short scene had only lasted several seconds. The silhouette had arrived in front of the partially open door without realizing the danger which had threatened her. And calmly, like someone who knew those inside, she entered.

II. The Clandestine Night Club

Couples squeezed against one another moving in time to the music. Sharp laughter, nervous shouts, an atmosphere blue with cigarette smoke floating in the low room. Floating, heavy perfume, the smell of alcohol, sweat. Soft lights, sometimes blue, sometimes red, gave a mysterious light to that clandestine night club. A suspicious, troubled, perverse atmosphere. The silhouette took off her overcoat at the entry. She appeared, young, attractive, wearing a low cut gown. Then she looked for a seat at one of the tables, for the most part occupied. Her look circled the dancing couples. For an instant a faint smile played over her face. She found a table and ordered a drink from the waiter. The orchestra played the opening of a slow waltz. A young and elegant man came toward her and bowed. She stood up. They went to add to the mass of dancers.

"Boss," Languille asked, as they danced, "may I finally know why you had me come here and why you came here yourself?"

"To work," Thérèse Arnaud replied, laconically, but she soon continued. "Yes, an idea that I have and that doesn't seem bad. I have the impression I'm not wasting my time."

"You've met the person you were looking for?" Languille inquired.

She didn't answer. Silent turns of the waltz.

"You don't know me any longer, Languille. I'm here alone. No more dances together unless you have special instructions to ask me. You're going to get attached to that lady there."

And with a discreet look she pointed out to Languille a foreign type of young woman accompanied by a middle-aged man.

"But that's Mata Hari," Languille said.

C.25 pretended not to hear. Then she gave precise instructions.

"Follow her when she leaves. Find out where she goes. Wait if necessary. Take notice of every act and gesture. Photograph those who approach her, those who talk to her, those who dance with her, in order to recognize them again."

"Understood," Languille said.

The waltz ended. Languille accompanied Thérèse back to her table. He took formal leave of her and returned to his place.

The atmosphere became even heavier. A kind of drunkenness floated in the foul air. Unhealthy desires hung about. The heat, the alcohol, the atmosphere exacerbated the nerves. The dimmed lighting favored those isolated to come together. A confused brouhaha of conversations and of laughter mounted.

Languille, while pretending to continue drinking and while dancing, began to take on the mission C.25 had given him. But he didn't understand the reason. He saw the Boss dance with the same man several times. By habit he noted several details about the individual: tall, wide shoulders, elegant, rather attractive man, distinguished bearing. Now Thérèse and her new dance partner were sitting at the same table, usual and ordinary in a night club! The conversation could be guessed: the man's compliments, the seductive words, the invitation for a meeting.

"Why do you want to put my sincerity in doubt?" said the man.

"You can't make me believe that these sudden feelings can be true," Thérèse said. "If I had not been here, another woman would have heard the same sentences, exactly the same."

The man made a gesture of vehement protestation. Then he drew close to Thérèse. His voice became softer, more seductive.

"We're going to leave, both of us! You'll come to my place. We'll end the night with joy. I have everything that's needed to satisfy you, however demanding you may be. Do you know the joy of opium? Doesn't that tempt you? Blue lights, a kimono, a pipe. And a dream, every dream. You've come here to get away from sad realities. Well! What I'm offering you is another, more complete evasion. And satisfactions more refined than all those of these beings who dance and drink. So? Is it agreed?"

He had seductively put his arm around Thérèse's waist. She didn't pull away. The man took this for consent.

"Shall we go?"

"No."

"Visible disappointment showed on the man's face. But she had already softened the severity of her refusal.

"No, not this evening."

"Why not this evening," he protested.

"Because it's impossible. You are tempting me, obviously. I don't deny it. But you must understand that a woman…a woman such as I, can in certain circumstances not have free use of her time."

"Yes! Yes!" the man consented, visibly disappointed. "But another day, another evening?"

"I didn't say no."

The man supposed it an acceptance. He took advantage of it.

"When? Soon? Tomorrow?" he urged.

Thérèse hesitated some moments. She reflected. Finally, she consented.

"No, not tomorrow. That's still not possible and for the same reasons. But would you like Thursday? Unless you will have forgotten me from now until then."

"Forgotten? Have no fear of that. The memory of this evening near you will follow me until then and even longer. When one has had the joy of being near you, dancing with you…"

Thérèse smiled and half closed her eyes. Then suddenly she shook off the slight drunkenness that seemed to have taken hold of her on hearing these banalities. She repeated:

"Thursday? Here? Toward midnight?"

"And this time you'll leave with me? You'll come to my place?" the man questioned.

"I'll leave with you," she said docilely.

Fleeting satisfaction showed on the man's face. Thérèse got up.

"Now I must go back."

Before separating from the man, she renewed her promises. Then she went to the entry hall. She quickly pushed a passage through the dancing couples. Languille, who was watching the Boss's departure, maneuvered so as to find himself in her path.

"Tomorrow, ten o'clock at the latest, at the house," she slipped to him. From minute to minute the atmosphere was becoming heavier. A kind of joyous rage had seized all the couples. Voices became louder, more strident, more nervous. The dances stopped and began again with more abandon, more languor, more mystery. From time to time the din of broken crockery could be heard dominating for an instant the noise of conversation. Niggardly daylight began to filter through the frosted glass windows. A wave of cold air came into the night club. The lights seemed to grow pale. And the gray shadow mingling with the blue lights lit up the tired faces, the worn-out make up, eyes overwhelmed with desire or drunkenness.

Languille left, following Mata Hari. Some steps in the dirty dawn. Two taxis were stationed at the corner of the Rue Fontaine. The dancer and the man accompanying her took the first. Languille hurried and opened the door of the second vehicle. He spoke to the chauffeur, who was asleep on his seat.

"Follow the other taxi!" The chauffeur acquiesced with a groan. The door slammed. The motor purred and the vehicle started down the empty street before the taxi carrying the dancer had disappeared in the horizon.

Languille, his eye on the glass separating him from the driver, remained on the lookout. At the bottom of the Rue Notre-Dame-de-Lorette, Mata Hari's taxi turned into the Rue Saint-Lazare. Some meters behind, Languille's vehicle continued on its way to the Montmartre suburb.

"Good God! Driver!" Languille groaned, trying to open the window.

The driver didn't even turn around. The car picked up speed. The window resisted, refusing to open. Steel plates rising on the panes transformed the vehicle in a hermetically enclosed cell. Languille jumped toward the doors. They were also locked.

"The pigs," Languille raged when he was convinced that he had been drawn into a trap, and that all effort to get out of that prison would be absolutely useless.

Daylight broke through; the Sun mounted in the horizon. The city awoke. And the taxi, faster and faster, carried Languille away a prisoner.

III. The Trap

At 2 p.m. there was a great deal of worry at the house of Thérèse Arnaud. The faces of Friquet and Marcel didn't even try to hide their consternation. There could no longer be any doubt. All hopes had disappeared one by one. It was useless to have any illusions. The reality was there. Languille had been kidnapped and no information had been gathered that would usefully guide any searches.

"Maybe Malabar has been luckier than we have," Marcel murmured.

"I hope so," C.25 answered, "but I would be surprised if he has."

Malabar entered a few moments later. This time he had not used the secret entrance. Questioning eyes rested on him. For any answer he held out a letter to Thérèse.

"Languille's handwriting."

Thérèse opened the message rapidly and glanced over the text.

"Where did you find this?" she questioned.

"Here. At the door. On the doormat," Malabar answered.

A pause while Thérèse thought. Then she read aloud:

"You are alarmed by absence. Not immediately in danger here. Held by Giroflées-Enghien. Come."

Marcel was already interpreting: "Les Giroflées villa at Enghien."

"Thérèse looked at him without answering. Now she began reading again slowly, pausing over each word.

"Strange, this text," continued Marcel, who was listening attentively. "Very strange. If Languille was in a hurry to write that letter as the telegraphic style at the beginning and address seem to indicate, why does he use words that have a double meaning and are useless in understanding the sense? Why *not in danger* instead of *no danger here* which would be in the same style as the rest. That's suspicious, as is the way that letter arrived at the entry door."

"Suspicious or not," Malabar said, "we have to go there immediately. Let's leave right now."

Thérèse was still silently studying the text.

"Fourteen," she said suddenly.

Her auxiliaries stared at her. And their astonishment grew with the enigmatic words Thérèse was pronouncing.

"Fourteen, that makes nine. And nine, that's D."

She went straight to a drawer of her desk. She rummaged through a box of pieces of paper. She took out a box which had written in big letters: D/9. Then she read aloud this strange formula:

"—2.3.5. 14. 1.4. 7.11.6.10.8.12.13."

"Marcel, write down all the list of numbers in that order to 14 (the number of words in the message). Omit the number nine which is the key. Take down the first letter of the words in the text, numbering them from 1 to 14 (always

57

with the exception of the number 9. E-P-A-N-S. P-I-E-D-I-R-G-E-V. Form words by taking the letters fitting the places indicated by the numbers of the formula."

Marcel rapidly executed her instructions.

"2-P, 3-A, 5-S," he murmured. Then he soon exclaimed: "That means: *Don't come. A trap!*"

"Don't come!" Malabar protested.

"That's certainly why we must go."

After thinking a moment, she distributed roles.

"You, Friquet, you'll leave alone as a rearguard. Objective: scout out the villa. Gather information. We'll wait at the station after we've found lodgings from where we can watch the *Giroflées* and wait for the proper moment to intervene."

"That job's for me," Friquet answered. "For me, who hasn't had a vacation, that's something!"

"Marcel will go alone. Malabar will act as my bodyguard."

Friquet left immediately. Each one got busy preparing the accessories necessary for the expedition.

A plan was already forming in the fertile mind of the intrepid agent. The warning Languille gave would be useful. A trap had been set. That was no reason not to try to free the prisoner and also foil the trap.

By the end of the day Thérèse and her agents were installed in lodgings on a circular street in Enghien.

"No traffic! Very quiet house," the proprietor had told Friquet when he had rented the bedrooms for a lady from Paris and her secretaries.

"No traffic," Friquet had thought when he observed the ease of leaving by the windows from the first floor. "That'll do. I took a prize in gymnastics at school."

When they had moved in, C.25 summed up the first information received. The Giroflées villa was situated at the edge of a lake. Its approach was through a large iron gate opening from the Boulevard Circulaire. The walls were high and rather thick, but they didn't look as if they couldn't be scaled. The iron fence of the villa could be seen from their windows. The building itself was a large, square, ancient structure without balconies, with three windows in the front. Two floors, and on the second floor all the shutters were closed.

There was no mystery. It was known that the villa was lived in all year round by an old gentleman who entertained a great deal. This justified the somewhat active comings and goings. An initial detail preoccupied C.25—the difficulty of surveillance. What happened on the other side of the lake was beyond any control. With a boat it was possible to enter and leave without drawing attention.

But Friquet, after having reconnoitered the surrounding area, reported:

"There are two wharfs along the lake. There are boats moored there. One of us can give himself the pleasure of a night boat ride, while the others can watch the boulevard. In that way nothing will escape us."

That's what they did. The whole night passed in perfectly useless stake-outs, in absolutely sterile guard duty. Nothing unusual, neither on the boulevard nor on the lake.

"It's exactly because we aren't noticing anything, because there isn't anything to notice, that something is happening!" C.25 said.

"An excellent reason to go there to see," Friquet said impatiently.

"Yes!" Thérèse agreed. "This is the time to go take a look around, to send someone up ahead."

"A volunteer? Present!" Friquet proposed.

"A vacuum cleaner? A broom?" But the servant who had opened the wrought iron gate repeated: "No! We don't need anything!" He was about to slam the gate on the intruder.

"To do the housework! No need to sweep! Your employer was interested. I've come to do a demonstration."

To be convincing, Friquet showed the imposing equipment. A few minutes later the servant, followed by Friquet, was walking down the path that separated the wall of the enclosure from the villa.

As an excellent salesman, Friquet was preoccupied with only one thing: to praise his merchandise, describe its many advantages.

"An astonishing gadget! It does away with all fatigue! Plug it in! And hop! In less than two minutes, no more dust!"

While Friquet's tongue was running on, his eyes didn't remain inactive. They photographed faithfully the layout of the villa in relation to the garden and the lake. Then, inside the house he noted all the necessary details to establish a sufficiently precise map a little later.

The servant was somewhat softened.

"So show your marvelous broom."

"Yes, but your employer would probably be interested. And as he's the one who'll pay, he should be present…"

"Oh! He really couldn't care less about that!" the servant said. "But I'll go look for him. Spread out all your clutter."

A look around. The servant had just left. Friquet was alone in a vast square room furnished in an ordinary way. It seemed to take the place of an office. Friquet hurried to prepare his electric wires. He stooped down quickly to plug it into the electric outlet. And he took advantage of the situation, as a practical measure, to affix a microphone to the bottom of a bookcase. Upon leaving in a short while, he had only to let the almost invisible wire play out, allowing liaison with the outside.

Friquet's wait dragged on. He remained alone for a long time. Finally, an old gentleman came in and listened courteously to the representative's demonstration. He asked questions. He took a lively interest in the perfections of the brand that Friquet was demonstrating. However, he didn't end the demonstration by buying. He asked to think about it. Then he took leave of the fake representative, who, putting away all his merchandise, left, accompanied to the wrought iron gate by the servant.

On the way, Friquet had noticed something strange about the villa which intrigued him. Beside the lake, an outside corridor, entirely glassed in, communicated directly with the left wing of the building by a kind of rotunda, also glassed in, constructed on pilings above the lake.

In order not to draw attention in case there was still a curious look on watch behind a window in the Giroflées, Friquet went on his way gravely toward the railroad station. And it was only later when he had gotten rid of all his paraphernalia as a fake merchant of vacuum cleaners that he reported on his mission to C.25.

Thérèse listened to her assistant's report carefully. She looked at the map he had drawn. She spent long minutes thinking.

"In essence, up until now, complete success! You got into the place without any problem. You didn't see anything there that would attract attention."

The rest of the day was spent on more surveillance. One watched from the boat. The second observed the comings and goings on the boulevard. The third listened for vibrations from the microphone. But the results at the end of the second day were all negative. Nothing to note, neither on the north façade nor on the south façade.

Time passing, silence, a spreading shadow.

"Listen! Someone is walking on the boulevard," Thérèse murmured.

"Yes! I hear!" Friquet, on surveillance, answered.

Thérèse drew near him. Two pairs of eyes were open; two pairs of ears listened. They saw nothing. They heard only *toc, toc, toc* at regular intervals. A silhouette became clear, little by little, emerging from the fog.

C.25 affirmed: "A wooden leg at the edge of the sidewalk. It would be so simple to walk some meters further in. The sidewalk isn't tarmac. That person *wants to signal his arrival.*"

In fact, the cripple disappeared while passing in front of the wrought iron fence, which had opened even before he arrived. Some time passed. Still fog and only the breeze which shook the tree skeletons. Another tapping in another rhythm on the edge of the sidewalk. In the silence all the sounds echoed. Everything resonated. Everything was distorted.

"It's now a double amputee," Thérèse murmured.

"It's a branch of the *Cour des Miracles*," Friquet joked.

But Marcel interrupted. He signaled the beginning of a conversation caught by the listening device. He described to C.25: "Two men's voices, one speaking in a commanding tone, the other very certainly a subordinate." Thérèse put on the earphones, and heard the following conversation:

"Have you understood completely?"

"Perfectly."

"You're armed. The prisoner is in the bedroom on the third floor. You're enough to assume guarding him by yourself while we're absent. Besides, it's only for a short time. We'll leave at ten o'clock. I think we'll be back about two o'clock in the morning."

"I'll do what's necessary!"

Thérèse handed the earphones back to Marcel. Then, taking Friquet's place at the window in order to watch the boulevard, she commanded in a low voice:

"Friquet! Get going! You'll bring Malabar up to date. Keep an eye on the lake. Find out if he has anything to report."

Friquet rushed off to carry out the orders. Shortly thereafter C.25 saw the wrought iron gate of the villa open. A powerful automobile, its curtains drawn, left and was lost in the night.

Thérèse looked at her watch. "Exactly ten o'clock," she murmured.

"Nothing to report on the lake," Malabar transmitted.

"No more conversation at the microphone," Marcel said.

Friquet's report said: "The boulevard is deserted."

"I'm going there. This is the time," Thérèse decided.

"I'm going with you, Boss," Marcel and Friquet suggested at the same time.

"Friquet will go with me just to the entrance," Thérèse corrected. "He'll watch to see that my entry goes off without incident. And immediately afterward he'll come back here to take up his job."

"But," Marcel objected, "what if danger comes up?"

"If I'm not back in an hour with Languille, you can go into action and come to my aid."

Two silhouettes, Thérèse and Friquet, rapidly crossed the distance from their lodgings to the villa. The wind was whistling furiously shaking the skeleton-like trees denuded of leaves. Huge clouds raced across an ink-dark sky. C.25 confirmed her instructions to Friquet.

A rope ladder, with hooks at one end, was fixed to the wall. Flat on her stomach, Thérèse inspected the garden and the villa. Only a third floor window gave off a thin light through the shutters.

"Everything's all right! Go back, Friquet."

The young man saw her disappear on the other side of the high enclosure. He remained for some minutes on watch, listening to the slightest noise. Nothing. Only the whistling of the wind. Then he rapidly returned to their lodgings.

C.25 cautiously examined the garden. Slowly, carefully, she went toward the villa. She was ready to be on the defensive. Four strong forms had come out of the shadows and jumped on her. They immobilized her. Before she had time to cry out, she was tied up. She was picked up. She felt that they were carrying her toward the house and a muffled voice was saying:

"It's done! This time we've got her!"

IV. Face to Face

"Good evening, beautiful lady," Karl Himmelfeld said ironically. His face was lit up with a large smile. "I certainly knew that you were curious and I've already told you that curiosity is a vile fault."

Thérèse looked at him without a word. She was waiting, calm in appearance. But she had already looked around the room in which she was a prisoner, alone with the spy. Windows padlocked. The only door locked. Any forced attempt at escape would certainly fail.

Karl, still mocking, began again.

"Really, I would have thought you more sensible. I was afraid of encountering more difficulties to accomplish the first part of my mission. It was enough just to let you install a microphone in the office and a trick conversation to bring you, like this, into the mouth of the wolf. You can be sure that since you came in here, the microphone wire has been cut. So, your faithful agents won't learn anything. And admitting that the fancy might take them to enter here, which is not as easy as you might believe, they would be met with all the honors due to them."

There was silence. The two enemies looked at each other.

"Do you know what you let yourself in for, charming lady, when you entered my place? To Karl Himmelfeld's? Enemy territory!"

Thérèse didn't answer. She looked at the German with contempt. Changing tones, the spy, after sitting down in an armchair and after having lit a big cigar, continued.

"Do you imagine you can play with me? Error! Karl Himmelfeld always takes revenge. ALWAYS! You escaped me at the Avenue de l'Opéra. At that time I had identified you, C.25, agent of the Deuxième Bureau. You put on a disguise that didn't gain you anything. You sent me on a little trip to dreamland. That didn't help you. Karl Himmelfeld's secrets are well guarded. You have proof of that!"

If Karl was talking about his "secrets" with such confidence, that meant that he didn't know that the safe on the Avenue de l'Opéra had been opened, that the code had been photographed and put back in place.

"Do you know the fate reserved to unwise people who put themselves in your situation?"

"Yes, death," C.25 said firmly.

"Please believe me, dear Madam, that the sentence would have already been carried out, if I were alone. It's easy. Especially when you take an evening walk in Montmartre along deserted streets. An accident: a revolver is taken out, and we have excellent marksmen."

Another pause. Karl blew another puff of smoke. With an abrupt gesture, he let the cinders of his cigar fall. Then, even more mockingly, he continued:

"A real loss for Captain Ladoux's services. You're a very precious agent. Brains, daring, courage. And at your age, there is still a long life ahead. What do you think? The one who offers to save your life in the situation which you've gotten yourself stuck in, would have a right, I estimate, to your gratitude. Or you would be very ungrateful."

Still the same disdainful silence from Thérèse. She was using the classic tactic: let the enemy talk, let him lay out his projects in a way that his weak point can be guessed.

"You aren't very talkative this evening!" the German stated. He looked at Thérèse whose resolute attitude threw him off track. He was disconcerted by so much calm. And he felt vaguely bothered about continuing, but it was necessary.

Karl insisted: "So, as for France, it's over! Give up all hope forever. But it would be regrettable that your very real talents were lost for everybody. That would be a shame! Sincerely! That's what we thought. What do you say? Let's avoid long speeches and not waste time. Stop this superior attitude. Don't forget that you are a conquered person, in the hands of the enemy. You are my prisoner. You are in *our* power. You are well guarded. Your case is clear. You've pronounced the sentence yourself a while ago. So you have to agree to what we want. Do it with good grace, whatever it may cost to your dignity and your patriotic sentiments!"

She now understood Karl's plans. His words were clear: work for Germany. C.25, agent for the Deuxième Bureau, answered with one word: "Never!"

Karl looked at her. He searched for a trace of nervousness, of anger. No, nothing but calm and contempt. And heavy fury began to mount in him. That resistance that opposed him, the conqueror! And by a beaten woman at his mercy! It was too much!

"I would have liked to convert you myself," he said. "That would have been a nice revenge. You don't want to be reasonable. Well! I'll carry out the instructions I've been given concerning you! And others will know how, and by other means that you'll perhaps appreciate more—willingly or by force—to make you do what we have decided!"

"Neither willingly nor by force. Never!" she said without even raising her voice. "I am in your power. Yes. Execute me, that's your right! As for forcing me to betray, no. No one will succeed in doing that."

Karl's rage broke loose, unchained by the calm and decisiveness of C.25. "Execute you! Yes! Myself! That would be for me a real joy to see you at the end of my revolver, waiting for the minute I decided to kill you. And I would make you wait, prolonging the agony, to see just how far this calm would last!

You would probably become less proud. You'd lower those pretty eyes then! I'd make you pay for your grand airs, your disdain!"

At the height of exasperation, Karl drew his revolver. She had not moved. The German, mad with anger, shouted:

"Yes, by my hand! By my hand! Point to the place on your temple where I'll make a hole."

But submission to discipline conquered his rage.

"Oh! Why was I given such precise instructions!" he said regretfully. And he quickly put his revolver back in his pocket.

A man came into the office and held out a letter to Karl, who frowned. An oath. A consultation. Comings and goings in the villa. The roar of a motor boat on the lake. Judging by the haste and the emotion this message caused, it must have been a matter of importance.

"Be patient," Karl concluded after he had given instructions to his aide. "We'll be back, C.25. We'll be back! And soon. We'll pick up this conversation. One of my men will guard you until I return."

She was taken to the third floor, to a room like the one she had just left as to exits and means of escape that it offered.

Karl himself came to verify that her bonds were in perfect condition. He verified the padlocked window. Then before closing the door that he locked with a key himself, he added, in guise of leave taking:

"I charitably warn you that no one has ever left the Giroflées villa alive. You are more isolated here and more securely than in the cellars of the Avenue de l'Opéra."

She heard the noise of a motor going away on the lake. Useless to look for a means of escape. There was none. Her only hope: the arrival of Malabar, of Friquet, of Marcel. But Karl's threats tormented C.25. Grave dangers certainly awaited those who were going to attempt to come to her aid and to that of Languille.

V. Assault on the Hideout

Three-quarters of an hour after Thérèse's departure, Friquet and Marcel could no longer wait. With common accord they decided not to wait any longer to intervene. To dominate their impatience, they had set up their plan of action. They would separate to divide the risk and, if one of them was not successful, to allow the other one to reach the objective. That method also had the advantage of separating the enemy's forces, attacking from two sides at the same time, if the alarm was given.

Friquet climbed the wall as the Boss had done. Marcel told Malabar about the departure toward the villa. Then, after that, he got into the hideout by the lake side. A rope ladder. Friquet was on the top of the wall. He had only to jump down.

"Oh! Damn! Fortunately I looked down before jumping into the void!"

Below, there was a triple barrier, fitted with sharp spikes like swords, coming out of the ground. To jump—however nice a jump it was—was to be inevitably impaled.

"Definitely, these gentlemen have charming intentions for us. I've already enjoyed the cellars on the Rue de l'Opéra. And now I'm going to make the acquaintance of a no less pleasant invention."

But Friquet immediately started thinking. "The Boss entered without any trouble a short time ago. It was *since* her passage that they put up that defense. So, we know she got in. Therefore we must act as soon as possible. To go back and try to enter by way of the lake is a loss of time. So..."

A storm had come up. The wind had doubled in fury, shaking the tree branches. Clouds rolled by, hiding the moon. A torrential rain was falling.

"This is as good as a play at the Châtelet Theater," joked the incorrigible Paris kid. "But there's no time to enjoy the performance. I have to get inside. How? A mystery."

A few minutes later Friquet tried to throw a rope around one of the tree branches. One trial, two, three. No success. New tries, still unsuccessful. Finally he managed to do it. The knot went over and tightened around the tree branch. Friquet tested its solidity.

"Yes, that will work!"

At a glance, he measured the distance, about four meters for the rope to deposit the man alongside the trunk of the tree. The arrival could be somewhat brutal! But it also had to clear the line of spikes which extended a distance of more than two meters and at different heights.

"Fortunately, I'm wearing my old trousers, because despite all my precautions I have a great chance of leaving a piece of them on the way! I'd be very happy if I don't at the same time leave a little flesh near those thorns."

A last look around, a last test of the rope that Friquet had attached firmly to himself like a belt. Some adjustments to get the maximum swing. And hop! The whistling of the wind masked the sharp sound of a tree limb breaking. Friquet, somewhat scratched by a point he had brushed against, fell at the foot of the tree.

"For a flying glide, that really was one! And in a little while I have to find another way to leave the Villa."

Friquet walked toward the Villa, approaching slowly. Nothing moved. A window with a light on the third floor.

"Good! We can climb up immediately," Friquet thought as he approached the steps, beneath the entry door. "I've put on my rubber gloves, so I can go in, but beware of what's behind the door," thought the Paris kid. "I remember a certain floor..."

The door opened without resistance. Friquet's electric torch showed a solid, immovable, floor and an empty, silent corridor.

"Beware of trick staircases," Friquet thought. "I like those at the Neuilly fair, but not here."

A walk, two, three, ten steps and not the least incident. A gust of furious wind, shaking the trees outside, the doors and windows slammed shut. The landing, a circular light for orientation, steps. Friquet felt the cold steel of a revolver against his temple while a voice said:

"Get your hands up!"

Friquet turned around. He raised his hands, but he had instinctively closed his fists. And he had obeyed so rapidly that his fists, while being raised, had violently encountered a head that moaned with a dull sound. A tall body collapsed on the floor. Another suppler and slimmer body jumped on him to take advantage of the victory.

A bark of a revolver in the night. Another shot from outside. A shout and the dull hammering sound of a furious fight. The blows rained down; heads hit the floor; the heavy sound of two chests out of breath, oaths.

"There! We've got you all the same," said a voice that wasn't that of Friquet.

"Not yet, pig!" the already very weak voice of Friquet articulated with difficulty.

During this time, Marcel had gone toward the lake, straight to the boat where Malabar was on watch. But the Colossus wasn't at his post. Had he also gone to look for Thérèse? If so, it was because he had noticed some unusual and worrying fact, since he had received no instructions of this type. If not, where was he? Drawn into a trap? Him, a prisoner too?

Marcel didn't wait any longer. He judged it more urgent to follow the plan he had agreed on with Friquet.

"I could hardly be any wetter in the lake. And at least I'll be waterproof."

Rapid strokes. The wind on the lake was raising little short waves that washed against the swimmer. Marcel swam straight toward the glassed pavilion. A few more strokes and the pavilion was reached.

"What's this?" Marcel said, astonished.

He had bumped into a fine grillwork of very tight mesh coming out of the water and rising more than two meters above the level of the lake.

"A nice net; let's go under it."

Marcel dived. And under it there was the same obstacle. Marcel's conclusions were clear: a kind of grilled cage totally isolated the sides of the Villa. An aquarium of iron wires coming from the bottom of the lake prevented access to the Giroflées.

Marcel swam, following the line of the netting. He was hoping to find a weak point, a possible way of getting in. No.

And the mesh was solid. Try to go above it? A foothold had to be found. A new examination, new dives, new hypotheses. All without any result.

Marcel, like Friquet, was thinking of modifying the plan and getting into the Villa through the boulevard. But he thought ahead rather logically. "Go back? Wasted time, without counting on the fact that the Villa is so well guarded from the lake side that it must be no less well defended from the boulevard side, which probably tempts the curious more."

Then after many searches, Marcel managed to get a foothold near the grill work in the lake.

"That gives a little rest."

A rope ending in a grappling hook. Two unsuccessful attempts. Then success crowned the efforts. Marcel ascended the tight rope. Once the obstacle was crossed, a dive into the other side. Fearing to encounter some electric current placed at the landing, Marcel tried to come to ground between two big trees. He got out of the water and made his way cautiously down the pathway. An explosion in the night.

"Booby traps with mines now! How hospitable these people are!" he sighed.

In the garden, Marcel went forward slowly. He cautiously opened the door, followed the corridor, moved toward the stairs, guided by the sound of a fight.

Suddenly Friquet felt the iron stranglehold paralyzing him loosen. The fingers around his neck loosened. The pressure of the knee on his chest relenting. The German spy was lifted off the ground by a vigorous fist striking him a solid blow. A majestic blow, well placed according to the purest rules of the art by a solid fist took away all thought of resistance.

Friquet stood up. "Thanks, old Marcel. There was one down. My legs gave way! And that dirty pig there would have knocked me out properly!"

Before the man had recovered his senses, he was tied up. And while he gently returned to reality, Marcel and Friquet exchanged impressions.

"No one in the house?" Marcel asked.

"Certainly not! Because with the boxing match that we've just offered as a free spectacle some amateur comrades would have come to umpire the scene," Friquet answered.

"The Boss? Languille?"

"We're going to ask our friend who's beginning to open his eyes—as far as he can open them, since they're vastly swollen."

Marcel's revolver was pointed directly at the spy.

"Take us to the two prisoners who are here. Useless to deny it. And be careful. You walk ahead. You open the doors yourself. The least resistance means your skin. Understood?"

The man hesitated a second. He rapidly saw the situation. He knew he was alone, a prisoner, unarmed. He had been made aware, a little brutally, of Friquet's ability in a fight. The revolver and the determined attitude of Marcel left him no hope. He made a sign of resignation. Less than two minutes later Thérèse and Languille were set free of their bonds.

"Now, let's go!" Marcel suggested.

But Thérèse, who was trying to stretch her numb arms and legs, immediately objected.

"Just a minute. Let's take advantage of our victory!" Then, speaking to the captive, she added:

"Give us a tour of the Villa. Show us the interesting corners, and no lying!"

The man remained silent.

"Let's go! Quickly!" Marcel threatened.

In the office C.25 scarcely hesitated. She glanced along the walls and a secret panel was fast discovered. It hardly resisted.

"Now, the word to open this safe?" she asked the prisoner.

"I don't know it! I don't know anything. No, really. I assure you that…"

"Don't waste your saliva," Languille smiled. "It looks like a brother to a safe I know. Four buttons! No reason it shouldn't open with the same word as its brother."

In fact the word "Carl" opened the safe. The harvest was abundant. Thérèse didn't even take the trouble to choose among the documents. The safe was liberally burglarized and the documents put in packets.

"Now we can leave," C.25 decided.

"Our friend will come along?"

"Of course," Thérèse answered. And turning toward the prisoner, she reassured him: "You can be reassured, we won't ask you to work as a French spy!"

"Walk straight ahead! You're very nice, but I'm always suspicious," ordered Marcel. "Open the door to the steps!"

The door to the corridor was locked. The man tried to turn the knob. Impossible. He explained:

"I don't know how. You can always enter without any trouble, but to leave…!"

Threats had no effect. He seemed to be telling the truth.

"You want to gain time, get us captured? Don't forget that your skin will answer for our exit. All of us out of here, safe and sound, with the documents, or you go down!" Marcel reiterated.

The man made a movement of fear. But he again renewed his gesture of helplessness as he tried to turn the door knob.

"The windows on the ground floor? The padlocks on the blinds?" Thérèse asked.

"I don't have the keys!"

At a glance, Languille, Friquet, Marcel and Thérèse realized the futility of attempting to use force. The blinds would resist.

"The window in the attic?" Thérèse suggested.

The man made a sign of agreement. Three floors. The dormer window and the roof glistening with rain.

"There's nothing else to do but go down!" Languille said. And with a glance he pointed to a drain pipe. The prisoner didn't budge.

"Go on, you have the honor of going first. Go ahead, go first!"

The man made a frightened movement.

"Do you have vertigo?" Friquet joked.

The man didn't answer. Languille insisted.

"Get going! Quickly! Show us the way."

There were no more false evasions. The man admitted:

"You can go down from here, but lower down there's an insulator, and underneath an electric current circulating…"

"Fortunately, we have some ropes. There are scarcely a dozen meters to get to the garden," Thérèse noted.

The descent was made rapidly without any additional incident. Marcel and Friquet had pointed out to Thérèse the traps which protected the entry to the Villa as well as those from the boulevard side and the lake side.

"Now, old brother," Friquet said to the prisoner, "we have to get out of here. You certainly know some magic word, some *Open Sesame!*"

"I don't know!" the man repeated with an unusually worried air.

"Come on, no tricks! Karl could come back at any moment," Marcel insisted.

"I don't know anything, I swear to you," the man defended himself. "We don't know much about the secrets. Only what's necessary to accomplish our missions. Only the chiefs have complete information."

The barrier of spikes made the wall inaccessible. The wrought iron fence was impossible to reach. It was triple guarded by the spiked barrier, by an electric current and by bobby traps that exploded when the door was opened, throwing their fire on the unwary who attempted to cross the forbidden zone. As for the lake, the mass netting prevented leaving the villa.

"Nevertheless, we're not going to stay here! We'll be caught like rats in a rat trap," Languille groaned.

The sound of a motor rose over the noise of the storm.

"A boat on the lake!" Thérèse murmured. "No doubt as to its passengers: Karl and his band."

"Pinched!" Marcel raged. "And all that because this damned pig won't show us a way out of here!"

"I think you can say your prayers," Friquet advised the prisoner who was not hiding a smile too well.

"We must find a hiding place and take advantage of circumstances," Languille advised Thérèse.

But Marcel wasn't wasting his time. He was trying to convince the prisoner.

"Then you've made up your mind? You don't want to say anything?"

Before he had renewed his gesture of ignorance, the dull sound of two fist blows resonated, accompanied by a shudder of pain. The noise of the motor was approaching rapidly.

"Too late! We're caught!" Languille groaned.

And there was again, elsewhere, dominating the sound of the very close motor, the shock of two hard fists against a head equally hard.

VI. What Malabar Was Doing

Malabar had seen the speed boat pull away from the Villa. He had immediately left his observation post in the boat. Jumping on his bicycle, he had rapidly reached the landing just in time to see the spies—five of them—get into a powerful automobile parked with all its lights out. Without losing an instant, the vehicle started in the direction of Paris. Malabar didn't give up following them. But the fight was too unequal. And from second to second the distance separating them grew.

"Nevertheless, I would really like to know where they are going," he groaned, while pedaling with rage along the Boulevard Circulaire.

Then the bicycle braked, stopping its impetus. It had stopped against an automobile parked outside a villa. Nobody inside. Ten seconds later and Malabar was inside. Two seconds more and the motor roared. Some minutes later the stolen automobile driven by the Colossus was racing in pursuit of the spies' vehicle. And the distance separating the two vehicles began to melt away. A frenzied race.

"They aren't even worried about knowing if they are being followed, they are so sure of themselves," Malabar stated with satisfaction.

Toward Paris. Traffic jam passing through St. Denis. Malabar lost time. The spies' automobile disappeared in the near horizon. And two dark streets opened. Which one?

"The most direct, probably! A bit of luck!" Malabar murmured.

The enormous foot pressed down on the accelerator. In the distance the first lights of Paris. The spies' automobile racing. A short stop at the tax station.

"You have to keep your eyes open in Paris or else they'll vanish. But impossible to avoid the formalities of the tax station."

A sharp whistle, promising a ticket, sounded. Malabar half-heartedly braked, seeing a policeman across the road. But just as the car was going to stop, the policeman stood aside and waved him through, leaving the road open.

"I don't understand why! But I'm in luck!" Malabar growled, while keeping the receding visage of the automobile he was following in sight.

Some detours in the little streets, and despite Malabar's skill, the trail was lost. Several times he went back over the road, hoping to again find the spies' automobile parked in front of a door. There, finally! So Malabar had located one of the hideouts of Karl's band.

"Another pretty little box where surprises await indiscreet visitors, very likely. We'll probably have occasion to visit it more in detail one of these days."

Malabar stayed posted for some time in the area, watching the access to the hideout. He didn't notice any abnormal comings and goings. He decided it would be imprudent, alone, to try to get into the place. No doubt it would be better to return to Enghien and warn the Boss. The Colossus had taken the time to draw a map of the locality and gather information concerning the house itself and its immediate environs.

When he returned to the stolen vehicle he saw that two tires had been punctured, and the spies' automobile had disappeared.

Malabar was offered two solutions: abandon the stolen vehicle? Repair it and get back on the road to Enghien? After thinking several minutes, Malabar decided:

"I could repair it faster and use the vehicle!"

And the Colossus noticed, not without astonishment, that the automobile carried a tricolored official license.

"That explains the policeman's attitude!" Then he began courageously to repair the damage.

Enghien. The Boulevard Circulaire. The auto rolled along. Fog. Rain. Darkness. Wind that whistled in waves. The automobile's headlights suddenly revealed a small group walking in the opposite direction. The car stopped.

"The Boss!" exclaimed the Colossus. "And with what a crew!"

"Oh! My old friend," joked Friquet. "It's not everyone who can, like you, offer a ride in a vehicle with an official tricolor license. You've become a minister!"

"We'll listen to jokes later, Friquet! Get in the car! It's urgent!" said Thérèse.

"You won't say we were nasty with prisoners," Friquet continued. "You see, you pig, we're going to offer you a ride in a minister's car. And nevertheless you broke my face."

"You too," Karl's auxiliary answered in a melancholy voice, mopping his puffy eyes and swollen nose.

How did Thérèse Arnaud and her assistants succeed in getting out of the Villa?

A few fist blows brought the German spies' silence to reason. Half knocked out by the fists which hammered his head, he had murmured:

"Maybe through the pavilion?"

Thérèse, her agents and the prisoner had taken refuge in the pavilion before the motor boat had landed. They had witnessed Karl and his band disembarking. They were hastening to the Villa to get back to Thérèse and Languille. The metallic mesh had been lowered to allow the boat to land. In his haste, Karl had not thought to raise it again. The night was almost ended. Caution was superfluous.

To jump into the boat with the prisoner and the loot before the spies entered the villa had been for Thérèse and her auxiliaries the affair of a moment. But the noise of the motor had drawn the attention of Karl and his acolytes. The revolvers started firing. Without any results, fortunately.

Once they had disembarked on the bank, Thérèse's situation was, however, scarcely less critical. Karl's band was certainly going to start searches and begin pursuing the fugitives. The German spies had automobiles which allowed them to drag the area and recapture the escapees who were reduced to traveling on foot.

"You've gotten us out of a difficult situation," Marcel told Malabar.

"I didn't do it on purpose. And that can be attributed to a desire for revenge!"

"Go a little faster, Malabar," Thérèse commanded. "We have to throw them off the trail."

"The weather is splendid," Friquet joked. "We can have a picnic on the grass. It must be cool!"

"Most probably," Thérèse smiled. "But we must first inventory our loot. Take us to Marcel's, Malabar. Before that we'll deposit our little man into the hands of competent authorities. It's useless for us to hold on to him any longer."

It was already late in the morning when the examination of the papers stolen from Karl Himmelfeld's safe was finished. C.25 had given orders to her aides either to photograph certain documents or to decipher others, or to take notes. After having returned, with rare coolness, the automobile he had "borrowed," Malabar was already present at the liaison with Captain Ladoux.

Thérèse had kept certain documents to herself. She examined them one after the other. Her brow wrinkled, trying to find the meaning of some incomprehensible words. But despite all the guesses, despite all the deductions, the entire enigma remained. One of the papers was a panoramic map.

"Obviously a railroad station," she guessed. The line of the tracks was clear. Before and after the station, important lines branched off from the main line. The details were very precise. Everything was labeled. Tracks to garages, the stationing of locomotives, the hangers for merchandise, signal boxes, out buildings. A bridge which overlooked the access to the station before the bifurcation separated from the central trunk line was surrounded with a big red circle.

"The objective to reach, what do you think, Marcel?" asked Thérèse, passing the document to the Chemist.

The Chemist in his turn examined the map very closely. Then he gave his opinion.

"It's very well done, very clear!"

"Yes, and then?" C.25 asked a little nervously.

"Oh! Not much after that: just my opinion," Marcel said.

"What is it?"

"With such information, a clever pilot couldn't miss the target. And the target, it's the bridge! In that way all the traffic on all the lines would be paralyzed. To destroy the station, that's well enough! But to destroy the bridge is a lot easier and the results are more important. The unfortunate thing is, there is no word on the map. Nothing. Not even a clue to know which railway station is in question."

Marcel still had the mysterious paper. He continued to examine it in every way, then for transparency.

"Do you see something?" C.25 questioned her aide.

"Unfortunately, no. Me, I don't find anything. But..."

"But..?" asked C.25.

"But," Marcel continued, "the supersensitive plate conserves clues which escape the most acute eyes."

"Try!" Thérèse commanded.

A few minutes later, Marcel gave her the following information. "Someone wrote on a paper placed on this map and probably with a very hard pencil, because the photograph has kept the mark of the traced words. It's a matter of an address, written in German characters which translate the French writing: 'The Commandant of the Aviation Base...near Lille.' Despite all my efforts," continued Marcel, who was examining the paper with a magnifying glass, "the name of the aviation base is impossible to read."

Thérèse examined the document in her turn. In doing so she reflected:

"Let's not be hasty. This mysterious map was simply used as a blotting pad. It was placed on a table. Someone leaned over it to write on a piece of paper or an envelope, an order or an address which has nothing to do with the map itself."

"What's more," Marcel approved, "this isn't the map of the Lille railway station for two reasons. Firstly, Lille is in occupied territory. Secondly, the Lille railway station is a closed terminal. The tracks don't go beyond the station. And the trains that go outside of Lille stop at the central station and are then directed to a dead end. The map indicates a station open in both directions."

"Right!" Thérèse approved. "Another hypothesis: aircraft flying out of a base near Lille can go bombard a French station shown on this map."

"Yes!" Marcel said. "That's logical. Everything seems to indicate that, since on this other document we also find: Lille. Therefore all these papers seem to be directed to the Commandant of the Lille base. This is information that the spies want to send to facilitate missions over our principal centers. But what is that important railway station?"

Marcel and Thérèse were silent.

"The railway station can be located. We'll check at the East Station and at the North Station. But even if the map has nothing to do with the handwriting, it's obvious that events are taking place at Lille that we should know about," C.25 deduced.

"Probably," Marcel said. "But how can we find out?"

"That's simple," C.25 concluded.

Marcel looked at the Boss with astonishment.

"Obviously, we just have to go there," she smiled.

Marcel was even more astonished. "Lille is occupied. You've just said so!"

Thérèse casually lit a cigarette. She shrugged. Then, blowing a puff of smoke, she calmly explained.

"Possibly! But that has no importance at all. You get upset by very little things, my poor Marcel!"

VII. In Occupied Territory

Ink black night. Deafening roar of the motor whirling at full speed. On the ground the dull rumble of cannons, the battle. The only stars in that dark sky of slaughter are the bursts of howitzer shells and rockets. Little by little, calm returns. Under the aircraft there is no longer anything, only an invisible black ocean.

"We've crossed the lines," the pilot murmured.

Minutes pass. A cold wind. The roar of the motor. The aircraft is flying at a high altitude over the territory occupied by the Kaiser's army. Suddenly there is silence, a great oppressive silence. And the aircraft begins to nose dive toward the ground. A few moments later, the descent is modified. The aircraft flies in large circles. The pilot is scouting a possible landing spot. A bump on hitting the ground. The aircraft rolls, then stops.

Thérèse jumps out of the cockpit. There are weighty seconds, very weighty. The pilot looks at the woman he has deposited in enemy territory. He'll return himself, but she will stay there. Alone, all alone! For a week she'll be an easy prey for a thousand dangers that at any moment will rise and multiply under her feet. The least error, the least lack of caution...or even an ambush learned too late, and everything will be finished. It meant death. A terrible mission. Not a word, just hearts beating a little more quickly. A firm handshake! Between men! Eyes which say "until we meet again." "Until we meet again," or "Farewell!" "In a week, Wednesday evening, here." The motor hums again. The aircraft moves forward and takes off. It passes above the tops of the fir trees that border the clearing. It veers rapidly and then flies straight into the night toward the French lines. The sound of the motor stops. The aircraft has disappeared. Thérèse has seen it dissolve rapidly into the darkness.

The Secret Service agent is alone in the darkness, in the cold that turns stiff arms and legs to ice. A terrible feeling clutches her, an indefinable sensation of solitude, not fear, not a lack of courage. A minute, a very long minute passes.

"All right, let's get going!" she commands herself. She walks in the night, following the compass into the forest. She must get as far away from the landing area as fast as she possibly can. While the valiant French woman's body is automatically walking rapidly, her mind is thinking of the goal: Lille. The mission: to find out what is taking place in that city and what information Karl's spies had sent to the Commandant of the neighboring aviation base; to determine if there existed any relationship between that information and the map of the Creil railway station discovered in the same stack of papers stolen at Enghien. C.12's rapid investigation of the East and North railways had determined that the map was that of the Creil railway station.

What could Thérèse think of doing? Set up plans for the success of her work? No, that was impossible. She was in enemy territory. She didn't have at her disposal the facilities that she had in France. She could count on no help. She must always be on guard, ready to flee or go on the defensive. She must, as often as possible, go unnoticed, always disguising herself, always deceiving an enemy that under the most diverse and most unexpected forms surrounded her *every hour, day and night!* And never, even in the most critical situations, must she hope for the least relief, the least help. Whatever the enormity of the danger might be, she must depend on herself alone to conquer it! And she had to conquer it or die!

All her mission could be summed up in a few words: get inside the enemy's projects, return at the date fixed to the clearing where the aircraft had landed in order to get back to the French lines. A simple delay and all was lost. It was simple, yes, but it was enormous! How many tricks? How much effort? How many perils? Impossible to prepare anything in advance. She had to bend with the circumstances. At 10 a.m., the Secret Service agent, after having walked without allowing herself the least rest, reached the Arras suburb. She was 60 kilometers from Lille. How could she cross that distance as rapidly as possible?

She was wearing a gray cap and she was dressed in the blue overalls of a mechanic that covered a dark tailored suit.

Nobody in the streets paid any attention to the young man who was walking very fast and whistling, a worker going to work. The Secret Service agent walked instinctively toward the railway station. She entered a little restaurant frequented by workers and employees of the railway. She ate with a good appetite, apparently indifferent to the comings and goings and talk. Nevertheless, she stared at people; she watched their comings and goings, and not a useful word of conversation escaped her.

"Otto, will you buy me a brandy?"

Otto looked at his watch and made an affirmative gesture. The glasses of the liqueur were placed on the counter.

"We have enough time. We're not leaving until eleven thirty-five!"

The engineer and the stoker, before drinking their brandy, exchanged melancholy thoughts. They complained of how hard the work was and of the lack of rest. A third glass of brandy was placed between the two others. And the conversation continued; they talked of schedules, services, trains. 11:35. A whistle. The hospital train of the wounded was leaving Arras.

The dead-drunk stoker snored in a car on the way to a garage for repairs. And Thérèse bravely began to stoke the furnace of the locomotive with large shovelfuls of coal.

"Once I'm in Lille, I'll certainly find out how to get out of here!" she thought.

Interminable stops. Lost time. Then slowly traveled kilometers which brought the fearless agent toward her goal.

At 2:00 a.m., at the arrival of the convoy at the Lille marshaling yard, to which the hospital railway train was sent directly toward its destination without going through the central station, the engineer renewed the statement he had made some minutes earlier to the chief of the Petit-Ronchin station:

The train was traveling at the required speed of thirty kilometers an hour. My stoker pointed out to me that a car was becoming over-heated. He left the locomotive cabin with an oil can. Holding on to the ramp, he went toward the front of the locomotive, on the right-hand side to apply the necessary oil. I stayed at my post watching the rails from the left-hand side. Shortly thereafter we crossed a train carrying materials, going toward Douai. At kilometer 253.700, I was worried about my stoker not having returned. He was no longer on the locomotive. I stopped the train to point out his disappearance to the chief of the station at Petit-Ronchin, who immediately caused searches to be made along the rails.

The locomotive was examined. There was no trace of blood. The searches made by the chief of the Petit-Ronchin station were without any result. An oil can was found, but no cadaver. And it was only a great deal later that in a little wood, rather far from the Douai-Lille train, they discovered, hidden under thick cover, a blue pair of overalls and a gray cap. They attached no importance to that ordinary find which could have had nothing to do with the disappearance of the stoker, because the stoker *hadn't disappeared.* The real stoker of the hospital train had showed up at the Arras depot. He was safe and sound.

Fallen, most probably, from the locomotive, how had he managed to reach Arras instead of going, as was logical, to the Lille depot, which was a great deal closer to the place of his fall? Why had he not told anyone about the accident which he had survived? Why had no one noticed him? How had he traveled the Petit-Ronchin-Arras return trip without being recognized? By what train?

The stoker could give no explanation. The shock had probably caused memory loss. And no memory, however vague, of the lost hours remained.

At 4 p.m., Thérèse Arnaud, dressed in a dark suit, reached the center of Lille. Her first concern was to find shelter. She rented a room in a modest hotel. She took some well-earned hours of rest. Then, she disappeared.

VIII. An Indiscreet Servant

Two days after her arrival in Lille, she was a servant in a small Lille inn. And very slowly, at her own timing, she approached the goal being sought. Having discovered the location of the aviation base, she went there, logically reasoning that it was easier to get documentation on the spot. Thus she had rapidly found that the pilots—and above all the officers—enjoyed relative liberty outside their hours of flight. They lived outside the camp, without having, sometimes, permission to leave. Therefore, of necessity, they had to be satisfied with the resources of the little village. And the resources were rare! Just an inn!

The pilots took most of their meals at that inn. The Commandant of the base had rented a bedroom there that he regularly stayed in, going to the base only during the day.

Thérèse had introduced herself at the inn as a servant looking for work, an energetic and hard-working servant not too demanding as to wages! The aviation camp was a source of profit, but also a source of work for the woman who owned the inn. She hired the Secret Service agent.

And since that time, each of them was satisfied, the inn-keeper and Thérèse Arnaud. The service had never been better. Everything was clean and neat. The meals were served with diligence. The bedrooms were kept in order. The many additional needs were accomplished rapidly and with good humor. What's more, an element very much appreciated, the presence of a young, pretty girl, not very unsociable—without her conduct being either provocative or scandalous—had brought in an upsurge of clientele.

Thérèse, on her side, had profited by her time. It's useless to explicitly state that the bedroom of the Commandant Von Krantz had been the object of the servant's every care. Dust had been cleared away everywhere! All the papers had been examined, the dossiers opened, the wardrobe explored. But the harvest was meager, if not nil. Von Krantz had no documents in his bedroom because he worked at his office in the camp. In his bedroom, nothing. Some notes of no importance, some information concerning the number of aircraft at the base and names of the pilots.

As a measure of precaution, the Secret Service agent had placed a microphone at the foot of the bed. But at night, Commandant Von Krantz was usually alone and he slept. The microphone transmitted to C.25 only loud snoring. When Commandant Von Krantz had nocturnal visitors, they were usually of a very particular kind. And the microphone picked up only amorous conversations and sighs that could not at all interest the Deuxième Bureau.

That particular evening C.25 had watched Von Krantz go into his bedroom. A feminine silhouette accompanied him. The fake servant hurried to finish her service in the inn and to go back to her poor lodgings. She immediately put on the earphones. Without being tired, she listened to the usual banalities accompanied by the various noises that are the music of amorous encounters.

"Then I'll see you Thursday," the woman was saying.

"No, not Thursday," Von Krantz answered sharply.

"Why?"

"Work," the Commandant replied laconically.

"Work. For the pilots possibly! But for you, the night from Thursday to Friday?"

"Me also! Everybody!" Von Krantz threw out sharply. "And now you have to leave. I'm tired. I have a lot of work to do. I have to get up very early tomorrow."

After various protests, the woman left. Thérèse still continued listening. Usually Von Krantz never sent away his companions until morning. And although he claimed to be sleepy, he didn't go to bed. A slight creaking of a window opening cautiously caused Thérèse, reclining on her bed, to stand up. She heard the call of a night bird. A man came out of the shadows. A rope ladder fell from Von Krantz's window. The man climbed up rapidly and the window closed.

"Then," Von Krantz questioned, "there was no problem? You found my fellow at the edge of the village?"

"Yes, he was filling up with gasoline," the man answered.

"And so?" the Commandant repeated as a question.

"So, it's done!"

"Thursday evening?"

"No change as to the date. Everything is confirmed. A troop movement has been noticed. The artillery depot that's near the station will be re-provisioned during the day."

"You have the papers?" Von Krantz asked.

"I have everything," the man assured him in a voice filled with satisfaction. "Everything is sketched a great deal better than on the maps you have. The emplacements have been well marked and the junctions, depot, and recent constructions are clearly indicated. Take special care of the bridge and 'la Folie.' So everything is going well. And we'll take advantage of it on our side. Coming here, I passed by the G.Q.G. You'll receive confirmation."

Thérèse's face showed lively pleasure, and at two different occasions. First of all, she had identified the man.

The sound of his voice was enough. It was the charming dancer who had paid persistent court to her and had insisted on taking her to his place when she had met him in the Montmartre night club. But before she had drawn all the conclusions from that discovery, two words struck her: *La Folie!*

"La Folie!" That was the spark that set all the machinery in motion. She remembered it perfectly. When she had shown the map to the chief engineer of the North railroad line company, he had answered, after examining it:

"That's the exact map recently created of the outskirts of Creil." He had moved a dossier and taken out another map not as complete, but on which was sketched much information. La Folie was a very important bifurcation situated near the artillery depot.

At that point the conversation between Von Krantz and the man became more precise. The spy was carrying to the Commandant of the aviation base the most recent information concerning an aerial operation against the Creil railway station. It was Creil that commanded the valley line of the Oise and the line of Boulogne-Calais through Amiens. The moment was chosen because troop reinforcements had to go through the station and, on the day set for the attack, so did the trains taking fresh supplies of munitions to the artillery depot.

Von Krantz's conversation with the woman confirmed the date of the bombardment given by the spy: Thursday evening. That meant in two days. The aircraft that was supposed to come pick up C.25 in the clearing was to let down on Wednesday evening, that is, in one day. Therefore it was necessary to get moving!

"You're going straight back?" Von Krantz asked.

"Yes, as soon as you've given me what's necessary for Karl."

At Karl's name Thérèse smiled again. So it was Karl Himmelfeld she again found in her path! He was the one who had sent the man to set a trap in the night club for the Secret Service agent of the Deuxième Bureau.

The two men continued to talk, exchanging information that she took down in shorthand notes.

There was a pause and the man said:

"I must not be late. The roads are bad."

Von Krantz's window opened. Karl's envoy touched the ground. Then he disappeared into the night. He crossed the village quickly. Some dogs barked angrily as he passed. An automobile was parked. A silhouette stood out some feet from the vehicle.

"Is it ready? Has everything been checked? Is the gas tank full? Can I leave?"

The questions were asked in a sharp voice, the tone of a commander. The man responded respectfully as a dutiful subaltern.

"All right!" Karl's envoy murmured. The silhouette gave a military salute and without waiting any longer, the mission terminated, he hastened to return to the camp.

The man looked at his watch. He lit a cigar. He put on a warm overcoat. He pulled up his collar against the cold. He put on his gloves and the car rapidly departed. Some kilometers, still more kilometers, the road glistening with rain, monotonous and straight ahead. The man automatically hummed a song to distract himself. Puffs of smoke floated around. The song was suddenly interrupted in the middle of a refrain. The man's hand left the steering wheel. The automobile swerved. Ten lean, muscular fingers clutched the spy's throat. Surprised by the unexpected attack, badly situated to defend himself, he was quickly the underdog. A brutal shock. The car, without a driver, smashed into a low wall. The man released himself from the stranglehold that was paralyzing him. He jumped out of the automobile, looking for his revolver. But he didn't have time to take out the weapon. The aggressor jumped at the same time as he did and the fierce combat began again. Two interlaced silhouettes rolled on the ground. A shot rang out in the night. A form was immobilized on the road. The other form rapidly stood up.

Thérèse Arnaud again leaned over the cadaver. She opened the heavy overcoat. She searched the secret pocket. She took out a big sealed envelope addressed to Karl Himmelfeld. A few short instants of hesitation and then, having carefully weighed the advantages and inconveniences of two methods, she made her decision. She undressed the cadaver and put on his clothes. She looked at the automobile.

"Unusable scrap iron now!" she groaned. "Obviously that would have been too nice! But you can't have everything."

And she fled quickly into the dark countryside wet with rain. Thus once more she verified the impossibility of working according to a plan set up in advance. She had taken advantage of circumstances. Some minutes after the spy had finished the important part of his conversation with Von Krantz, thus furnishing C.25 enough information, she had left the bedroom. The microphone couldn't tell her anything more! Through the corridor where the window opened to another façade of the inn, she had reached the ground before the spy. She had gained ground and waited for him in the passage. She had followed him and crouched in the shadows waiting for the proper time to act. When the soldier entrusted with guarding the automobile had left, C.25 had taken advantage of the spy's preparations. While he was putting on his overcoat, she had slipped into the back of the car. And there she had waited to attack until the car was in the middle of the countryside.

The Secret Service agent was satisfied. She had been successful at Lille. She was bringing back enough information to foil the enemy's plans. And in addition she had stolen a stack of documents from German sources destined for Karl Himmelfeld, her old enemy.

But the game wasn't won. Far from it! The loss of the automobile complicated the situation and left her in the middle of dangers which would multiply as hours passed. With the car it would have been relatively easy to cross, before the spy's cadaver was found, the 75km that separated her from the clearing where the aircraft would land the next night. She would have been hidden all day near the place of the landing. She would have been at the rendezvous at the set time. And back across the French lines, she would have given the warning sufficiently early for the État-Major to take the necessary measures to foil the aerial attack against the Creil station.

But alas! It wouldn't be that way! She had no method of transport. It would have been in vain to make a forced march to get as far away as possible from the place where she had gotten rid of Karl's envoy. She couldn't get away from searches. The cadaver and the debris would be very quickly discovered, with daylight at the latest. And from that moment, the vice would tighten relentlessly around the fugitive. There would quickly be a relationship between the crime and the disappearance of a servant in the inn where Karl's envoy had gone. The alarm out, the mesh of the net would be tightened. And to get through it!...An agonizing problem when 75km full of danger remained to be crossed. Thérèse walked following the compass. She took as a landmark the railway tracks of Lille-Douai-Arras. The dawn was beginning to disperse the night. The day was in the process of birth, adding even more to the difficulties. C.25 had already, by way of caution, avoided the villages. She went around them, thus adding some kilometers between herself and the goal.

She reached the railway tracks. It was also necessary to avoid the stations where the presence of a woman traveler would be quickly noticed. That would be the surest way to attract attention. As for renting an automobile, that was the last method she could dream of. And for several reasons. It would be unwise. It could easily be traced. Then, next, she had left in such haste that she hadn't taken enough money! Nevertheless, it was not humanly possible for her to cross on foot the distance that separated the landing spot of the aircraft, given the detours she had imposed on herself. So?

Still some hours of walking. A winter day, fog and rain. She was walking along the railroad tracks. The raucous whistle of a train. A heavy train of material was advancing, having trouble climbing an incline. A jump to cross the palisade. Another jump to reach the outside foot rail.

"Phew!" But the fugitive wasn't safe. At the first station they came to, they would point out a man hanging on the side of the train. The train had picked up speed. It rolled along in the approaching day carrying the valiant French woman, alone, immensely alone in this fracas, in this hornet's nest of dangers.

The brakes screeched. The convoy slowed down. Thérèse took advantage of it to reach a flat-bed car filled with beams, which she hid under. Broken by fatigue, in that uncomfortable position, she crossed the kilometers which brought her to the clearing. A very short stop at the entry to a station. It was 9 a.m. Some minutes later she saw, not without astonishment, the train stop in the Douai station. She had a premonition of a new danger. Without leaving her shelter, she moved forward to investigate. A quick movement threw her back into her hiding place. The whole length of the train, soldiers aligned on both sides of the convoy. Fortunately the train was very long and the last cars remained out of the station. No doubt the alarm had been given. The train was being searched.

To remain there guaranteed discovery. She didn't hesitate. With a glance she looked for another hiding place to escape the searches. She left her shelter. She slid between two railway cars. Then, flat on her stomach on the railway track, she continued. In this way she passed under two railway cars, grazed by the sharp stones. She had noticed that the next to last railway car of the convoy was covered with a tarpaulin. She stood up between the chains attaching the cars. She reached the tarpaulin. She slid under it without knowing what she was going to find. She didn't have any time to do anything else. She heard heavy footsteps running over the railway tracks. Some voices reached her. It was the search, an operation that seemed to be followed with rare minutia. She had only several seconds of rest. In a minute the soldiers would lift the tarpaulin. They were already at the other end of the railway car. She thought she could already feel hands seizing her.

The enclosed railway car was especially built to carry a 380 artillery piece. What refuge could she find there? Once the tarpaulin was lifted it was over. A gesture decided her. The cylinder head of the 380 opened. Voices were approaching. Without hesitating, Thérèse got into the canon. A sign of relief that was of short duration. In her refuge she heard the movement of some men who had undertaken examining the entire heavy piece of artillery.

Some deadly seconds. She was holding her breath. If someone thought of looking inside the interior of the canon...then there would no longer be any hope for the Secret Agent to escape. Finally the noise came from a distance. The search continued without incident. Then the train started again slowly, carrying Thérèse toward her goal. A little before Arras, she left her shelter. She started walking again.

"After all! More anxiety than real trouble," she thought. "I'll be on time for the rendezvous with the airplane."

Night, a glacial winter night. The rain had stopped. The Secret Service agent reached the clearing. Another anxiety not less cruel. Would the aircraft come? Would it manage to cross the lines without any hindrance? Heavy minutes. The hour for the rendezvous passed. Finally! Her ears heard in the night sounds the roar of a motor. The sound approached. Then suddenly it stopped. She saw the airplane circling the clearing. It skimmed the ground. It landed. It rolled several meters. It was going to stop. C.25 gave a sigh of deliverance. She approached the airplane running. A great flame burst out. An enormous flame which lit up all the sinister lights. A column of smoke mounted to the sky. The gas tanks had exploded. The aircraft was in flames.

Twisted body, steel turning red, clouds of smoke like a whirlwind. A terrible human scream. The cry of the pilot who hadn't been able to get out and who was aflame, a human torch.

And she watched that terrible spectacle, powerless. She could do nothing, attempt nothing.

The inferno discharged terrible heat. Several seconds of the most terrible discouragement. Events were in league to prevent the Secret Service agent from accomplishing her task. Fatigue, isolation, the many difficulties already overcome, added to the prospect of other danger, still greater, to conquer, conquered Thérèse. The prospect of work to accomplish, to reach the lines! She, she all alone! To cross the zone of the German armies, to reach the first enemy lines. To cross them, and to reach the first French sentinels. No method of transport! On foot! Avoiding the inhabited centers, the patrols! The task impossible, superhuman! And death an ambush at each step! These thoughts took up only a few seconds. She shook off her discouragement.

"The bombing of the Creil railway station is supposed to take place Thursday evening. It is Thursday morning now. I have to be in Paris today; 200km, more than half of which are in enemy territory." She straightened up. "I'll be there! I HAVE TO BE THERE!"

IX. A German Aircraft Toward Paris

On Thursday evening, the Bourget military airfield was on alert. The D.C.A. of the C.R.P. telegraphed: *A German aircraft has flown over our lines. It escaped the chase squadrons and is heading toward Paris, flying at a high altitude, following the Oise Valley.*

Some minutes later the aerial flotilla that Gallieni, with great trouble, had obtained for the defense of the capital, took off. One part of the aircraft flew in front of the enemy with great urgency to make it turn back. The other part flew in circles around the capital to forbid it access should it have still escaped. Telegrams followed one another without stop. Other D.C.A. transmissions emitted the same message, thus marking the flight path of the enemy aircraft.

A German aircraft flying at a high altitude and following the Oise Valley is flying toward Paris.

Some minutes later and this telegram:

Hit by convergent fire, the German aircraft is down.

But soon there was a correction.

The German aircraft is not down. It made an amazing tailspin descent. But it soon was upright again and it continued its flight after that feint that put it out of range of our fire.

Then some communications that seemed bizarre.

The aircraft, without having encountered our patrols, rapidly changed direction. It left the Oise Valley and descended straight toward the south.

Always flying at a high altitude, it was spotted in the regions less well defended by aerial incursions. It thus avoided the fire of the batteries of the D.C.A. of the north and east of Paris.

Because of that tactic, it is supposed that it intends to go around the city.

The following minutes confirmed in all respects that hypothesis. Some transmissions noted the German aircraft over the Haute-Seine, then above the Fontainebleau forest. The chase squadrons had not been able to reach it. The patrol squadrons had seen nothing and continued their futile rounds.

The telegraph suddenly became quiet. Nothing. No more news of the aircraft.

Where had it gone? What mysterious goal was it following? What did it mean to do? It's strange itinerary left room for all suppositions.

Actually, the danger was small. Some hours without the least useful information. The last information had come from a station in the area of Corbeil.

Solution to the problem: the aircraft must have fallen. But where? The Police stations were immediately alerted. Measures were taken to locate the aircraft. It hadn't vaporized. They ought to be able to find it. Both it and its equipment. Perhaps intact. The aircraft: a pile of scrap iron and one or several cadavers. At least one spy...

Nothing but hours without news. At 7:00 a.m. the aircraft was found. It had landed in a field near Milly. No trace of an accident. The aircraft was in perfect condition ready to resume its flight. But the gas tank was empty. As for the crew, no trace. The aircraft had been abandoned. The problems became more focused. What had become of the crew of an enemy aircraft after it landed in the vicinity of Milly?

New suppositions. Was an automobile waiting for the spies in a predetermined location? Police searches closed in on the landing spot. No one had seen anything; no one had noted anything. And nothing abnormal had happened during the first hours of the night.

At 7:15 a.m., there was the report of a stolen bicycle at a garage in a village situated four kilometers from the landing spot. A rapid calculation determined that the flight had taken place about 50 minutes after the calculated time of the arrival of the aircraft on the ground. 50 minutes represented the usual time to easily cover the four kilometers that separated the two points.

At 8 a.m., the testimony of an employee of the P.L.M. railway reported that he had been shoved while on his job at the entry to the platforms of the Villeneuve-Saint-Georges station. A man, arriving at the last minute, had entered the station by jumping over the barrier. The employee approached the traveler and demanded to see his ticket. The traveler had answered by butting the employee in the stomach with his head and by jumping had caught the last car of a train headed toward Paris. A new calculation determined that the time of that incident corresponded perfectly with the time of arrival of a bicycle, ridden perfectly, that left the area around Milly at the time of the flight.

At 8:20 a.m., the special commissariat of the Paris P.L.M. station, alerted by the Villeneuve-Saint-Georges station (the train didn't stop at the intermediate stations) had arrested a traveler without a ticket as he got off the train. All news gathered in the interval led to the belief that the traveler without a ticket was the pilot or one of the passengers of the mysterious aircraft.

At 9 a.m., the Deuxième Bureau of the Ministry of War let all telegraph posts, Police units, anyone on alert, know that all searches concerning the passengers of the German aircraft had been halted. Shortly thereafter, the telegraph brought the Bourget military airfield, information coming from the G.M.P, extremely precise orders concerning aerial operations which would take place the following night.

Chasse aircraft! Bombardment aircraft! Veritable action stations for combat! There soon were added other telegrams emanating from the main aviation centers at the front and the interior to operations and to reconnaissance flights ordering them to act in concert.

In Captain Ladoux's office, after she had turned in the secret paper intended for Karl Himmelfeld, and which, soon, in translation, showed itself to be of major importance, Thérèse Arnaud told the story of her mission.

She furnished details of the events that had transpired from the time the French aircraft had dropped her in the clearing.

A servant in an inn near Lille. Searches with no result in Von Krantz's bedroom. Conversations with Karl Himmelfeld's envoy, who was also the man who had tried to draw C.25 into a trap in Paris! The details of the bombardment of the Creil station. The escape. The departure by automobile. The assassination of the spy. The dangerous trip and the refuge in the 380 artillery piece. The landing of the French aircraft and its burning.

At that time Thérèse had had some moments of real discouragement. But the sound of a motor had brought hope. Perhaps a second French aircraft. Illusion! An aircraft had landed in the clearing, drawn by the light of the fire. But it was a German aircraft. The pilot and his co-pilot had stepped to the ground. They had approached the French bird that had just finished burning. They thought some accident had caused the death of one of their comrades.

They had recognized the remains of a French aircraft. There was no doubt for them as to the mission of that aircraft. And they were looking around to find out what had happened. Their thoughts had been interrupted by a violent roar of the motor. They had jumped forward, but too late! The propeller had been put in motion and Thérèse had jumped into the cabin. The German aircraft had taken off under the noses of the two pilots, powerless to prevent that kidnapping.

The German lines had been crossed without great danger, but at the French lines, peril had begun. Thérèse, frozen by the wind, had undergone fire by the posts of the D.C.A. At several times she had thought she was lost. Shells were exploding around the aircraft. Then, thanks to a spiraling tailspin, pretending to be hit, she had been able to escape and cross the French lines.

To avoid facing new barrages, she had turned around, trying to get as close as possible to Paris. But, because the aircraft had run out of gasoline, she had

had to land near Milly. The rest was only child's play for the intrepid C.25. Some kilometers on foot! (She was used to it.) A stolen bicycle! (It wasn't the first.) And the shoved ticket taker was the only French victim of that extraordinary escapade!

Captain Ladoux listened with admiration to his agent's story. He couldn't find words to congratulate her. Words that would have been worthy of the courage and of the boldness expended. But his throat tightened with emotion. He had to be content with remaining silent a long time.

The Bureau had already brought the Captain the translation of the documents destined for Karl Himmelfeld. The Captain went through them at a glance and his face lit up.

"Another beautiful operation," he said, "and one that will spare the lives of numerous Frenchmen and their allies. Not only your trip; a little movement in Flanders, is going to allow us to oppose, by every means in our power, the bombardment of the Creil station and the destruction of the artillery depot, but still you bring to us elements of major importance as to the German organizations..." Captain Ladoux hesitated a moment. Then he concluded in a vague tone: "About the German organizations abroad."

C.25 took leave shortly thereafter.

"I'm glad," she told Captain Ladoux, "to have done my duty. But at the same time I still put one over on my excellent friend, Karl Himmelfeld, who wanted to take revenge on me. And that causes me unimaginable pleasure!"

THE SECRET OF THE VILLA

I. Help!

A sad November day with rain pouring from a low, gray sky. A glacial wind whistling. The Gentilly plain presented a gloomy and sinister aspect. It was a spot that even under a clear sky was hardly enchanting. A vast deserted expanse. And at the end, toward the horizon, six modest pavilions close together.

To reach these villas there was a little, badly cleared path completely lined with trash which led from the Bicêtre road. The pathway had no exit. It ended in a dead end against the ditch of the Paris to Sceaux railway, which at that spot made a very sharp curve. Because of this fact, the railroad bordered the path on two sides.

This pathway had to be taken to reach those pavilions. Whoever wanted to get there by going across the plain, would run into quarries that made access absolutely impracticable.

That particular day, about noon, a fog came in, limiting visibility. Suddenly, from the direction of the pavilions, a sharp cry rang out:

"Help! Help!"

The appeal was heard. The inhabitants of the villas immediately came outside. They saw a woman (one of their neighbors who had spent the morning working in a field she possessed bordering the railroad) fleeing, still shouting her frightened appeal:

"Help! Help!"

A man, thin as a skeleton, was following her. They were running forward. The man was going to catch the woman whose flight emotion and fear had stopped. It was done. The man reached the woman. In his turn he cried out: "Save me! Save me!"

Then, as if effort had exhausted all his strength, he collapsed. A few minutes later the neighbors had revived the man. They began to ask him for explanations of his strange conduct. The man looked around him, casting astonished eyes on the little group surrounding him. Then he began to laugh.

"Why did you do that? Where did you come from? Where are you going? What do you want here?"

The questions crossed each other. The man didn't answer. He continued to look around at those assembled like a trapped beast. Then he started to laugh again.

During this time the woman who thought she was being attacked, explained:

"I was returning from my field. I was walking quickly. Suddenly, when I was passing in front of The Roses villa…whose owners have been gone more than six weeks—I saw that man, thin, frightening, his face bloody, trying to climb the fence. I was afraid. I started to run. The man chased me. Then I called for help!"

The man continued to remain unable to understand all these questions. He continued to laugh. Then, from time to time, he murmured: "Save me!"

II. The Mad Man

With a bored look, Monsieur Martel, Gentilly Commissioner of Police, re-placed the telephone on the hook.

He looked sadly out of his window on the gray day. He pushed back his chair. He took several steps. The sight of the frozen pavement whipped by a sharp wind, drew from him a deep groan of discontent.

His secretary looked at him with questioning eyes. Monsieur Martel grumbled:

"It's down there, toward the quarries."

"Serious?" the secretary asked.

"Maybe! I don't know. A business that seems to hold some surprises."

Then in a tone of importance he concluded:

"I sense it. I foresee it. It's a matter of instinct! It's a dirty business! That's never deceived me in the course of my long career. Nothing simpler in appearance."

After a short pause to stir up interest, he continued:

"I was informed that they discovered at The Roses villa a man who had been confined in a little shed attached to the house. That individual was in a deplorable state. He was hurt while fleeing and seems to have lost his mind. Something absolutely incomprehensible: although the house had been shut for six months, they found large stocks of fresh food in the shed.

"And there was nothing abnormal in six months?" the secretary asked.

"Nobody noticed anything," the Commissioner continued, "but now, naturally, the neighbors remember having heard strange noises at night, cries. Probably the cries of the unfortunate confined man."

"And that man's identity?" the secretary questioned.

"Unknown. A doctor has been called. He'll inform us. Is the man really insane or is it only a temporary loss of memory. When we get there, we'll get all the details," the Commissioner finished.

There was a short silence. Monsieur Martel took his overcoat off the hanger. Then he turned toward the third person in the room who had listened to the whole scene without saying a single word.

"I gladly invite you to go with us," he said ironically. "A nice little outing! And in a pretty neighborhood! A 15 minute walk in the cold, the wind sharp enough to cut off your nose!"

"Great! I was just wishing to get outside! My Boss sent me to you to get the information that you have obligingly made available. And after that, she says I can have the day off. So, I'm going to take advantage of the charms of the countryside," joked the incorrigible Paris kid, Friquet, the valuable assistant of Thérèse Arnaud.

"Then, let's go!" the Commissioner decided.

On arriving at The Roses villa, the Commissioner's first concern was to inquire about the victim. A man came forward toward Monsieur Martel. They shook hands.

"So?"

"So nothing can be learned from the man," the doctor answered. "He's insane, crazy enough to be locked up. I examined him. He has no trace of a wound, or of bad treatment. Only some superficial cuts, not very deep and not at all serious, that he got himself when he escaped. He is astoundingly thin and dirty, which leads me to believe he has been a prisoner a long time. In any case, the first thing to do is get him to the hospital. I'll do what's necessary and send you my report."

"Didn't they tell me that food had been found in the shed?" the Commissioner inquired.

"Yes! And that's the strange thing. The food had been brought in recently."

"Therefore," Monsieur Martel deduced, "someone knew about the victim's location and regularly brought him something to eat."

"Regularly? That's not proven. A man can remain a long time without nourishment. And the food found today is perhaps the first for a long time..." the doctor guessed.

"Dirty business! Dirty business!" the Commissioner grumbled, raising his collar as the doctor walked away. To be thorough, Monsieur Martel questioned the unknown man. He could get no satisfactory response. He didn't insist.

"Let's look at the villa," he said.

"The results were in every way negative. The visit to the villa brought no information, no enlightenment. The entire mystery remained.

Out of habit, Friquet noticed the layout of the villa.

"The Roses is made up of four little rooms. On the first floor: a kitchen and a dining room. On the second floor, two bedrooms."

Monsieur Martel finished his job.

"Nothing in the cellar, not even wine. It's a basement for junk," said an inspector.

"Dirty business! Dirty business!" the Commissioner summed up once more.

The group of policeman made their way toward the shed. But there, just as everywhere else during the visit, the minutest inspection didn't turn up anything interesting.

While the inspectors and the Commissioner were going into obscure places, Friquet stayed in the garden. He was enjoying the fresh air, while looking around him. He suddenly bent down and straightened up again almost immediately. He looked around to see that no one had seen what he had done. He put a torn and dirty, rain soaked envelope into his pocket.

Soon afterward, having given instructions to his subordinates, Monsieur Martel left The Roses villa.

"Dirty business!" he continued to rage.

Friquet said goodbye to him. And while the Commissioner returned to his office, Friquet hurried toward Thérèse Arnaud's house to carry her the information that he had been sent to get from the Gentilly Commissioner.

III. The Real Villa

"What's this, Friquet? I told you I wouldn't need you before tomorrow," Thérèse Arnaud said in astonishment, seeing her assistant come into her house through the secret door.

"I didn't like the air in Gentilly, Boss," was all Friquet said.

Then he calmly reported on the mission on which he had been sent. Thérèse took down the information furnished. When she had finished, Friquet handed her the envelope he had picked up in the garden of The Roses villa.

The secret agent, without understanding, looked at the dirty paper. Then suddenly the expression on her face changed. She became serious, attentive, and frowns creased her forehead. Friquet followed the Boss's various changes of expression, evident signs of rapid thought.

"What is this?" C.25 asked.

"Apparently it's an envelope," Friquet answered calmly, without any hurry.

"I see that!" she answered impatiently. "But why are you bringing me this?"

"Just a thought…It's as you might say a souvenir of the outing I took to Gentilly."

"Let's have a truce with the jokes, Friquet," Thérèse said in annoyance.

More seriously, Friquet explained: "I picked up that envelope. Just as I was about to throw it away, I noticed some pencil annotations."

"I see them also," C.25 said impatiently.

"Those annotations don't say anything. But I thought that perhaps they could say something."

"Possibly. Maybe just words that mean nothing except for the one who wrote them. Or a hidden meaning. A secret coded message. Take that to Marcel. I'll wait here for the results. And come back here to tell me how…"

"Then you think that…"

"I don't think anything," Thérèse said. "I notice that in the middle of some words these two letters linked together: *af* or *AF*. It could be some sort of abbreviation, the initials of a proper name. That could mean all sorts of things. But A.F. are also the initials which the German Espionage Service use to identify its agents. Now on this envelope I can read not only AF, but also the number 65. A.F.65 which is translated: Agent 65 of the German Espionage Service. Now, quickly, don't waste any more time."

A few hours later, C.25 having been brought up to date by Friquet about the mysterious story of the Gentilly mad man, was waiting, with her assistant, for information from the Chemist, to whom the envelope had been given for examination. They didn't have long to wait. Thérèse's sliding bookcase wall in her office was pushed back. Marcel, who had taken the secret passage, appeared.

"Well?" Thérèse and Friquet asked at the same time and with the same impatience.

As his only answer, Marcel held out the envelope. Thérèse looked at it a moment. She exploded in anger.

"What? What? Him again? So is he everywhere, mixed up in every case?"

"Karl Himmelfeld," Friquet said in astonishment.

In fact, on the envelope Friquet had picked up, there now appeared under the address, half effaced by the rain, the following words: *Herr Karl Himmelfe….* The end was missing because of a tear in the envelope.

"There's no possible doubt. It's really a question of Karl," the Secret Service agent murmured. Then after thinking a few seconds, she asked:

"Marcel, how did you get that new superscription to appear?"

"Very easily, Boss," Marcel answered. "By placing the envelope into some chemicals. I don't deserve any credit. The ink used is of an excessively simple composition."

There were some long instants of silence. Thérèse was thinking. Suddenly she decided.

"Go get Malabar and Languille!"

"We're going to take a walk this evening?" Friquet asked.

"Obviously!" C.25 answered.

"So, I've got it! We're going to Gentilly."

Thérèse, smiling, looked at him and said: "You've found that out? And you already found the envelope. You're finding a lot of things today!"

C.25's agents soon arrived and each one hurried to prepare the things needed for the expedition. Then, without waiting any longer, they started. On the way, she explained to each one the role they had to play. The explanations were clear and precise. The Secret Service agent decided that it would be better not to enter The Roses villa through the path pointed out by Friquet. She thought that, perhaps, in order to clear up the mystery surrounding the discovery of the demented man, Monsieur Martel might have had the villa watched. But she guessed that it would be very easy not to alert the Police. Therefore she would get to the villa by way of the railroad tracks to avoid the quarries. What's more, following her usual practice, she didn't want her assistants to go with her. However, that tactic had already brought dangerous misadventures!

Everything went as planned. At 1 a.m., Thérèse, Marcel, Malabar, Languille and Friquet climbed the embankment of the railroad. They separated after having walked toward the quarries and around the villa.

C.25's agents went to take up their posts.

The courageous Frenchwoman, after having scaled the wall, entered the villa.

No agent of Monsieur Martel had been seen. It was probable that the Commissioner of Police had thought it was enough to set up watch at the only entry to the pathway, which allowed normal access to the villa.

Thérèse, who was carrying an enormous case, again went over the visit made some hours earlier by Friquet, without any more success.

"Obviously there's nothing! And it's because there's nothing that there is something!"

She knew, from having already come face to face with Karl Himmelfeld, that locales the most innocent in appearance and shops the least suspicious were always admirably organized hideouts.

She didn't stop on the first and second floors. The outside surveillance of the pavilion had been decided on. She went down to the cellar. A first inspection revealed nothing. The cellar seemed to be used for junk. Some miscellaneous objects were stacked up. Among those objects, a ladder.

The presence of a ladder in a basement used for junk was nothing surprising. However, Thérèse's intuition told her that the ladder wasn't there by chance. She had a use for it. She began a new examination and her perseverance was quickly recompensed. She discovered a trap door which opened easily. That trap door hid a narrow stairway that led to a second cellar.

"Of course!" she murmured. "The usual concrete room, like that of the Avenue de l'Opéra. No way out but through the stairway. And this time perfect material: sending and receiving posts for the wireless. Stacks of explosives or chemical products. And a telephone."

C.25 took down some details on a map she rapidly sketched. Then, as a measure of security, knowing how dangerous explorations in spies' houses are, she took the time to dress entirely in a rubber suit that protected her.

"I've already paid for carelessness!" she thought.

When she was finishing, a ringing sounded. A moment of surprise. The ringing began again. Her face lit up in a smile.

"The telephone!"

She didn't hesitate. Thinking she would learn some information destined to the spies, she picked up the receiver. Soon she heard a voice she knew—that of Karl Himmelfeld—who was saying:

"Curiosity is always punished, C.25. I've already told you that. You've escaped me twice. This time you're caught, and definitely caught."

There was a burst of laughter and Thérèse answered:

"Karl Himmelfeld, I've already escaped you twice. I'll escape you again this time as I did before."

"Certainly not, C.25. Believe me!"

And she didn't hear anything more.

IV. A Night of Terror

There was no pretense in Thérèse's laughter. Actually, she could laugh at Karl's threat. The other time that she had fallen into her enemy's power, she was not armed. This time, foreseeing a fight more and more relentless, she had taken the most minute precautions. And whatever the trap, she was certain to get out safe and sound from The Roses villa whenever she pleased.

In fact she had with her a complete kit of the most up-to-date tools from which no security door, no lock, however complicated it might be, could resist. In addition, she was, when she chose, in communication with her agents outside the villa. She could, when she wanted to, give them instructions, tell them her exact position and the danger she was facing. They were at the receivers, ready to intervene at the first call. And they too had tools which could overcome all obstacles. When she had scaled the wall of the villa, she had let the wire of a telephone that connected her to Malabar unwind. Because of that, Karl's threats were absolutely vain. And what was even more, it was not Thérèse this time who would be Karl's victim. It would be Karl and his agents who would fall into the hands of C.25.

After the few minutes of reflection that it took Thérèse to see the situation, her decisions began to reach Malabar. By telephone, she sent all the information concerning the second cellar and the way to enter it through the trap door in the first underground basement. Naturally, Malabar offered to send reinforcement immediately to the Boss so as to ward off any eventuality. But the Secret Service agent refused. She didn't need to have any assistant near her. She was running no danger. She could get out of the cellar, but she intended to stay there to serve as bait. No doubt was possible. Karl's telephone call certainly indicated that the spies were going to come to the villa, intent on terminating their enemy. They had been alerted to her arrival. The envelope Friquet found was again a trap. Therefore, she reserved another job for her agents.

While she remained in the lower basement, they must set up a trap and capture everyone trying to enter the villa.

Several minutes later, carrying out the orders Malabar received, the following steps were taken: each of C.25's agents watched the villa from a certain distance on one side—Friquet toward the railroad track, Marcel toward the Bicêtre road, Languille toward the quarries. Malabar, while keeping in telephone touch with the Boss, was in charge of guarding the pathway, a post having a smaller zone of surveillance because of the narrowness of the path. Therefore the villa was encircled for 100 meters around. No one could enter without being seen.

Thérèse's auxiliaries were linked by telephone extensions. A dog bark was the alarm signal. The plan was thus agreed on: to let the enemy enter the circle under surveillance; to wait without action, in case there were many spies, until they all had entered the zone. Then noiselessly tighten the circle by simultaneously approaching the villa without at any time, breaking off surveillance so that no one could get out. Then follow the orders that Thérèse would transmit. Thérèse had at her disposal four determined, well-armed aides; therefore, five persons. No surprise was to be feared. It was enough force to overcome an enemy even greater in number.

While her auxiliaries around the villa were carrying out her orders and getting ready for the fight, C.25 was making sure not to leave any room for anything unexpected, in case, totally improbable, the spies might use a secret passage to enter the villa without drawing the attention of the watchers. Malabar had just transmitted to C.25 the assurance that each one was at his post. The cave's silence was suddenly interrupted by a series of crackling sounds. Thérèse understood very quickly. The wireless receptor was transmitting. It took only a moment to put on the listening device. And to the degree that the crackling sounds continued, the face of the brave young woman relaxed. She smiled with satisfaction.

After the wireless message, she looked for a small code book in her bag. And with no difficulty she translated: *A.F.65, 23, 42 will cross the Swiss border Thursday to reach Gex to put themselves at the disposition of Karl Himmelfeld. Instructions at A.F. if necessary.*

She quickly set up her plan. It was necessary to reach Gex before the arrival of the three German spies, to capture them. Therefore, there must be immediate departure for Gex.

She thought again for a few minutes. That new mission was going to oblige her to abandon Karl Himmelfeld and his agents. Too bad! Besides, she had decided to get rid of Karl definitively. It was henceforth useless to let him stay free in order to discover other details of the German organization, thanks to him. There was no doubt that she had nothing more to learn from Karl. She had blown her cover with him. And the character of the fight C.25 had undertaken against the German spy was definite. No quarter any longer. One or the other of them had to disappear.

In order not to break off the surveillance around the villa, C.25 decided to telephone Malabar with the necessary instructions. She would then leave the cellar, and thanks to her powerful automobile, traveling without losing a minute, she would be able to reach the border well before the spies. But the telephone that was to reach Malabar wasn't working any longer. Maybe a fight had broken out around the villa?

She didn't try to telephone any more. She went to the stairs that should take her to the upper level cellar.

Sparks of electricity streaked across it. She received a shock.

"Fortunately I'm wearing my rubber suit," she thought. But even that protection was not enough. Enormous apparatus similar to Rumkorf coils threw deadly electrical waves into the cellar. A trap door fell quickly, barring access to the stairway exit. In the floor a circular opening a little larger than that of a manhole cover opened up. Soon she had only two solutions: to die struck down by the electrical currents or to jump into the void! The void! A gaping black hole putting out a smell of mold.

Thérèse still hesitated, looking for another method of defense, a corner to hide in. But she convinced herself very quickly that she could hope for nothing. All the space in the cave was streaked with the electric charges, stronger and stronger. Just enough time to deploy the rope ladder with knots at one end. To put it on the side of the open hole and instead of throwing herself into the void, to hang down by means of the ladder. Her preparations were quickly made. She descended into a kind of well. After descending several rungs, as soon as she felt herself safe from the electrical discharges, she descended more slowly. She examined the walls of the well. She threw a small piece of lead into the empty space below. She counted the passing seconds, waiting to hear the sound of its arrival, so as to measure its approximate depth. Many seconds, then the sound of a softened noise, the sound of a hard body falling into the water!

"The rope is too short! And the bottom of the water! Karl Himmelfeld does things well," she murmured, worried.

The Secret Service agent remained immobile on her ladder, looking for some way to escape inevitable death. Suddenly she realized that the ladder was dropping on one side. Probably one of the knots had come undone and was sliding slowly on the cellar floor. That could be a fatal fall to the bottom of the well. And if the fall wasn't fatale, she would be drowned!

Everything was calm around The Roses villa. No human presence except that of the four watchers, who were alert, flat on the ground, listening to the least sound. But they discovered nothing. Two hours went by. The circle set up between Thérèse's agents functioned regularly. The same sentence from quarter hour to quarter hour passed from one to the other. "Nothing to report! Nothing to report!"

At the end of this time, Malabar became uneasy. There was no longer any news from Thérèse. And Malabar's call remained unanswered. Was that a reason to be alarmed? No, not yet. In fact, Thérèse was busy with other tasks and she couldn't answer. It was also possible to suppose that the German spies had succeeded in getting into the villa (or that they were even there before the arrival of C.25) and that the spies were currently there.

The Boss's orders were firm: do nothing without instructions except in case of alert. As disciplined soldiers, the four agents continued to mount watch, waiting for instructions that weren't coming. The hours flowed slowly and were heavy with worry. Malabar's new calls received no answer. And the prolonged silence of the Boss became more and more incomprehensible. However important C.25's discoveries in the cellar were, her silence toward her auxiliaries was inexplicable. And the lack of news increased the fear that some new trap had closed once again over the courageous Thérèse Arnaud.

Before the dawn had begun to wipe out the night, Malabar could hold out no longer, giving the order to shut down the surveillance operations in the way agreed upon. The four auxiliaries then began to creep toward the villa. They each climbed a wall from their side. The small garden and the shed were quickly inspected. Then Thérèse's agents divided into two groups. That of Marcel and Languille were in charge of visiting the villa. The other, that of Malabar and Friquet, undertook without further delay the exploration of the underground rooms.

Malabar and Friquet reached the first cellar without any trouble. Thanks to information given them by the Boss on the telephone, they easily found the trap door in the underground that opened onto the stairway.

Shortly thereafter, they got into the lower cellar. It was empty. There was no trace of disorder, No signs of a fight. Everything was perfectly in place.

"Nevertheless, the Boss was here!" the Hercules exclaimed.

They searched in vain for a long time for signs of Thérèse's having been there. Nothing. Absolutely nothing. The first group that had gone to search the villa came to join Malabar and Friquet. But the new searches undertaken couldn't gather the slightest information. Thérèse Arnaud had disappeared.

It was evident that C.25 had spent some time in the concrete underground chamber and it offered, visibly, no other exit but the stairway leading to the first cellar. The Secret Service agent was no longer there, but how had she gotten out, since none of the four men during their surveillance had noticed the least human movement of any kind, neither on the inside or outside of the villa? Each began searching for some trap door, for some secret passage.

"The existence of that secret passage would explain everything," Marcel theorized, "the arrival of the enemy spies and the disappearance of the little one."

The house was again searched from the second floor down to the basement, and always with the same result. Friquet, who had been absent for a few minutes, returned. The news he brought only doubled the anxiety clutching the four men. The telephone wire linking Thérèse and Malabar had been cut and that had been done *on the first floor of the villa*. Therefore, while Thérèse was in the cellar, *someone was there at the same time as she.*

So, how did that person enter? How did he hide? How did he leave? And how did Thérèse get out of the villa? And admitting that she had been made prisoner, she wasn't a woman to let herself be kidnapped without resistance. From this, it could logically be concluded that not only a single, but several enemy agents, had been present. But that hypothesis, which seemed to resolve the question as it concerned her disappearance, made the problem more obscure. How could several men be hidden? How could they have entered and left the villa, since the villa was surrounded?

One fact deepened the mystery, the first telephone call from C.25 to Malabar. She had said:

"I have just searched the whole house. There's absolutely no one there. I'm certain. Right now," she had said, "I'm in a second cellar."

"So?"

Then the four assistants of C.25 were totally confused. They didn't know what to think. And their worry had foundation.

Daylight was breaking. It was useless for Malabar, Friquet, Languille, and Marcel to work relentlessly to find any trace in the villa. They conferred rapidly and arrived at the following decisions by common accord: Languille and Friquet would leave immediately to try to gather some information around the known operations of Karl Himmelfeld. There they might pick up some trail, some movement, some trace of activity that would orient the searches. As for Marcel, he held onto the following reasoning:

"Maybe the madman that the Police had hospitalized yesterday might furnish some enlightenment. Since he had been confined in the villa, he ought to know the existence of a secret exit, of some sort of passage allowing the spies to enter and leave without drawing suspicion."

That new supposition, had opened up a line of hope. Marcel had begun immediately to verify it. Therefore Malabar remained alone at The Roses villa. He couldn't make up his mind to abandon the search. And his reasoning always struck the same insoluble problem: the Boss *must* be in the villa. She wasn't there any longer. Now she couldn't have left without being seen. Therefore, if she left as a prisoner without any of the agents seeing her, there was a secret passage. And despite all the searches, they had found no exit, no clue, nothing!

The Roses villa remained the central place where, when they had finished their mission, C.25's auxiliaries had to come back to in order to coordinate with Malabar.

Marcel's visit to the unfortunate mad man brought no precise information. On the contrary, it managed only to further obscure the mystery. The man had recovered some calm. Marcel had been able to see him and interrogate him. The man didn't seem to comprehend the questions put to him. He paid no attention to them. It seemed he was following his own personal thoughts. Despite all the patience which Marcel showed, he hadn't been able to make himself understood by the demented man, who continued to repeat without any connection, the same leit-motif:

"You can't get out! It's impossible! And the people who enter disappear! They disappear forever!"

That sentence repeated many times in a vague, absent tone, coming back like a refrain, resonated gloomily in the mind of the Chemist. Was the insane man talking about The Roses villa? *They can't get out and the people who enter disappear forever.* And Thérèse? Nevertheless, Marcel repeated his questions tirelessly.

"They can't get out? Are you sure of that?"

The man looked into space without paying attention to the question. Then, picking up the thread of his elusive thoughts, he murmured a sentence that culminated Marcel's astonishment.

"Warn the Deuxième Bureau. Only they will never know about it because those who enter disappear and that continues."

"What Deuxième Bureau?" Marcel questioned. "Tell me. Explain to me so I can warn them."

"You, warn them?"

He laughed sharply and that was all.

On leaving the mad man, Marcel was even more perplexed. Who was the mad man? Probably Karl's agent? That hypothesis justified the fear of the man, who, in his delirium continued to doubt that the Deuxième Bureau had been warned.

Marcel returned to Gentilly. He found Malabar desperate. The searches of Languille and Friquet were still futile. Marcel's story caused anxiety in Thérèse's agents. There could no longer be any doubt. The man's words took on a tragic significance. *Those who enter don't leave.*

Only the mad man possessed the key to the enigma which might allow finding a trace of the unfortunate Thérèse Arnaud, victim of the implacable fight undertaken against Karl Himmelfeld.

V. Electrocuted and Drowned

The rope supporting Thérèse suddenly slid toward her. One of the knots coming to the edge of the well opening had thrown all the equilibrium off. And the second now was also beginning to slide. C.25 didn't have enough time to climb back up to the lower cellar. Besides, to go back up was to expose herself to the deadly electric currents she had miraculously avoided and which wouldn't give her a second chance.

So? What was to be done? Nothing! The Secret Service agent was on a rope ladder that was hanging over a well opening. Shortly afterward, a loud cry! Some seconds later, a sinister *Floc*! The ladder had fallen into the water. Then, silence. A silence of death.

"Phew!" Thérèse sighed. "That was close! Some minutes more and Karl Himmelfeld's predictions would have come true. He would have been rid of me! Fortunately, I'm accustomed to gymnastics! Logically, I ought to be electrocuted and drowned! But I'm here!"

She flashed the ray of the electric torch all around her, murmuring, "Here? I don't know where. But, temporarily safe."

Just as the rope ladder had fallen, she had discovered in the wall of the stone well, a kind of niche. In an unbelievable effort, she had jumped. Looking more carefully into the hiding place, where she had taken refuge, she said: "This isn't a niche; it's a corridor!"

In fact, the niche wasn't enclosed. A very narrow and very low opening where you could only enter by creeping remained open. Without hesitating she entered the casing.

"I don't have anything to hope for by remaining in the well, so I might as well follow this path."

Minutes, painful quarters of an hour later, at the expense of the greatest efforts, and despite immense fatigue, she continued, flat on her stomach.

Turning at a right angle, the corridor became wider. After a while she could continue on her way on her knees in the oily ground. At different times she stopped to orient herself. The corridor, seeming to go up toward ground level sometimes went down more deeply. Despite her hurry, she didn't neglect any of the precautions her situation demanded. What was this corridor? Where did it come out? What new traps were hidden?

At the end of another hour, she could increase her speed. The corridor was getting bigger, rising higher and higher. It was soon possible for her to stand up to go on her way.

The Secret Service agent didn't forget the goal she was following. To go to Gex and capture the three German spies who were that night crossing the Swiss border. If possible, to go into action even before the enemies had reached Gex and, following Karl Himmelfeld's instructions, spread out into our territory. While making her way along, Thérèse was thinking intensively.

Karl must know about the arrival of those three agents that the German espionage service is putting at his disposition. He must have become aware of it at the same time as C.25. In fact, the long range wireless message intercepted by Thérèse had certainly been received by other wireless posts set up in the spy's hideouts.

She still had one ace: Karl must think she was electrocuted or drowned. He must think he was through with her. Therefore he wouldn't be on guard against her. That was what gave the brave Frenchwoman the greatest chances for success. Then, once she had taken care of the three German agents' fate, she must set about getting rid of her dangerous adversary. And to succeed, she must reach Gex!

Now, at the moment when every instant was important, she was going along in a subterranean passage which seemed interminable! Where was she going? Where would she come out? Would she even manage to leave this corridor?

"Ah! Now I know where I am," Thérèse suddenly said, breathing a sigh of relief. "Getting back to the surface is only a matter of patience!"

She walked faster, neglecting precautions. She had nothing more to fear. The subterranean passage had led to the catacombs. Another half-hour of walking, then the stairs, a door that would scarcely hold out against the simplest tools. Still more stairs.

And the young woman, muddy, a little dazzled, mingled with the crowd walking around the Place Denfert-Rochereau. A taxi. She didn't even go to her house. She had herself taken directly to the garage. Her powerful automobile, always ready to take to the road, was there. On the road, directly toward Gex. It was about 3 p.m. At 4 p.m. she stopped for several minutes. She had already traveled 100 kilometers. Resting? Yes and no. The time to throw some nourishment into a stomach which was crying out in hunger. And also instructions to give her auxiliaries.

At the first attempt no response to her telephone call. Friquet and Languille were trying to gather information at Karl Himmelfeld's hideouts. And Malabar was keeping a futile watch around the villa. Finally, at a new stop caused by needing to fill up the gas tank, and no longer having to fear running out of gas if circumstances required a longer trip, she reached Marcel by telephone.

It would be impossible to describe the Chemist's joy on hearing the voice of the Boss—long distance, it's true—that he thought dead. But Thérèse cut short his emotion. She immediately transmitted directives. Marcel was told to go let Malabar know he was to join her in Gex the same night, by any means possible.

"At Gex, tonight?" Marcel, alarmed, asked.

"Yes, at any cost," she ordered.

"But even with the most powerful automobile, it's impossible," the Chemist objected.

"I've already told you that you let yourself be weighed down by useless considerations. Impossible by automobile, take a plane!"

Before Marcel had time to answer, she had hung up and paid for the call.

C.25's car rolled along in the night, surrounded by a dense fog.

"Fog!" she groaned. "They have all the luck! That's going to help the border crossing."

Her thoughts were logical. But if the fog was favorable for the plans of the German spies, it was a great deal less favorable to the high speed touring car at night, on roads with poor visibility.

While driving along, C.25 had established her plan. She had consulted her map. She had studied the hills that were the easiest to climb by the spies who must try to avoid the authorities and throw off surveillance. From all the evidence, only two routes were possible to reach the road separating the Swiss border from Gex.

As the hour advanced, she found herself behind the schedule she had set up. Despite C.25's impatience, the fog required her, despite all her lack of caution, to maintain a speed considerably less than that which was necessary to be sure to arrive before the spies on the other side of Gex, where the two roads separated.

She was afraid she might not be able to manage to get information about the famous A.F.16, the German spy in charge of facilitating the border crossing of his fellow citizens. C.25 had logically deduced that it was necessary for her to get to the three German spies before they succeeded in joining A.F.16. This agent must have received instructions directly from Karl. These would be in direct contradiction to those that she *herself* had heard given to the envoys of the espionage service.

It was past midnight when Thérèse's auto reached the first houses of Gex. The village was asleep, dark, wrapped in a winding sheet of fog. In order not to attract attention uselessly, she crossed the village slowly and followed the route toward the border.

"Now, to go any further would be dangerous. Nothing indicates which hill Karl's friends will come from. And they must prefer to take the little paths rather than the big roads."

She parked the automobile, all the lights off, against the road side and began surveillance. She was there more than a half-hour. All at once she had an idea. A little behind the automobile, in such a way that a vehicle coming from Switzerland would pass her, the agent strung a rope across the road. In that way, any motorcycle or automobile coming from Switzerland and stopping at her signal would have nothing to fear. But whoever tried to pass beyond would shortly thereafter hit a barrier that would cause an accident.

Some more time passed. Then she heard a roar. No doubt, a motorcycle. But the noise was coming from the opposite direction from that which she had foreseen. A motorcycle coming from Gex was going toward the border. However, on the road straight ahead, she didn't see any light. She was going to put the rope a little forward in order to avoid the accident it would cause, but she didn't have time. The sound of a fall, and a German obscenity. Before the man had time to get up, the Secret Service agent had jumped on him. Surprised by that attack, as he had been surprised by his fall, the man hardly resisted. Thérèse guessed that the motorcyclist was A.F.16, going to meet the three spies.

"What road are they taking?" she asked.

"I don't understand!" the man growled.

"You understand perfectly well. Point out immediately the road that A.F.65, A.F.23, and A.F.42 are taking to go to Gex. You received instructions to go meet them."

"I don't know; I don't understand," the man repeated.

"I'm going to make you understand; I guarantee it!"

But with a superhuman effort the spy was getting loose. He tried to stand up. He succeeded, and in his turn he jumped on Thérèse, who, although prepared for the attack, couldn't hold out against the onslaught.

VI. Malabar's Trip

Malabar was crouched in the little garden of The Roses villa when Marcel rushed up to him and in a happy voice said:

"Quick, Malabar! Let's get on the road!"

"On the road!" Malabar said, astonished. "You've found the Boss. Where?"

"Where? I know precisely nothing about that," Marcel informed him.

"So?" Malabar growled, disappointed.

"I only know one thing: she's alive and you're to leave immediately!"

"Me?" stammered Malabar, who was, however, accustomed to the most diverse orders from the Boss.

"Yes, you," Marcel continued. "You have to reach the Swiss border tonight, at the intersection of two roads. It's very clear on the map. You can examine it on the way."

"This very night! Impossible!"

"Impossible, no. By plane!"

"Yes, that can be done," Malabar said, convinced. Without waiting any longer, he got up and with wide strides left his sentry point, where he had lived hours of terrible worry about the fate reserved for the Boss.

"Am I going alone?" he asked.

"No. To save time carrying out the orders given, I have already sent Friquet ahead to take charge of doing whatever is necessary to find the aircraft we need."

"Then everything's all right! And what am I supposed to do over there?"

"Something I'm sure you won't tell anyone," Marcel smiled.

"What! Are you doubting me now?" the Hercules said angrily.

"No, not at all, my good Malabar. But, as I don't know myself, I can't tell you. Thus, I'm absolutely certain that nobody will find it out. From us, at least!"

Malabar and Marcel hurried off to find the taxi on the Bicêtre road that had brought Marcel and was to conduct the two agents to the Bourget Airfield. When they arrived, the taxi wasn't there.

"What does this mean?" Marcel raged.

"A person in a hurry who found a taxi," Malabar suggested.

"Yes? A person in a hurry who took a taxi with a rather tidy sum already showing on the meter! You're getting senile, Malabar."

"So? What do you think?"

"I'm not thinking anything, Malabar, but this area is almost deserted. Clients for taxis are rare. Draw your own conclusions."

"The conclusion is easy!"

And at the same time the same name dropped from the two agents lips:

"Karl Himmelfeld!"

For a few steps the two friends were silent. Then, picking up the cadence of their walk:

"That's something that risks making the trip dangerous!"

"Bah! We'll see about that," Malabar said. "The important thing is to get to the Bourget Airfield. Once in the aircraft we have nothing more to fear. And whoever could reach us and keep us from being at the rendezvous with the Boss would have to be very bad people."

Malabar and Marcel's suppositions were correct, if not in details, at least in fact. The taxi's disappearance was another trick of Karl Himmelfeld and his acolytes. Malabar thought he was alone at the villa when the Chemist had come to join him. But their conversation had had a witness who had not lost a word of instructions Marcel had given. A microphone had been placed in the garden, and an agent of Karl Himmelfeld, on a chimney of the roof had been at the earphones. Even before the Hercules and Marcel reached the Porte d'Orléans, Karl Himmelfeld had been alerted. He learned with a rage that he didn't for a moment try to hide: 1. Once again C.25 had escaped him. 2. That she certainly knew about the arrival of the three German spies. The fact that she was setting up a rendezvous that very night with one of her agents in the vicinity of Gex was a sufficiently clear fact.

From that point, an unusual agitation took hold of the German agent. Telephone calls, messages sent over the wireless. A veritable call to combat action stations. For the moment Karl renounced doing away with C.25. There would be time later to definitely terminate her. At the moment he had a more pressing mission to complete: to prevent C.25 from reaching the spies on their arrival in France.

Himmelfeld didn't fool himself that he had the bad hand in the game. Thérèse was seriously ahead of him. But nothing was lost. Since Thérèse's agents, who were just a short time ago at Gentilly, could be this same night in the vicinity of Gex, Karl's envoys, who were right then in Paris, could reach the same town at the same time. From that point, Karl used every method to slow down Malabar's departure, so as to allow his agents to gain time.

Thus, near the Swiss border, where C.25 was waiting for the Hercules, she would meet Karl's agents. And that was enough to modify all the plans of combat and change C.25's almost certain victory into an irremediable defeat.

When they arrived at the Bourget Airfield, Malabar and Marcel found Friquet impatiently waiting for them. The aircraft was ready. A few men were finishing the preparations for departure. Without waiting any longer, the Hercules and Friquet put on their flying suits and shook hands with Marcel.

Full of gasoline. Full of oil. A trial of the motor. Some misfiring.

Friquet was surprised.

"A while ago, in a trial run, while waiting for Malabar to arrive, the plane's motor functioned perfectly."

"It's possible it was working a while ago," the pilot said, "but now it's not working and I can't leave with this situation."

"How long before we can take off?" Friquet asked.

A vague gesture was the only answer he got. Some attempts to get another aircraft were tried. And the absolutely incredible answer came back:

"Impossible! We have only two aircraft available for these types of cases. All the others are on patrol…We can't use them!"

Malabar began to go into a rage. But Friquet, cleverer, had already asked:

"Two aircraft, you say? The one we're supposed to take and that's currently out of commission, that makes one. We'll take the other one!"

"The other one? Impossible!"

"Why?"

They heard the roar of a motor. The man Friquet had asked raised his arm in the night, pointing, and said:

"The other aircraft, that's it; it's taking off!"

A double oath came from the throats of Malabar and Friquet. Nothing to do but wait. Despite themselves C.25 's two agents resigned themselves. Nevertheless, Malabar couldn't stay in one spot. He went toward the aircraft where the mechanics were trying to repair the motor. The Colossus watched their work.

"All right! Let's look at this motor!"

Somewhat surprised, the mechanics let Malabar work on the motor. In a few minutes the motor began to turn over regularly.

"This time, let's go!"

But this time, one of the mechanics came to report that gasoline was leaking out.

"Good God!" Friquet said, beside himself, "it wasn't leaking a while ago."

And the same answer came back: "That's possible. A while ago it wasn't leaking, but it is now. So, it has to be repaired."

"That won't take long," consoled the other aviator, who was part of the flight as co-pilot.

Malabar was again supervising the repair. When he returned, his face revealed an expression that astonished Friquet.

"What's wrong with you, Malabar?"

"Nothing," he said, elusively, evading the question. "Nothing."

"Is it only because we're late that you're looking like that?"

Malabar didn't answer. Addressing the two aviators, he asked:

"All right, is it finished? The motor is turning over, the gas tank isn't leaking any longer. We can leave."

One of the aviators looked at his watch and then said calmly: "Yes, we can leave now that everything's as we wanted it."

Friquet, at the same time as the aviator, looked down at his wristwatch. "We've lost an hour and a quarter," he declared.

It was, in fact, an hour and a quarter since the second available aircraft had taken off. Malabar and Friquet strapped in. The aviators started the aircraft. The motor roared. An arm was lifted. A rumble, and the plane took flight.

VII. In the Aircraft

For more than three hours, the aircraft flew regularly in the fog. Malabar was following on the map and paying attention to the route followed. Friquet was thinking. The flight was going without incident. Since the departure from the Bourget Airfield, Malabar and Friquet had exchanged only very brief words. C.25's two agents seemed preoccupied. Friquet, usually quick with repartees and facetious sayings, remained silent.

What was bothering Friquet, to the point of making him lose his good disposition, was Malabar's attitude. Friquet had never known him to put on such a face!

The motor continued to turn regularly. The fog, which had been surrounding the aircraft since the departure from the Bourget Airfield was becoming thicker. Suddenly, obeying the pilots command, the aircraft approached the ground. It flew in big circles several times. The pilot and the co-pilot looked at each other. Then the aircraft flew higher. Motor roaring regularly. Fog. The minutes passed.

"We must be coming in?" Friquet asked.

"Yes! Now's the time to keep an eye out," Malabar said.

Then, without moving, Malabar decided to confide to Friquet the reason for his worry.

"My friend, I repeat to you, this is the time to keep an eye out. As you've guessed, we're approaching Gex. And because of that, we could have a very unfortunate accident. Don't move. It's useless to attract the attention of the other two. Listen to this little story. The motor at the Bourget Airfield had nothing wrong with it. Nevertheless, they took a long time to repair it. During that absolutely unnecessary repair which I myself oversaw, a second aircraft, *the only other one available,* took off. I imagine it carried people as much in a hurry as we are and for the same reason."

"What are you saying, Malabar. I don't get it."

"I'm saying that once the motor was in good shape, the gas tank began to leak. And again I looked for myself. That leak had been deliberately caused, just a simple turn of a screw. Now, unless you're as thick as a plank, you ought to understand."

"Understand what?"

"That the pilots are very likely Karl Himmelfeld's agents. The most astonishing thing is that they're flying us in the right direction. And that's what makes me afraid that the closer we get to our destination, something unfortunate will happen to us. We're an hour and a quarter behind the first aircraft that left. It could only seat two people. That was not space enough for the mission Karl had in mind and that the Boss wanted to oppose. Do you now begin to understand?"

"Yes, I understand," Friquet said, "that these dirty bastards want to take us down brutally."

"If we give them enough time," Malabar said, looking at his watch.

The co-pilot turned toward the two passengers. The pilot once more descended to try to get his bearings in the thicker and thicker fog. Suddenly, after having picked up altitude, the aircraft veered sharply toward the south. Malabar and Friquet pretended not to be aware of the change of directions. A look from Malabar to Friquet.

With the same movement, the two friends rose from their seats. While with one quick gesture Friquet snatched the co-pilot's glasses off and with a firm hand applied a mask soaked with chloroform to his face, Malabar's fist slammed down on the pilot's skull. The aircraft began to pitch. The pilot had been knocked unconscious. Malabar climbed on top of his seat. Then at the risk of breaking his shoulder, he climbed into the pilot's place. Taking the unconscious man's seat belt off, he passed him as rapidly as possible, and without taking too many precautions, to the rear of the cabin. Then he strapped himself in. It was just in time. The aircraft had begun a rapid dive. It took all Malabar's skill to manage to re-establish equilibrium and right the aircraft. However, the co-pilot Friquet had attacked was offering more and more resistance, fighting fiercely against the effects of the narcotic. Malabar, as soon as he was in command of the aircraft, left the controls for a moment. With a well applied fist he put an end to the co-pilot's resistance.

"That does it. He got what he deserved," yelled the Colossus, while calmly taking back the aircraft's stick.

"Phew!" sighed Friquet, "I believe that we're coming back from some distance."

"Yes," agreed the Colossus. "However, everything isn't over. We're near the end. But we have to find a landing spot. And we must get started looking for the Boss."

"Tell me this, my little Malabar, if, at Bourget Airfield, you were suspicious of the two pilots, why did you say nothing?"

"So as not to raise the alarm, to be able to reach Gex at the intended time, and at the same time, with a little luck, get rid of these two."

"That doesn't matter, my big fellow!" Friquet concluded. "To put us in the hands of Karl's accomplice, you don't lack guts!"

"This isn't the time to lack it! To land in such a fog."

The aircraft descended slowly, making large circles, but alas! the ground remained invisible. For more than a quarter of an hour, the aircraft turned above the point Thérèse had indicated for the rendezvous. Malabar was beginning to get desperate.

"It's enraging, even so," he grumbled, "to get to the end despite all the changes and be obliged to turn about like sheep in a pasture. It's absolutely impossible to land."

"I like wooden rocking horses, but I'm beginning to have enough of them," joked Friquet, whose good humor was restored.

The circling continued. Suddenly, a light came up through the fog.

"A flare!" Malabar rejoiced.

"And another!" Friquet added.

The aircraft flew toward the point indicated. During this time the two men exchanged their thoughts.

"Don't rejoice too quickly," Malabar said. "These flares are certainly for us, but who's sending them?"

"What do you mean, who?"

"Damn, my little friend! Don't forget that the aircraft carrying Karl's two envoys left an hour and a quarter before us. And they may be the ones who…"

"You're reasoning all wrong, Malabar," Friquet joked. "Admitting that it was Karl's agents that sent us those signals, don't forget one thing. The aircraft, our aircraft, is piloted by their comrades. At least they think so. So they have no interest in making us smash up the landing. On the contrary, it's to their advantage to have us land in good shape…to more surely and more properly execute us on our arrival."

"You're right, Friquet," Malabar answered. "And in that case, we have the ability to answer them. I even have a grenade in case of danger!"

New circles. Two more flares. Malabar checked out the spot indicated. He flew the aircraft very carefully. The aircraft motor cut, it began to descend. The two men could see a clearing surrounded by high trees. Still some meters from the ground. A sudden fall followed by the noise of wood and broken metal. The aircraft had hit a tree.

VIII. A.F.65, A.F.23, A.F.42

Thérèse's blackout from A.F.16's blow was of short duration. A fist blow intended to stun the intrepid Deuxième Bureau agent had passed well over the mark. C.25 had ducked rapidly. Moving forward with his blow, A.F.16 couldn't hold up under the blow to the stomach when Thérèse butted him with her head. Again, he fell, knocked out. And the Secret Service agent hurried to tie him up.

"One down!" she murmured.

However, time was passing. And if she had mastered A.F.16, as far as the three German agents were concerned, she was not any further along than when she left Paris. They must now have crossed the border and be traveling toward Gex. She dragged A.F.16 across the ground as far as the automobile. Then she hoisted him into the interior. He rapidly returned to consciousness, but he didn't seem disposed to hold a conversation with his conqueror.

"You see," she told him, "I'm afraid you'll take cold. The nights are bad. You'll be a lot better off in my car than running around the mountains. So, tell me, where were you going? Which direction are A.F.65, A.F.23, A.F.42 coming from?"

For a moment the man remained silent. Thérèse used this break to tie her prisoner more firmly.

Finally, he said:

"Me, I'm captured. I'm lost. I know what awaits me. But you won't get the others. Great Germany will hold onto three faithful servants."

"Unless it loses all four of them!" C.25 objected.

"In any case," the man continued coldly and proudly, "I won't be the one who caused their loss. It's useless to interrogate me. I won't tell you anything, neither by persuasion nor by force. You can kill me. That would spare me the firing squad. But you won't find out anything!"

C.25 understood that she wouldn't get anything out of the prisoner. Then leaving the automobile, she returned to her observation post. Nothing. The widespread silence of the mountains. The wind blowing through the leafless trees. The animal calls. The rustling of the leaves. The thousand diverse sounds. No trace of the spies. Suddenly a thought passed through C.25's mind. She turned back toward the prisoner. He saw her coming toward him and smiled. Perhaps he knew, given the time, that the envoys from the Nachrichten Bureau had successfully reached Gex. Perhaps he had received instructions saying that the spies had reached a pre-determined point. She knew that her limited resources were not sufficient to set up a trap from which it was impossible to escape. It was relatively easy for the spies to avoid danger, temporarily, from C.25. Temporarily, yes. But tomorrow morning the three men would be at Gex. And there, however much care they might take to pass unnoticed, the battle would begin again, and they were very much in danger of losing the game.

Thérèse had the best reasons to want to move quickly. Leaning over A.F.16, she said:

"Since you don't want to talk, you don't need to keep the power of speech. You might cry out and raise the alarm. It's absolutely useless!"

And she put a solid gag in her prisoner's mouth. He couldn't resist, but he showed visible signs of rage at that measure.

"Well! Does that bother you?" C.25 continued. "So my idea wasn't bad? You were counting on giving the alarm to your friends when they approached? Then, without knowing it, you've just admitted that the envoys from the German espionage service are coming by here. And, because the trap I've set up could capture them, let's not neglect any precaution."

Saying this, she lifted out the back seat of the automobile. That seat covered a vast chest.

"I'm sorry," Thérèse continued, "but for the moment I can't offer you any other housing. Be quiet. Everything is taken care of. It's rather uncomfortable, but you can easily breathe."

She toppled the spy into the opening where the seat had been and put the seat back in place. Almost another hour of watching. The roar of a motor. Accustomed to identifying sounds, she was not wrong. It was not the sound of an aircraft motor, but of a motorcycle. The noise approached rapidly. She placed herself resolutely in the middle of the road. She signaled with the automobile lights. A motorcycle with three men came out of the fog, but without slowing down. Thérèse renewed her signals. The motorcycle stopped. No possible mistake. Three men with their hands on their revolvers. She didn't flinch; she knew the recognition sign for the three German spies. At that discreet sign, the three men responded. Going forward then, she held out a paper to the driver of the motorcycle. The three men stepped to the ground.

"Everything is ready," Thérèse said.

They didn't move. Three dim lights were directed toward the automobile where Thérèse was holding the door open, saying:

"I'm going to give you some light."

The interior of the automobile lit up. The three men walked briskly over and climbed inside.

Taking her place at the steering wheel, the Secret Service agent pushed on the accelerator and on a hidden lever. As she did this, she quickly lowered her head. A revolver shot rang out and passed above her. The windows of the automobile were already being replaced by steel panels. The doors would no longer open. The vehicle had become a rolling prison.

"Fortunately, the panels are covered and the material is solid," Thérèse thought, getting the speed back in hand.

"I bothered Malabar for nothing," she was thinking. "I don't need him! Everything went better than I had hoped. A.F.16, A.F.65, A.F.23, and A.F.42, a good day! Another good defeat, the best I have ever inflicted on Karl Himmelfeld!"

C.25 was taking her prisoners for an outing by driving around in circles in the Gex area while waiting for Malabar. She was beginning to get worried, fearing that her faithful auxiliary had been the victim of some enemy machination, when the sound of a motor reassured her. This time there was no mistake. It was an aircraft. She immediately started toward the clearing which she had noticed while driving around and, which, in a pinch, could act as a rather passable landing spot. She heard the aircraft pass overhead several times. A flare exploded! Two! Four! She was already rejoicing when she saw the aircraft suddenly fall as if out of control. Must she, in complete victory, have to deplore the death of her auxiliaries? Fortunately, no! The accident was serious! But Malabar and Friquet got out of it with a good shaking up, violent emotion, and some scratches of no seriousness.

"The Boss!" the Colossus exclaimed.

"It's been a long time since we've seen you," Friquet joked.

"And we were afraid that we would never see you again!" Malabar finished the sentence.

"No! Not this time," Thérèse answered unconcernedly.

"But are you alone?" The Alsatian asked.

"No, I have a lot of company."

"So do we," Friquet added.

"But," Malabar worried, "the first German aircraft that was coming before the three agents?"

"Haven't seen it. No trace," Thérèse said. "Nevertheless, it would be better not to stay here. Besides, we've finished our job."

Before going back to the car, Friquet asked:

"What are we going to do with our passengers?"

"What passengers?" the Secret Service agent asked.

"Two friends of that excellent Karl Himmelfeld who were extremely obliging in piloting our aircraft here…and to whom we showed our gratitude by sending them to dreamland…so that they didn't send us to a more distant land!"

"We're going to take care of them," C.25 said. "The friends of our friends are our friends! However, my automobile is already full."

"Full!" Malabar exclaimed.

"Exactly! I didn't come here for nothing. And we're going to have the pleasure of accompanying A.F.16, A.F.65, A.F.23, and A.F.42 to Paris where we will put them in the hands of the authorities."

"Four and two," Friquet calculated. "Six!"

Malabar carried the two aviators who were in the rear seat of the aircraft to the automobile.

"Now it's full! We don't need to capture any more before Paris!" he declared.

"Next time, Boss, a vehicle will have to be requisitioned to transport your prey!" Friquet joked.

And with Malabar at the wheel, the automobile got on the road toward Paris.

"Be careful," C.25 advised Malabar. "This isn't the time to have an accident."

IX. What Languille Did

Languille had gone to look for Thérèse Arnaud, thinking he could find clues by searching Karl Himmelfeld's hideouts. Not knowing the Boss had been found, and that she had given instructions for Friquet and Malabar to go meet her in the area around Gex, he had gone to Karl's hideout at Enghien. He suddenly noticed unusual comings and goings around that nest of spies. He was going to alert Marcel by telephone to ask him for immediate reinforcements.

"Don't worry about the Boss," Marcel said. "But above all, don't budge. I'm going to call you back immediately."

While watching the outside of the hideout, Languille was brought up to date by the Chemist about the different events of the day. What he needed to know: that Thérèse Arnaud was at Gex. That Malabar and Friquet had just left by airplane to meet her.

"Everything leads me to believe that the Boss has discovered in the Gentilly villa, information that caused her to leave urgently for Gex," Marcel deduced. "Now there would be nothing astonishing in the fact that Karl Himmelfeld had gotten wind of the affair and had undertaken to thwart her projects."

"That's very possible!" the Acrobat approved.

"It's even more possible," Marcel continued, "that diverse small details remain unexplained. Notably the disappearance of the taxi that had taken me to Gentilly. Then, too, certain delays in the departure of the aircraft that was to transport Malabar and Friquet. Then also the flight of the first aircraft, the only one available, while our friends remained at the Bourget Airfield and couldn't get a flight! Each of these facts is, in appearance, rather insignificant. But in putting them all together, and adding to them the activity you are seeing there, I think we can again be useful to the Boss. But let's not get carried away."

Languille gave Marcel a detailed account of what he had noticed in the course of the afternoon. In going over the times and putting things together, Marcel and Languille soon reached the following points: 1. The activity going on in Karl's lair had begun some minutes after Marcel's transmission to Malabar in the garden at Gentilly ordering the departure for Gex. 2. The time of the flight from the Bourget Airfield of the first aircraft corresponded to the departure of an automobile carrying two individuals coming from Karl's place.

"Don't we have any information as to the business which called the Boss to Gex?" asked Languille.

"None," Marcel responded.

Then after a short pause, he continued:

"I've drawn my conclusions. There's no possible error. The taxi that disappeared, the aircraft, the departure of the two people, Malabar and Friquet's breakdown; all that is tied to the business at the Swiss border."

"But what's to be done?" Languille questioned. "Should we also leave to take help to the Boss. I'm afraid she's going to find herself faced with important forces."

"Impossible! We'd arrive too late," Marcel stated.

"There…a telegram delivery person!" Languille said.

"Oh! A telegram," Marcel objected, "has no importance! Karl and his spies have more up-to-date ways to communicate between themselves, more rapid and that leave fewer traces."

"That's to find out," Languille murmured. "Stay there. I'm going to dash to the post office that's the wireless station and I'm going to find out the text of that telegram. Don't forget, Marcel, that the telegraph is still useful if there's nothing else. There's not always a telephone handy, and an even stronger reason, a wireless set."

"Agreed!" Marcel said.

A short time later Languille returned.

"So?" Marcel demanded.

"So my idea wasn't bad! This telegram tells us something…when you've translated it, Marcel."

Marcel examined the text that Languille handed him.

"Yes, obviously, but at the moment there's one word we can understand."

"What word? I didn't see anything" Languille said.

"Yes you did," Marcel explained. "Laumes! Doesn't that tell you anything? Laumes is a rather important town in Bourgogne on the Dijon road."

"On the Dijon road," Languille repeated.

"Or also on the road to Gex, if you prefer! I'm going to dash and translate this text and I'll be back."

There was no difficulty in Marcel's task. The telegram, translated into clear language read:

Fog. Forced to land in Laumes, on the edge of the departmental road. Aircraft damaged.

"So," Marcel said some moments later, "our suppositions were right and are verified. The first aircraft that left certainly carried Karl's agents. No doubt. Besides, the time of the departure, the time the flight took, the loss of time to find the post office: everything fits."

But Marcel didn't have time to carry his deduction any further.

Languille was saying: "And here are the results of the telegram received."

In fact, a very powerful vehicle had just stopped in front of the spies' hideout. Before Marcel was able to stop him, Languille had gone toward the automobile, murmuring:

"Useless to wait any longer to give them their change from their bills."

And two minutes later, two tires of the automobile were flat. The door opened. A silhouette appeared.

"Karl Himmelfeld!" Marcel and Languille said at the same time.

It was he. He was accompanied by a tall man who seemed a subordinate. He kept a respectful distance from the Chief.

The car started off, but it soon stopped, and Marcel and Languille hidden behind the supports of a carriage door, watched, assuming that the haste with which the repair was done was motivated by Karl's bad humor.

A little afterward, the repair completed, the driver got back behind the wheel. A little smoke. A screeching. A blast of a horn.

"On the road!" Languille said.

Then, leaving Marcel stupefied, he jumped up and going across the street, with one prodigious leap he caught the automobile on the fly and clung onto the baggage rack. The vehicle disappeared at the turn of the avenue.

X. On the Road

Two powerful automobiles cruising along in the night in opposite directions on the same road. One of them, driven alternately by Malabar and Friquet (while Thérèse took, finally, some hours of well-deserved rest), had left Gex at 5 a.m. and was traveling toward Paris.

C.25 and her auxiliaries were satisfied. They were coming back victorious. Tomorrow morning they would reach their goal. And they would put their collection of six German spies into the hands of the military authorities.

The other vehicle had already covered many kilometers at a mad speed since it had left Paris. In that vehicle a man was thinking. That man was Karl Himmelfeld. His restraint was worn away. He was enraged. But he was going to get revenge. Karl's plan was childishly simple. For these reasons he had the greatest chance of success. Karl had for a moment been taken aback when his agent, left on surveillance at Gentilly in The Roses villa, had transmitted to him Marcel and Malabar's conversation. So, C.25 who couldn't be captured had once again fled! That bordered on the miraculous. And Karl hadn't been able to find any satisfactory explanation for that escape. But where his rage had attained its height was when some seconds later he had learned about Thérèse Arnaud's departure for Gex, where she had immediately summonsed her agents. In that way, the uncapturable C.25, not satisfied with having escaped his revenge, was actively thwarting his projects.

Karl hadn't hesitated an instant. The Secret Service agent's presence at the border had a direct relationship to the arrival of the three German Agents. Karl immediately guessed the situation. He knew what adversary he was dealing with! Serious danger was going to await the envoys of the German espionage service as soon as they set foot on French soil.

Up to that point all Karl's efforts had been directed toward the same goal: to warn the three spies, to put them on guard; and if need be, to modify their itinerary. And to do this, Karl had used the following means:

First of all, he had slowed down the departure of Thérèse's agents. Then he had arranged that the pilots of the plane carrying him were his own men. And Karl wasn't satisfied with that maneuver. Thus he killed two birds with one stone. He sent two of his own German agents to the German spies to warn them to be on their guard. Then on landing, the pilots were to immediately execute Malabar and Friquet. Thus, instead of the reinforcements she was counting on, she would be met by two more agents, who would join the two agents who left in the first plane. In that way, Thérèse would have to fight against eight men (four leaving from Paris at two different times.)

And Karl was again congratulating himself on this plan which would do away with C.25 accidentally, and thereby exonerating him from his failure to execute the earlier orders concerning C.25. But fate had already changed this plan. The two men who had left by air were halted by fog at Laumes. And the three spies would have only A.F.16 and the two pilots who had flown Friquet and Malabar to help them combat C.25's ambush. And, although the late hour left Karl no hope of arriving at Gex at the desired time, he had decided to go himself to the location. Perhaps by an active and energetic counter-offensive he would be able to win the fight on the point of being lost by his agents.

Now, Karl's automobile had picked up, when passing through Laumes, the two aviators. It was therefore a reinforcement of five men (including the driver) who were going to confront C.25, who was presumed to be alone.

Still some kilometers in the night and in the fog. Two automobiles traveling the same road, in opposite directions! Two powerful headlights ahead shining into Karl's automobile. Karl's driver moved to the right without slowing down. A minute. And the two automobiles passed each other, each following its own route. Karl jumped, an instinctive movement!

"No, that's impossible! Absolutely impossible!" But nevertheless, he wasn't dreaming. The passing of the two automobiles, one near the other, had lasted only an infinitely short time, long enough, however, for him to recognize the occupants of the car racing toward Paris, all the curtains drawn back. C.25 herself and her two agents who had left yesterday evening from Paris in the aircraft flown by his agents, those two auxiliaries who, now, should be definitively sleeping in some woods or some clearing! And C.25 wasn't a woman to quit a fight, as desperate as it might be, to go back to Paris. Therefore, she had won!

These thoughts lasted only as long as a lightning bolt in Karl's head. No! C.25 hadn't yet won! In desperate situations, the most daring methods were used. A brief order through the automobile's intercom. Karl's vehicle stopped suddenly. A new order. The driver turned the vehicle around. Then, driving as fast as possible, he raced toward Paris with the aim of overtaking C.25's automobile.

The roar of an engine in the fog. The trees bordering the road flew by at a dizzying speed. At the end of a few minutes, Karl saw in front of him the rear lights of the other vehicle. He gave instructions to the three men accompanying him. They got out their revolvers. Brief instructions to the driver.

"At whatever cost, overtake the vehicle in front of us. Pass it. Then force it off the edge of the road, to force it to stop!"

Several minutes passed, during which these orders were carried out. The distance separating the two automobiles regularly diminished. Karl calculated the chances of victory. Five men on his side. On the side of the enemy: Malabar, Friquet, Thérèse Arnaud. Karl's vehicle passed that of C.25, driven by Malabar.

"Watch out!" Friquet suddenly said.

At the same time Karl's driver began to approach at the edge of the road. Malabar, to avoid stopping, quickly turned the steering wheel to the right. Two revolver shots whistled past the ears of C.25 and her auxiliaries. Immediately, in response, Malabar again pulled ahead of the German vehicle. A burst of fire! The maneuver planned by Karl was badly executed. It was C.25's automobile which squeezed his off the road.

The two automobiles stopped. In the darkness, red flashes came out of the revolvers without ceasing and died out. The vehicles were used as shields, each group hiding behind the cars, shooting without stopping.

Languille himself had been surprised by the sudden about-face of Karl's vehicle. Still clinging to the luggage rack, he was ready to act, waiting for the right moment. He had guessed there was something wrong. Shortly thereafter, recognizing the Boss's automobile, he had slid to the ground. And his agility had kept him from serious injury. But, instead of joining Malabar and Friquet, Languille had hidden himself in the darkness! And Karl and his crew had suddenly heard shots coming from another direction. Who was this new enemy joining C.25?

A moment of uncertainty! A cry! One of Karl's men was down! Ammunition was becoming short! Karl's agents were still firing, but attacked from two sides, they were trying to answer in all directions. Their shots lacked precision.

"Be careful!" Thérèse ordered.

Malabar looked at the Boss. He discharged his revolver. Another cry from the enemy. Malabar's hand moved back and forth in the darkness, his arm extended.

The sound of an explosion! Thérèse, Malabar, and Friquet, wearing masks now, rushed toward Karl's automobile.

The enemies were lying on the ground, half asphyxiated.

"They don't like gas grenades," Friquet said.

Languille soon came running to join his friends. The battle was over. There was nothing left to do but pick up the prisoners.

"Fortunately, we still have spare rope to tie up all this!" Friquet joked.

It was a total victory for Thérèse. Karl and all his staff were in her hands, alive, except for the driver, who had been killed outright.

"Good idea you had, Languille," Malabar stated. "You won't be one too many to help us carry everybody to Paris."

The two vehicles soon got on the road toward Paris. C.25's automobile, driven by Friquet and Languille, carried the load of spies taken at Gex.

"Don't complain!" Friquet had told Karl. "You're going back to Paris in your old clunker!"

In the early hours of the morning the two vehicles arrived in Paris without incident.

XI. The Secret of the Villa

The same day several incidents occurred which passed perfectly unnoticed except by Thérèse Arnaud and her agents and several of the initiated. The connection between them and the fact that they occurred at the same time were a great deal more striking than the facts themselves. First of all, at noon, The Roses villa was destroyed by a huge fire. Nothing but the wall remained. The investigation carried out by Monsieur Martel, the Commissioner of Police, couldn't determine the exact cause of the disaster. A short circuit in the wiring was mentioned. And that was all. Naturally, for C.25, the explanation was different. The fire had been started…or had taken place, following an explosion which had entirely destroyed the installations in the second cellar. Almost at the same time, the laboratory in the beauty supply boutique on the Avenue de l'Opéra burned down. And despite the efforts of the firemen, nothing could be saved. Shortly after that, the villa at Neuilly, the private residence of Karl Himmelfeld, went up in flames in its turn. Finally, before the end of the evening, Thérèse Arnaud learned that the Les Giroflées villa at Enghien had also been destroyed by fire, while an explosion of an unheard of violence had reduced to bits the house where Karl Himmelfeld had established for some time his general headquarters, and from where he had left the evening before to go to Gex.

At her office, C.25 lit a cigarette.

"We have definitively terminated Karl Himmelfeld this time," she told her agents. "But we haven't finished with the German spies. Very much to the contrary, there should be seen in that systematic destruction of all the hideouts we know about a will to hide the strength of the German agents in Paris. Everything has been destroyed so that we can't learn anything. And in the process, Karl and his agents won't talk. We won't learn anything! Even so, German espionage is still as strong. With Karl gone, the others will continue their work. Other hideouts, as well organized, furnished with all the perfections will function from

116

this evening. And other agents will come with the mission of avenging the death of their chief!"

"Absolutely! I believe that we have our plates full!" Friquet concluded. "And the battle that we undertook against Karl is only a war of children beside what the future holds for us."

"Possible! Let's wait to see what happens," Thérèse said calmly.

"I have a feeling we won't have to wait very long!" Malabar sighed.

What Thérèse had foreseen was verified. Karl and his agents, meeting in a counsel of war, refused to talk. No confession. No information. They all met their condemnation to death calmly.

"We are disappearing because we are vanquished," Karl said proudly. "But others will come who will triumph where we have failed!"

On the morning of his execution, Karl Himmelfeld, with bravado, made the following declaration:

"Now, before dying, to show you that, despite everything, you know nothing, I'm going to reveal the secret of The Roses villa. Monsieur Martel, Police Commissioner of Gentilly, had closed the file on 'The Mad Man of Gentilly,' some days before. Once again, he concluded: 'Dirty business!' In fact, the man had not been identified. Despite the searches undertaken, there had been no result. The man would remain X whoever until the day he died. The doctors had declared his case to be without any possible hope of improvement."

Karl Himmelfeld now gave the name of the Gentilly mad man. Or rather he gave him his official service number. The Gentilly demented man was an agent of the Deuxième Bureau who had joined the fight against Karl. He had been taken prisoner. And with an unheard refinement of cruelty, the German spies had managed to drive him mad. They had put everything in operation to achieve this result! Sequestration, bad treatment, subjections to massive doses of drugs.

Karl concluded with a threat which was not concealed. "She will find out how we take revenge! And we will take revenge! We will get revenge!"

Those were the last words of Karl Himmelfeld, head of German espionage in Paris. He died courageously, in the Vincennes pits where ten stakes had been prepared for him!

THE VIOLET MASK

I. The Business Luncheon

Noon-day traffic was as usual backed up the entire length of the Rue Caumartin. Long lines of automobiles used that street which linked the Boulevard Haussmann to the great Boulevards. The sidewalks were crowded with pedestrians, workers escaped from the neighboring workshops, male and female office employees getting away from the noise of typewriters and office worries. A few of the luxurious establishments and the bars which were open principally at night were opening their doors to some of their earlier clients.

At the Royal Peacock, a restaurant currently in vogue, a rather large crowd was gathering to have lunch around little tables elegantly decorated with flowers. Well-trained waiters were already discretely identifying a minister and two deputies among the patrons. A few steps away, a famous actress, with her entourage, attracted everyone's attention with her daring outfit. The perfectly trained staff were attending to other clients, all very "chic," but less well known.

In a corner of the room, a woman was dining alone. She had not had the least trouble getting that somewhat secluded place. Then, under the surprised look of the maître d'hôtel who had hurried forward, she had ordered her lunch. He had expected the classic response:

"Not right now. I'm expecting someone." There was no such comment.

The client, apparently paying no attention to what was going on in the room, to the comings and goings of the waiters, to the arrival of new clients, seemed only preoccupied with doing honor to the lunch she had ordered. However, as time went on, the Royal Peacock's room filled up. The murmur of conversations grew louder, sharper, accompanied by the noise of crockery. The waiters, always in a hurry and always attentive, moved silently over the thick carpets. Suddenly, a new group, composed of two men and one woman, came into the restaurant. The three people offered a rather striking contrast. One of the men and the woman were very suitably dressed, but without that affectation and elegance which seemed to characterize the regular customers. This couple, without showing excessive timidity, seemed somewhat astonished at the luxury of the establishment and looked around curiously at the sumptuous décor that they apparently saw for the first time. The two individuals seemed a little disoriented. They hesitated to move, fearing to bump into some waiter. On the contrary, the third person seemed perfectly at ease and affected the casual manner of the regular customer, of a man who was accustomed to frequenting first-class establishments.

He had responded with a nod to the question of the maître d'hôtel, who had come forward to welcome the group. And glancing around in a distracted, slightly bored, blasé manner at that kind of décor which was distinguished by no originality, he let himself be guided toward a table, almost pushing ahead of him the two people accompanying him. There was no doubt that it was this third person who, having chosen the Royal Peacock, had brought along the two people with him. There was also no doubt that he was the one who, later, would pay the bill. In fact, with the good manners of a head of household, the man—tall, thin, clean shaven—saw to it that the couple was comfortably seated. Still deferential, he passed to his guests the menu which the maître d'hôtel had presented him. Then, different signs showed he was insisting, encouraging his two guests to order more expensive courses than they, by discretion, had ordered from the set menu. When the maître d'hôtel had taken the orders, when the wine steward had received the necessary instructions, the couple seemed to relax somewhat, and got ready to enjoy pleasure and comfort they were not used to.

This trio, that nothing indicated was out of the ordinary, occupied the table next to that where the client dining alone continued to eat with a good appetite. Only a profoundly observant mind would have been able to note that, since the trio's appearance, she seemed to have slowed the cadence of her meal, and was making an effort to make it last as long as possible. Beginning with the hors d'oeuvre, the three clients appeared to come alive. The couple, a little like a child living a dream, began to eat with a good appetite. With more discretion, the host served himself and smiled somewhat while considering his guests. After leaving his two guests the time necessary to get accustomed to the restaurant's atmosphere, the clean-shaven man began to speak.

At the first words, the two guests almost stopped eating. You would have thought that they had been caught by some surprise which had taken away their appetite. Nevertheless, the host showed the most exquisite good manners and was careful to see that his guests lacked nothing. Little by little the uneasiness of the beginning of the conversation dissipated. The couple, who, at first had listened with unfeigned surprise, stopped being mute and risked posing a few timid questions. And it appeared that the clean-shaven man's answers only added to the two guests' astonishment. Before the hors d'oeuvres were finished, the conversation became more precise, more coherent, broken by questions from the three diners.

Echoes of that conversation carried on in a low voice reached the client at the neighboring table, who lent an attentive, indiscreet ear, while still slowing the cadence of her meal and still seeming preoccupied with her own thoughts. Continuing to look as if she was thinking of something else and nothing in her facial expression indicating the interest she took in the interview between her neighbors, the solitary diner positioned herself so that none of the words exchanged by the trio escaped her.

Gently, patiently, always with a friendly smile, like someone attempting to win someone over, the clean-shaven man answered the questions put to him. He refuted the objections the couple raised. And he tirelessly continued his discourse. While the maître d'hôtel was bringing the fish course, the host went on:

"Come now, why are you hesitating to accept the situation I propose to you? It has nothing that isn't attractive to you. And there's no shortage of people who would be delighted with the proposition I'm offering you."

"I'm not disagreeing that it's very good," answered the other man, who seemed to be the spokesman for his companion, who remained almost mute and limited herself to expressing her surprise by little movements. "It's very good; it's even too good."

"It should never be complained that the bride is too beautiful," the host advised.

"Even so, we'd really like to know what accepting the offer you're making us would obligate us to."

With a reassuring smile, while filling the wine glasses, the clean-shaven man explained:

"Nothing! Absolutely nothing! Please note: I'm not proposing a contract to you, that is to say, a business arrangement where each one of the signers has rights and obligations. This is simply an offer, just an offer which doesn't hide any trap...Would you, yes or no, like to entirely change the mediocre situation in which you find yourself?"

"Obviously!" the man agreed.

"Then it's simple. Take my offer. In two days you'll live in a sumptuous modern apartment on the Champs-Elysées. You'll have all the necessary personnel to serve you."

"To have servants, that's all very well," the young woman's companion answered judiciously. "Still, at the end of the month, salaries have to be paid."

With a grand gesture which swept away all petty preoccupations, the host assured him:

"A matter of details! A matter of details that you won't have to worry about. You'll have everything necessary befitting the residence that will be yours. You will be generously paid for all the expenses that your new social position will entail. According to the situation, according to the external expenses you'll have to incur, I'm able to assure you that the monthly sums that will be paid to you—I'm not talking about salaries, but the sums needed to cover only your household expenses—will vary between 3,000 and 15,000 francs. Even in exceptional cases and if the need became felt, that last amount would be increased. I tell you again that you will have no need to be concerned with questions of money."

"Then what are we supposed to do?" inquired the young woman's companion. "It isn't usual that such offers are made without our being obligated, in exchange, to carry out some job, to..."

Still with the same smiling reassurance, and still refilling the wine glasses while the maître d'hôtel was bringing the main course, the clean-shaven man assured him:

"You'll have absolutely nothing to do! Nothing. No work will be required of you..."

"Then?"

"Then, in exchange for the life I'm offering you (a princely life, you'll admit) I'll ask you for only a small amount of obedience. Oh! Don't expect anything extraordinary. A little bit of obedience for some questions of detail which will be regularly furnished to you, twice a day. For example, to begin with, I'll require you to stay in the apartment I'll have rented for you and under the name I'll have chosen. One name or another, what does it matter to you, right?... As for the other obligations, I can give you an example. It might be that on a certain day I'll ask you to receive a certain person or to give a dinner at which I would choose the guests. There's nothing in that itself that you might find disagreeable. And you don't need to fear that you won't find yourselves up to the level of the circumstance, because I'll surround you with personnel chosen by me who'll be capable of doing what's necessary."

The effect of these propositions was visible. The couple manifested more and more obvious surprise. Temptation shone in the guests' eyes. To accept the offer, wasn't it to see themselves realize a dream, a fairy tale? Wasn't it to have a life of great luxury, princely, free from all material cares? The clean-shaven man's propositions made the young woman's eyes shine. Nevertheless, despite everything, a doubt still tormented the man and the woman. They tried to guess what masked such offers. Evidently they suspected some trap. And there, there only, was the reason for their hesitation.

The neighbor at the next table, having finished her meal, had ordered coffee and left the room for a moment. Then, after a short absence, she came to take her seat again, while the clean-shaven man was again going over the advantages of the propositions he had formulated. At each of the host's new temptations, and perhaps under the influence of the meal and the drinks which were only a prelude to the grand life promised, the couple's hesitations were melting away. Objections were less and less frequent.

"So? Is it agreed? Can I count on you?" summed up the clean-shaven man after having once more clarified the really unbelievable conditions of that magnificent affair. But before the answer was formulated he added:

"Ah! I was about to forget one clause, an important clause of our moral contract: the most absolute secrecy about the propositions I've made to you and the greatest discretion in case you should be asked questions. No one needs to know who you are, where you come from! Do you understand? Overnight you'll drop your two personalities. You're no longer the two individuals you are today. You are Monsieur and Madame X...I'm creating a new personality for you, another kind of life, another national identity, another existence. I'll take care of everything. Is it yes this time?"

After having consulted his companion with a look, the man answered:

"It's yes."

The host showed evident satisfaction with that answer. He smiled engagingly.

"Agreed! You won't regret having listened to me and having let yourselves be convinced. But don't forget: the secret. From now on, those who entered here a while ago no longer exist."

With a nod of the head, the couple agreed.

"Now don't worry any more about anything. You'll hear from me shortly. Be ready, beginning this evening if necessary, to take on your new functions."

The acceptance of that strange bargain had led to the end of the meal. The host didn't prolong the conversation any longer. As soon as the coffee was served he asked for the check with the ease of a man accustomed to expenditure. The maître d'hôtel gratified him with the obsequious "thank you" due to every royal tip. Then, on an unspoken question from the clean-shaven man, the couple rose and the trio made their way toward the exit. A few steps behind them, the solitary diner, who also had finished her meal, left the Royal Peacock.

On the Rue Caumartin sidewalk, the clean-shaven man took leave of his two guests. He appeared somewhat in a hurry to get busy with the installation of the couple. Two taxis carried them away, in one the couple and in the other the clean-shaven man. Two other cars took off immediately behind those two taxis. The solitary diner had gotten into one of them…into a waiting car, driven by a chauffeur of remarkable stature—and into the other a tall, thin young man who had exchanged a rapid, knowing look with the solitary diner.

So, Thérèse Arnaud and Languille, whom the Boss had alerted by telephone, had dashed off on the trail of the three strange clients of the Royal Peacock. Toward what new adventures, toward what new dangers, were the valiant agents of our Deuxième Bureau rushing?

II. Monsieur and Madame Varlet

At the end of the day, Thérèse Arnaud organized the information she had gathered relative to the three clients of the Royal Peacock. Her research and that of Languille had acquired the following facts: The clean-shaven man who had made such strange propositions to his two guests was a man named Joseph Lusseaux, who lived at 339 Rue Davy, where he had a rather honorable reputation. There wasn't the least suspicion attached to his life. In appearance he lived as a peaceful middle-class man with some private income. To augment his income, he operated a private detective agency called *Fast/Discreet,* but the office seemed to have clients infrequently. On the other hand, Joseph Lusseaux's life style didn't seem to put him personally in a position to keep the commitments he had made to the two guests. It was clearly evident that the fortune of the private detective would not have permitted him to underwrite, even for a month, a couple leading a life as luxurious as that he had described. But there, too, there was nothing suspicious in the actions of Monsieur Lusseaux. He could very well not have been acting in his own name, and be nothing but an intermediary, a spokesman charged with transmitting the offers of a third party.

On leaving the Royal Peacock, Joseph Lusseaux had immediately gone to a real estate agency in the vicinity of the Madeleine Church. With an employee of the agency, he had visited several luxurious apartments in the neighborhood of the Place de l'Etoile. Then, without making a decision, or at least without letting the real estate agent know his decision, he had gone back to his domicile, where he had not received any visitor.

In the course of his investigation, Languille had gathered the following details: Joseph Lusseaux, although at an age to be drafted into the army, had not been inducted because he was afflicted with a double hernia and had difficulty seeing out of his right eye.

From the beginning of the affair which she was conducting, Thérèse Arnaud found herself faced with several problems. From all the evidence, Joseph Lusseaux, in attaching himself to the couple to whom he had promised a luxurious existence, was not acting for himself. Nevertheless his authority was sufficient for him to make decisions, since on his return to Rue Davy he had not received any visitor...and his apartment didn't have a telephone. Therefore, in those conditions, without checking with anyone whatsoever, Joseph Lusseaux could direct the affair. But who was the third party, the mysterious X who had thus directed the private detective? There was another problem just as important. It was very obvious that the services that the couple would require after they moved in would be of a very special nature. In fact, the most elementary logic led to the deduction that unknown persons could not be given a princely existence, defraying all their expenses, paying them for their simple domestic expenses monthly sums varying from between 3,000 and 15,000 francs, without expecting services justifying these monthly expenditures. Third point: businesses which could afford to risk such sums in simple expenses conducted business on a grand scale. And the simple examination of the facts, the simple nature of the propositions made to the couple, and Joseph Lusseaux's insistence on making them accept the offer, easily demonstrated that it could only be a matter of foreign business. In fact, to conduct normal business, however important it might be, it was not at all necessary to procure unknown people an establishment on the Champs-Elysées and surround them with such luxury. What established the accuracy of that hypothesis was again the modification of the civil status of the couple, the absolute secrecy demanded...and the obligation to take each day, twice a day, by telephone, instruction from an X who would give them directions...

The information concerning the couple gathered by Thérèse Arnaud, shed no light on the affair. Languille, who had from the next day remained tied to Joseph Lusseaux's footsteps, telephoned the following results to the Boss:

Still without having received any visit, without having even received any mail, without going to the bank to get money, Joseph Lusseaux had gone to the real estate office, had rented a luxurious apartment on the Champs-Elysées and had immediately paid the first month's rent. In the course of the morning, the couple moved into the domicile chosen by him, by the private detective. Numerous suppliers of household goods began to stream through Monsieur and Madame Varlet's apartment. Suppliers who brought important deliveries without, however, Monsieur and Madame Varlet's having ordered anything at all. All the deliveries had been paid for in advance. So Joseph Lusseaux's promises were being fulfilled point by point. And Monsieur and Madame Varlet, astonished, dumbfounded, were present in a dream come true. The constant file of suppliers transformed the Champs-Elysées apartment, adding even more to the luxury of the situation.

While André and Josette Varlet were taking possession of the apartment, Languille, who had received from the Boss the mission of continuing to follow the private detective, communicated by telephone the following information, which broadened the problem. After having left the real estate agency and after having given André and Josette instructions, Joseph Lusseaux had gone back to his apartment. Therefore, all the deliveries made to the Champs-Elysées were filling orders already made…or were purchases made on the spot by someone other than Joseph Lusseaux, perhaps by the mysterious silent partner.

In the course of the afternoon, a young man arrived at the domicile of Monsieur et Madame Varlet. He stopped an instant at the concierge's lodge.

"Monsieur Varlet?" he asked.

Without doubt obeying instructions, the concierge questioned: "Who's inquiring?"

Without the least hesitation, the young man answered:

"That's right! I forgot to tell you. I'm sent by Monsieur Joseph. I'm the new valet." And before the concierge had been able to answer, the future servant asked:

"Is this a good situation? Couldn't you tell me! I'm asking because right now good employers are rare. Monsieur Joseph, who sent me, told me I would have an excellent position here! But, just between us, Monsieur Joseph seems a little out of it…so, I prefer to ask you."

"Me? I don't know anything!" answered the concierge. "The new tenants arrived this morning. I gave them the keys, as I was ordered. That's all I can tell you. In any case, to rent an apartment like that, you can be sure that your new masters have money."

"Good! Then everything's all right!" concluded the future valet. "What floor is Monsieur Varlet on?"

"The third."

The man sent by Monsieur Joseph left the lodge and went into the vast vestibule. He walked slowly, looking around him curiously, as if to size up the house, to find out the income that could hire him for such a position. Just as the future valet was about to reach the service elevator door, two forms jumped out. There was a short scuffle, a scuffle in which the outcome wasn't in doubt. The man sent by Monsieur Joseph was dealing with two adversaries who had just overcome him by surprise. Therefore the future valet's defense was rather weak. And the domestic was soon "out." One of the forms immediately spread out vast, gray canvas packaging material in which Monsieur Joseph's inert envoy was wrapped. And then, as if he were only a wisp of straw, one of the aggressors picked up the package, thus formed, under his arm.

"Let's go, Friquet! Quick, to the car!"

"Okay, Malabar!"

Quietly, like two furniture men come to make a delivery, Thérèse Arnaud's agents left the building where André and Josette Varlet had just moved in. They carried under their arms, peacefully, the future valet sent by Monsieur Joseph. Driven by Malabar, the car rapidly reached the house of the Boss. The valet de chamber, still wrapped in his packing material, was taken out of the car. And, carried by Malabar, was taken up to Thérèse Arnaud's office. The famous secret agent took a quick look at Monsieur Joseph's envoy, who, with rather legitimate reasons, was protesting about the aggression of which he had been the victim.

A slight smile lit up Thérèse Arnaud's face. "Obviously this unfortunate man is wondering what has happened to him!" A new look at Monsieur Joseph's envoy by C.25 led to this conclusion:

"He doesn't know anything!"

Nevertheless, to be sure, she asked the prisoner a few questions. The answers were spontaneous and the tone really sincere. The captured man swore he didn't know Monsieur Joseph. He had seen him only once, in the morning. He had been sent to him by a placement bureau. The private detective had made the candidate valet undergo a rigorous interrogation. He had taken some time to examine his references. Then, without any more explanations, he had given him Monsieur Varlet's address, telling him to go there as soon as possible, presenting himself as sent by him.

"Good!" Thérèse Arnaud concluded in an enigmatic tone when the prisoner had finished.

"But why am I a prisoner? What have I done? What do you intend to do with me?" inquired Monsieur Joseph's envoy.

"To use you as a model," smiled Friquet, who, at the beginning of the interview had gone to pick up a make-up kit. And with the art he brought to each of his transformations, he applied himself to copying the domestic candidate's features. The candidate, more and more surprised, didn't resist the Paris kid's little tricks. He couldn't hold back an exclamation of surprise.

"You'd swear it was my portrait!" he exclaimed when Friquet had finished.

"Thanks for the compliment!" the Paris kid said mockingly.

Thérèse Arnaud had watched that scene without saying anything. Since the interrogation of Monsieur Joseph's envoy, she was thoughtful. She suddenly interrupted her train of thought. She looked at Friquet's transformation. "Good!" she said. "Now, you know what you have to do?"

"Yes. As soon as I have a result, I'll get in touch."

"All right!"

The Paris kid promptly left.

C.25's plan was clear: to capture someone who was supposed to go into the Varlet household, sent by Monsieur Joseph, and replace him with one of her assistants. Thus Thérèse Arnaud would have someone on the spot! Someone who could watch everything and furnish her with the elements necessary to solve the problems she was up against...someone who could also furnish her with the first point of departure which would allow her to actually discover the real motives of Monsieur Joseph, private detective...and the Varlet couple...who were now strangely preoccupying Thérèse Arnaud. She had witnessed the conversation in the course of which they had accepted Joseph Lusseaux's offer. But, just to what point had they been in good faith? Admittedly, they had raised objections; they had hesitated. But when they received the orders of the mysterious correspondent, would they carry them out? Would they become accomplices? To what extent was the Varlet couple in good faith? And to what moral decline would their love of luxury, of money, lead them? To what shady operations? To what complicity? That's what she had to find out.

Malabar had remained in C.25's office, still watching the valet. Suddenly, Thérèse Arnaud, who seemed to have forgotten the presence of her assistant and the prisoner, shook herself.

In a sharp voice, she ordered:

"Him? Into the holding room."

"Me? But..." began Joseph Lusseaux's envoy.

Malabar looked at the Boss in surprise. He didn't understand the decision. C.25 shrugged nervously. Then, in an annoyed tone she threw out to the Colossus: "Oh, yes, Malabar, oh, yes! Into the holding room! And under good surveillance! It's impossible for him to have told the truth...or at least, the whole truth...and it's fortunate that he lied!"

III. A Model Valet

When he was presented to the Varlet couple, Friquet was immediately accepted. There was no doubt that André and Josette had been informed and had been told of the arrival of the future valet. The Paris youth was immediately aware of that by the questions asked, questions of pure formality, very insufficient to take on the services of a domestic. One point remained mysterious. Since there was no telephone in Monsieur Joseph's apartment and the instructions came to the Varlet couple while the private detective was at his apartment, who telephoned? Who pulled the strings of the two marionettes that were André and Josette Varlet?

127

That was what Firmin-Friquet couldn't find out. What's more, neither was it possible for the Paris kid to know the tenor of the communications which the Varlet couple received. During the two days since Thérèse Arnaud's assistant had assumed his position as valet in the service of the Varlet spouses, life continued to be normal in the Champs-Elysées apartment. The fairy tale continued to unfold point by point. The household suppliers followed one after the other. Now there was a line of tailors, dressmakers, shoe makers, shirt makers, lingerie suppliers who, always coming on behalf of the famous Monsieur Joseph, brought André and Josette the many costume accessories necessary to maintain their role.

As a perfect valet, Firmin discretely looked into the mail, which was in reality very meager, that the couple Varlet received. But that indiscretion of the Deuxième Bureau agent did not clarify anything. Thérèse Arnaud was daily brought up to date about everything André and Josette did. But the famous secret agent seemed not to take an interest temporarily in the affair, or at least to wait for other events to move into action. What events? Only C.25 knew that. Her instructions were always the same. She had not changed her plan of combat. Friquet should, until further instructions, stay in his valet role, gathering information by every possible means. As for Monsieur Joseph, at his every outing he had an assistant of the famous spy tailing him. But on that side, the business was moving slowly. Nothing in Joseph Lusseaux' actions yet allowed precisely pinning down the role he was playing in that affair.

The third day, Firmin noticed in the Varlet couple's mail, an invitation to a masque ball. André and Josette, on learning about the invitation, looked at each other.

"A masked ball at the home of Raphaël Mortier! Raphaël Mortier? Raphaël Mortier..." André repeated.

"I don't know him," Josette remarked.

Monsieur Joseph's two protégés remained undecided as to what to do. Should they consider taking advantage of that invitation from an unknown person? Josette's shallow character leaned toward the affirmative. More reserved, André hesitated. No decision was made. Suddenly the telephone rang. Coolly, Friquet, the Paris kid in the kitchen also took up the listening device of the microphone he had installed in the apartment office as soon as he arrived. The telephone call came from Joseph Lusseaux. The private detective asked if his two protégés had received an invitation for the masked ball to be given the next day at the home of the sculptor Raphaël Mortier. On André's affirmative answer, Monsieur Joseph ordered the Varlet couple to go to the ball.

"Don't worry about anything! Whatever is necessary as regards your disguises will be taken care of."

Now, that evening, when Thérèse Arnaud was apprised of her assistants' reports, she observed the following facts: at the hour Friquet indicated, Monsieur Joseph was in his apartment, Rue Davy, in an office that did not have a telephone. Nevertheless, Joseph Lusseaux had telephoned the Varlet spouses without leaving his domicile. What could be deduced from that fact? Did there exist another person who, in the name of Monsieur Joseph, was giving orders to the Varlet couple? Or rather did there exist a secret telephone line linking Joseph Lusseaux to the Champs-Elysées apartment?

As soon as she learned of the instructions Monsieur Joseph had given ordering the Varlet couple to attend Raphaël Mortimer's masked ball, C.25 immediately went into action, suddenly taking up again that affair that she had limited to surveillance. All the assistants of the famous spy were called in. To each of her colleagues, C.25 distributed the role they would play in the course of the masked ball.

And while waiting for the evening of the ball, Friquet and Languille continued their surveillance without bringing the Boss the least precise fact capable of furnishing useful information. In the Champs-Elysées apartment that Firmin-Friquet had searched many, many times, there was nothing suspicious. No secret exits, no compromising papers, no furniture which could be used to hide documents. Absolutely nothing. The life of the Varlet couple seemed to be limited to receiving decorators, trying on costumes, and taking short walks. The mail brought nothing useful. Monsieur Joseph's telephone calls even became commonplace and most often announced that some decorator was coming…or asking if everything was going to the satisfaction of André and Juliette. To that point the Varlet couple seemed not to have been mixed up in any shady business. It still remained to be determined with what tasks Monsieur Joseph or the powerful unknown person that he represented, intended to employ André and Juliette, who seemed susceptible of becoming unknowingly the accomplices of an unknown person's activities.

Finally, the day of the masked ball arrived. In the course of the afternoon, Monsieur Joseph arrived at the Varlet couple's apartment. It must be noted that since André and Juliette had been installed at the Champs-Elysées, Monsieur Joseph had never visited his protégés apartment. And that abstention was hard to comprehend. Therefore what motives did the private detective have for not coming to find out for himself the situation of the couple?

Joseph Lusseaux's first concern was to assure himself that the disguises that André and Juliette were to wear had been delivered. After having carefully examined the costumes, Joseph Lusseaux shut himself up in the office with André and Josette.

"Well! These bad-mannered people who don't talk in front of their faithful valet!" joked Firmin-Friquet. "Fortunately the faithful valet has taken his precautions even so to find out what you don't want to talk about in front of him!"

And, smiling, the Paris kid went to the kitchen. He picked up the listening device connected to the microphone hidden in the office where the three persons were shut up. And he heard nothing! Absolutely nothing! Not the least sound of conversation. Thérèse Arnaud's assistant quickly realized that the wire had been cut. The cut had been made in the office itself, because until then the wire existed. Who had noticed the presence of a microphone? Who had cut the wire? Didn't that discovery make Firmin-Friquet's situation dangerous?

"Ah!" groaned the Paris street kid, "my little Friquet, you should watch out. And besides, if your bosses and their dear friend Monsieur Joseph aren't exchanging secrets, why take so many precautions to be sure they aren't overheard?"

By gluing his ear to the door, the Paris kid tried in vain to catch some snatches of the conversation taking place in the office.

"Nothing doing," he concluded.

Passing near a window looking out on the Avenue des Champs-Elysées, Friquet noticed on the sidewalk the silhouette of his comrade, Languille. There was nothing in that to surprise the Paris kid. Languille, still attached to the steps of the mysterious Monsieur Joseph, was waiting until his prey had finished his conversation with the Varlet couple.

"All right! Everything is going well..." Firmin-Friquet sighed. "But everything would be going a lot better if I could hear what my employers and Monsieur Joseph are planning."

Languille's presence reassured Friquet. In fact, since the telephone wire had been cut, the alarm had been given. The situation of the valet had become dangerous. But Friquet wasn't alone. Still on watch behind his window, Friquet was waiting until Languille raised his head. And Thérèse Arnaud's two assistants exchanged a sign of recognition.

Suddenly, just as Friquet, after having signaled to Languille, had left the window, he was seized from behind and pulled violently. An iron fist closed tightly around the body of the Paris urchin. Despite the suddenness of the attack, Firmin-Friquet resisted as well as he could. Unfortunately, his situation wasn't good. He was dealing with an adversary of uncommon strength. Despite his heroic defense, Friquet was quickly reduced to immobility by Monsieur Joseph. André Varlet, drawn by the noise of the fight, came into the room.

Joseph Lusseaux said simply: "No need! It's done! He won't bother us anymore."

A few steps behind André, Josette entered, her arms full of dresses. She didn't seem to show any surprise on seeing the Paris kid reduced to immobility. The private detective simply asked: "The cords!" André Varlet rummaged through the pockets of his dressing gown and soon took out a package of solid cords which very certainly had been prepared with that operation in mind.

Very rapidly, skillfully, like someone who had done the same work many times, Joseph Lusseaux and André Varlet tied up Thérèse Arnaud's assistant. But, during that operation, the street kid saw, bulging from Joseph Lusseaux's outside jacket pocket, the shape of a revolver. Still having one hand free, the Paris urchin, grabbed the revolver and fired twice, but, his movements limited, without managing to wound his adversary.

"That's a lot of noise for nothing, my little friend," Joseph Lusseaux mocked. "So let me work without bothering me."

Then, after that ironic remark, André Varlet and Monsieur Joseph finished trussing up the street urchin like a sausage, under the amused eyes of Josette. When they had finished, they quietly tested the solidity of the bonds. They verified, that in the position he found himself, Thérèse Arnaud's assistant couldn't make the least movement. Josette, still smiling, opened the door of a wardrobe.

"While waiting," she said, pointing to its vast inside.

"Yes, very good!" Joseph Lusseaux answered.

And with André Varlet's help, Monsieur Joseph transported the package that constituted Firmin-Friquet to the wardrobe. He deposited him in the cubby hole. He locked the door.

"We'll take care of you later!" he threw out at him.

In his cell, Friquet still heard for several seconds the murmur of voices. There was no doubt the three accomplices were conferring about how to proceed. They were preoccupied with Friquet's fate. What had the Varlet couple and Monsieur Joseph decided? It appeared, since they hadn't immediately finished off their adversary, that they had their reasons. What were they hoping? What did they want to do with Friquet? In his wardrobe, the Paris kid, without worrying too much about his situation, which, however, wasn't brilliant, was thinking:

In the course of his functions as a valet, Firmin had discovered nothing that might put the investigation on the right track and demonstrate complicity between the Varlet couple and Monsieur Joseph. Nothing had been found that indicated that the actions of the trio were reprehensible. By capturing Friquet, the Varlet couple and Monsieur Joseph had denounced themselves. If they hadn't had some interest in hiding the true nature of their actions, they wouldn't have had to consider Firmin's possible indiscretions. On the other hand, now that the alarm had been given, the trio was on their guard.

However, Friquet summed up his situation, which remained critical. Admittedly, to be in the hands of the enemy wasn't an enviable position. But all contact with the Boss hadn't been lost. C.25 knew that he was working for the Varlet couple. On the other hand, Languille, who was on surveillance duty on the sidewalk, would again pick up Joseph Lusseaux's trail as soon as he left the Champs-Elysées apartment…So, all hope wasn't lost…Still, it didn't take but a second to execute a prisoner!

Several hours went by, during which Friquet reflected sadly. Suddenly the wardrobe door opened. André and Josette appeared. The couple checked the state of his bonds to reassure themselves that he hadn't managed to untie them. Friquet immediately noticed that André and Josette were dressed, ready to leave.

"Have a good time," André ironically invited. "We're going to dinner…and then we're going to the ball."

"If anyone asks for us, Firmin," Josette added, "you'll answer that Monsieur and Madame are out."

They closed the wardrobe door again, but a thought by Josette led to the door of the cubbyhole being opened once more.

"Be careful! We need him alive. We don't want him to be suffocated in there!"

André seemed to hesitate a moment. He examined the enclosure.

"Yes, obviously," he agreed, "if we're away a long time."

The couple went away, leaving the door shut but not locked so as to let the prisoner be able to endure a long captivity without the risk of dying from lack of air. When the couple had left, Friquet joked ironically: "Monsieur and Madame are out. In those conditions, their faithful Firmin would like to take advantage of his employers' absence to take a little walk downtown himself." But Firmin's wish wasn't easily realized.

"I now have the time to try to get free of all these cords. Since they've gone out, I won't be disturbed in getting started on my little operations," the Paris kid sighed. And he immediately began trying to get free. Unfortunately Monsieur Joseph and André were specialists in tying, and his efforts produced no appreciable results.

"This is going to take a long time," Friquet groaned, still continuing his attempts. Having succeeded in loosening his bonds somewhat, he added: "It will take a long time, possibly, but it will happen…Unfortunately, when I'm free again I'll be too late to go to Raphaël Mortier's masked ball. Too bad!"

IV. Thérèse Arnaud Steps In

After having answered Friquet's signal, Languille remained on watch in front of the building inhabited by the Varlet couple, waiting for Joseph Lusseaux to come out. When he had finished tying up the unfortunate Paris urchin, Joseph Lusseaux didn't stay long with his two accomplices. He gave them the last instructions concerning Raphaël Mortier's ball and left them to their preparations. Coolly, like a person taking a walk, Joseph Lusseaux went back down the Champs-Elysées as far as the Place de la Concorde, Languille trailing behind him. At the Rue de Rivoli, the private detective hailed a taxi. Shortly afterward, he arrived at the Boulevard Saint-Michel, still followed by the Acrobat. Joseph Lusseaux entered the Steinbach brasserie. As soon as he entered, he went directly to the owner. He asked:

"Monsieur Maurice?"

"He has already been here, Monsieur. He waited. Then he left."

"He didn't leave any message for me?" Joseph Lusseaux interrupted.

"Oh, yes, he did, Monsieur," the owner informed him. "He said he would come back here for an aperitif and he told me to ask you to wait."

Joseph Lusseaux's expression, which had clouded over, brightened. He said only, "That's fine."

Leaving the owner, he went toward an unoccupied table. He sat down. A waiter hurried forward.

"A glass of beer," the private detective ordered.

Then he coolly took out his cigarette case. He lit a cigarette. He took a large swallow of beer. He took a newspaper from his pocket. And paying no attention to the comings and goings of the clientele, he appeared to be absorbed in reading an evening newspaper.

On the trail of his prey, Languille had gone into the Steinbach brasserie. The Acrobat had noticed the rapid conference between the owner and Joseph Lusseaux. Then Thérèse Arnaud's assistant had sat down on a barstool next to the table occupied by Monsieur Joseph and he, too, had taken a newspaper out of his pocket.

The attitude of the owner of the brasserie clearly demonstrated that the private detective was known in the establishment. That was for Languille an accepted fact. Maybe by putting the Steinbach brasserie under surveillance, Thérèse Arnaud might discover some fact that would shed light on the affair preoccupying her. The Acrobat was continuing to examine, surreptitiously, the patrons, when a couple entered who, after a short hesitation, and a glance around the room, walked straight toward the table occupied by Monsieur Joseph. The owner rushed ahead of the two arrivals.

"Ah! Monsieur Maurice! Monsieur Joseph has just arrived!" Then, greeting the young woman accompanying Monsieur Maurice, the owner bowed:

"Good Evening, Miss Fernande."

Mr. Joseph exchanged handshakes with the new arrivals, who sat down at the table with him. New drinks were brought and the three individuals became absorbed in a rapid discussion. His ears open, Languille tried to grasp the meaning of the trio's conversation. But the discussion seemed to be of little interest.

"Nevertheless, Monsieur Joseph didn't come here without a reason," Languille thought. "Neither was it to pass the time of day that he was waiting for someone. So?"

However, the conversation between the three individuals continued without bringing Languille the least useful information. A hypothesis came to the Acrobat's mind. Perhaps Monsieur Joseph and his two friends were waiting for the arrival of a new person? And it would only be when the group was complete that the conversation would become interesting? While continuing to listen, C.25's assistant examined Monsieur Maurice. Couldn't that be the mysterious X? The man for whom Monsieur Joseph was the agent...and who installed the Varlet couple in the Champs-Elysées?

The first examination refuted that supposition. First of all, Monsieur Maurice didn't look like a man who could pay out considerable sums of money. He was decently but not expensively dressed. He looked like some average employee, a middle class bourgeois. In addition, the attitude of the two men was not that of the inferior to the superior. They seemed to treat each other as equals. On the contrary, if Monsieur Maurice had been the mysterious X, Monsieur Joseph, in his presence, would have taken a deferential attitude and would have, undoubtedly, awaited the instructions of the man who was his superior. Now, there was nothing like that, at least in appearance. At the same time, Languille was trying to discern Mademoiselle Fernande's role. At first look, this role wasn't easy to establish. Mademoiselle Fernande had nothing unusual about her on which to focus an examination. She was a petite brunette, rather insignificant in looks, with an almost pleasing figure. From time to time, her eyes brightened with strange lights when she looked at Monsieur Maurice. She took part in the discussion, but contributed only ideas without the least originality. And every so often it seemed she didn't exactly understand the meaning of the interview, and she limited herself, in order to satisfy a desire to talk, with approving and pronouncing absolutely insignificant statements. What was Monsieur Maurice to Mademoiselle Fernande? There was nothing there either to lead anywhere. No sign of intimacy. No special mark of sympathy, of friendship or of tenderness…

After a quarter of an hour of conversation, Monsieur Joseph paid for the drinks. He consulted the time. The trio got up and started toward the door. Before crossing the threshold, the three individuals shook hands, like persons who, having finished their conversation, were going to separate immediately after leaving the café. In fact, Monsieur Joseph was the first to leave, while Monsieur Maurice and Mademoiselle Fernande exchanged a few polite words with the owner. Languille was getting ready to take up his shadowing again when the brasserie door opened…at the same moment that Monsieur Maurice and Mademoiselle Fernande got to the exit. Thus, the client who was entering found himself face to face with the couple who were leaving. There was a brief confused moment. The man arriving quickly drew back, as if to stand aside and let Monsieur Maurice and his companion pass. Languille, who was behind the couple, continued to walk straight ahead, forcing the couple in front of him to do the same.

"Well, Malabar…" said the Acrobat to the client who had stepped back.

"Well, my little Languille, it's done…Help me stick them in the automobile…"

Like lightning, Malabar, when he had found himself face to face with the couple, had handcuffed Monsieur Maurice and Mademoiselle Fernande, who were rather stupefied by the rapidity of what had just happened. Although resentful, they offered no resistance. C.25's auto was parked in front of the Steinbach brasserie. It took only a few seconds for Thérèse Arnaud's two assistants to push in a dumbfounded Monsieur Maurice and a trembling Mademoiselle Fernande. Before getting in with the prisoners, Languille asked:

"But in these circumstances, Monsieur Joseph…"

"Don't worry," Malabar reassured him. The Boss has prepared for this. I've brought Loulou as reinforcement. And according to what happens, either he will help me bring back the prisoners…and you'll continue to shadow Monsieur

Joseph…or otherwise, he'll take charge of Joseph…and you'll help me…So, it's taken care of. Leave Joseph alone. Loulou'll take care of it."

At her house, Thérèse Arnaud was waiting for the return of Malabar, whom she had charged with arresting Monsieur Maurice and his companion. As soon as the two prisoners arrived, C.25 began the interrogation. The captives made no difficulty about answering the questions asked them, without, however, ever stopping complaining about their treatment. They didn't understand why they had been arrested. It came out from that interrogation that Monsieur Maurice was the "friend" of Mademoiselle Fernande. They both worked at the same printing company. That was where they met. Now, Monsieur Maurice was married. And his wife, jealous, having some suspicions about her husband's behavior, had hired Monsieur Joseph, a private detective to investigate her husband's actions. But Monsieur Joseph had a bizarre conception of his role. And, although his agency had as its motto, "Quick/Discreet," the first thing the detective had done was to go alert Monsieur Maurice that his wife was suspicious…and that he was going to be watched. The purpose of that approach by Monsieur Joseph was to get Monsieur Maurice to pay him a certain sum of money so that in exchange the private detective would furnish false information to the jealous wife. In fact Monsieur Joseph's maneuver had worked. And in order to be left in peace and continue to see his "friend," Monsieur Maurice had immediately paid Monsieur Joseph the sum of 2000 francs. It was a new demand for a payment of 500 francs that had motivated the meeting between Monsieur Joseph and Monsieur Maurice that evening at the Steinbach brasserie.

Thérèse Arnaud had listened to the corroborating explanations furnished by Monsieur Maurice and his companions, interrogated separately. There were no contradictions between the two explanations. Malabar, who with Languille had been present at that scene, showed some surprise. He didn't understand why the Boss had decided to have these two individuals arrested. They seemed to have only a tangential connection to Monsieur Joseph and their role in the affair C.25 was working on, was non-essential. The two individuals seemed likely to be immediately set free. At the end of the interrogation, Monsieur Maurice continued to protest…and Mademoiselle Fernande started to cry again. Thérèse Arnaud looked at them a long time and then she commanded in a sharp voice:

"Take these two back to the holding room."

Malabar let out a stifled exclamation, and while obeying the orders of the Boss, he grumbled:

"The real valet Monsieur Joseph sent to the Varlet residence was a good guy…and the Boss shut him up in the holding room. These are also good people: they're going to the holding room! I don't understand it at all!"

And parallel to Malabar's reflections, Thérèse Arnaud was murmuring: "Those two…exactly like the valet Monsieur Joseph sent to the Varlet apartment. They're lying. And it's fortunate they're lying."

And without taking any more thought about the captured couple, Thérèse prepared for Raphaël Mortier's masked ball.

V. The Masked Ball

At about 9 p.m., excitement was the rule in the vast apartment occupied by Raphaël Mortier. The sculptor's receptions were always well attended. They were even sought after. To be invited to Raphaël Mortier's receptions was to be sure of finding oneself in a milieu comprised of the greatest industrial, political, commercial, artistic and diplomatic powers. Raphaël Mortier assembled in his salons the most outstanding personalities belonging to all these worlds.

The guests were assembled in little groups, according to their preferences and formed inner circles which continued to discuss business or politics. The attractive costumes, the intrigues that the masked ball permitted heightened even more the brilliance of the soirée. The reception rooms offered the most unusual and the most attractive sights. The guests had rivaled each other in ingenuity and cost in choosing their costumes. It was the most amusing and the most anachronistic spectacle it was possible to imagine. In all the reception rooms, in the corridors, there was a constant parade, swirling of costumes, of songs, of gaiety, of laughter. The unreal and the real became phantasmagoric, imposing and superimposing on each other. Personalities foreign to each other, who would have been thought never to have met, brushed up against one another and mingled. A Pierrot flirted with a Venetian lady endowed with every charm. A harlequin flirted with an odalisque. Skipping about in farandoles were Spaniards and Hollanders. The history of France rubbed elbows with the Comédie-Italienne, which also mingled with the fairy tales of Perrault. The Opéra Comic mixed its heroes with those from romantic drama and ancient mythology. The Arabian Nights had sent its Scheherazades, Persian princes, slaves, Hindus. The *Cour des Miracles* had mobilized its gangsters and its prostitutes. Under these disguises were ministers, ambassadors, all Parisian and foreign high society.

Thérèse Arnaud's assistants, following the instructions of the Boss, wandered through the reception rooms, mingling with groups, trying to gather interesting information arising from the brouhaha of laughter and conversation that the suspects, under the cover of the possibilities offered by the masks and sex roles, would be sure to exchange.

Languille had been especially charged with trailing the Varlet couple. It was through them the suspects would be unmasked. In fact, since the couple had received special instructions from Monsieur Joseph to attend the Raphaël Mortier ball, it was very obvious that André and Josette had been given a mission. It was the purpose of that mission that had to be discovered. From all the evidence it seemed that it was at Raphaël Mortier's ball that André and Josette Varlet would begin carrying out the activities for which Monsieur Joseph had engaged them.

From the beginning of the evening, the Boss had the feeling that some event she didn't know about had occurred. Friquet, who had received special instructions to leave the apartment on the Champs-Elysées as soon as the Varlet couple had left and come to the ball also, had not yet arrived. It was unusual for C.25's assistant to be late. Since the Varlet couple was present in Raphaël Mortier's reception rooms, nothing should have prevented Friquet from being there. So, C.25 sent Marcel to the Champs-Elysées. The Chemist rushed to the Varlet apartment. As soon as he entered, he found the Paris kid getting ready to leave.

"Is that you, Marcel?" Friquet asked, astonished. "I'm sorry you didn't think about coming sooner. You could have helped me get untied. Now I'm late! I'm going to miss the first dances! That's too bad. I would have had the pleasure of dancing with my boss, that dear Josette…"

"Is that right? No long stories! Let's get going. You can tell me what happened on the way," the Chemist decided.

Shortly thereafter Marcel and Friquet arrived at Raphaël Mortier's ball. The first thing the Paris kid did was to inform C.25 of what happened in the Varlet apartment in the course of the afternoon. For C.25, Friquet's capture clearly denounced Monsieur Joseph. At the same time, there was no longer the shadow of a doubt as to the complicity of the private detective and the Varlet couple. Since André Varlet had helped Monsieur Joseph tie up the captive, since Josette had witnessed the scene, it must be admitted that if they were perfectly innocent at the time they had accepted the private detective's propositions, André and Josette had very quickly consented to do everything the man who was offering them luxury commanded. On the other hand, it was equally evident that Friquet's capture had warned Monsieur Joseph and his accomplices. They were therefore on their guard. And knowing that C.25 was having them spied on, Monsieur Joseph must have had to give special instructions to the Varlet couple, surrounding themselves with an excess of precautions.

Thérèse Arnaud was at that point in her thinking when she had a slight moment of surprise. She had just recognized, among the wave of arrivals, Monsieur Joseph, very recognizable under his disguise! And behind the private detective, was Loulou, faithful to the mission that had been given him. Loulou was continuing to shadow that mysterious person.

What had Monsieur Joseph come to do at Raphaël Mortier's ball? Was he going to do something himself? Did he have a goal? Did he personally have a task to fulfill? Or was he just coming to watch the Varlet couple? In any case, since the complicity of the three people was no longer in doubt, C.25 had nothing more to do than wait for what would happen.

The Boss immediately sent her aides the following instructions: Malabar was primarily to follow the movements of Monsieur Joseph; Languille was to remain assigned to André and Josette Varlet; Friquet would help the Acrobat just in case André and Josette separated during the evening.

Loulou and Marcel would act as liaisons between the different groups and carry to C.25 the results of what the other assistants found out. In addition, they would also hold themselves ready to replace whichever of their comrades had important situations to bring to the attention of the Boss. In any case, Thérèse Arnaud would not remain ignorant of any of the movements or actions of the Varlet couple and Monsieur Joseph. And it was important that C.25 be alerted to everything that happened as soon as possible so as to take action. Having thus arranged her troops and settled her plan of action, C.25 herself began to watch the groups.

From the first moments of his arrival, Monsieur Joseph had gone rapidly through the reception rooms. He made an imperceptible sign of recognition when he encountered André and Josette Varlet, but he didn't stop near them. He continued to go through reception room after reception room as if searching for someone. He obviously was not finding the person he expected. He consulted his watch several times. Then he again went through the rooms, showing a certain worry. This did not escape Thérèse Arnaud. Monsieur Joseph, therefore, hadn't come to Raphaël's ball just to watch his two accomplices. He had some other goal. He was waiting for something else. He was hoping to find other people with whom he was connected. Who? Perhaps just simply the mysterious X, for whom he was the intermediary? Perhaps also other accomplices.

C.25 smiled slightly. "He may be looking for his two friends…those I have at my place, locked up in the holding room."

Just then, Languille came to invite Thérèse Arnaud to dance. The Acrobat had left Marcel in surveillance near Madame Varlet while he went to confer with the Boss. While dancing, Languille rapidly told C.25 that he had noticed the rather strange attitude of a young girl in the reception rooms who seldom stopped looking at Josette Varlet and arranged it so that she could always come back near her. That young girl was wearing a magnificent purple costume and a violet mask.

At the end of the dance, Languille went back to his post while Thérèse Arnaud went to the buffet, where the presence of the young girl in the violet mask had been pointed out to her. C.25 intended to watch the execution of the plan she had just conceived and that she had ordered Languille to carry out. The Acrobat was supposed to strike up a conversation with the young girl, pretend the beginning of an attraction for her and use every pretext to stay close to her. From the beginning that pretext succeeded admirably. Undoubtedly flattered with being sought out, the young girl in the violet mask welcomed very favorably the advances of Languille that she very willingly accepted as an escort. She made the rounds of the reception rooms, seeming extremely gay, going from group to group, without, however, stopping at any.

While Thérèse Arnaud was dancing with André Varlet, she heard a sentence which attracted her attention. Near a window, a group comprised of four men talking with a certain animation, all near the spot where Josette Varlet was talking with Malabar. A phrase suddenly emerged just as C.25 passed near the group. "Hydraulic brake of the 75…" It seemed at this moment, through the slits of her violet mask, that Josette Varlet's eyes gleamed in a strange way.

After having left André Varlet, C.25 went back toward the group where she had heard the phrase that drew her attention. The group of four men was continuing a discussion with the same animation. Even certain gestures seemed to indicate that the discussion was becoming more heated. But, unfortunately, it was now impossible to approach the group that was protected by Josette Varlet, very smiling, her eyes still shining under the violet mask…and by the young woman Languille was escorting. Suddenly Josette Varlet walked away. She left the reception room.

C.25 went closer to the group of four men. They were making no effort not to be heard. They continued to argue. It seemed they were discussing the current price of steel.

"Too late!" Thérèse Arnaud murmured in rage.

What's more, the group dissolved shortly afterwards. Languille's young dancing partner, escaping from her escort, disappeared. The Acrobat immediately dashed after the young girl. But he had to stop his pursuit at the door of the Ladies Room. Languille and Loulou, who had followed Madame Varlet to the same spot, lit a cigarette and exchanged some small talk while waiting for their prey to decide to come back to the reception rooms. Shortly thereafter, Josette Varlet, gay, carefree, again went to mingle with the flood of dancers. The Acrobat, following the girl in the purple dress, went toward the buffet.

C.25, who had noticed the absence of the two women, suddenly frowned. She also went to the buffet near Languille who was using his charm to persuade his flirt to accept another glass of champagne.

"All right!" the girl consented, "but this will be the last one."

"What do you mean? The last one? Why?" Languille quickly asked.

"Because I'm not going to spend the night here. I'm not bored with your company. On the contrary! But I must return home early…As soon as I finish this glass of champagne, I'm going to get my coat. I'm not telling you goodbye but *au revoir*, dear sir, and…I must dash off."

A new frown crossed Thérèse Arnaud's forehead. On the sly, she had continued to observe carefully Languille's dancing partner. C.25 trembled imperceptibly. She had just noticed that the violet mask that had matched the young girl's dress perfectly (even marvelously matched, since it was made of the same material as the dress) was a little paler.

Still escorted by Languille, the girl left the buffet. She led her partner from group to group, shaking many hands. She moved toward Josette Varlet, with whom she also exchanged some polite words. Then she walked away toward the vestibule.

"Don't leave her for an instant!" C.25 told Languille, who, while the girl was putting on a large cape, had made himself unrecognizable in the men's room next to the cloak room with an ingenious disguise.

Leaving Raphaël Mortier's salon, the girl went directly to the Champs-Elysées. She was on foot in the Spring night, walking with rapid steps, without the slightest hesitation. Arriving at the Hotel Claridge, the girl stopped. After a short moment, she entered the lobby of the hotel, greeted by the porter who hurried to accompany her to the elevator where a gentleman had just arrived a few steps before the girl. Arriving at the elevator door, the gentleman had courteously stepped back to let the woman in the violet mask enter first. He followed her into the elevator. He asked politely:

"What floor are you stopping at, Mademoiselle?"

"The fourth."

The elevator stopped at the landing of the fourth floor. The girl got out, followed by the gentleman, who remarked pleasantly:

"We live on the same floor."

After a rapid acknowledgement, the girl went down the corridor, while the gentleman closed the elevator door and sent it back down again…without losing sight of the girl who soon disappeared into a room.

"Since the Boss told me not to leave her, I'm going to stay on guard duty in the corridor," murmured Languille.

VI. The End of the Ball

Despite the late hour of the night, the liveliness of the Raphaël Mortier ball didn't lessen. On the contrary, the atmosphere seemed bubbling over. Flirtations strengthened, mutual intimacy was born. Laugher became less strident, softer. The words murmured became tenderer. They were getting ready to elect a Queen of the Evening. This harmless game made the women become more gracious and flirtatious. Suddenly Friquet gave a start. A woman had come to meet Monsieur Joseph and had exchanged some words with the private detective. It was the sound of that woman's voice that had caused the emotion of Thérèse Arnaud's assistant.

"Madame Varlet! Josette Varlet, my employer!" murmured the Paris street kid.

Josette Varlet! That fact in itself had nothing surprising. On the contrary it was very natural that Madame Varlet had an interview with Joseph Lusseaux in the course of the evening. The accomplices could have needed to consult each other. Or Josette Varlet might have needed instructions from Monsieur Joseph. It was not that encounter and that conversation that had caused Friquet's astonishment. If that woman who had come to meet Monsieur Joseph were Josette Varlet, she wasn't dressed the same. There actually was in the reception rooms a woman standing near André Varlet who, in everyone's eyes wore the same dress worn a short time before by Josette, who, now in another dress, was talking with Monsieur Joseph. Why this subterfuge? Why had Josette Varlet transformed herself? Why had another woman taken her place and was playing a role next to

André Varlet?

Friquet went immediately to alert the Boss. Thérèse Arnaud simply answered:

"You're just now seeing that, my good Friquet! You didn't understand what happened in the Ladies Room? What does it matter? My decision is made. I'm just waiting for the departure of the suspects to arrest them without a scandal. Since you're near me, you're going to be in charge of taking my instructions to Marcel, to Malabar, and to Loulou…for the exit."

When Josette Varlet arrived, Thérèse Arnaud had decided to make a mass arrest. Those to be apprehended:

1. Monsieur Joseph

2. André and Josette Varlet

3. The woman currently playing the role of Josette Varlet in the reception rooms.

To do this, Malabar, Marcel, Loulou and Friquet were to act separately. C.25's car, which had been parked in a neighboring street, was to be driven to the door of the building. As soon as the individuals to be arrested came out, they would be immediately apprehended and put into the car. C.25 had taken into account the situation where all the suspects would leave at the same time. In that case, C.25's, troops were to surround the group and, if necessary, use force. But everything seemed to indicate that the suspects would leave separately. Unless they did, it was useless for a false Josette Varlet to continue to pull the wool over everyone's eyes in the reception rooms, if Monsieur Joseph's accomplices intended to leave together.

Thérèse Arnaud's instructions were immediately communicated to the famous agent's assistants. And each one got ready to execute the orders when the time came.

What had happened in the ladies' room that had escaped the eyes of C.25's assistants? It was very simple, a ruse of Monsieur Joseph that the famous agent had succeeded in foiling. A few moments apart, Josette Varlet and the girl in the violet mask had gone to the ladies' room. When Josette Varlet arrived, another woman was already there. There the two women changed costumes. Then Josette Varlet had taken down on the reverse side of her violet mask the information that she had gathered while listening to the conversation of the group discussing the Hydraulic Brake 75. Then Josette Varlet had given her mask to the woman who now looked like Josette. When the young woman in the violet mask in her turn arrived at the ladies room, a simple exchange of masks had permitted the transmission of information Josette had gathered.

It was that exchange of masks that had warned C.25 when she had noticed the girl in the purple costume. She had previously worn a mask made of the same material as her dress, but she now wore a mask of a slightly paler shade of violet. Then, when Josette Varlet went back again into the reception rooms, the false Josette Varlet went to take the place of the real one near André Varlet. In truth, why this subterfuge was needed didn't yet seem clear to C.25.

Then, while this was going on, the girl in the violet mask had left Raphaël Mortier's ball carrying the information gathered. That was why Thérèse Arnaud had ordered Languille not to leave the girl. Since C.25 had decided to make an arrest en masse, why had she not had the girl immediately apprehended? No error was possible, since they would have found the telling evidence on the guilty girl herself: the violet mask. But in reacting this way, Thérèse Arnaud would have broken the chain. Once the girl was arrested, it was over. There would no longer be any way to follow the trail. What was going to become of the information contained in the mask? To whom was this mask going to be given? It was to obtain this information that Thérèse Arnaud had left the girl in the violet mask free. It was that girl who, in spite of herself, would let C.25 reach the accomplices.

Little by little, the reception rooms were emptying. One by one the dancing partners were disappearing. The party would soon be over. Thérèse Arnaud's car had for some time been parked directly in front of the building, ready to receive the prisoners. Loulou was already on guard in the street. The other agents of the famous detective continued to watch all the individual suspects. Monsieur Joseph continued to talk to Josette Varlet in a low voice. The false Josette, on the arm of her false husband, after having shaken several hands, was making her way toward the vestibule. When the Varlet couple reached the vestibule, Malabar and Marcel hastened to rejoin Loulou and to wait for the couple at the building's exit. The arrest of the first couple went off without the least incident. As soon as they were on the sidewalk, André Varlet and his companion were immediately surrounded by Thérèse Arnaud's three assistants. There was no fighting, no shouts, no scuffles. Marcel's resolute attitude and Malabar's size took away from the suspects any desire to resist. Immediately captured, André Varlet and his companion were taken to the car where they were tied up and left for Loulou to guard.

During this time, Friquet, on the trail of the real Josette Varlet, left Raphaël Mortier's ball. Josette arrived on the sidewalk just as Marcel and Malabar had finished with the couple. She tried to go back into the sculptor's ball. Even though she had no doubt how the fight would turn out, Josette still attempted to resist and call for help. The cries were quickly stifled by Malabar's huge hand over the girl's mouth. Before Josette's cries had managed to draw attention, the so-called Josette Varlet rejoined her so-called husband and the woman who had played her role during the last part of the evening.

Nothing remained to do but to arrest Monsieur Joseph, who in the sculptor's reception rooms, was watched by Thérèse Arnaud. While Malabar and Loulou remained in the street watching over both the exit of the building and the car holding the prisoners, Friquet and Marcel went back into Raphaël Mortier's apartment. They found Thérèse Arnaud mystified. Monsieur Joseph had mysteriously disappeared. He had gone to the men's room soon after the departure of the Varlet couple when Josette Varlet had left him. He had not reappeared. The door to the men's room was not locked when Marcel opened it. But the place was empty. Nevertheless, Thérèse Arnaud was certain of it, Joseph had gone into the men's room. On the other hand, Thérèse Arnaud's assistants, who were in the street, were absolutely certain that Monsieur Joseph had not left the building either by the main door or by the service door. A rapid search explained the mystery. A small window had facilitated Monsieur Joseph's escape, following which, taking advantage of a drain pipe, he was able to reach the ground, thus descending two flights into the void. The searches which immediately took place in the courtyard of the building and in the cellar, didn't turn up any trace of the fugitive. Thérèse Arnaud didn't seem unusually affected by that failure.

"There's no use losing any more time! That fellow is long gone!" she stated when she went back to her car. There, Malabar and Loulou confirmed the information previously gained. Monsieur Joseph hadn't left the building by the usual exits. How had the private detective's suspicions been aroused? How had he known that flight was his only means of salvation? That was the mystery.

VII. The Violet Mask

Languille, faithful to the commission the Boss had given him, in order not to lose the girl in the violet mask, mounted guard in the corridor on the fourth floor of the Claridge Hotel. So as to avoid being surprised by some domestic or some guest coming in late, the Acrobat, whose presence would certainly have seemed suspicious, had hidden in a corner behind a small table holding a big green plant. From that observation post nothing could escape the eyes of C.25's assistant. He could see the door of the bedroom into which the girl in the violet mask had disappeared. For more than two hours, Languille remained watching like a hawk. Only two hotel guests passed by. Suddenly the elevator stopped on the fourth floor. The door clanged. A dull purr indicated that the elevator cage was going back down toward the first floor. A silhouette was profiled in the soft shadows of the corridor. Languille couldn't hold back a moment of surprise. The individual walking down the corridor was none other than Joseph Lusseaux! The amateur detective! Without the least hesitation, Monsieur Joseph walked toward the bedroom of the girl in the violet mask.

"Yes! What's he doing here?" murmured Languille.

The door closed on the amateur detective. Five minutes later Monsieur Joseph came out. For a moment Languille was uncertain. What should he do? The Boss's instructions were definite: don't leave the girl. But...the girl was in her bedroom and apparently wasn't at all disposed to leave it before daybreak...On the other hand, Monsieur Joseph's arrival complicated the situation and changed the events. The Acrobat didn't know the purpose of the detective's nocturnal visit. However it was very easy to deduce that Monsieur Joseph had come looking for something. In fact, whether it was following instructions or from some other information, Monsieur Joseph had used the telephone. Therefore, since the detective was going to some trouble himself, it was a matter of picking up something or bringing something.

While the Acrobat was making these reflections and wondering what action he should take, Joseph Lusseaux came back toward the landing. He held an object in his left hand that he was grasping as if it were very valuable. With his right hand, the detective searched in the left pocket of his overcoat. He took out his wallet, a voluminous wallet, in which he carefully enclosed the object he was holding in his left hand. That activity took place while Monsieur Joseph was passing down the corridor right in front of the Acrobat. Despite the soft lighting, Languille distinguished a mask perfectly...a violet mask...the girl's mask. It was that violet mask that Monsieur Joseph had come to pick up, in the middle of the night, in the hotel bedroom.

For Languille, that was a revelation! You would have had to be very stupid not to understand that Joseph Lusseaux would not have put himself out personally to come looking for an ordinary mask. Therefore, evidently, if the amateur detective had taken the trouble to come looking for that mask, that was because it had some sort of importance...some significance...or that it contained something in itself. It wasn't for the girl that Thérèse Arnaud had ordered her assistant "not to let her out of his sight." It was for the mask she was wearing. It wasn't the girl who had to be watched before everything. It was the mask. From that point, the Acrobat's mind was soon made up. To follow the Boss's orders strictly was not to follow the girl, but to follow the mask.

Monsieur Joseph was rapidly descending the stairs. Languille immediately left his hiding place and dashed after the detective. In the hallway, without any hurry, Joseph Lusseaux lit a cigarette. Then he left the Claridge. In front of the hotel, he called a taxi. There was no other car in sight. The least hesitation meant letting the detective escape...and most of all it meant letting the violet mask escape...that mask that must be of great interest, since Monsieur Joseph seemed to attach so much importance to its possession. As soon as the car started off, Languille jumped and clung to the back of the vehicle. The auto sped rapidly through nocturnal Paris, almost empty of all traffic. It passed the Place de la Concorde, the Rue de l'Opéra, the Rue Lafayette, the Porte de la Villette...and left Paris. "Nice outing!" the Acrobat murmured. But an outing leaving much to be desired in the way of comfort. The auto continued its course a long time in the night. It was beginning to grow light. In the distance, streaks of dawn were trying to break through the darkness. The auto stopped near the Bourget airfield. Languille slid to the ground and hid behind a tree. Monsieur Joseph ordered the chauffeur:

"Wait for me here..." The driver began to raise objections, citing the hour. Monsieur Joseph quieted him. "Don't worry. You'll be amply paid. Besides, I won't be gone very long. It will be only a matter of ten minutes."

Following the road, Monsieur Joseph rapidly walked toward a small, pathetic-looking hotel. He rang the bell. After some time, the door opened. The detective disappeared. Shortly afterward, Languille saw a light go on in one of the second floor windows. A new doubt tormented the Acrobat. What to do? What was going to become of the violet mask? The proximity to the aviation field established too clearly the goal of the pseudo-detective's nocturnal drive. Evidently the violet mask was going to change owners. Monsieur Joseph was only the go-between. He had taken possession of the violet mask in the girl's bedroom and he was bringing it to some accomplice who would be in charge of taking it to its destination. Then? When Monsieur Joseph came out of the hotel—arrest him? He would no longer be carrying the precious mask. Should he attempt to get into the hotel to find out what was happening? Languille rapidly evaluated the risk he would run. He was just about to decide to break into the house when, suddenly, an auto arrived at full speed. Before the Acrobat had recovered from his surprise, Malabar and Loulou jumped to the ground.

"Quickly! Where is Joseph?" the Colossus asked.

"Over there!" Languille answered, pointing to the hotel.

"That's good. The information was correct," the Colossus muttered. "Let's not waste any time. Let's go."

The door of the hotel opened at the first knock by the agents of the Deuxième Bureau. Without any more explanation, Thérèse Arnaud's agents pushed aside the hotel keeper, who opposed their intrusion without first knowing why they were there. In a hurry, Languille, Loulou and Malabar climbed the stairs. With one blow of his shoulders, Malabar broke the door into pieces.

"Raise your hands!"

The speed of the operation had been such that Monsieur Joseph and the man he was talking to hadn't had time to put up the least gesture of defense or to attempt flight. A pistol shot was followed by a cry of pain. Monsieur Joseph had tried to throw himself out the window. Loulou had stopped him in the middle of his jump. The pseudo-detective had been slightly wounded in the shoulder. C.25's assistants reorganized rapidly. The accomplice to whom Monsieur Joseph had brought the violet mask was a pilot usually charged with flying the mail of German spies. Monsieur Joseph, given first-aid and tied up, was grimacing in pain and shouting oaths. His accomplice, on the contrary, feeling any protests were useless, realizing that all defense was useless, seemed to resign himself to accepting his fate—a fate which he undoubtedly knew. Shortly thereafter, Thérèse Arnaud's assistants packed their prisoners in the automobile, which immediately started back to Paris.

How had Malabar and Loulou arrived so opportunely? How had they known that Monsieur Joseph was in a Bourget hotel? The explanation was very natural. When Thérèse Arnaud and her assistants had realized the uselessness of searching for Monsieur Joseph in Raphaël Mortier's building, they had immediately begun to interrogate the prisoners. André Varlet had refused to say anything. The real Josette Varlet remained equally mute. The only response C.25

could get from the couple was: "We don't know anything! Ask Monsieur Joseph!" The false Josette Varlet seemed crushed since her arrest and never stopped moaning. C.25 surmised that she had a weak personality, which made her susceptible to telling what she knew. The woman didn't display the least resistance. She furnished all the information.

And this is what they learned: that the woman in the violet mask was an accomplice of Monsieur Joseph. That she had picked up in the ladies' room the mask on which Josette Varlet had noted different information gathered during the evening at Raphaël Mortier's, and diverse communications destined to the *Tiergarten*. That during the evening the mask would be picked up from the girl (H.678) with the violet mask by Monsieur Joseph, who would then carry it to the traitorous pilot enlisted into the *Tiergarten* under the number A.L.546. C.25 also learned that for a long time that flier, always volunteering for special missions, took advantage of each of his trips to carry mail destined to the *Nachtrichten Bureau*.

Without being questioned any further, the false Josette Varlet pointed out the residence of the flier, to whom at different times she had been instructed to carry various communications. Given these facts, Thérèse Arnaud had immediately dispatched Malabar and Loulou to the Bourget Airfield, telling them to wait for Monsieur Joseph to arrive and to proceed to the arrest of the aviator and the private detective. The next morning the girl in the violet mask was arrested at the Claridge Hotel before she had left her room. C.25's prisoners were turned over to the military authorities with the exception of Monsieur Maurice Lagoupille and Mademoiselle Fernande, who were immediately set free.

Sometime later, after a rapid trial, the woman in the velvet mask, the Varlet couple (enrolled only several days in the ranks of the *Tiergarten* by Joseph Lusseaux, but who in reality were pathetic individuals) and Monsieur Joseph finished their careers in the *Caponnière de Vincennes*.

THE GREEN LIGHT

I. The Mysterious Automobile

A faraway bell ringing. 8 p.m. A winter night, dirty, thick with fog. Large dots of flashing lights weave in and out the Rue Buffon: a few rare street lights. The houses aligned on one side of the street with windows blinded for the night. On the other side of the street a high wall: the Jardin des Plantes.[10] Sometimes the muffled roar of an automobile engine, the angry roar of an impatient motor, or the mournful howl of a frightened or nostalgic wild animal. And everything again falls into silence. A few rare passers-by walk quickly to escape from the bombardment of the North wind whistling down the street and the oppressive fog. A few shadows: hats pulled down to upturned overcoat collars. A man pacing up and down on the sidewalk along the wall of the Jardin des Plantes. A monotonous walk. Walking slowly, walking fast. And not tiring, the man walks. He occasionally interrupts his walk for a short moment. He lifts his eyes toward the houses, probably searching to distinguish some trace of light behind the closed shutters, some shadow. Then, without a word, in the same regular and mechanical step, he begins to walk again.

A faraway voice begins to come closer rapidly, repeating its monotonous refrain:

"*The Intran!* Buy *The Intran*, latest edition!"[11]

The man crosses the street. The newspaper hawker approaches. "*The Intran,* latest edition!" The voice fades away.

The man returns to his observation post. He leans against a light post and he unfolds the newspaper he has just bought. His glance runs distractedly over the front page. The man turns to the second page; his eyes glance over the third. Then he suddenly seems absorbed in reading an article. The man has without a doubt found what he was looking for. He no longer does anything else. Only read, learn. Then, dropping the newspaper, which fell into the gutter, the man left in a hurry in the direction of Walhubert Square. The man quickly walked faster. In a short time he had increased his speed from walking to running. Then, still as if he were being chased, he began to run at full speed. Nevertheless, behind him: no one following. While continuing to run faster and faster, the man, in a mechanical gesture, pulled his hat down over his eyes.

---

[10] The Paris Botanical garden founded in 1793, containing the Ménagerie, a small zoo.

[11] *L'Intran* or *L'Intransigeant*, the largest evening daily of the right during the 1920s.

The Rue Buffon came to its estuary. A somewhat denser movement of tramways and cars. The man dashed forward to cross the boulevard without looking in any direction except in front of him, toward a goal that only he knew. A soft cry. A screech of brakes. The shock threw the man's hat into the gutter. And the man remained under the automobile, a powerful limousine. No witness to the accident except a policeman who was on duty at the crossroad who heard the cry, saw an automobile coming at full speed, suddenly stop, but that was all. He wasn't exactly sure of what had happened. He automatically walked toward the stopped automobile. Two men stepped out of the stationary vehicle. They looked around. They murmured a few words. The car slowly went into reverse to free the individual who was underneath. Then one of the occupants of the car leaned over. He put his hand on the victim's heart. The examination was rapid. The driver straightened up. He said: "Dead!" Then, without consulting each other, the two passengers leaned over with the same movement. They picked up the corpse, one by the head, the other by the feet. The door was opened. The two men and the cadaver disappeared into the automobile. The interior was immediately lit by a green light. An impatient roar of the motor resounded, followed by a long honk of the horn. The policeman was within some meters of the automobile when it left at full speed. Blowing his whistle had no effect. Instead of obeying the signal to stop, the automobile picked up speed. And it disappeared into the horizon before the policeman was able to take down its license number.

Sadly, understanding nothing of the rapid drama which in several seconds had found enough time to be born and take its course without leaving the least trace, the policeman went back to take up his post on Walhubert Square.

"Bizarre, even so!" he grumbled. "Nevertheless, I certainly saw a man crossing in front of the automobile...Where did he suddenly go? Under the car probably! Unless he recognized some friends and got in with them. However, I saw two shadows get out of the car and look under it! So? And why was there a green light inside the car?"

II. The Mystery Deepens

The policeman meditated for a long time over the mysterious facts he had witnessed. Then he passed on the facts—or rather what he knew about them—to his superiors. And by way of the hierarchy, the reports, drawing attention by their oddity, had ended up in the office of the Chief of the Police. That civil servant was attracted by the enigmatic side of the affair. What was that automobile with the green light? And why had it fled instead of stopping at the command of the policeman? What had happened during the short time it stopped on the Boulevard de l'Hôpital? What had happened to the man who ran across the street in front of the vehicle? Accident? Kidnapping? Crime? Many telephone calls brought the Chief of Police no precise information. The policemen, of a necessity posted for a certain time along the road followed by the suspicious automobile, turned up nothing. From another direction, none of the missing persons reported corresponded to the man who might have been kidnapped or attacked at about 8 p.m. near the Walhubert Square.

Monsieur Dupuis, Chief of Police, had called in the traffic policeman, the witness of the mysterious facts. Nothing to clear up the situation had been furnished. The policeman was limited to repeating the facts in his report without adding neither the slightest additional facts nor the least detail which could be used as a basis for any kind of investigation.

"This is shady business!" Monsieur Dupuis grumbled. "We have to find that car, whatever the cost!"

The subordinates of the Chief of Police confirmed his diagnosis. Their intuition warned them that it was a matter of an important case. What could serve as a basis? What were certain facts? A man was crossing the street. An automobile was coming at great speed. The car stopped. Then everything had disappeared. Automobile and man! As for the cry the policeman heard, it could be interpreted in different ways. A cry of fright by the pedestrian who saw a car speeding toward him. The agonized cry of a man who recognized enemies. A cry for help! The Chief of Police and his subordinates were not unaware that it would be hard work to clear up the enigma. They would have to rely on luck to bring up some detail which would allow the course of the events to be reexamined. Obviously to find the man would be to take a first step toward the solution: to find the car. But everything had disappeared. Just then Monsieur Dupuis was told a female visitor was asking to see him.

"All right! I'll see her."

A few moments later, Thérèse Arnaud entered the office.

"Ah! What about that!" the Chief of Police exclaimed. "You've come just as I was thinking of calling you. But let's do things in order. What business have you come to see me about?"

"Maybe for the case that you wanted to call me about?"

"The mysterious automobile on Walhubert Square?" Monsieur Dupuis asked.

"Yes, the car with the green light," answered the famous agent. "I wanted to find out what exact information you possess."

"Nothing! That is to say, unfortunately nothing," the Chief of Police answered.

He repeated to her the story the policeman who had witnessed the mysterious events had told him. He showed her the reports which confirmed that story without shedding any light on it. And he concluded:

"That's all! The automobile has disappeared! The man also…dead or living? We have no trace! Not the least little detail, not the least object, not the least little thing, however insignificant it might be."

C.25 rummaged in her raincoat pocket. "Here's what you're missing!" she said.

"What!" gasped the Chief of Police, astonished.

He looked curiously at the object Thérèse Arnaud was holding out to him. It was a soft hat, ordinary, worn, without a manufacturer's mark, without initials.

"This hat...?" Monsieur Dupuis asked in a worried voice.

"This hat," she explained, "is the one worn by the man crossing the boulevard just as the car struck him..."

"Where did you find this hat?" questioned Monsieur Dupuis.

"In the gutter, some meters from the place where the facts we don't know took place," Thérèse said coolly.

"And in your opinion, what does this hat mean?"

The agent made a vague gesture. The Chief of Police continued:

"Let's not get carried away. Does this piece show there was an accident? If there had been a fight, as short, as rapid as it might have been, the policeman who was coming toward the automobile would have seen something. He never indicated that the shadows came together, and he never saw three shadows together! Only two...two who got out of the automobile...So?"

Thérèse Arnaud just repeated: "Yes...So?"

Then after a few seconds of reflective silence that Monsieur Dupuis was careful not to interrupt, she got up and took leave of the Chief of Police.

III. The Mail Box

Leaving the office in the Rue des Saussaies, Thérèse Arnaud went back again to the place of the mystery. She had re-established the itinerary the unknown man had followed right to the point where the automobile had stopped and where the hat had been thrown into the gutter. There was no doubt about it. The man was coming from the Rue Buffon. The famous agent had fixed her campaign plan from that point. It was easy to set up surveillance on the Rue Buffon because it had only two exits and it wasn't crossed by any other street. Therefore, Friquet and Languille had already been posted on guard duty for the last two nights, one on each end of the street. But they had not yet reported any useful information having, or seeming to have, a direct rapport with the mysterious automobile. At the beginning of the third night, when Thérèse Arnaud's assistants were beginning to despair of ever obtaining any useful clarification, Friquet suddenly saw, coming down the boulevard, a powerful limousine, its interior lit by a green light! Friquet looked at his watch: 8:15 p.m., the hour at which the mysterious facts had occurred.

The car had turned into the Rue Buffon and was coming at full speed past Friquet. To jump on his bicycle and begin the chase was the matter of only an instant for Friquet. A special whistle warned Languille to be on his guard. But Friquet was quickly outdistanced and when he came to the end of the Rue Buffon, the car had disappeared. He thought that Languille, more fortunate then he, might have been able to follow it successfully. And in order not to disobey the precise instructions of the Boss, he didn't go any further. He came back calmly, pushing his bicycle along the wall of the Jardin des Plantes to again take up his watch at the corner of the Rue Buffon and the boulevard. Darkness enveloped the peaceful and almost asleep street. Friquet noticed a silhouette coming from the opposite direction on the other side of the street. It was that of a man walking casually along, whistling a popular song rather loudly. Suddenly Friquet saw the man, who was walking in front of the houses, stoop down rapidly as if he had dropped something. Then he immediately straightened up. But Thérèse's assistant had clearly seen that, when he straightened up, he was holding a rectangular package. The man bent over a second time, in the same spot. Then, just as rapidly, he straightened up. *He no longer had the package!* Then he continued his walk down the Rue Buffon.

The man was walking casually along, like someone talking a stroll. He took no precaution to see that he was not followed. Friquet let the man get somewhat past him. He then went quickly across the street and turned around. In a few rapid steps he came to the exact spot where the passer-by had twice bent over.

"A cellar window," Friquet murmured. Leaning over then, he rapidly drew up a box.

"That's the package my man had when he straightened up the first time!"

Friquet looked at the box. "Obviously, it's empty now."

He put the box back where it was, then he hurried to catch the man whose silhouette was disappearing in the fog. Then, so as not to let him know he was being followed, Friquet kept a certain distance between the man and himself. To have gone any closer would have been imprudent. Besides, the Rue Buffon was deserted and the man couldn't take any other street. Friquet would catch him at the other end. In spite of the instructions from the Boss, the Paris street kid judged that the discovery was of sufficient importance not to let the prey escape…and to leave the street surveillance, where, it seemed likely nothing more would happen.

Still being followed, the man turned into the Rue Linné. At the corner of the Rue Monge, just as the man was going to cross, an automobile arrived. It stopped for just a second. A hand came out the window. And went back in holding a bundle of papers. And the car sped away. The scene had been so rapid and the car had sped off so quickly that Friquet didn't hesitate.

"You shouldn't release the real prey to go chase the shadow! On my bicycle, I don't have any chance to catch the car with the green light! But I've got the essential, the man." Therefore, Friquet stubbornly stayed on the trail of the man who continued to walk casually along. Another thought came to Thérèse Arnaud's auxiliary's mind:

"What's happened to Languille? Since I let him know about the passage of the mysterious automobile in the Rue Buffon, he would usually have started in pursuit. So?"

Should he believe that the powerful auto driving around in the neighborhood, waiting for the man's arrival, had thrown off Languille? Should he think that, in following the automobile, Languille had made an important discovery which had obligated him, him also, to abandon surveillance of the Rue Buffon?

Walking and walking in nocturnal Paris. "Me, who hasn't eaten," Friquet grumbled, "I'm taking a walk for my digestion."

The man, still not taking the least precaution to hide himself, continued on his way, truly a rather strange path. At midnight, still continuing his shadowing, Friquet had passed La Place de la Bastille, L'Opéra, the Madeleine Church, the Place de l'Étoile. Then he had gone in the opposite direction. A sudden detour. And the man disappeared in a nice looking house, near the Champs de Mars.

"He's probably a fellow visiting Paris!" Friquet grumbled. "Now there's nothing else to do. Wait until he comes out! If only I could get in touch with the Boss."

Alas! There remained no other means at his disposal. To leave his post would perhaps be to let the individual escape. So, Friquet resigned himself. The next day at noon, the man not having come out, Friquet still remained at his post.

IV. Anxious Hours

The next morning, at Thérèse's house (while Friquet was still at the Champs de Mars) the situation presented itself in the following way:

Malabar, who was supposed to relieve Friquet at surveillance on the boulevard side of the Rue Buffon, hadn't found anyone there. He had immediately made the Boss aware of his worry about Friquet. And the minutes passing without bringing the slightest news of the Paris street kid added to C.25's worries. As for Languille, who had been temporarily replaced by Marcel, at the surveillance of the other end of the Rue Buffon, he gave Thérèse the following report:

"Yesterday evening, a little after 8 p.m., I was alerted by a signal from Friquet. Almost immediately I saw the car with the green light arrive. I followed it. The vehicle followed a strange route, seeming to turn in the area of the Jardin des Plantes. Where streets crossed, it disappeared. I found it again. I rushed after it. The car stopped at the Place Maubert and I noticed that this wasn't the same vehicle. There was no doubt possible. Another trick to throw off the trackers. Those who occupied the car with the green light had noticed they were being followed. They had led me into a street where a different car was parked...the one that I had trailed while the real vehicle with the green light had gotten away from me."

"Finally, Languille, do you have the details?" Thérèse asked.

Languille gave some precise details: the kind of car, its horsepower.

"The number," Thérèse questioned.

"5643J6," Languille answered.

Alas! The attempt at verification gave no result. As it was easy to foresee, the license number was false. And the real vehicle number 5643J6, quickly located, was another kind of car of a very inferior horsepower.

Thérèse's anxiety grew. What had become of Friquet?

Before going to search for her assistant, the secret agent dictated the following orders: "Malabar will remain until given other instructions on surveillance at the Rue Buffon. And you, Languille, you'll go back to the Rue Buffon, to your usual post. You'll relieve Marcel, who'll come to rejoin me here. While Malabar and you are watching the places we're currently interested in, I'll begin the search for Friquet with Marcel."

That's what they did.

Languille had already been back at his post for two hours. He hadn't noticed anything abnormal. And the minutes were passing slowly. Languille seemed to take the greatest interest in the work of a painter who was working with a brush painting the letters for a boutique sign on the Rue Buffon. The man noticing himself the object of Languille's attention, seized the first pretext to start a conversation.

"Don't you have anything else to do but watch others work?" he inquired.

Languille, so as not to raise the least suspicion, launched into an unlikely story of a rendezvous with a young woman who was supposed to bring him news of his mother.

"Maybe she hasn't been able to come. She's the maid of all work, so she'll take advantage of when her employers send her on an errand to come meet me here."

The painter was listening distractedly. Suddenly, he suggested:

"Then come on. We're going to go have a glass! That'll warm you up since you've been hanging about."

Languille declined the offer, but the worker insisted: "All right, come on. I'm buying! A glass has never hurt anybody!"

To refuse any more would have been awkward. Languille followed the worker. There was a bistro two doors further down. Its façade was drab and the boutique was so dark its lights flashed night and day. The worker entered, followed by Languille, who, not to lose sight of any movement in the street, stayed near the door. Two drinks were lined up on the zinc counter.

"To your health!" the painter said.

Languille responded in a friendly way, while observing three inoffensive drinkers, further away, who were playing dice. The Acrobat quickly emptied his glass and set it on the counter, then he turned aside a little to let a new client enter. He thought he would take advantage of the open door to return to his post. He started to leave. The new client barred the passage.

"Excuse me, sir," said Thérèse Arnaud's assistant.

Before he could make a movement, he was immobilized. The painter had seized his arm; the three inoffensive drinkers had jumped him. The man who was entering quickly closed the door.

"We've got him!" several voices said.

And in a few seconds, Languille was tied up. Rapidly, without saying a word, the five men picked him up and carried him to the rear of the shop where a small stairway opened, descending toward the cellar. The brave boy was quickly deposited there. Then, after a last examination of the bonds that immobilized the prisoner, the men left, abandoning him in the cellar, the door of which they closed after them. Not a word had been said.

"Yes! I've been caught," Languille thought. "Everything was prepared in advance. They noticed me; they drew me here. It was simple…and I'm in the hands of the enemy. But which ones?"

Hours passed. The Acrobat tried in vain to get free of his bonds. Wasted effort! From time to time he heard comings and goings in the shop, sometimes laughter. All of a sudden it seemed to him there was more noise in the bistro with more numerous sounds. Laughter, sometimes even bits of conversation, came down as far as to him in the cellar.

"Well! They're talking about me! I may be going to learn the fate they've reserved for me," he sighed.

In fact, a conversation was taking shape, the sounds coming down to the prisoner.

"He's down below…in the cellar. And there's no danger he'll get into the bottles…" one voice was saying.

"What are we going to do about him?" another voice questioned.

"We'll see," the first voice answered. "We'll soon have instructions about him…when the pick-up is done…"

"That shouldn't be very long from now?"

Languille was listening with both ears and the sounds he heard made sense, little by little. Several times as the customers were speaking that same phrase returned: "when the pick-up is made." The pick-up? Then several other conversations relating to the same subject:

"I've just posted my letter," said one of the customers, "and it was heavy!"

Languille then next heard someone affirm that he had just mailed news about Château-Thierry which "would please the Boss."

A confused brouhaha seemed suddenly to greet the arrival of another customer. And Languille understood, little by little, his ear adjusted to the murmurs he heard.

"I've come from over there, and it's heating up," one of them was saying.

"Château Thierry?" several voices asked.

"No…the 4."

No more doubt! Languille was persuaded that he had fallen into the hands of German spies. Various ones were returning from diverse missions. They had met there.

"Quick!...I'm finishing my report and I'm carrying it to the box," one of them continued.

"Hurry up!...It's eight o'clock."

"The mail box isn't very far away," Languille heard. And that sentence was punctuated by a rough laugh.

What was that mail box the spies were talking about? And also that mail and that pick-up? All questions Languille's brain was trying to piece together...but in vain. Little by little, there was silence again. Languille could no longer hear anything but a murmur of conversation without being able to understand the least word. Then the door of the bistro slammed two or three times. It was the noise of the outside steel safety doors they were drawing down. And then nothing...only the steps of a late passer-by.

V. The Skirmish

When evening fell, Thérèse Arnaud had to admit that all her searches with Marcel to find Friquet had been useless. They had no clue as to the place from which the happy Paris street kid had disappeared. Despite their worry, the Secret Service agent and her assistants didn't lose sight of the affair which they were working on. C.25 had therefore revised her dispositions for the night guard on the Rue Buffon. Surveillance would be carried out by Malabar, who would relieve Languille. Malabar, therefore went first of all to the boulevard side of the Rue Buffon. He went down the street to let Languille know that he could take a little rest.

"Hello, my big boy!" said a happy voice.

"You! You!" exclaimed Malabar, excited.

"Yes! Me," answered Friquet.

"But where did you come from, you dog? We were looking for you everywhere!"

"Don't worry! I've just checked in with the Boss. And…I have an idea. It's almost eight o'clock. We're going to see something."

Still recovering from his joy at finding his friend again, Malabar remained silent some instants. Then he suddenly returned to reality.

"So, Friquet, did you relieve Languille?"

"Languille? Do you think he cares?"

"What's that?" Malabar, astonished, asked.

But Friquet was continuing:

"While I was standing watch in the street, Languille was in the bistro; he was drinking alone. Talk about a strange friend…"

But Malabar asked rapid questions, and Friquet immediately explained. As soon as he had finished his mission at the Rue de Mars, he had returned to Rue Buffon to check certain facts. He had told Thérèse. And when he arrived at the corner of the street, he saw Languille leaving and going into the bistro.

"And, my friend, if he's been drinking ever since he went in, he must have quenched his thirsty by now!" Friquet joked.

"Ah!" Malabar was thinking, "That's undoubtedly unusual. It might be useful to go see."

"Let's wait a little…a few minutes," said Friquet. "And afterward we'll see about it."

Friquet's purpose was simple. He had thought to return to the Rue Buffon and do what he had seen done the night before: walk down the sidewalk, lean down, empty the box of its contents…and take back his harvest to C.25 who would certainly be interested in that crop.

But a quick examination had convinced Friquet of the impossibility of his attempt, or, at least of the impossibility of taking the box without attracting attention. He had in fact noticed that the box was constantly watched. Two windows on the first floor of the building opposite each side of the cellar window were occupied. Friquet had seen shadows behind the curtains. Therefore any attempt at grabbing the box would be immediately known by the enemy. Friquet had, as a consequence, modified his project. And if he asked Malabar to wait a few minutes before finding out about Languille, it was to convince himself that the facts observed the evening before would be renewed every evening at the same hour. Once there was that certainty, the only thing left to do was to choose a day to carry out the Boss's orders with every chance of success. The business was only pushed forward, because you could be sure of finding an interesting harvest every evening.

A clock struck eight times far away in the distance. Malabar and Friquet hid in the shadows. They saw a man arrive who bent over in passing near the cellar window. Once, twice.

"I'll explain it to you later," Friquet whispered to Malabar.

A car, speeding, came into the Rue Buffon. When it passed in front of C.25's assistants, Malabar exclaimed, astounded:

"The green light!"

"Yes…" Friquet said. "Don't make anything of it, my friend. We'll get it again…another evening. Now, I'm satisfied in that direction. But I'm still worried about Languille."

"Well, then, let's go," Malabar decided.

When the two comrades entered the bistro, they made out in the low and smoke-filled room a dozen customers playing cards. The murmur of conversations immediately stopped. Standing in front of their drinks, Friquet and Malabar each looked around. In just one glance, they could see Languille wasn't there.

"It was impossible for him to have left without my having seen him," Friquet whispered in the Colossus's ear.

"So?…Yes! I understand," said Malabar.

The two men had their drinks refilled often. Both agents of C.25 noticed a strange fact. None of the customers had decided to leave. They went on playing cards, seeming to pay only mediocre attention to their game.

"They suspect us," muttered Malabar to Friquet. "I have a feeling that things are going to heat up before very long."

And while drinking to each other's health, the Hercules gave his companion instructions for the fight.

"You, you'll guard the door. And anyone who wants to leave you'll tap on the head…if they get as far as you. But before they get that far, they'll go through my hands."

"Malabar, there are ten of them…including the owner…" Friquet said.

"Well, yes, there are ten of them…what difference does that make?" the good giant answered coolly, rapidly emptying his glass. Then he quickly turned around. The clients exchanged significant glances. Suddenly a signal rang out in the relative silence.

"Ha!"

"Get going, my little friend," Malabar ordered.

Friquet took his battle station.

Malabar had picked up a table around which four players were sitting. A terrible whirling around, the table at the end of his arms. And shouts. Four combatants, their heads more or less damaged, had just been put in a condition (temporarily at least) to cause no more trouble.

Shots rang out.

Malabar had taken cover behind the zinc counter so as not to be attacked from behind. Currently, six men remained standing. Two bottles thrown by

Friquet knocked out two combatants

"It's lucky I'm not fat," thought the little Parisian, quickly dodging a well-thrown stool.

Malabar walked straight up to the five men still standing. He was still brandishing his table above their heads. And, instinctively, the heads were lowered. But one of the men jumped toward the assailant while another grabbed the table in an attempt to disarm the Colossus. The man who jumped on Malabar rolled three feet away, accompanied by the sound of crushed bones. The table rolled away. The four survivors of this fight rushed forward, but they immediately retreated. Malabar, having seized one of the wounded men by the leg, was again twirling him around, while Friquet continued his bombardment with bottles. Shortly afterward, there were four men remaining, driven into a corner by Malabar, who was generously distributing blows with his fists and feet. You could hear the panting.

One of the first ones wounded, tall, slim, had only been stunned. He returned quickly to consciousness. He rushed forward again, expecting to surprise the giant from the rear. Luckily, Friquet was watching. He butted him in his stomach with his head. But lithe, subtle, the enemy had jumped to one side. And Friquet, drawn forward by the momentum, almost fell on the floor. He recovered rapidly and before his enemy was able to profit by his victory, he dealt him a superb blow with his fist. If it didn't have the force of those of Malabar, it was nevertheless precise enough to make the one who had received it see 36 candles. Still, the man continued to fight with Friquet. A fight of fake passes and agility. The blows passed to one side or didn't hit the enemy hard enough to put him out of the fight. As for Malabar, he had sufficient work dealing with his three enemies.

Suddenly, there was a whistle. And Friquet's adversary stumbled, lassoed. To finish making him powerless was for Friquet the business of a moment.

"Phew!" the Paris street kid breathed.

At the same time, Malabar's last adversary fell over, knocked out.

"The combat has ended for lack of combatants," Friquet joked. "That doesn't matter, my big Malabar. You didn't pull any punches."

"There's no time to lose," Malabar answered. "Where's Languille?"

C.25's two agents began a survey of the battle field. "Languille, Languille!" called Friquet. Soon a voice responded to his call. To knock in the door of the cellar with a blow of his shoulders was for Malabar child's play. Languille was quickly freed.

"You're a disgusting person," Friquet joked. "While we were freezing in the street, you were drinking in this shop and you were sleeping while we were beating up people."

"If you think it's possible to sleep with the noise you made," Languille answered, "you must be a sound sleeper."

"Nevertheless," Friquet assured him, "there are clients upstairs asleep."

Back upstairs in the shop, Languille, a little in pain, and Friquet guarding the prisoners, Malabar telephoned C.25 asking her to come immediately to take delivery of the vanquished.

VI. After the Battle

Thérèse soon arrived. And she wasn't stingy with her congratulations to her two collaborators. It was a fine capture.

"A beautiful picture!" she said. "If the quality is the same value as the quantity, this will be a fine operation! We'll see about that, provided Malabar hasn't damaged them too much and they can still talk…"

While Languille and Friquet were busy bringing round the wounded, the woman agent was already thinking of following up the operation. The success wouldn't be complete until the contents of the box had fallen into her power. Of course, as Friquet had foreseen, it was easy to try force. But that would be to give the alarm and at that hour of the night, risk not finding important loot. It would be necessary to operate at about 8 p.m. On the other hand, they had to act before the story of the fight and the arrest of the spies got out.

"So, that will be for tomorrow," Thérèse said. "And if we can, we have to arrest every individual who comes in bringing any kind of message."

A fast visit to the placement of the cellar window—which Friquet showed her from the sidewalk facing it—germinated an idea in the famous agent's fertile mind. "The letter box is in the cellar. Now, surveillance is done from the ground floor. Therefore, whoever could get into the cellar without giving the alarm, could gather up the contents of the box without the men posted on the ground floor being aware of anything. In essence there is only the distance of two buildings to cross. Therefore to dig two passages into the cellar would allow the bistro's cellar to be used to reach the one where the letter box is. Thérèse told Malabar about her project. He answered:

"That's more work for me! I'll work discretely. All in all, that means a passage leaving here and ending up at the neighboring building, and another one from the neighboring building into the next. It's simple. It'll be done, Boss. I'm going to start to work."

While Malabar, aided by Friquet and Languille, undertook that task, the Boss and Marcel took care of the prisoners. Interrogations followed. Several of the spies refused absolutely to answer, to furnish the least information as to their missions and the nature of the information they had communicated to their chief. The search hadn't produced anything.

"All right! All right!" said Thérèse, who was coming up against the mocking silence of the last prisoner. She lit a cigarette. Then, speaking to the Chemist, she stated:

"You'll have some work tomorrow. As soon as we've finished here, you can go get a few hours rest and prepare all that's necessary for chemicals. You should also get some special brass plates." Then, speaking to the prisoners, she added:

"Now, before telephoning the Deuxième Bureau to come take delivery of these gentlemen, we're going to take off their shoes."

At the announcement of that measure—very elementary, however, because shoe heels were very often used by spies as hiding places—the prisoners' faces showed a great deal of anxiety. The operation was rapidly and methodically done. Each pair of shoes was examined. The heels looked into were emptied of their papers. And before the paddy wagon arrived, C.25 had collected an important haul that she classed methodically: maps of the armies' placements; information concerning the movements of troops and depots for goods and equipment and for ammunition; recently drawn maps showing the placement of artillery; some notes written in code (which Marcel would ultimately decode); some information about the organization of the espionage service and the make-up of an agency situated in Switzerland that facilitated crossing the border into France.

"Well," Thérèse said, on examining those notes, "it seems the little business of Gex obliged the German espionage service to change its plans."

Several hours later the prisoners were sent away in a fortified military vehicle. Thérèse alone remained on the battlefield, while in the cellars Malabar, Friquet and Languille occupied their time usefully. She was still worried.

"A nice success for your work," said Marcel, coming to join her.

"Oh!" Thérèse said modestly.

The Chemist protested: "Not satisfied? You are truly difficult."

For a moment the famous agent remained silent. Then she explained to Marcel.

"That's not it. I'm not hard to please. Of course I'm satisfied with the results achieved today. But my job would be very incomplete if I were content with that."

Marcel opened his eyes wide in astonishment as C.25 continued.

"From all the evidence, the individuals that Malabar made it possible for us to arrest this evening are small fry. Some of those who don't reach the great chiefs of German espionage in Paris. They carry out the missions they're given, and then they come to unload their reports in the mailbox…that we'll empty, I hope, tomorrow. That's very good. But the mystery of the automobile with the green light hasn't been cleared up."

"How's that?" Marcel asked.

"No, Marcel. The enigma is still there. The information gathered is clear. Every evening, about eight o'clock, a man makes the drop. The automobile with the green light passes by and carries away the documents. But we're missing the most important element. How, by what means, following what complicities do these documents, these reports, finally reach a destination?"

Marcel made a gesture of agreement. Thérèse continued.

160

"Obviously, we can make some guesses. But how many dangers, how many set-backs before the guesses are changed into certainty! Where does the automobile with the green light go when it has made the pick-up? It's for that reason that tomorrow we must, at any price, avoid arousing their suspicions. Unless we do, we'll lose the trail and the criminals also. Tomorrow the pick-up must go as usual…when, even so, the real documents will be in our possession."

After a moment's silence, the Chemist questioned timidly:

"What are you suggesting?"

"It's simple, only it's monstrous! To retain all their usefulness, I imagine that these documents must be sent to the enemy as rapidly as possible. So, the most rapid method of communication…"

"By air?"

"Yes, Marcel, by air," Thérèse continued. "And that's where the business becomes monstrous. A plane leaving the Paris area (the radius of a car making the service regularly every evening) is rather limited. So, an airplane leaves the Paris area every evening carrying papers it must carry to the enemy. The importance of that treason is such that, despite everything, I can't believe it."

"Then," Marcel asked, "what other way is there?"

"I don't know…not yet…!" said Thérèse. "But I'll find out. I have to."

VII. A Fruitful Harvest

In the early morning hours, Thérèse was told the work Malabar had undertaken was finished. There now existed a useable passage which, by going through the neighboring buildings, allowed them, without arousing suspicion, to go through the bistro cellar to reach the adjacent cellar where the mailbox was situated. Thérèse had decided that the bistro would open as usual. Malabar would take the place of the owner. He would be helped in his job sometimes by Friquet, sometimes by Languille, acting as waiters. They would be the liaison to her. Whichever one of the two assistants wasn't working behind the bar, would have charge of watching the mailbox. Thérèse reserved for herself, as usual, the most dangerous role: to enter the enemy cellar and take out the letters. As for Marcel, his task was already laid out: to photograph and translate all the documents brought to him. These dispositions taken, it was understood that C.25's associates would receive orders, according to the circumstances, when the usual hour of the pick-up arrived.

In the morning, after having taken some hours rest, Thérèse returned to the theater of operations. Malabar and Friquet were doing marvelously in their new occupation. Thanks to the secret passage—and thanks also to her suppleness—Thérèse penetrated the spies' cellar without too much difficulty. There were already four letters in the box. Thérèse removed them and replaced them with an equal number of similar envelopes…which contained false documents. Then she got out to take her harvest to Marcel. Passing into the bar of the bistro, she gave orders to the bar waiter to pick up, regularly, every hour, letters left in the box and to replace them with others containing false documents. A tiny mark on the envelopes would identify the documents brought by the spies and those put there by Thérèse and her aides. At 4 p.m., Thérèse returned to the Rue Buffon.

"This is working," Malabar told her. "Business is good. I've had a lot of customers! Only…they won't come back tomorrow!"

Thérèse frowned in worry. "What's that? What's wrong? Have they been alerted?"

"No," Malabar said. "It's just that, to keep them from talking…if they noticed anything …then…"

"Then?" questioned Thérèse.

"Then," Malabar finished, "when they had had a drink, I served them a little something for their digestion. A good blow of my fist but not too strong, not to knock them out, just enough to stun them and tie them up. And…there are 17 of them waiting in the cellar."

"Ah, good," Thérèse smiled. "You scared me."

Friquet had also followed his orders. And Marcel, without letting up, was photographing, translating, submitting the papers to the most diverse chemical processes possible. Languille, on watch outside, had equally used his time in a profitable way. The number of passers-by who leaned over when they came abreast of the cellar window was considerable. He had to renounce, at least for the moment, following them, and arresting them. Somewhat after having dropped their unusual mail, the spies crossed the path of a young man walking nonchalantly along. Perhaps to facilitate future operations, with the aid of a minute photographic apparatus hidden in his sleeve, he took their picture.

As the day went on, Thérèse's auxiliaries, began to be worried, without, for all that, neglecting the least in the world their jobs. Was the warning out? What would happen at the pick-up time? And the automobile with the green light?

8 p.m. came. Malabar had at that moment 27 clients in the basement of the little café. Friquet had just come back from the spies' cellar after having exchanged the last letters deposited. Languille was watching in the Rue Buffon the area around the "Post Office."

Rapidly, accompanied by a loud blast of the horn, an automobile passed by. In the interior shone a green light. A few seconds later, a man stooped down in front of the cellar window, emptied the letter box, and put it back in its place. Then he continued walking. Languille saw him stop at the end of the Rue Buffon. The automobile with the green light stopped for a few seconds. Then the horn sounded, a louder roar of the impatient motor. Then the car with the green light sped into the streets of sleeping Paris. Behind, another automobile just as powerful, appeared. Languille had just enough time to see Thérèse and Marcel in the second automobile.

VIII. Airplane Shot Down

The two automobiles went across Paris rapidly. Thérèse's task was relatively easy. Quiet streets, almost no traffic. No fear that the car with the green light would disappear at a traffic jam. Besides, the occupants seemed to think they were perfectly safe. They weren't worried about throwing off someone following them whose presence they probably didn't even know.

"We're going in the direction of the Bourget airport," Marcel said to the Boss. "Am I wrong?"

"No," Thérèse answered laconically.

She was a little pale, because her hypothesis was confirmed. The mail destined to the enemy left regularly each evening by airplane. Right up to the last minute, Thérèse had hoped that her reasoning was faulty. Despite everything, she had refused to believe in so much treachery on the part of a French aviator. Marcel, almost guessing the Boss's thoughts, asked:

"Isn't it possible for a pilot to carry this mail without knowing the nature of what's been given him?"

"To be ignorant of what he's transporting and to whom he's giving the letters? And where he's going? Can a French flier land in occupied territory or in enemy territory believing that he's in France? To hand over the letters to whatever German État-Major, believing he was giving them to the French authorities? And getting across the lines? And? No, you're dreaming, my poor Marcel. Now I see very well that the idea of treason by one of our aviators must be admitted. But, even in accepting that idea, as repugnant as it may be, there are still some facts I don't understand. Planes which depart from Bourget airbase are controlled. They have a well-defined mission each time they take off and it's not always the same. And what throws me off the track in this business is the frequency and the ease with which a French aircraft can get into Germany."

"Yes," Marcel agreed. "It's even more extraordinary that a French plane can cross German lines without being greeted by intense fire and without being immediately pursued. So the passage of that aircraft is expected. His coming was anticipated. How is it that the French authorities have never noticed that a French aircraft crosses the lines each night at the same spot…and isn't the object of any German fire?"

Thérèse listened to Marcel. When he had finished, she said in a strange voice:

"Yes, Marcel, your reactions are correct. There is that…and there's also a great number of other things, all as inexplicable, all as inadmissible."

The road to the Bourget airport stretched out, gleaming and black. Thérèse pressed down on the accelerator. The motor roared. Little by little the distance separating the two vehicles melted away. C.25's automobile passed the spies car and picking up speed, arrived first at the Bourget airport.

Thérèse had taken precautions during the day. Without giving the details of the case she was working on, she had had Captain Ladoux alert the Bourget Airport, in order to find there all the information she might find useful. The agent left Marcel on the outskirts of the billeting area with instructions to watch for the arrival of the vehicle with the green light and to follow the actions of its occupants. She foresaw that a man, just any pilot, must come to meet them to take delivery of the mail. Despite her identification, the French Secret Agent was stopped at the guard gate. That was a rule which had no exception. A man was immediately detached to accompany her to the office of the Commandant. Without wasting time, she asked for necessary details. She thus learned that several pilots were entrusted with diverse reconnaissance flights.

"This evening," the Commandant said, "there's not a great deal of activity. Outside of patrol squadrons, only seven pilots have been scheduled for night flights."

"None has yet taken off?" she asked quickly.

"None! Besides the departures this evening are only scheduled toward eleven o'clock," the Commandant informed her.

Thérèse Arnaud remained silent a moment. Then she asked: "Are the flights known by the pilots in advance?"

"No," the Commandant explained. "I choose the pilots, but they don't know for what mission. They only know that, in principle, they will make only one flight a night. I say 'in principle,' because sometimes certain departures are canceled at the last minute following diverse circumstances."

"Good, good," Thérèse quickly said, evasively. "Then exactly when do the pilots know the details of their mission?"

"A few instants before taking off, actually," said the Commandant. "Generally the pilots themselves help in the final preparations. They want to be sure—and that's understandable—that everything is perfectly in order. They themselves look over the various operations which precede the flight. It's at that time that a superior officer gives them verbally all the required information. Besides, the men we've assigned for these kinds of missions—always extremely dangerous—have proved themselves many times. They're not only regular French air force pilots, but also true men who have frequently given proof of their courage and their strength. All have been decorated and have been given the most flattering citations for their audacity and their temerity."

Thérèse shook her head without saying anything. There was again a short moment of silence. Then she suddenly asked the Commandant:

"No one can enter the camp?"

"No one! There are strict orders. Whoever tries to enter is arrested by the guards and brought here. You've been able to see that yourself. However, you have official identification. The orders are even more strict for those who try to enter without any official identification."

"Perfect!" Thérèse said thoughtfully. "At what time," she almost immediately continued, "must the pilots assigned for the night flights be present?"

"In principle, they must not leave," said the Commandant, "but practically..."

Thérèse cut him off quickly: "Is it possible to know if all the pilots scheduled to leave tonight are currently present?"

"It's easy to be sure. But right now I can answer you in the affirmative."

The Commandant gave some rapid orders to a junior officer, who left in haste. He came back some minutes later bringing the following details, which were communicated to Thérèse:

"The seven pilots are present in the camp. They ate in the mess hall. And no one left after the meal."

"None left after the meal," C.25 repeated slowly.

Before taking leave of the Commandant, she set out to see the aircraft which were supposed to fly during the night. The Commandant let her leave; accompanied by a junior officer she walked across the field. The airplanes were outside the hangers. A group of men were working around each of them: skilled technicians, mechanics, laborers, pilots. Thérèse's glance counted, with no possible doubt. Eight aircraft. She walked toward an aircraft where there was less activity. The pilot wasn't there. He wasn't helping with the final preparations. She continued her visit. She verified that the seven pilots were very near their plane. Then she went to rejoin Marcel.

"So?" she asked him quickly.

"It's done, Boss. The mail has been given to a pilot. One of the occupants in the car with the green light got out of the car about 100 meters from the camp's entrance. He was immediately met by a man who was waiting, hidden near the wall. The interview lasted only a few seconds. Not even the time to start a conversation or to give orders, just time to hand over a package, which after that the pilot carried under his arm when he went back into the camp."

"Yes," Thérèse said. "I met him then when I was leaving. I saw his silhouette. And he was walking rapidly toward the eighth airplane which is parked at the extreme right of the group on the departure line."

A dull silence, then the conclusion. "Then there's no possible mistake!" A pause and then a question from Thérèse in a very different tone: "And the car with the green light?"

"It immediately went back in the direction of Paris," the Chemist informed her.

The agent shoved Marcel into her car immediately and at full speed the car raced toward Paris. Not a word was exchanged between Marcel and the Boss during the short trip. C.25 went directly to the office of Captain Ladoux. And 15 minutes later, the following message was received by all the posts of the D.C.A. within the C.R.P.: "Order is given to watch all the movements of an aircraft coming from the interior and flying toward the front line of the armies." Exact information and the description of a biplane which was—clarifying the message—to be considered an enemy aircraft to be shot down and destroyed. (The seven other aircrafts which regularly left the Bourget airfield were monoplanes.) The message was transmitted at 11:05 p.m. Order was also given to forward the results and an account of the results of that measure. Minutes passed. Gloomy. Silent.

A laconic message sent from a D.C.A. post in the vicinity of Creil announced: "Identified biplane shot down, fell at Lamorlaye."

Thérèse didn't wait any longer. And the car again raced in the night. A mad drive. Marcel gave up trying to understand. Not a word left the lips of the Boss. She was leaning over the steering wheel. Her foot never left the accelerator and despite the fact the automobile was going at its maximum speed, Thérèse Arnaud still found it too slow to suit her.

A loud blast of a horn sounded behind C.25's automobile. What vehicle was trying to pass the automobile speeding at more than 100km/h? Thérèse didn't budge; she gripped her steering wheel harder. Despite everything, shortly thereafter a vehicle began to appear beside that of C.25 and little by little passed her car.

Thérèse groaned: "Good God!" while Marcel, shocked, said in astonishment:

"The car with the green light!"

"Obviously, they've been warned," Thérèse exclaimed. "Their clandestine listening stations picked up the message. And they're rushing to reach the spot where the airplane was shot down in order to save their mail."

And the two automobiles continued their race through the night.

166

IX. Still a Mystery

Troops had immediately moved to the spot where the biplane had been shot down. The aircraft was broken in pieces. The pilot had been killed. By good luck, the gas tank hadn't caught fire. First efforts were to disengage the aviator's body caught in the metal debris. When the bust was free, the men went through the pockets to establish the identity of the victim. And there was immediate consternation. It was absolutely incomprehensible! However, the orders received from Paris had been carried out exactly. There could have been no mistake. It was the exact aircraft identified. The officers were thunderstruck. It was a French officer whose name was known not only in aviation but in the entire world who had just been shot down. An officer who had to his credit 20 aerial combats in which he was the victor. An officer whose name German pilots never pronounced without fear.

There was an error. But where did it come from? An order badly transmitted? An erroneous order? Where lay the responsibility? Whose fault? And also what sanctions would follow that act? Nevertheless, the D.C.A. post had followed instructions exactly. On officer still doubted the reality.

"Perhaps these are not the victim's identification papers," he hazarded. The cadaver having been taken out of the plane, the officer came forward. "Oh, but yes! It's really he!"

His picture, many times reproduced on the occasion of each of his glorious actions, had popularized the features of the hero of aviation.

Shortly afterward, when the officers were still hesitating, alarmed, a high powered automobile arrived. A passenger got out. He explained that he was on the road and that he had seen the airplane shot down. He hurried over to help, to bring aid if necessary. While he was talking, a second passenger had gotten out of the vehicle. He had examined the aircraft debris, while his companion continued talking. Then, seeing that their services were useless, the two men got back into their car. And they turned around. Before going back to their auto, they had exchanged the following words in a low voice:

"It's done. I've found it intact."

"Then let's get the hell out."

And one of the two men—the one who had examined the debris of the airplane—was carrying a little purse which he was hiding under his over-sized overcoat. The scene, from the arrival of the car until its departure hadn't lasted five minutes. The car with the green light crossed C.25's car just as she arrived at the scene of the accident.

"They found what they were looking for," Thérèse murmured. "Their mail! Obviously."

And she smiled, slightly, thinking that the mail contained only the false news and the erroneous information that she had deposited in the Rue Buffon "mail box." Thérèse showed her credentials to the officers who were near the fallen aircraft. One of them handed her the military record book and Thérèse couldn't hold back a cry of protest:

"That's impossible! Absolutely impossible!"

"That's what we said also," a lieutenant remarked. "However, there's no doubt. He was really the one brought down by the French battery." He stepped to one side, showing the cadaver lit by the moonlight. The famous Secret Service agent stood still, in a state of shock. Without waiting any longer, she got back in her car. She again took the road to Paris, always at full speed. She drove mechanically. Thoughts were rolling around in her mind, tumultuous, contradictory. She had been certain that the pilot who had been shot down was carrying mail destined to the enemy. And the proof of it was that the spies, learning about the crash of the aircraft, had rushed to save their mail. Therefore, there was no error possible. The plane that was shot down was clearly the one identified, the one she herself had pointed out. And she hadn't been mistaken. The only mystery was the identity of the pilot. Absolutely above suspicion, having a thousand times given proofs of his conception of "duty," how could that officer, that ace of aviation, pilot the airplane carrying messages destined for the enemy?

Also, why had the Commandant of the Bourget Military Airfield declared that seven planes would take off, when eight aircraft were prepared for flight?

"The key to the enigma is at the Bourget Military Airfield," murmured C.25.

As for Marcel, he remained mute. He too had recognized the dead man. And for him, no doubt was possible. It was a matter of a horrible mistake. The Boss's message had caused an ace of aviation to be shot down. Gloomy journey in the night. Suddenly, the famous woman agent slammed on the brakes. The car spun out of control on the oily road. A magnificent skew despite the mastery of the driver.

"What's the matter?" Marcel asked.

"It's fortunate I saw it in time. If I hadn't, given the speed we were driving, we wouldn't have escaped alive," Thérèse assured him.

The woman agent quickly jumped to the ground, followed by the Chemist. Across the entire width of the road had been placed a road barrier studded with spikes.

"I recognize that weapon," C.25 said. "It's the same system as was used at the wrought-iron fences at the Enghien villa. The spies were enough ahead of us. They stopped long enough to place this toy intended for us."

She rapidly pulled back the dangerous barrier which was supposed to produce a mortal accident by blowing out the tires. Then the car continued on its way toward the Bourget Military Airfield.

"This is the first attempt against us since we started following the car with the green light. It's probably the beginning of hostilities," Thérèse remarked.

"I'm even somewhat astonished at the ease with which everything went off this evening," Marcel murmured.

"Why? They were so confident they didn't notice anything. They only became suspicious when they intercepted the message announcing the crash of the plane carrying their mail! And they still don't know the most important thing: that their real mail is in our possession."

During these last thoughts, the car had picked up its maximum speed and raced in the night toward the Bourget Military Airfield, where Thérèse hoped to find the key to the enigma. Less than an hour later, with no incident, they arrived at the Airfield. She immediately went over her information. The Commandant of the airfield gave her the following explanation:

"The information I gave you," he said, "was perfectly correct. Only seven aircraft were supposed to take off tonight."

"Nevertheless the eighth one was prepared just like the others," Thérèse Arnaud maintained.

"Yes," the Commandant continued. "But the pilot, the glorious officer who died near Lamorlaye, was not stationed at this base. He was part of a squadron from the front lines. However, given the special nature of the missions he flew, he was often called to Paris. He received direct orders. And, very often, given the capital importance of the information he carried into occupied territory, he came himself to give additional verbal explanations. In those conditions, he enjoyed a favored position. He landed here and went to Paris. Then, following the orders given him, he left again shortly afterward."

"When did he arrive?" Thérèse asked.

"Yesterday morning."

The woman agent shook her head and then went on:

"And…he asked that his plane be ready to fly in the evening?"

The Commandant made a vague gesture.

"I don't know! As I told you, he was not under my direct orders. But, I'm going to find out."

Still worried, Thérèse was thinking while the Commandant of the field gave some orders and asked for some explanations from the Ministry of War and the Deuxième Bureau by telephone. The answer was stunning, deepening the mystery. The pilot wasn't supposed to take off in the evening. He had been given no mission either by the Ministry of War or via the Deuxième Bureau. What's more—an incomprehensible circumstance—he had asked his superiors for a 24 hour leave. Naturally, given the officer's brilliant service record, that permission had immediately been given.

Thérèse listened to these facts without saying a word. Her forehead was creased with a deep frown. Why, having obtained a leave, had the officer left? Why? And also, how had the necessary instructions for preparing the airplane and putting it in condition to fly in the evening, been given? New searches by the Commandant brought forth the following facts:

The pilot had telephoned to the warrant officer in charge of the positioning of the planes. He hadn't talked about permission. He had—as he did each time he was given a mission—demanded that his plane be ready to take off. The warrant officer had many times received similar instructions. He had, therefore, immediately done what was necessary without surprise, and without even referring the matter to the Commandant of the field.

"So," Thérèse said, "a fact I didn't know has turned up which changed the pilot's intentions. He first asks for leave. Then, after he gets it, he changes his mind and decides to rejoin his squadron at the front lines or to leave on a mission without any orders? Why?"

A requested confirmation brought the following details:

The aviator had obtained his leave during the early afternoon. The telephone call asking for the aircraft to be made ready was received at the Bourget field about 5:00 p.m. There were again long moments of silence during which Thérèse tried in vain to solve the enigma.

"During his stays at Bourget, did that officer take lodgings in the camp?" she asked.

"No," answered the commandant, "but I know he had rented a little room in the area."

"Could I have the exact address?"

The Commandant furnished the requested information. Thérèse went immediately to the pilot's domicile. The officer lodged in an unremarkable hotel room. There was no trace of disorder. The bed wasn't unmade. Thérèse found a letter on the table containing only these words, written in a feminine hand: "Will you be in Paris Wednesday? I would very much like to see you." And the signature, "Beth." An examination of the dates stamped on the letter indicated that the officer had received the letter that same morning. It seemed likely that it was because of that letter that he had asked for his leave. And that woman who wrote the letter? A trap to draw in the officer? Just a simple and ordinary rendezvous with a woman?

And that question without a believable answer still remained: why, after having received that letter and after having arranged to have free time, had that officer left that evening piloting the aircraft transporting the spies' mail?

Following her method, Thérèse deduced that an explanation could probably be furnished by means of the letter's signature. But who was she? There was no trace of an address, no indication of a name, only the signature "Beth," that Thérèse guessed was a diminutive of Elizabeth. Clearly insufficient information on which to base an investigation. There wasn't even any indication of the area where the famous Beth lived. The letter had been mailed at the Post Office on the Boulevard Haussmann…the perfect spot for people just passing through.

The officer's bedroom, used only for short stays between two flights, contained nothing. No personal objects. No papers. Only the necessary toilet articles and extra linen in a valise. Thérèse looked through this meager baggage, searching for some clue which would let her go back over the course of the events.

Nothing! Suddenly, she saw something satisfactory. Among the linen, she had just found a woman's photograph. The woman who signed the letter without a doubt. Thérèse continued her search. A smile. A smile which immediately changed into a pout of disappointment. She had just found a second woman's photograph. Now she looked angrily at the two photographs. Two different women! Which one was Beth? The agent's hope of a moment before faded away. Would the famous woman agent not be able to solve the mystery of the aviator's death?

The next morning, after absolutely fruitless searches during the night for some orientation on which to base the solution of the enigma, Thérèse Arnaud went back to the Bourget Military Airfield. In Paris she had found reassuring news about all of her auxiliaries. Everything had come off perfectly on the Rue Buffon right up to the bistro's closing time. In order not to give a warning, Malabar had delivered his prisoners to the authorities, one by one. The papers and the documents found in the mail box had been photographed and turned over to Captain Ladoux. Instructions for the next day were given: continue to keep the cellar window on the Rue Buffon working and, as the evening before, replace the mail skillfully.

But for Thérèse, the problem, far from being resolved, was becoming complicated. There were still three mysterious facts remaining. Where was the man who had disappeared just as the automobile with the green lights passed through near Walhubert Square and whose hat Thérèse still possessed? How could the presence of the pilot, the aviation ace, in the aircraft transporting the mail to the spies be explained? Finally, how would the mail found the next day in the mail box on the Rue Buffon be sent on its way? Thérèse was sure that mail would also leave, despite the death of the pilot. So? The Secret Service agent returned to the unfortunate flier's bedroom. Why? She could give no logical explanation for her act. Her instinct, her flair, drew her back to that bedroom that contained nothing, that she had explored, and where, it seemed, she had nothing more to discover. It was 8:00 a.m. C.25 went methodically back over her search. She again rifled through everything and the result was the same. The bedroom contained nothing, with the exception of the linen, and the two women's photographs. At 8:05 a.m. the bedroom door suddenly opened. The man who entered had a moment of surprise. Thérèse was stunned. That was one of those moments when reality verges on the unbelievable. The aviator whose cadaver she had seen the night before beside the fallen aircraft near Lamorlaye, was there...in front of her, his arm in a sling. So?

X. Toward the Truth

In a few moments, Thérèse Arnaud had laid out to the aviator the motives for her presence in his bedroom. She rapidly brought him up on the facts which had motivated her intervention. And the further C.25 explained to the pilot the story of the mail transported to the enemy, the more anger rose to the officer's face.

"That's unbelievable," he said. "Absolutely unbelievable. According to your story, you saw me last night in an aircraft that had been shot down. And you recognized my cadaver?"

"Yes," Thérèse confirmed. "Besides, I wasn't the only one. And all the officers present recognized you just as I did."

"And in addition to that, my plane was transporting mail destined for Germany?" he asked in a rage.

"Exactly! The proof of it is that as soon as the news of the accident was known, the spies left to reach the point where your aircraft was shot down to retrieve their precious letters—or rather a packet of false documents that they thought were valuable."

"And my plane had been readied to leave yesterday evening?" the pilot asked.

"You telephoned the Bourget Military Airport yesterday about 5:00 p.m." Thérèse informed him.

"Telephoned? Me? Yesterday? Not on your life!"

"Nevertheless, the telephone call was received by the petty officer responsible for moving the planes. He immediately did what was necessary," Thérèse clarified.

They both remained silent a long time. Thérèse, the first, began to formulate a fragile hypothesis. "Let's admit these things: someone telephoned in your place, a person perfectly familiar with your actions and gestures. Good. The spies knew that you would be in Paris all night. They took advantage of it to have your aircraft made ready and to use it. That's not impossible."

"What is impossible," the pilot objected, "is that people recognized my cadaver in the area around Lamorlaye while at the same hour I was in Paris…where certain diverse strange things took place which I will tell you about in a little bit. However, since it was I it seems who fell with the aircraft, it was therefore I who got into it yesterday evening. My usual mechanics, my fellow pilots, what do they say?"

The seven pilots left on a mission. They haven't returned," Thérèse said. "The men haven't yet been interrogated about that."

"And" the officer continued, "to get into the airfield, I went by the guard at the gate. Did anyone see me?"

Thérèse and the aviator got on the road to the airbase. Verification was easy and clear. The non-commissioned officers on guard at the gate confirmed having seen the aviator pass through. The men putting the aircraft ready for flight were also adamant. Thérèse immediately telegraphed orders to have the cadaver of the pilot shot down in the vicinity of Lamorlaye taken to the center of Bourget.

"Now," she said, "it's my turn to ask questions. You talked to me a while ago about strange events. They may put me on the way to the truth. Maybe, but I could say, probably. And first of all, what's wrong with your arm in the sling?"

"I'll tell you in a moment," said the aviator. "It's some story. Many little facts which I didn't pay attention to suddenly take on a very clear meaning. It's better to start at the beginning. The arm in the sling is the conclusion."

Thérèse and the aviator went to the mess hall and sat down. The pilot told Thérèse the following story:

"Some time ago I met a young woman, charming. And things took their course…what usually happens in such a case."

Thérèse held out to the officer the two photographs she had taken from his bedroom. And she asked: "Which one?"

The pilot smiled slightly and pointed to one of the two photographs.

"I'll have to ask you for them later," said Thérèse. "Now would you give me the name and address of that young woman. Then you can go on with your story."

The officer quickly did as C.25 asked, after which he continued:

"Myself, I didn't attach any great importance to that conquest, but I quickly noted that my…partner didn't have the same indifference. She looked for every opportunity to meet me. The most often when I came in from Bourget I found in my apartment a letter like the one you saw. Naturally, I didn't have any real motive not to respond to the invitation. Most often I returned to the Bourget Military Airfield only a few hours before taking my flight again."

"To this point," Thérèse said, "I don't see anything suspicious. "Nevertheless, how long did that affair last?"

"About two months," the officer answered without hesitation.

C.25 repeated: "Two months." And she seemed absorbed in thought. Then, suddenly:

"So? During those two months you didn't notice anything whatsoever of a nature to raise your suspicions?"

"No, to tell the truth, nothing, if it wasn't the way my girlfriend seemed to know my arrivals. I told her so. She told me it was a matter of intuition."

"Is that all?" C.25, quickly interested, asked.

The officer thought several seconds. "I also noticed that when I slept at my girlfriend's house I slept deeply. When I awoke I always felt groggy. That didn't draw my attention. I blamed that sleepiness on the duration of my flights and the excellent meals that awaited me at each of my arrivals."

"Yes…obviously," Thérèse thought, saying, "There, regularly, you woke up very late in the morning, just at the time of departure, or almost."

"Exactly!" agreed the officer.

"Then what are the strange occurrences?"

"They happened last night. I arrived at my girlfriend's house shortly after having left the Ministry of War. Nothing suspicious in the evening. It was only toward 11:15 p.m. that my girlfriend was called to the telephone. We had dined very late and we had hardly finished. She left me for several minutes to go to the telephone. When she returned, she wanted to go out. For me, I saw nothing inconvenient in agreeing with her wish. We went to a clandestine nightclub on the Rue Mansart."

"Yes, I know," Thérèse smiled.

"There," the officer continued, "an argument between my girlfriend and me broke out for absolutely no particular reason. We broke up and I left the establishment alone. I took a short walk in the Rue Mansart. There I was attacked by some brigands…"

"Can you give the precise details of that attack, above all of the description of the aggressor?"

"The details, yes," the officer said. "The description, no. Here's why: just as I was coming to the corner of the Rue Blanche and the Rue Mansart, I ran into a man who asked me for a light. I held out my cigarette, suspecting nothing. The man jumped me and before I had time to set up the least gesture of defense, I was attacked from behind. A fight followed. Fortunately, I'm rather strong, but I was dealing with a strong party. I finally managed to get away. I took to my heels. Two revolver bullets grazed me. A third hit me lightly in the arm. I went down the Rue Blanche at a gallop. I looked back once to see if I was still being followed. I saw a powerful automobile that came out of the Rue Chaptal. The men following me got into the automobile which rapidly disappeared."

"Didn't that vehicle have any unusual identification? Didn't you notice anything?" Thérèse asked.

"I was too far away to make out the details very well," the officer explained. "I don't know, for example, the make of the automobile or the number, but my attention was drawn to the light shining in the interior, a green light."

"Perfect!" said Thérèse. "I understand."

The officer quickly finished his report, which told C.25 nothing new.

Some minutes later, after having given some instructions by telephone, Thérèse Arnaud, accompanied by the aviator, went to see the cadaver of the pilot shot down in the Lamorlaye area. There, the officer could confirm the perfect resemblance, feature by feature, that the spy had to him.

Then Thérèse gave the following explanation:

"The enemies discovered this double that would fool even your friends. And they employed him in their service. Each time you were kept in Paris near your girlfriend, your plane was flown, piloted by your double."

"But, tonight's attack," the officer objected.

"Its object was to make you actually disappear, since your double was dead. The telephone call which alerted your girlfriend coincided perfectly with the time when the spies had just learned of the death of the aviator downed near Lamorlaye. They tried to draw you into a trap to make you disappear. A double vengeance. First of all to get rid of you. Next to avenge the death of one of their own. And also to let doubt overshadow me, Thérèse Arnaud, who gave the order to fire on your plane."

Everyone approved the reasoning of the woman spy. Other news came to confirm these explanations. Marcel, sent by C.25 to shadow the aviator's girl-friend, telephoned that he had arrived too late. Beth had left in a hurry, carrying little baggage. An automobile—which had to be the car with the green light—came to pick her up during the early morning hours.

"Obviously that woman's cover is blown. The spies preferred to have her flee, since the trap had been discovered…"

There was a silence. "That explains a number of things, but that's not all," Thérèse thought. "The job isn't finished." And she immediately left the Bourget Military Airfield to return to Paris.

XI. Thérèse Arnaud's Victory

Thérèse Arnaud had solved the problem of the aviator's death. And given the complexity of the problem, it had taken her very little time to find the correct solution. She was relieved. For a moment she had, despite everything, feared having had an innocent man killed. But now, satisfied with her victories over the spies, she continued her task. She went directly to the Rue Buffon. She was afraid of finding yet another enigma. Now the alarm had been given. The spies now knew she was on their trail, since they had met her way back from Lamorlaye. Therefore they had been able to take their precautions. And they had even perhaps already delivered some reprisals to C.25's auxiliaries.

Fortunately, nothing had been done. None of the famous detective's aides had disappeared. Malabar was still at the bistro on the Rue Buffon. And he had coolly dispatched 58 clients to the cellar, first of all, and then into the hands of the military authorities. Friquet and Languille were still acting as waiters at the counter, as the agents picking up letters from the mailbox on the Rue Buffon and watching the exterior of the said mailbox. As for Marcel, as soon as he had left during the night, he had gone back to photographing the massive number of documents which continued to arrive.

Thérèse thought the situation couldn't go on forever. The spies were rapidly going to realize—if it was not already an accomplished fact—that the "post office" on the Rue Buffon was in the hands of C.25 and her assistants. Therefore they would immediately modify their plans. Nothing more would be collected from the Rue Buffon and all C.25's agents would risk would be a fist fight with the German spies. As a matter of caution, they had to abandon the Rue Buffon, where they could learn nothing more. And in that case, there was no reason to wait any longer to pick up the two mysterious drivers of the car with the green light. Thérèse hoped to be able to pick up the trail again and find out how the mail would be sent toward Germany.

Shortly after the Boss arrived at the Rue Buffon, Languille, Friquet and Malabar found out that an important mission would be attempted that evening.

Each of them waited impatiently to learn the role the Boss was reserving for him in that affair. At 6 p.m., the following steps were taken: the two agents watching the mail box from the windows of the ground floor had been put out of commission and had joined Malabar's prisoners in the cellar. The business had been done without any noise. From the basement, Friquet had pierced two little openings in the first floor. Then, through these holes, he had poisoned the two agents with the help of a very powerful gas supplied by Marcel. Thereafter the letter box, interior and exterior, was in the power of C.25. She no longer ran any risk of a surprise from the German agents assigned to the surveillance of the mail box.

At 8 p.m., the pick-up time, the automobile with the green light came hurtling into the Rue Buffon. Malabar, installed behind his counter, saw it. Shortly thereafter, the man charged with picking up the letters arrived in front of the cellar window. As usual, he whistled rather loudly to signal and not be obliged to wait in front of the cellar window. A hand came out holding the box and the man bent down. But he didn't rise up again. The hand holding the box had imprisoned the hands delivering the box and drew them toward the cellar. A form immediately came through the window of the ground floor and fell on the man bent double. The man was reduced to silence and was powerless. He was immediately taken to Malabar, who also served him a fist-cocktail and took him down to the cellar. Two minutes later, Languille, carrying the false documents, wearing the man's overcoat and hat, left Malabar's bistro and went down the Rue Buffon whistling the same tune that the German spy had been whistling some moments before. Friquet came up behind him, passed, and went to alert Thérèse of the success of the first part of the plan of attack. Malabar also left his zinc counter and made his way toward the meeting place where Languille was supposed to meet the car with the green light. No incident. Languille continued on his way. The car with the green light arrived at the Rue Monge. It stopped. A hand came out the door. Languille advanced and held out the packet of mail, and then tried, as instructed, to grab the hand held out. But he didn't have time to complete the act. He was seized. The door opened and Languille was pulled into the green automobile, which drove away rapidly. Two shots were fired from either side of the vehicle, which passed near Friquet and Malabar. Behind the automobile with the green light was Thérèse Arnaud's automobile in hot pursuit. At the same time, Malabar and Friquet leapt on the running board of each side. The doors opened. Marcel, Thérèse, Malabar and Friquet were all in the automobile following the vehicle with the green light.

"They took Languille prisoner," Friquet announced to Thérèse.

"I know! I saw it!"

The two vehicles once again raced across Paris at full speed, then through La Porte de Pantin and onto the road toward Bourget. The night was dark, dirty, heavy with fog. The spies' car drove into the obscurity at full speed. Thérèse's car didn't lose any ground. Two high powered cars racing in the night. Thérèse tried in vain to pass. Impossible. The speed indicator oscillated between 110 and 120km/h. The distance between the two vehicles didn't diminish. Suddenly, there was nothing in front of C.25's car.

"They've turned to the left," Malabar groaned.

A turn of the steering wheel. A jolt. And the chase continued on the narrow and badly paved road. No more houses. It was the open countryside.

"They've turned to the right!" Marcel informed.

Another quarter hour of chase with sudden turns without the spies' vehicle being able to throw Thérèse's off the track. But in this game, the distance between the two automobiles didn't get any smaller. On the contrary, little by little the spies increased the distance.

"They're going to escape us once again! And they have Languille as a hostage," Friquet groaned.

Now, by a sudden new detour, the car with the green light had returned to the main road. At a dizzying speed, the trees formed a ghostly, black line.

Thérèse swore.

"The motor is beginning to give out. We can't hold on long at this speed, and they don't seem to be running out of steam," Thérèse said to Malabar.

"So?" the Colossus asked.

A new effort by the female agent to force the car to exceed its maximum speed.

"So we have to end it, and quickly. I'm pushing the car. It can keep going, painfully, for some minutes, but after that, finished…"

"Let's do it…"

A roar of the motor, Thérèse clenching the steering wheel, her foot on the accelerator down to the floorboard. Two doors opened from the interior.

Malabar on one side, Friquet on the other, revolvers in their hands. Two shots! Then two more! The two back tires of the automobile with the green light had just blown out. In response, a hail of bullets hit C.25's car. Thérèse bent over quickly to avoid the shots. The pursued car swerved. It stopped against a tree. The occupants jumped out. Two men in the spies' car had fled, discharging their revolvers without hitting anything. Thérèse's agents followed, creeping in the obscurity along the edge of the road. The revolvers barked without stopping.

"There's only one of them left," Malabar whispered.

In fact there was more than one shadow near the vehicle. But the other silhouette came back, pushing in front of him Languille, who thus found himself between the two camps. For C.25's agents to fire on the spies meant the risk of hitting their comrade. The revolvers on C.25's side were silent. The two Germans profited by their advantage. They continued to water their opponents with their shots. But they were shooting a little at random. There was no longer any shadow visible. Thérèse, Friquet, Marcel, and Malabar had disappeared into the shadows. The occupants of the car with the green light were leaning behind their vehicle to avoid being surprised. Then they stopped wasting their ammunition. They searched the shadows. One of them, using the car's headlights, directed the lights along the edge of the road, trying to find the French agents.

Languille was always some feet in front of the two spies, handcuffed, immobilized, no possibility to budge. In addition, the least movement would be death for him. Suddenly, the automobile with the green light was put in reverse. The two spies leaning against the back of the car didn't have time to watch out, and they rolled under their vehicle. Malabar's voice sounded from the other side of the spies:

"Quick!"

Friquet, Thérèse, and Marcel jumped out from their hiding places. Malabar, who in the shadows had managed to crawl past the car, had then used his Herculean strength, and pushed it back on the enemies. The car was surrounded; Languille was released from his bonds. And the two spies were prisoners under their own car. Threatened by revolvers, they come out and were immediately tied up.

Not a word came out of the mouths of the two captured men. They seemed not to hear the questions Thérèse asked them.

"They're not very talkative, these clients," Friquet stated.

"Let's not insist," Thérèse decided. "Let's get on the road!"

Malabar, who had just frisked the prisoners showed Thérèse the billfold of one of the men. Thérèse looked at it quickly. She couldn't help being surprised. The headlights of the automobile shining on the face of one of the prisoners lit up a haughty face full of arrogance.

"Yes! It's I," he said proudly.

Thérèse's victory was complete. One of the occupants of the car with the green light was a German Prince (certain members of the German nobility solicited, in fact, the honor of being part of the Nachrichten Bureau services.) Thérèse's car, damaged by the crash, was abandoned on the roadside. Malabar hastily put the spies' car back in shape by switching out the two damaged tires. Thérèse and her four agents got in, surrounding the two prisoners. The famous green light still lit up the interior of the comfortable vehicle. Malabar was at the wheel. And that was the return to Paris.

During the trip, the two prisoners remained mute. However, Thérèse noticed that, since they had entered the car, a mocking smile played over their faces from time to time. Nevertheless, the men hadn't the least possibility of making the smallest movement. They couldn't budge. On the other hand, reduced to impotence, two against five, they could hardly hope to flee. As for help from the outside from a friendly automobile, the result seemed very problematic. Thérèse was still observing her prisoners. More and more satisfaction could be seen under their self-willed impassive mask. Thérèse noted a look the two men exchanged.

"Stop immediately, Malabar! Everybody jump out!" Thérèse suddenly shouted.

The car, which was arriving at the outskirts of Paris, stopped. Thérèse's agents jumped out, dragging the prisoners.

"Quickly, let's get far away," Thérèse ordered sharply.

The little group hurried away and had scarcely covered 50 meters when a terrible explosion detonated, followed by a high, mounting flame, while the automobile debris fell like rain around the spot where Malabar had stopped.

"Yes," Thérèse explained. "That's why they were so glad to see us take their car. One of the two activated a time bomb with his feet. They would sacrifice their lives…but we have stopped them."

A half hour later, two taxis let out their passengers and put them in the hands of the military authorities. The identity of one of the prisoners caused great surprise. In a haughty tone, the man demanded to be set free from a part of his bonds before answering the interrogation. He was given satisfaction. But before having answered the first question asked him, the man, taking advantage of the relative freedom of movement given him, bit into the gem setting of his ring. He said simply:

"People like me aren't shot." Before anyone was able to intervene, he died, poisoned by a quick-acting product contained in the jewel.

"Such a quantity of prisoners of all classes, and such an abundance of the most interesting documents, what a harvest!" marveled Captain Ladoux while Thérèse Arnaud smoked a cigarette in his office. "You've explained everything: the astonishing story of the aviation officer and his double, the German spy. You've arrested the two occupants of the car with the green light. But have you penetrated the mystery of the man who disappeared at the Walhubert Square, just as the car with the green light passed by?"

"Yes," Thérèse answered. "The man was assassinated."

"One more crime attributable to the spies," said Captain Ladoux.

"Oh! If they weren't committing others," Thérèse explained, "the harm wouldn't be very great. The victim was an agent of the German espionage service. I suppose his superiors had doubts about him. So an accident was staged. The proof of that is in the way the cadaver disappeared, carried away by the murderers."

"Perfect," said Captain Ladoux, "but how did you establish that the victim was an agent in the service of German espionage?"

"I found his hat," Thérèse explained. "That was enough for me. Hat linings sometimes contain useful clues, a little obscure. But thanks to Marcel, I was able to decipher them. And I had already made up my mind when I showed the hat to the Chief of Police.

Just then a dispatch was brought to Captain Ladoux, who sent it immediately to be deciphered.

"Wait a minute," he said to Thérèse, who was getting ready to leave. "I won't be very long. And considering the source of this telegram, I wouldn't be surprised if it weren't something to interest you."

Five minutes later, Captain Ladoux explained to Thérèse: "This message announces the arrest of Herta Grunberg, a notorious spy who's been living in Paris for several months. She was known under the name Elizabeth Verville..."

"The aviator's girlfriend," exclaimed Thérèse.

"Exactly! She was arrested just as she attempted to pass into Switzerland, crossing the border in the vicinity of Gex..."

"Gex again!" Thérèse smiled, concluding, "one more prisoner."

"Yes, and now everything has been explained," finished Captain Ladoux.

"No, not yet," Thérèse Arnaud corrected.

THÉRÈSE ARNAUD VS MATA HARI

I. In the Monte Carlo Gardens

Coming down from a clear and pure sky the reflections of the Moon turn the multi-level terraces of Monte Carlo silver. A fairy décor. A dream night in which everything seems unreal or unearthly. Behind the scaly trunk of a huge palm tree, a light suddenly makes a wound in the fluid shadows. A red point begins to spread slowly at the extreme end of a big, smelly cigar. He walks patiently up and down. He seems to be waiting for something…or for someone. Faster, a shadow left the casino through the door reserved for entertainers and goes in the direction of the gardens. Now the light of a cigar faces the light from a cigarette. The two men exchange handshakes.

"You're going back to Nice tonight, de Bergh?"

The Baron de Bergh hesitated scarcely a second. Then in a voice which, nevertheless, betrayed a slight hesitation or a vague secret, he answered.

"Exactly, Saracco."

"Good. Then here it is."

Quickly, after having made sure there was no indiscreet witness in the vicinity, Saracco searched in the inside pocket of his jacket. He took out a large portfolio. He opened it. He took out a large envelope on which the brown stains of five wax seals could clearly be seen. He held out the envelope to Baron de Bergh and repeated, but in a different tone, almost like that of a superior giving an order.

"It's clearly understood, isn't it! You will return to Nice immediately. No stupidity."

The Baron de Bergh nodded in agreement while he also made the envelope disappear in his turn into the inside pocket of his jacket.

"Goodbye," Saracco said.

Two hands were again extended. Saracco had already begun to walk away. He came back two steps and slipped in another recommendation:

"Be careful, alright? It's important."

Another look around to be sure no one had been able to overhear the conversation. The two men separated. Same rapid steps. Saracco goes back toward the casino while, like someone taking a stroll, calmly finishing his cigar, Baron de Bergh continues his slow walk. But Baron de Bergh's walk then became more and more uncertain. A more and more clear hesitation appeared. Suddenly, probably following an abrupt decision, the Baron walked obliquely toward the casino. He was going to enter, but he stopped short and remained motionless for a few seconds. Then, unwillingly, he turned around, probably preoccupied with

181

the order received, or thinking about the pleasant night that he could finish in that atmosphere of luxury. Or did the attraction of the gambling (that gambling where, in a single evening some people win or lose a fortune) glisten with seductive illusions in the Baron's eyes? But the final, irrevocable decision had been taken. With a firm step, after having turned around to be sure no one had witnessed his hesitation and the start of his disobedience, the Baron, like a soldier who faithfully carries out a superior's orders, no matter what it costs him, left the casino. He went resolutely toward the city, toward the train station.

Now the Baron de Bergh was walking rapidly into deserted and asleep Monte Carlo. Although he showed no apparent worry, he was careful to turn around rather frequently in order to throw off anyone curious who might have followed him. But the Baron's caution turned up no suspicious presence. Nothing! Nothing but the deserted avenues bordered with palm trees. Suddenly, after just having turned around once again, the Baron, reassured, was going to continue walking when a shadow suddenly detached itself from the trunk of a tree. It came to the Baron's side. Before he had time to make a move to defend himself, to jump backward, he was immobilized. A shot rang out. The Baron's body fell.

The shadow leaned over the ground. Searching the interior jacket pocket, it removed the envelopes with seals. Then it was careful to place an exactly similar envelope in the pocket. Then the shadow kneeled down over the Baron's corpse. It closed the still warm fingers of the right hand on the trigger of the revolver used to murder the unfortunate man. It murmured: "A bullet to the right temple. The revolver in the right hand. Suicide! That's clear. And the Baron's financial situation will confirm that hypothesis." Then the shadow disappeared in the night.

II. Saracco's Emotions and Anger

The Police Commissioner was calmly leafing through a dossier. An agent entered, saying a gentleman wished to speak to him. The Commissioner stifled a yawn and made a bored gesture. The policeman made the following clarification:

"Sir, it's about the suicide of Baron de Bergh."

The Commissioner shrugged and replied, "The Baron committed suicide following gambling loses. The investigation is over. The Ambassador from Holland, who was responsible for the victim, has been told. The affair has been closed."

"Nevertheless, this gentleman has strongly insisted on being heard," the policeman pointed out.

The Commissioner resigned himself.

"All right! Have him come in," he sighed, closing his file.

The visitor entered. Tall, big shoulders, severely but elegantly dressed. He appeared very moved.

"You've asked to speak to me? I'm listening, sir," the Commissioner said, in a not very engaging tone. The man took out his portfolio, showing diverse pieces of identification, which the Commissioner, bored, didn't even look at.

"Sir, I am Saracco."

The Commissioner's attitude changed immediately. And it was with a very friendly voice that he hurried to say:

"The Director of the Ballet of Monte Carlo Theater. Oh! Pardon me. I was…"

Saracco made a wide gesture. Then, still somewhat moved, a little preoccupied:

"It's a matter of that unfortunate Baron de Bergh."

"Yes! Still young! Too bad! Alas! Here it happens every day, so commonplace…"

"I know, I know, Sir, but that's not the question here."

"So?"

With some slight embarrassment, while watching the effect of his words, Saracco slowly continued:

"I have a…a favor…a service to ask of you, Commissioner." And gaining confidence, he became bolder as he went along:

"It's a very little thing, very simple, but perhaps from the administrative point of view it's not very regular…"

"Oh, Mr. Saracco, for you, please believe me, if it's in my poor power to help you, I'll gladly do so."

Saracco breathed a discreet sigh of joy.

"I thank you, Commissioner. Here's the problem. Just yesterday evening, a few moments before the unhappy Baron put his fatal determination into execution, I had a few moments conversation with him. I had had dealings with him many times. I had known him a long time. He was going back to Holland. Given the circumstances, I gave him a letter that he must get to the person it was addressed to as soon as he arrived at The Hague."

The Commissioner looked at Saracco with curiosity.

"That letter was strictly personal…and….rather intimate. As a director of a ballet company you will understand, you aren't any the less a man and can hold a certain admiration, completely artistic, I maintain, for a woman. So…"

"So?"

"Then I would like, if possible—and I would be particularly grateful to you—if that letter were not placed in the file, so as not to fall into strange hands. It's a matter of things that concern only the person to whom it was sent. It would seem painful to me and absolutely useless, not to say injurious, if this letter were surrendered to the malicious public. There are so many people, avid of scandals! The least indiscretion can have dreadful consequences when it's a matter of a woman's honor and reputation."

"Yes…yes…obviously," the Commissioner agreed.

"Besides," Saracco finished, "that letter no longer has a purpose as the person it was sent to, arrived this morning in Monte Carlo."

Thinking a short moment, the Commissioner decided.

"The reports on this business haven't yet been scheduled. Nor have the objects and various papers found on the body of Baron de Bergh been inventoried."

"But...that letter?" worried, Saracco quickly asked.

"That letter," the Commissioner smiled amiably, "as a personal friend of yours, I'm going to be able to give it back to you."

"I thank you a thousand times, Commissioner, because..."

The Commissioner cut off Saracco's flow of words. To show his importance, he made it clear:

"It's obviously completely irregular from an administrative point of view. But I will take personal responsibility for that."

Then to justify his reputation as a man of the world, he smiled: "Since it's for the honor and reputation of a pretty woman."

Saracco rapidly furnished the information which allowed the retrieval of the letter.

"It's a large mauve envelope closed with five wax seals, sent to the following address: Madame Mata Hari, 16 Nieuwe Uitleg, The Hague."

Saracco left the Commissioner of Police. Crossing the threshold, he let out a new sigh of relief deeper than the first. Then he returned to the theater.

In his office he dealt with several small current tasks. He answered a few telephone calls. He was clearly in an excellent mood. His features were relaxed. His lips murmured a happy little tune. And he didn't seem at all saddened by the sudden loss of the excellent Baron de Bergh. A smile played over his clean-shaven face. A few moments of reflection. Saracco took the letter destined for Mata Hari out of his portfolio. He examined it. While pursuing his thoughts he turned it over in his hands. He opened a secret drawer in the desk. He threw in the envelope. Just as he was throwing the envelope in, he thought to himself:

"I can effectively complete the dossier before sending it off."

For several minutes after having locked his office door, Saracco wrote slowly, using a code to draft his text. He dried his oily ink. He tore off the leaf of blotting pad. He burned it in his ash tray, taking care to spread out the cinders. He took out an envelope from the stationery rack. But he didn't write any address. To enclose the pages confided the evening before to Baron de Bergh, Saracco unsealed the envelope the Commissioner had kindly returned. He removed several folded sheets of paper. He unfolded them. He put the page he had just finished on top. He attached a seal. His look was one of fright.

"Oh! Oh!"

Saracco now leaned over the sheets of paper. He turned the pages rapidly. He read them. His expression became livid. His hands began to tremble. His mouth fell open. No sound came out, only unintelligible groans. "Oh! Oh!"

Anger strangled Saracco. He wiped his forehead, pearled with drops of sweat. Minutes went by. Saracco stayed there, in front of the dossier, his head buried in his hands. In a brusque gesture he threw the entire dossier into the secret drawer, that, pushed violently, slammed shut. He took the telephone off the hook. He shook the apparatus with feverish impatience.

"Hello…Hello…Miss, give me…give me…"

Taking stock, Saracco hung up the telephone, and groaned: "Ah! The villains!"

Then, striding across the room, he tried to vent his anger on his office carpet. And a whole flood of insulting words finally came out of his throat. Saracco's finger pushed the bell. He went to his office door. Then he waited for the valet to come.

"What do you want?" he asked him roughly as soon as the servant entered.

"But you rang and…"

"Rang? Me? No! Leave me the hell alone!"

Astonished, the servant looked at the ballet director without understanding.

"Nothing, I tell you! Nothing! Leave me the hell alone."

When the servant had left, Saracco went back into his office. He turned over the contents of a drawer to find a telegraph form to fill out. He began writing. He stopped, tearing up the pages he had just written.

"No! No!" and he burned the telegraph form.

Saracco again took up his excited pacing. He circled his office like a caged beast, his face congested, his eyes rolling in his head.

"It's urgent to get the warning out! Ah! The swine! The swine!" he raged on. "And who? Who could be suspected? I put the papers in the envelope *myself*. I gave them to de Bergh. The letter didn't leave the inside pocket of my jacket from the moment I sealed it until the instant I confided it to de Bergh. The envelope was sealed when the Commissioner gave it back to me. The writing on the envelope was my writing. The seals were the same. And, even so, the papers were replaced. Yes…replaced…that's worse than stolen. Stolen, that's still understandable…but…replaced by *false documents*…"

The ballet director again locked his office. He opened a secret door that led to an elevator. A quarter of an hour later, back at his desk, his anger had given way to a kind of gloomy depression. His head in his hands, the ballet director was thinking, thinking. From time to time some sentences showed the direction of his thoughts.

"The documents stolen. De Bergh…committed suicide…The letter closed with seals…Who? Who? Who had time to take the envelope, replace it with another one, in the short time after de Bergh's suicide and the moment his cadaver was discovered? I left the Baron at 11:30 p.m. It wasn't yet 1:00 a.m.

when they found his body. It's impossible in an hour and a half to put together that collection of false documents. Then, was de Bergh murdered? Was de Bergh a traitor who could have given the real documents to a third person? And worse still, treason that's here in my business, in my life, surrounding me. It's not only the incomprehensible story of that letter, but also, today, my secret wireless service which is shut down. So, who? who?"

Still some moments of deep reflection. Saracco fought against the incomprehensible. He set up hypotheses; he looked for some way, some clue. He searched through his memory to find some small fact that would furnish a point of departure. He found nothing. Absolutely nothing. He observed nothing, picked up on nothing. Nevertheless, the facts were there. The documents given to the Baron had been stolen and had passed into other hands. *Into whose?* And who had prevented the ballet director from giving the alarm by the only method that couldn't be traced? *Who?*

"I'll find the guilty party," he thought, "and then you'll see what Saracco's vengeance is like, because I will get revenge."

III. A Trip with a Friend

An ordinary rental vehicle rolled along the road from Corniche to Beaulieu. Blue atmosphere, blue air. Mediterranean blue, a symphony of all the azure colors. The palm trees stretched out their scaly trunks to the Sun and their rheumatic branches seemed like tired arms. In the distance, in the moving horizon, the sky and the sea mingled all the aquarelle colors. As a good guide, the driver turned toward the travelers, to point out with a wide gesture the magnificent panorama unfolding. Hills ran along the sea and hid the horizon, over there on the Italian cost. The two travelers made a vague gesture of silent agreement.

"No way to say two words with this witness." They had the car stop. Then they walked toward the sea.

Friquet looked at the Boss with astonishment. Since her arrival on the Côte d'Azur, Thérèse Arnaud was no longer the same. She was no longer recognizable. She sometimes manifested incomprehensible nervousness, which puzzled those who had always known her to be so perfectly calm, so in control of herself in the time of greatest dangers. Here, on the contrary, she became irritable very easily, and for facts that seemed without the least importance. She seemed no longer to think of anything…if not of a man.

"Beautiful country," the Paris street kid said mechanically, but he couldn't explain to himself why the Boss had taken him to a cove in the area of Beaulieu. Almost happily, Thérèse answered:

"Yes a beautiful country. So much the better if you like it. You're going to have leisure to admire it just as you please. You'll be alone here, free. And you'll be able to lead a pleasant life."

"Alone? But you…?"

"Me," C.25 answered calmly, "I'm leaving!"

"Ah!" There were a few short moments and Friquet's joking personality soon reappeared.

"Tell the friends in Paris hello for me…That old dirty and slimy winter Paris, probably waiting for you with some very dark and very complicated new case for which Captain Ladoux is recalling your brilliance."

"No, Friquet, I'm going to take a pleasure trip."

"A trip for pleasure!" Friquet repeated, dumbfounded. "You scared me. I thought you were going to say a honeymoon trip."

A little irritated by Thérèse Arnaud's laugh that had greeted that remark, Friquet responded,

"Even so, Boss, I'm not as completely stupid as I appear. And I can see clearly."

"I would be delighted to know, my dear Friquet, what you saw! An occasion to teach should never be lost," C.25 joked.

"I've seen, and that's enough," Friquet affirmed sharply.

"Ah! What did you see?"

"That's easy. Among the people you've given the mission to watch, there's one whose actions and movements especially interest you. When I talk to you about others who seem, however, more interesting and sometimes suspicious, you invariably answer me: 'That has no importance. What's Van Vith doing?' News is received that there's a German submarine in the Mediterranean: 'That's not important. What's Van Vith doing?' Your only worry is what Van Vith is doing. Besides, he's not doing anything. You look for every opportunity to be with him, to meet him. You dine at a table neighboring his. And when you are not with him, you're looking for only one thing: to know what he's doing! And I've seen you either happy or sad, in a joyous or bad mood according to whether you've met him or not! You can't do without him."

With a big, carefree, young laugh, Thérèse Arnaud, corrected him.

"Say rather that now it's he who can no longer do without me. That would be a great deal more exact."

"Pardon, Boss, I'm not asking you to confide in me."

"Just because of that, I'm going to. The time has come for me to explain certain things to you, certain facts, certain of my actions which might have seemed strange and incomprehensible to you. Don't worry. I won't tell you everything."

"Thanks anyway for trusting me!"

"I'll tell you enough," Thérèse Arnaud continued without worrying about the ironic interruption, "to permit you to employ your time here usefully."

During some silent paces, Friquet waited impatiently for C.25's explanations. She suddenly asked:

"Friquet, were you really stupid enough to believe I was in love with Van Vith?"

"The man's good looking!" was the only statement Friquet made.

"Yes," Thérèse smiled. "I grant you that. He eats heartily and, most of all, he takes his drinks straight. But I'm not the least in love."

"Oh! And yet…"

"Yes, and I acted exactly as if I were, proof that my strategy was able to deceive someone who knew me well, you. With Van Vith I acted as if I were attracted to him with a very tender sympathy. And I was right, because after a very cold beginning where he seemed not to notice me, or not to be interested in me, the Ambassador from Holland to Nice became civilized. He had always been very courteous and correct. But I wanted something more."

"And when you want something, Boss…"

"No, not always, Friquet, unfortunately! Not always! I would have wanted Van Vith to fall in love with me. Really in love. And I partly failed, I admit."

"Nevertheless…"

"Nevertheless, I'm leaving tomorrow with him."

"Well, in that case, Boss, you've won."

Thérèse Arnaud laughed again. Then she spoke again after several seconds.

"No, I haven't won. Not yet! It's just that in the course of our conversations—by a chance that exists when you bring it about—we found quite a few mutual ideas! We often saw life from the same point of view. I warn you that Van Vith's point of view isn't very sharp, but rather obtuse instead. Our reading brought us together. The man got used to my being near him, to that presence I worked at slowly for two weeks to impose on him, despite him, instant by instant. A sort of camaraderie was created between us. He doesn't love me. No! And besides, he was frank enough to admit it to me. I appeared very saddened. Finally, he doesn't love me, not yet. But he has to spend a rather long period in Holland. The thought of finding himself alone seemed insupportable to him. He suggested that I leave with him."

"And you accepted with joy," suddenly concluded Friquet, who finally understood. "All the patient comedy that you played with him had only that as its purpose."

"This time I think you've guessed it," Thérèse agreed.

"Boss, you've taken away my last illusions," Friquet joked. "How can I now believe in women's sincerity?"

"There's never an end to illusions, Friquet. A bottomless sack holds them, a sack with a double bottom! And, besides, leave sincerity alone. The Service comes first."

"I'm at your service!"

"Now you're going to find that men's sincerity is not any better than that of women. During my absence, you're going to stay on the Riviera, until you receive new orders. And you won't be bored. Mata Hari arrived in Monte Carlo this morning. Your mission: insinuate yourself into her company."

"Understood, Boss!"

"No, Friquet. Pay attention! It's not a question of getting near her as a servant, but of getting asked in. To become a friend, if possible. I don't say a confidant, that would be asking too much! Inspire confidence in her and try to find out…"

"To find out what, Boss?"

"What I'm looking for, Friquet."

"And what are you looking for, exactly, Boss?"

"If I knew, I'd look for it myself."

Friquet thought a few moments. "I've got it. I saw Ruy Blas a while ago. You order me to make that woman love me."

"Yes, if it's necessary."

"Must he also become…"

"If it's necessary. That's not important," C.25 cut him off.

"After all," Friquet concluded, "that might not perhaps be disagreeable."

"Agreeable or not…"

"It must be done…" Friquet finished the sentence. "I understand, Boss. I'll do my best."

Again a few more steps in the cove. Then, returning slowly to the automobile awaiting them, Thérèse continued. "At the same time, Friquet, you'll keep an eye on Saracco. That will be easy. I have an idea that he'll meet Mata Hari often, and a great deal more often than believed."

"All right!"

"That's all I have to tell you. You'll get my instructions as they're needed. You'll follow them scrupulously, without trying to understand. Before my departure tomorrow, I'll give you all the necessary information to send me a report on your mission. So, everything is going well."

"Everything is going well!" Friquet confirmed. However, before reaching the road, the Paris urchin couldn't help asking: "All the same, Boss, the report about the German submarine in the Mediterranean, that's a case of the type which would seem to be of interest to you."

"Just so. It interests me a great deal."

"Yes?" Friquet said, astonished. "It interests you and just when you would be able to take care on the spot, you fly away to Holland."

"Yes, Friquet, exactly!"

"Ah!"

Friquet knew C.25 well enough to know that it was useless to insist. He wouldn't learn anything more.

IV. The Fisherman's Cabin

Thérèse had been away from the Riviera in the company of the Ambassador from Holland to Nice for a week. The last news Friquet had received had given him some unexpected information. They told him that the Boss and Van

Vith had embarked at Vigo on the steamship *Hollandia,* which served the British Islands.

The mysterious disappearance of Mata Hari one night prevented C.25's auxiliary from beginning his work. So, despite himself, he was almost reduced to inactivity. An inactivity, however, that he, to distract himself, used to shadow Saracco the Director of the Monte Carlo ballet. If you didn't let yourself get dazzled by appearances, certain particularities of Saracco's life were not without a seeming strangeness. The most abnormal fact in Friquet's opinion, was Saracco's trips to sea. The trips always took place at the old Monte Carlo port. Saracco always took the same minute precautions to disguise himself. Leaving the Theater from the stage entrance, he never wound up at the old port without making many detours to confuse anyone trailing him. He even went so far as to enter a small villa with two entrances and exits so as to confuse eventual curio-seekers. And while by all appearances the ballet director was resting, he had skipped out.

For some evenings, Friquet had felt a passion growing in him. He had suddenly discovered a desire to fish. He had also rented a motor boat. And regularly, each evening, Friquet left Nice at about 10:00 p.m. His boat took to the open sea, then obliquely turned in the direction of the Italian coast. For anyone curious, these trips must have seemed bizarre, just for the simple reason that Friquet was fishing alone (with what?) for part of the night. And when he returned no one could find the least trace of fish in the boat.

A clear night, the sky paved with stars. A Mediterranean rocking dreamily. And over there the lights of Monte Carlo. Friquet's boat rocked along without a destination, it seemed. Then, suddenly, after the passage of a second boat leaving the Monte Carlo port, Friquet stopped lying at anchor. He executed a sharp right turn in the direction of Italy. Suddenly the motor boat that Friquet was shadowing, veered around.

"Damn! I've got myself pinched! Clumsy!" Friquet groaned, stopping.

Saracco's boat turned in circles several times, as if he had reached a predetermined spot and was waiting.

"That's romantic! Saracco has a rendezvous in the middle of the sea," murmured C.25's auxiliary.

The ballet director, still watched by Friquet, continued to circle around. Suddenly, silhouetted by the Moon, a boat of fishermen in a sailboat with triangular sails, hoisted a red light three times to the top of the mast. A similar signal answered from Saracco's boat. The two boats approached one another. Then, after remaining some moments side by side, they went their separate ways. The sailboat went in the direction of Monte Carlo. Saracco continued to navigate toward Italy. And Friquet continued to shadow without tiring. He saw in the distance the lights of Ventimiglia, those of Bordighera and of San Remo. A little later, the ballet director rapidly approached the coast, where the very indented coast offered an uninterrupted line of coves, small beaches, capes, and bays.

190

"He's going to land. The areas around the coast are too dangerous and require extensive knowledge."

A quarter of an hour later, after having maneuvered with extreme care in order not to raise the alarm and in order, nevertheless, not to lose Saracco's trail, Friquet, in his turn, landed in a rocky cove. He had pulled his boat up on a little beach of sand. Then diving into the water, he swam around a little cape where he had seen Saracco's boat enter a short time before. Two silhouettes that the Moon had clearly outlined.

"They're not far away! They've disappeared into those rocks. And what's more, their boat has remained on that little beach," Friquet surmised.

C.25's auxiliary explored the near horizon in vain. However, the inlet Saracco had chosen measured about 30 meters. It was closed by two promontories of rock both toward San Remo and as well as toward Ospedaletti. An abrupt wall of rock stood toward the interior of the country. Well hidden behind a pile of rocks, Friquet saw a fisherman's cabin. And he joked: "I've fallen into the middle of a novel. They claim that romance is dying. Saracco is madly in love with a beautiful Italian girl that he meets by the sea outside Ventimiglia. And this is a poetic fisherman's cabin that discreetly hides the idyll." Friquet continued to examine the site.

"Even so," he continued, "I'm curious to meet the ballet director's conquest. They'll certainly have to leave. Their boat is on the beach! They won't escape. I have only to wait."

Friquet's patience was put to a hard test. At the end of three hours, hidden, set up behind a rock from which to watch the door of the cabin and the cove where the boat was waiting, but which painfully bruised his back, he groaned: "The lovers have gone to sleep." No event at daybreak. The cove was deserted. Nothing was moving in the cabin. Saracco's boat was there. And Friquet still kept his gloomy watch. The Sun began to heat up the waves. Friquet still waited. Two hours later he made a decision.

"Even so, I'm not going to give up and go back empty-handed. I've waited five hours. That won't be for nothing. After all, I'm risking very little. I'm just a person taking a walk. I see a cabin. I knock on the door in passing. One idea like another. And if they get angry, I'll apologize."

In a few steps, Friquet was in front of the cabin. He knocked. No one answered. He tried again. Same silence.

"Since no one's inviting me to leave, let's go in!"

The door wasn't even locked. It opened immediately without the slightest difficulty. And the cabin was empty!

"Damn! Damn!" Friquet raged. "For a rabbit, this is a superb rabbit. I've waited five hours to get this result! Nevertheless, I'm sure they disappeared here. They couldn't have reached the top of the cliff while I was swimming around the cape. It's physically impossible. I arrived at the cabin fewer than five minutes after they disappeared. In addition, the wall of the rocks is sheer. There's no other path, nothing! So?"

The secret agent plunged into silent reflections.

"There's no shilly-shallying, since I myself saw them disappear here at the site of this cabin. The cove has no way out. The boat is still there. And they aren't there any longer! A director of a ballet company is not a magician. He can't make his companion disappear and volatize himself next."

Friquet began a methodical inspection of the cabin, an operation which he conducted with scrupulous meticulousness. It was, after all, very simple: no furniture; just the walls, the flooring, the roof, the coal heater, the ground, straw on the hard earth.

"Not very luxurious, my bachelor! It lacks modern comfort. They aren't hidden in the wardrobes; there aren't any! Therefore the only solution: the thick wool of the oriental rabbit must hold some surprise for us."

Friquet was flat on his stomach. He spread aside the straw methodically. After a few minutes of this work, he let out an explanation of surprise and satisfaction.

"Here's what I was searching for!" Friquet had just discovered, hidden under the dirt, a metallic plate with a ring.

"There, I was just in the anti-chamber! No use waiting for a servant to announce me! Let's go in! But let's keep our eyes open."

Before proceeding any further, Friquet verified in a few seconds that he had on him a wide choice of diverse instruments.

"I have all my material on me in case of a surprise. Then let's get started."

The trap door lifted with no difficulty, opening onto a dark, narrow stairway.

"Everything is going too well!" C.25's assistant joked. "I'm brave and I don't like work that's ready-made. It's ease that tires me."

He descended slowly, cautiously, counting the steps. "No elevator!" he grumbled.

The stairs ended in a grotto.

"It has light. It even has air. But it's scarcely inhabited," Friquet continued.

In fact, an opening in the middle of the wall revealed a whole panorama of the Mediterranean. The grotto opened naturally very deeply into the sea. But the passage was too narrow for Saracco's boat to be able to approach it directly.

"And there's still no one in that cabin where, nevertheless, a while ago two silhouettes disappeared. This continues to be strange."

In a corner of the grotto, Friquet noticed a pile of diverse materials.

"Oh! There's something that complicates the situation!" Friquet murmured. "Those aren't provisions for a snack piled up there. Barrels, kegs, of all sizes. A complete supply of oil and gas. Yes, all that's needed to re-provision a submarine. "And continuing his search, Friquet added: "Somebody has even been here not long ago. There are still fresh traces."

Friquet continued his examination. He went to the edge of the grotto. He entered the water, swam to the end of the cavern. They he came calmly back. Looking around, he sized up the grotto's contents.

"Yes, they can restock the depot, not by the sea, but by the cabin. Just any kind of vessel that comes as far as the beach. It's easy."

He climbed the stairs again. He verified the possibilities of the operations. He again went over some details that made his hypothesis more and more likely. Then, satisfied, he murmured:

"Good! Everything's perfect!" and he went down again into the grotto. Like a conscientious worker who has time to take great pains with his work because he's not in a hurry and because he's not at all afraid of being disturbed, Friquet summed up the effects of his preparation.

"Me, I'm not the director of a ballet," he mocked, "but nevertheless everything will dance! As for a beautiful fireworks show, this will be one! And he calmly finished adjusting the Bickford cord to the stick of dynamite. He took another few moments to check his finishing touches. Then, whistling, he stood up. Taking a cigarette out of its case, he pressed his cigarette lighter. He inhaled a whiff of smoke. Then he set fire to the dynamite fuse.

"Now, in about seven minutes," he said, "it would be better to be found elsewhere. It would be totally unhealthy to stay too near, so much more so since the fuse is short!"

By swimming, Friquet escaped through the natural opening in the grotto. He swam around the cape. He came to shore on the little neighboring beach where he had left his boat.

"My boat!" he exclaimed. He looked around. No mistake. The boat had disappeared. However, there was no human presence around.

"And my fireworks show that's going to explode!" C.25's assistant sighed. A second to size up the situation. Would the rock wall crumble? No. Impossible. The operation would be long and dangerous. There wouldn't be enough time. The sea? Continue swimming? Impossible to be far enough away at the moment of the explosion!

Friquet decided. "Work backward! I can return and snuff out the fuse. But there won't be a second to lose."

He hesitated no longer. He went back by way of the sea, going around the rocks. He rushed off.

"Halt! Put up your hands!" shouted a voice.

And before the secret agent had time to obey, a bullet whistled past his ears, probably as a warning that it was useless to resist.

V. Aboard the Hollandia

The nocturnal sky was gray, low, and framed with clouds that the wind pushed rapidly toward an agitated sea completely decorated with white embroidery. Low waves crowded against each other, slamming against the pitching hull of the *Hollandia*. The liner had just recognized the lights of Ouessant. The Island of Molène was disappearing in the fog which the Créach light house had trouble slicing through.

"Gloomy weather!" Van Vith grumbled. "What a morose crossing. And how much I would have regretted not having gone by way of Italy and Switzerland to reach The Hague if you hadn't been with me."

Thérèse smiled at the banal compliment and Van Vith, taking her smile for a compliment, continued his flattering remarks.

"A companion such as you is enough to make the most tiresome trip enchanting. A series of charming hours! One is never tired of listening to you! You know so many things! You've seen a great deal, traveled a great deal! And most of all you have traveled intelligently! That means everything!"

The night was becoming cooler. Carrying a light fog, the wind was bringing in droplets of a penetrating rain.

Thérèse Arnaud, wearing a warm coat, leaned against the guardrail, looking into the distance at the circle of the lighthouse beams. Suddenly she shivered. The attentive Ambassador noticed the instinctive reaction to the cold.

"You're cold," he said, full of concern. "We shouldn't stay here. You're going to be ill."

"You're right," Thérèse consented with a smile. She walked away, faithfully followed by Van Vith.

"All these passengers are idiots and boring," he said. "It's only ten o'clock. Impossible to sleep now. Admittedly, this somewhat rough swaying will allow us to get some rest later on. So I'm going to suggest the shelter of my cabin. We'll find some of those excellent cigarettes you like there; some drinks knowledgably mixed with my care—and you're aware I know what I'm talking about. These will help us endure the rolling and pitching. And we'll be able to devise other pleasant things…a little bit of everything. Do you want to?"

Thérèse gladly accepted. Delighted with that acceptance, Van Vith whispered: "I have a feeling this will be our best evening aboard."

"Why?" Thérèse asked.

The Ambassador made a vague gesture that was lost in the darkness.

"I don't know, or rather, oh, yes I do! Because you'll be there, near me, you, the most charming of comrades."

"You don't mean a word of it," Thérèse cut in.

While making their way down the corridors to reach the cabin reserved for Van Vith, Thérèse Arnaud, smiling and mocking, continued:

"Oh, no, don't defend yourself. I repeat, you don't mean a word of it."

In a serious voice the Ambassador answered: "You don't know. You can't guess. I have many times been impressed with your perspicuity, your intuitive intelligence. But you can't conceive of the transformation of feelings that move beings. It's psychological."

Lightly, in a mocking voice that only she could assume, the French Secret Service agent retorted: "No, psychology isn't my strong point."

"That's too bad! Yes, truly a great shame," Van Vith sighed. "You have in front of you, and in my own person, a veritable tempest inside a head."

"Hopefully, that won't make the boat pitch any higher!" Thérèse joked.

"You're laughing, but for me the next hours will perhaps be decisive."

The conversation continued in Van Vith's cabin. Comfortable chairs, cigarettes, alcohol. Drinks carefully prepared with experience by the Ambassador. Van Vith got up his strength before bringing up the big sentimental question. He downed in succession three full glasses of whiskey. Then, having warmed up the motor, he let out the clutch.

"Psychology, my dear friend is the key to everything! The secret motives that govern our behavior! The change in feelings that we nourish without knowing it! I was sincere, yes, completely..." Van Vith watered down his sincerity with another copious ration of whiskey. "Sincere when I told you not so long ago in Nice: 'I don't love you.' But I would be less sincere if I told you so this evening..."

"Is this a proposal?" asked Thérèse, who was attentively following the Ambassador and who wasn't sorry to see the level in the bottle of alcohol rapidly lowering.

Before answering Van Vith emptied his glass.

"A proposal! That would be commonplace! And you aren't a woman to be satisfied with anything ordinary. You need..."

"What I need," Thérèse interrupted, "is a glass of that excellent whisky."

Van Vith immediately obeyed. He refilled the two glasses. He emptied his, which he hurried not to leave empty. He drank it. He made a disdainful grimace.

"Obviously this whisky isn't bad. It's Scotch! But you'll see, since you seem to appreciate fine things, when we arrive at The Hague, I'll have you taste a Schiedams...one of those Schiedams which leaves this Scotch very far behind." And as a sign of disdain for the Scotch, he emptied all the contents of the glass while Thérèse's enigmatic smile became more apparent.

"This Schiedam," resumed Van Vith, who had forgotten his declaration of love to think only of the qualities of the alcohol, "this Schiedam, I think I still have a bottle, the last, in my baggage."

"You're telling me such complimentary things that I'm in a hurry to get to know its taste," Thérèse answered.

"Your least wishes...wishes..." sighed the diplomat whose tongue had become thick. "No, I won't finish that. That would be ordinary...Still one..."

A five-minute search. A cry of triumph: "Here it is!"

A little time flows past tranquilly. Cigarettes are smoked. The air in the cabin fogs up. Van Vith's thoughts get slower. The bottle of whiskey, three-quarters empty, is beside the bottle of Schiedam, the level of which is dropping in distressing proportions. A moment of inattention from the diplomat who is searching in the void for the rest of his proposal. C.25 leans a little toward him, over the table where the two empty glasses are waiting. Another ration of alcohol. Van Vith sighs: "Really extraordinary, this Schiedam."

"Yes! Really!" C.25 smiles, watching the Ambassador carefully. The Ambassador, who is shaking, sits down on a chair...and he goes to sleep...a profound sleep as much from drunkenness as from the narcotic that C.25 has made him absorb in his last drink.

"So there! I won't be disturbed for a part of the night! No time to lose! And be careful," murmured Thérèse, who began to work immediately. She worked methodically and with precision, without the least trace of nervousness, taking care to put everything back exactly in place, being sure that no small detail afterward revealed the careful attention she paid to all the Ambassador's luggage. Every object was looked into, rummaged through, examined, verified, as if documents interesting to C.25 might be faked or concealed in whatever small hiding place. Alas, however meticulous the visit which took several hours of Thérèse's uninterrupted attention, the result was nonetheless absolutely negative. The papers and dossiers of Van Vith brought C.25 no clue, no enlightenment. The wallet of the sleeper, who was snoring and groaning, taken from his pocket, gone through, and replaced, revealed absolutely nothing.

C.25 began her search again, this time on the Ambassador himself, looking for some secret pocket hidden in clothing. Nothing! Absolutely nothing!

"Nevertheless," Thérèse said stubbornly, "I would have sworn that drunkard has the proof I'm looking for in his baggage! I've gone through everything. I've found nothing."

C.25 picked up Van Vith's hat that was on a coat rack. She turned back the lining. She smiled, but her smile soon faded and, disappointed, she said:

"The booty is scanty."

She had taken only an envelope from the hat, an open envelope on which there were five wax seals. Nothing in the envelope. Still nothing!

"The same writing as on the envelope of the letter confided to the Baron de Bergh," murmured C.25. And also the same address: Mata Hari, 16 Nieuwe Uitleg, The Hague."

The pale winter day filtered through the portholes. A thin ray of the Sun already high in the horizon, lent a little gaiety in the cabin. Van Vith, his head heavy, his mind like blotting paper, his hair tousled was slowly returning to reality. The reality: a cabin absolutely orderly, and on the table two empty glasses and two bottles of alcohol. A few instants later, the diplomat had returned to very clear consciousness and his face was worried, grave, preoccupied. He walked slowly about the cabin. He seemed to be searching for something he didn't find. He opened his valises. He verified that all was perfectly in order. He even noticed that different objects that he had placed in a particular way so as to have proof in case of an indiscretion were exactly in the position he had placed them himself.

"However, I certainly have the impression that…I didn't dream it!" he growled.

For a long time, he also relentlessly tried to discover some indication of the search made of his baggage. No, nothing! But despite the negative result, he remained distrustful. A secret presentiment had warned him. He had retained very clear memories of the proposal scene. And suddenly: nothing more. A nothingness, nevertheless, in which Van Vith had not completely lost consciousness. He had the feeling that he had been searched. Without anything apparently changed in his camaraderie with Thérèse Arnaud, Van Vith kept himself on guard. And although she didn't miss any occasion to get information and to follow up her search, she arrived at The Hague with the Ambassador without having discovered anything…except the envelope of a letter addressed to Mata Hari…by Saracco.

VI. The Mystery Dispelled

Friquet, his arms raised, turned around to face his enemy. A double cry of surprise rang out.

"You, Malabar!"

"You, Friquet!"

But without trying to understand any further, the Paris kid said quickly: "Old boy, no jokes! Not far from here, there's a lit fuse ending in a little stick of dynamite. And before anything, there's not a minute to lose. It has to be extinguished."

While saying that sentence, Friquet started off. Malabar's laugh stopped him.

"Don't run, little one. It's done! I put it out myself. And I certainly didn't know it was you who prepared that little explosion. Compliments, it was good work."

Friquet breathed a deep sigh.

"Thanks, old boy! Whew! I was afraid I'd be too late!" Then he immediately went on: "But by what luck are you here?"

And Malabar told how he had found himself in the fisherman's cabin. He had received orders directly from C.24 to watch Mata Hari, who had left Monte Carlo to go to Bordighera for a purpose as yet unknown. Now, Malabar, in the course of his surveillance, had discovered that the dancer took a boat at Ventimiglia almost every night and left by the sea. He had joined up with the Boss from a fishing boat and thus he had learned the purpose of those nightly promenades of Mata Hari that he saw leave by sea and return to Bordighera by automobile. Difficult shadowing had led Malabar to the fisherman's cabin the evening before. But not wanting to break his cover and knowing he could catch his prey the next day, he hadn't gone into the dwelling. Malabar had watched the dancer depart in a boat last night. Then he had left directly by land toward the

197

cabin. But, running into bad luck just as he wanted to mount his bicycle, he found it had been stolen. There was no train service to a station near the cabin. The Colossus had therefore lost time before finding the owner of a garage who would agree to lend him a bicycle, and he reached the cove where the cabin was hidden with considerable delay.

Deciding to enter if he had to, the Colossus went in. He found no one. But the trap door Friquet found was very visible. Malabar didn't hesitate; he descended by the narrow stairs (all this while Friquet was leaving by way of the grotto). Coming into the oil and gasoline supply depot, he saw the fuse Friquet had lit. He too had to move quickly. A delay of a few seconds and it was all over! A quick examination of the fuse told Malabar that it had been lit recently. Therefore the author of that attempt wasn't far away. Malabar started a search and he discovered a man that he had immediately knocked out and tied up, while the woman—Mata Hari—got away in a boat moored on the beach (Friquet's boat).

"So, where is your fellow?" asked Friquet.

"In the cabin, well trussed up," the Colossus informed him.

"I'd be delighted to make his acquaintance. Besides, you probably don't need to introduce me," Friquet joked.

C.25's agents reached the cabin in a few steps. Malabar pushed open the door and pointed Friquet to a package twisting about on the floor, trying in vain to break the ropes paralyzing him. At the first glance, the Paris kid identified the prisoner:

"Saracco! Everything is coming off well! It's a good catch!"

"You said 'Saracco?'" Malabar asked.

"Yes, old boy. It's true you yourself don't know him. So...pardon me." And Friquet ceremoniously made the introduction: "Malabar...of the Deuxième Bureau, not at your service! Mr. Saracco, director of the Theater of Monte Carlo Ballet."

Joining in the comedy, Malabar bowed and murmured: "Delighted to make your acquaintance, sir." Then he continued: "Even more delighted since I received instructions concerning you. I believe we'll have the pleasure of traveling together."

Then, leaving Saracco to answer his jokes with an outpouring of terrible swear words, Malabar explained the Boss's instructions. Her orders, received yesterday evening, told Malabar to stop watching Mata Hari momentarily and to start shadowing the ballet director without interfering with his functions. According to C.25's instructions, the operation should be done discreetly, without causing anyone to notice. Next, the prisoner should be urgently moved to the Antilles Aviation Center, where instruction had been directly transmitted to transfer Saracco to The Hague by air.

"Besides, my old Friquet," Malabar finished, "we're part of the trip! I was ordered to get in touch with you for that operation and to send you to the country of the tulips."

"Then let's be on the way to the tulip country, as they say in the final act of the Folies Bergères night club show. That'll give us a little change from the Côte d'Azur!"

C.25's two agents began to carry out the practical means of transferring the prisoner.

"That's simple," Friquet decided. "We have here at hand everything necessary. Since Mata Hari borrowed my boat, we have nothing left but that of our prisoner. So we can remove him from Italian territory without too much trouble and avoid the complications which his transfer by land might cause us. And, fortunately, in order not to call any sort of attention, we have all that's necessary for supplies. There's no shortage of gas here."

The two agents began to fill the gas tank of Saracco's boat.

"Now we have nothing more to do but wait for night to leave. And head straight in the direction of Antibes."

But on thinking about it, Friquet modified the plan, however logical it seemed at first. He thought about the fact that Saracco's capture had a witness: Mata Hari. Therefore by staying all day in the cabin, they might have good reason to be afraid that the dancer would, with reinforcements, attempt some attack to rescue the prisoner. So, after having told his fears to Malabar, who validated them, Friquet suggested an immediate departure. Only, instead of heading to Antibes directly, the boat would head straight to the open sea. Then when night came, they would veer toward Antibes so as to leave Italian waters more easily.

"But before our departure, Malabar, we have something to do," Friquet said.

"Yes! Obviously! What you started and that almost blew me up," the Colossus answered.

"Then this time, let's do it!"

They attached another fuse, considerably longer, to the end of the charge of dynamite. Then the boat was dragged to the beach. Saracco, lifted like a feather by Malabar, was installed in it.

"You see, old boy, we're almost your guests," Friquet joked. "You took us to your coast, but as considerate people, we'll let you avoid the worries and fatigue of that activity!"

Saracco, who hadn't been present at the two agents' talk, didn't know the fate awaiting him, and answered only with another outpouring of swear words. However, he wasn't without visibly showing a certain worry. And so he was far from all possible help, because he had thought that Mata Hari would try to rescue him.

"Everyone ready to board?" Malabar asked.

After looking around again carefully, Friquet answered: "Yes, get ready!"

Malabar went back into the cabin. He came back out rapidly some seconds later. As nimbly as his weight allowed, he jumped into the boat. The motor purred. The propeller beat the water. Leaving behind it a whitish wake, the boat headed toward the open sea. Suddenly a formidable explosion, the noise reverberating in the distance from echo to echo, split open the cabin, and a red light mounted toward the sky. The gasoline and the contents of the cabin had caught fire.

The voyage came off without the least incident. And as Friquet had foreseen, the boat left the Italian waters that night and headed toward Antibes.

"We have to enter at night in order not to draw attention to our rabbit," Friquet said.

"In that case," Malabar suggested, "it would be better not to approach the Antibes port, but make use of a break in the coast to disembark."

"Exactly right!" Friquet concluded. "Besides, between the Cape of Antibes and Juan, we'll find what we want."

Some hours later, with no problem, Saracco's boat approached the coastal region. And shortly thereafter it moored in a cove.

"Point du Jour, everybody out! Everybody pay at the exit!" Friquet joked. Then he asked:

"Malabar, will you take charge of unloading the package?"

"Yes, little one. Don't worry about it."

Saracco, who had made the trip huddled at the bottom of the boat, was swearing and struggling when Malabar, in water up to his knees, picked him up in his arms.

"Let's go. Be quiet!" the Colossus growled. But he had hardly spoken when there was a plop! Saracco, twisting around as much as his bonds permitted, had escaped from the hold of Malabar, who was trying to put him under his arm to carry him to land. And the ballet director fell into the sea!

"I certainly told you not to act like an idiot," said Malabar, who had only to bend over to retrieve a coughing, spitting, vociferating ballet director. And Friquet, who was watching that scene bent double with laughter. While Saracco, paralyzed with fear, recovered from his emotion, Malabar took a precaution to throw the curious off track. Leaving the ballet director guarded by Friquet, he turned over the boat. He opened a small breach in the hull using a tool taken from the kit on board. Then after having again righted the boat, which swerved away from the beach, he started the motor. He abandoned the boat, which left toward the open sea and sank shortly afterward.

"There!" said Malabar, returning to Friquet and Saracco. "All we have to do now is wait—until tonight—not to arouse suspicion, and then to proceed to the Antibes Aviation Field."

C.25's two agents looked at the ballet director. He was so pitiful, shivering, still spitting, that they couldn't help giving another gentle laugh. Malabar bent down and untied his prisoner's legs. He replaced the ropes on his arms with handcuffs. And Friquet, understanding the purpose of that action, said charitably:

"Your legs must be stiff. So you can walk to relax a little."

But Saracco protested and refused straight out to take a step. Friquet and Malabar didn't hesitate. They each drew their revolver. They pointed them at the ballet director. And while raising his massive fist in the air, Malabar commanded in a voice that couldn't be ignored:

"Go on! Get started! And don't act the fool!"

Saracco looked at the revolvers. Then, continuing to swear and blaspheme, he got up. And his stiff legs began to take resigned steps, while, mocking, Friquet stated:

"Fear is the beginning of wisdom. My mother always told me that—and yours must have told you that also. You see, you should always listen to what your mother tells you."

Saracco growled unintelligible insults.

"What's he saying?" Malabar asked.

"He said my mother was right," Friquet translated freely.

At the Antibes Aviation Field, everything was ready for the immediate departure of Malabar, Friquet, and their prisoner. A pilot had been given necessary instructions and was waiting for the arrival of the agents from the Deuxième Bureau. An aircraft was ready for flight. But Saracco began to show new fears.

"You don't like flying?" Friquet joked. "Too bad! You're going to!"

Saracco's fears also had another cause. He had heard the conversations of the pilot, Malabar and Friquet. So he had learned the destination toward which he was headed. And he knew that to reach Holland, no matter what precautions were taken, what detour was made, the lines had to be crossed…and also the territory occupied by German troops. And that perspective made Saracco's shoulders—that the walk had dried after the forced sea bath—shiver. However, the pilot gave Malabar and Friquet reassuring information.

"This isn't the first time I've made the trip to Holland…or elsewhere. Everything is set for the landing because, naturally, I'll calculate my speed to arrive at night. The French front will be alerted about our passage. But damn, after that it will be less amusing! We'll try to get through anyway. Since I've already done it, why wouldn't I succeed once again?"

Some minutes were used to send wireless messages in code and over special long wave radio frequencies. The messages arrived without delay.

"Everything's going well! Everything is ready for us to avoid the most difficulties possible! Let's go!"

Saracco, who was trembling more from fear than from cold, was hoisted into the cabin despite his protests.

"I don't think it's worth the trouble to tie him up any longer," Friquet joked. "He doesn't seem to want to make an exit in the course of the flight."

Malabar gestured widely. Then, taking his revolver out of his pocket, he simply said:

"Besides, if the fancy takes him, I have something that will bring him quickly back to reason. I'm in front of him and you're behind, so…"

"And then…" Friquet finished, "he wouldn't get very far."

A rumble from the impatient motor. The pilot's lifted arm. A slight bump…and the aircraft left the ground, turning above the airfield to gain altitude and then disappeared behind Mount Estérel.

VII. Preparations for an Offensive

As soon as she arrived at The Hague with Van Vith, Thérèse Arnaud settled in not far from the Ambassadors' residence. But she noticed that as soon as she had taken possession of the premises she was the object of a vigilant and indiscreet surveillance by the Holland Police. Every time she went out, she had no trouble verifying that she was being followed. She verified it quickly. And she found with certainty that her telephone was connected to the Police telephone switchboard. So, as a measure of simple precaution, she avoided any visit and all communication with the desk agents at The Hague. And she remained isolated. Who had given the warning! Was it Van Vith? Was it some enemy agent who on the Côte-d'Azur had noticed C.25's activities? Besides, the source of that surveillance mattered little. Whatever the cause, the results remained the same. Thérèse Arnaud couldn't correspond with anyone whatsoever without the Holland Police being immediately informed. She had only been able, thanks to the intermediary of an agent passing through The Hague and returning to France, to have coded telegraphic instructions sent to Malabar, who was instructed to carry them out. But C.25 hadn't been able to be kept up to date about the results. That was the agent who was also charged with preparing for the landing of the plane carrying the Secret Service agents to the vicinity of The Hague.

One afternoon, Thérèse was told by her servant (a woman more than likely paid by the Holland Police) that a gentleman was asking to speak to her. She asked that she see him immediately. At first sight, she recognized Friquet, who had made himself unrecognizable. With a quick wink she let her auxiliary know that the slightest words of the conversation would be immediately reported to the Police. So, Friquet introduced himself as a friend coming from Germany who, having learned that Thérèse was at The Hague, wanted to say hello. The interview was commonplace and mundane.

But as a measure of precaution, hoping for a visit from another of her agents, she had prepared coded instructions that she passed to Friquet, who had done the same. Therefore, despite the Police surveillance, C.25 was again in contact with her agents.

Friquet's report told her that Malabar and Saracco, still a prisoner, after a difficult landing, had arrived safely at The Hague. The French agents were lodged in a safe house retained for them by the intermediary agent who had transmitted the Boss's messages. Saracco was secure and her agents weren't waiting for anything more but her instructions.

But the most important point of the message was the following: Friquet announced that, to his great surprise, the day after the aircraft landed, he had met Mata Hari at The Hague. Was that trip of the dancer only a coincidence or, on the contrary, wasn't it motivated by the kidnapping of Saracco? In that case, how had Mata Hari been able to pick up the trail since, from the time he had left the fisherman's cabin the ballet director hadn't met anyone. The entire journey from Antibes had been done by sea and at night. The boat had been sabotaged. And after a short stop at the Aviation Field, where Saracco had been locked in an empty office and put aboard an aircraft without any workman being able to notice his special situation as a prisoner, he had been locked up.

C.25 considered that information for a long time. However, again, it mattered little how Mata Hari had arrived so rapidly at The Hague. The fact existed; she was there. And there were two possibilities: did the dancer know about Saracco's presence at the capital of Holland? Or, rather, was she ignorant of the ballet director's location? That's what it was important to know, because according to one or the other possibilities, the course of action was very different. If Mata Hari knew where Saracco was, she would no doubt try to rescue him. If she didn't, the dancer came to The Hague for reasons it would be useful to know.

"Well," Thérèse said, "we'll soon know."

On their side, her auxiliaries knew the Boss's orders. They were simple. Until they received further instructions, Saracco would remain a prisoner. Every precaution should be taken that he was seen by no one. They were told to beware of the Holland Police. Special caution was recommended in everything and for everything. Malabar was in charge of guarding Saracco. As for Friquet, C.25 had reserved another more active mission for him. He was to take a job as valet to Van Vith, who didn't know him, having never met him at Nice except under various disguises. It was not necessary to furnish any more precise orders to the Paris kid. He knew what wearing the livery of a valet meant for the envoys of the Deuxième Bureau. Their only qualifications for a good domestic servant was to know how to see and listen...by any means possible. Indiscretion was greatly appreciated. C.25's orders were quickly carried out.

Saracco was locked in the cellar despite his protests. And The Hague newspapers carried the next day the story of a mysterious crime by a person unknown. Investigations had turned up no trace. A man had been found murdered at the outskirts of the city, a knife wound to the heart. Nobody had seen anything. The Police had used their best detectives, who had only suppositions. Theft wasn't the motive for the crime. Vengeance, then? The victim was in reality a somewhat disreputable character whose passion for gambling had several times put him in difficult situations. However, he was a perfectly upright domestic servant, very well-trained, perfectly satisfactory, in the service of his employer, Van Vith, the Holland Ambassador to Nice, who had highly recommended him.

The next day, Friquet, who wasn't unfamiliar with that sudden vacancy for a valet for the exact same person with whom C.25 had ordered him to get employment...after having furnished the most flattering and the most serious references of indisputable authenticity.

Several times during walks and with the help of various stratagems, Malabar and C.25 had managed to exchange letters and mutual reports about what had taken place. Friquet's entry into Van Vith's service had facilitated communication between C.25 and her assistants. In fact, Thérèse sometimes went to the Ambassador's residence. And Friquet, correctly accompanying her to the door, didn't waste time. But relations between Van Vith and Thérèse seemed—since their arrival at The Hague—to be a great deal less frequent, a great deal less regular. Van Vith often used as a pretext state business, questions of the highest importance to take care of, to call off a rendezvous at the last minute.

Three days after he had been on the job, Friquet began to install microphones. Unfortunately, the requirements of his job didn't allow him to remain at the receiver and, therefore, he missed the most important conversations which took place during the day in the Ambassador's office or drawing room.

To remedy that situation, Malabar was secretly put into Friquet's bedroom and during the daytime he took down scrupulously all Van Vith's interviews. Then in the evening he returned to guard Saracco, who was waiting dejectedly in a basement where Malabar had reinforced the locks.

Thus the French agents captured interesting conversations between Mata Hari and Van Vith who were in close contact. One evening, Van Vith's valet, after he had finished his work, secretly left his bedroom. He went directly to Malabar's house where he also found Thérèse, who had managed to throw the Holland Police off her trail. The three spies rapidly organized the steps to take. And the battle plan was soon established.

VIII. The Trap

The goal of the French agents was the capture of Mata Hari. Thérèse told her agents: "We have an excellent method. The presence of Saracco, who is always available to us, will facilitate the task."

"At last he's going to be useful for something!" Friquet joked. "He's been fed and lodged doing nothing for a long time, that fellow. And he might not be sorry to leave his basement..."

C.25 reflected a long time. Then she decided to send for the prisoner on the spot. Friquet took charge of getting him.

"Excuse me for disturbing your sleep," he said mockingly to the prisoner. Saracco who understood the futility of any protest, quietly allowed himself to be taken away. He regarded with curiosity C.25 who was preparing an envelope on letter paper. Then:

"He had a pen on him when you captured him?" she asked.

At the affirmative response of Malabar, who held out to her the object asked for, she continued, pointing to a chair at the table.

"Sit down there and write what I dictate to you. Take care! With your most natural handwriting, right?"

"And without shaking," Friquet joked.

"The envelope first of all," C.25 continued. "Mademoiselle Mata Hari, 16 Nieuwe Uitleg."

Then she began to dictate the letter. But at the first sentence, Saracco put down his pen and declared firmly: "I won't write!"

Thérèse repeated the text of the letter in a calm voice. And in a voice that didn't require an answer, she commanded:

"Go on! No problems! I'm in a hurry!"

"No, I understand and I won't lend myself, willingly or by force, to your maneuvers. It's shameful!" Saracco exclaimed.

C.25 took out her revolver. She put it against the ballet director's jaw. She looked at her watch. She repeated the first sentence of the letter once again and said:

"You have one minute to decide. Write or be blown away."

The ballet director was pale with anger and trembled all over. Thérèse Arnaud looked at her watch.

"So?" she asked, her finger ready to press the trigger.

With a cry of rage, Saracco picked up his pen. And he wrote the text dictated. When she had finished, she added: "And now sign."

Saracco put down his pen a second time. "That letter is an infamy. I won't sign."

"I'm in a hurry," C.25 said. "I don't have time to start the same comedy over again. Sign...or..."

Feeling the coldness of the revolver against his temple, Saracco, appended his signature.

"There!" C.25 approved.

"It wasn't as hard as all that," Friquet joked.

"I'll get revenge," Saracco threatened. "And if you kill me, others will avenge me!"

C.25 didn't seem to hear that threat. She picked up the letter and re-read it. She examined the signature.

"Everything is correct," she concluded, "despite the fact that the signature is a little shaky."

She put the letter in the envelope and ordered Malabar: "Now you can take the prisoner back to his cellar."

Moving near the prisoner before he had gone out the door, Friquet told him:

"Just between us, old boy, I think you did well to obey the lady! First of all, you have to be courteous and never refuse ladies anything…most of all when they know how to ask it nicely!"

When Malabar had accomplished his mission and returned, C.25 explained the expected outcome of events.

"Mata Hari will come on receiving that letter signed by Saracco setting up a meeting to put back you know what. You know the place of the rendezvous," C.25 continued. "It's near the place where you landed…and where the plane remains in an underground hanger. Therefore kidnap and then depart for France. Friquet will get free under whatever pretext. As for Saracco, we can't unfortunately take him with us. You'll leave him in his cellar. He'll get out the best way he can. We'll pick him up again as soon as he returns to France. Malabar will be our pilot since the aviator who brought us is on another mission somewhere else. The operation doesn't present any difficulty. As you know, the area where we operate is very deserted."

Everything arranged, C.25 left her agents. Before going back to her own lodgings, she made a long detour. She stopped at several popular cafes where presence would be reported to the Police. Her absence, during which time all trace of her was lost, hadn't lasted three quarters of an hour. Friquet returned to the building where Van Vith lived without any trouble.

The day of the meeting arrived. In the morning, Van Vith left his house without leaving his valet any instructions. The valet—as a faithful servant of the Deuxième Bureau—hurried to take advantage of his employer's absence. The desk drawers were methodically gone through. Some papers that seemed the kind that might interest Captain Ladoux made their way into Friquet's pockets. The safe didn't hold out very long. There the Paris kid made a first class discovery: the new secret code between Germany and Holland. Without wasting a second, Friquet went back up to his room. He opened his valise and took out a small, perfected, very sensitive camera. He carefully photographed each page of the document, murmuring:

"Here's something that will cheer up our friend Marcel and make up for not having accompanied us on this interesting trip."

Then the secret code was put back in place and the safe closed. Friquet looked at the time.

"Now let's get on the road!" He went upstairs again to his room. He took out from his valise everything that might be useful. Then he joked:

"Damn! I forgot to give my two-weeks' notice."

An hour before the time set for Mata Hari's arrival, C.25, Malabar, and Friquet, each having taken a different way, were united in the underground hanger where the aircraft was waiting. Malabar carefully made the last checks. The plane was filled with gasoline. Everything was ready. Thérèse gave everyone his role. When Mata Hari arrived, C.25 would go to meet her. Malabar would rush out of the ditch where he was hidden. And the two agents would dash back immediately toward the hanger where Friquet was waiting. The action would take only a few minutes, just the time to take out the aircraft where Mata Hari, well tied up, would have been deposited—a sortie Malabar's Herculean strength would facilitate. Then, gain altitude in a hurry! A last look at the aircraft, a last thought by Thérèse. Everything was ready.

"Malabar," she said, "go stand guard duty in the ditch. Wait until I'm rather near Mata Hari...and move quickly."

"Understood, Boss!"

As soon as the Colossus had left, C.25 prepared a big envelope stuffed beforehand with false documents that she held in her hand.

"Now, let's go," she murmured.

For several minutes she walked slowly on the road. She looked like a tourist taking advantage of the first rays of a springtime sun.

"Ah! What if she should be late!" murmured C.25.

Still another few minutes of waiting. Although she showed no outward sign, the French Secret Service agent felt a vague impatience mounting in her. Finally, on the horizon, a clear silhouette that C.25 identified quickly, but she immediately raged: "Ah!" And two minutes later, masking her bitter disappointment under a perfectly courteous smile, Thérèse Arnaud held out to Mata Hari, an envelope stuffed with documents...under the impassive eyes of Van Vith, murmuring..."from Saracco."

"Thank you," was all the dancer said.

Malabar, who had come out from his hiding place, had a rapid sign from C.25 telling him to remain quiet.

And, grumbling, the Colossus went back into hiding. "Bah! I could have taken both of them! It wasn't that big herring of an Ambassador who would've bothered me. I'd make short work of him."

Mata Hari and Van Vith returned to The Hague. Thérèse Arnaud made a long detour before coming back to the underground hanger where she found Friquet and Malabar very disconcerted.

"Friquet," she ordered, "go back to your job until you get new orders. You must get back to Van Vith's before he does. The ambush didn't work. No point in putting the Holland Police hot on our heels."

And as Friquet looked significantly at the aircraft thanks to which it would be easy to thumb their nose at all the Police, C.25 added with rage:

"I don't want to go back to France empty-handed!"

Each of the three French agents quickly returned to their occupations. Friquet went back to his job with Van Vith, who might very well not be aware of the disappearance of certain papers until a great deal later, the disappearance of which wouldn't immediately throw suspicion on Friquet, the impeccable valet. And the code, the famous secret code, key to all the important messages between Germany and Holland, was back in place. Unfortunately, the photographs were not yet in France, and Friquet's discovery, so long as they were in his possession, had no usefulness.

Malabar found Saracco back in his cellar. Thérèse, rage in her heart, evaluated that day of defeat.

"In all, I managed to slip Mata Hari some documents. Their importance won't be lost on the Tiergarten...but for some time they will upset the arrival of reinforcements to the French front. And, on the other hand, as there is a discrepancy between the source of these documents whose origin they're sure of and those coming from sources no less sure from other enemy agents, the État-Major will have something to keep him busy looking for the truth."

But a set-back, however enraging it might be, wasn't enough to keep down the indefatigable Deuxième Bureau agent.

"Mata Hari has escaped me this time! I have to make other arrangements. As for my situation vis-à-vis Van Vith, it is becoming rather strained."

Obviously C.25 was aware of the danger of that failed expedition. She knew she was already being watched by the Holland Police as suspicious. It wasn't the meeting with Mata Hari that would resolve things...still, C.25 had in this way appeared to be very devoted to German interests.

But any detail risked making her stay at The Hague impossible. And arrangements had to be made to be able to flee at any minute...along with the two faithful agents. Therefore, if some new attempt to make sure of getting Mata Hari must be attempted, it had to be done quickly. And C.25 tried for a long time to lay out a new campaign plan allowing her to bring the dancer back to France. There was no doubt of her guilt.

"After all," murmured C.25, "I was wrong a while ago...to capture the Ambassador of a neutral country...that would have somewhat heavy consequences for me...even though there's no longer any great doubt of Van Vith's guilt. Only..."

And after thinking again, Thérèse concluded:

"All hope isn't lost!"

IX. An Indiscretion That Turns Out Badly

At about 6 p.m. the next evening, Van Vith, who had gone out during the afternoon, came back home carrying a little dispatch case that he was holding as something valuable. Before going to his office, he rang for his valet, who respectfully asked his master's wishes.

"I have to work. I don't want to be bothered by any pretext. I am at home for no one. Absolutely no one, you understand. The order is strict and there is no exception!"

Friquet bowed formally. "Understood, Sir!"

As soon as the door had closed on the Ambassador, Friquet murmured:

"You…you're going to do some more funny work. I'm not curious, but I would really like to know what the contents of that little briefcase you must hold onto are."

Fewer than five minutes later, the bell rang again. And Friquet hurried to his employer's office.

On the table, the open attaché case revealed an important packet of documents. Certain ones that the Ambassador had already opened or examined, were spread out in front of him. And with an experienced eye, Friquet recognized maps and typographical lay-outs.

"I've thought about it." Van Vith said. "I'm absorbed in important work. Don't bother about my dinner. I may go out when I've finished. You're free for the evening."

Friquet thanked him and left. He went immediately to his bedroom. He was thinking:

"I'm more and more determined to explore the contents of that famous briefcase! But how? If Van Vith goes out, I'll take advantage of his absence…but being cautious since I probably won't have a lot of time. He's going to eat in a hurry."

But a doubt worried Friquet: "Why doesn't he take his papers?"

Friquet searched a long time for a plan that would allow him to procure the documents. Alas! He found no way that satisfied him. The only possible way was violence, to burst into the office with a revolver and do the superb and classic "Hands Up!" But the consequences were serious. He would lose his cover immediately. After that, only one thing was left to do, flee! Flee with the Holland Police on his heels.

"If I knew, if I were sure the papers were worth risking the job," Friquet murmured, "I wouldn't hesitate! But maybe demolish all the Boss's plans for some insignificant documents….the consequences are too great."

Friquet was at that point in his reflections, deploring the impossibility of asking C.25's advice on how to proceed, when there was the sound of a telephone ring, very muted by the space of the two floors separating the Ambassador's office and the domestic's bedroom.

"Well! My microphones may tell me!" grumbled the indiscreet valet. And he immediately picked up his receivers.

As he listened to Van Vith's conversation, Friquet's large smile expanded.

And in his naturally joking disposition, he ironically remarked on Van Vith's replies.

"But, of course, my dear friend…what's that! Oh! But of course…with great pleasure…What an excellent idea! At eleven o'clock! Yes…thank you very much dear friend…See you soon!"

And when Friquet heard the sharp sound of the receiver being replaced, he began a joyful dance.

"A rich idea…a marvelous idea, delightful!" he rejoiced. "It's definitely worth something to listen, if not at doors, at least to know what's said behind them! My mother wasn't right when she told me not to listen to what other people said!"

The telephone call that had just come to disturb Van Vith during his absorbing work was a result of the diplomat's hurry and the timber of Mata Hari's voice. And the answers were sufficiently clear to guess the questions without possible equivocation.

Friquet knew that Mata Hari was dancing that evening at a charity ball where she was giving an act. She had asked Van Vith to have supper with her and the diplomat had willingly accepted the invitation.

"So," Friquet concluded, "he's going to skip out to *cherchez la femme*, about eleven o'clock. Then they'll go together to some chic nightclub. Van Vith will have a good appetite. Having a charming woman at his side will put him in a good mood. That will lead him to offer champagne…He loves champagne, this good Van Vith. He won't be in any hurry to return. Then to go have supper with Mata Hari, he won't take his precious little papers. He'll lock them in his safe. But the safe's a joke for me, it's my old friend, it can't refuse me anything! So, I have a good part of the night…to allow me to document myself. Now, patience. I just have to wait until eleven o'clock."

The hours passed slowly, Friquet used them to smoke cigarettes. A little before 11 p.m., the slammed door told the domestic that Van Vith had left his office. Friquet looked out his window and saw Van Vith walking away.

"Don't hurry, in case he forgot his cigars or his umbrella. I prefer him not to find me in his office."

Despite his impatience, the Paris street kid, waited another quarter of an hour. He reached Van Vith's office. He had taken only his kit of tools needed to open a safe and a pocket light. He didn't want to use an electric flashlight for fear that it might be noticed by someone passing by, by some friend who, meeting the diplomat later, would raise the alarm.

"You can never worry too much about these details," remarked C.25's assistant, with just reason.

A little later he continued:

"I wouldn't be lucky enough that, in his hurry to go meet the very charming dancer, he had forgotten to put up his papers and left them on the table! Too bad! Today's employers no longer have enough confidence in their faithful domestics!"

The documents were not on the table.

"Now it's just between us!" Friquet joked, approaching the safe. And he set to work. Shortly afterward he exhaled a sigh of satisfaction.

"There! It was a cinch. A key wouldn't have opened it any easier. Now, let's get the papers."

The interior of the safe was lit. The documents were in hand's reach. Van Vith hadn't even taken the trouble to replace them in the briefcase. At the time appointed, he had stopped working; he had gathered up the spread-out files and placed them at the front of the safe to pick up when he returned.

A rapid examination caused Friquet to emit a joyful but stifled exclamation:

"This is really some business!"

There was a whole dossier concerning the organization of the underwater defenses in the Mediterranean. Letters for the submarine commanders addressed "In Care of Van Vith, Holland Ambassador to Nice," valuable notes concerning the movements of fleets in Turkey and the Adriatic. Friquet hesitated.

"Should I pocket them or photograph them? Impossible to photograph them; I don't have enough light. So." A decision. Friquet put the documents in his pockets. Then he advised himself:

"Now, my little friend, some good advice. Let your friends know about your departure and get out quickly, without..."

The door opened. The ceiling light turned on. The silhouette of Van Vith and the Police.

"Hands Up!"

"Now we've got them!" Van Vith said. "That one and his accomplices, the French woman and the Colossus. We've had our eyes on them for a very long time."

Before the words "Hands Up!" were out, Friquet with his revolver had shot out the overhead light. With one leap he was at the window while Van Vith's voice was finishing the threatening phrase.

"Thanks for the information!" Friquet thought.

Confused scuffles, orders: "Go down by the stairs!" At the same time shots exploded in the darkness as red lights lit up the end of the revolvers.

The open window. And two floors separated Friquet from the ground. About six meters!

"Fortunately I got a prize for gymnastics at school. But, even so, six meters, it's a bit risky," grumbled the Paris street kid. He had no choice. It was the jump or the Police...So...

Not hurt too much when hitting the ground, thanks to his suppleness and agility, Friquet stopped a moment to get his breath. Shots rang out from the window, while two shadows hidden behind the door jumped toward him. Jumping to one side, he evaded them. He shot twice at them; they responded with two shots. And Friquet ran, still followed by the two policemen. Deserted streets. The pursuers were not tiring. They maintained their distance without seeming to be short of breath. Several times Friquet tried to throw them off the track by sudden detours. Alas! in vain. Finally, the Paris kid was able to slow down a little. The policemen were falling further behind. One more street, and then a sudden detour. And then nothing!

"Even so, old boy, you've come some distance. Be careful not to fall back under their paws."

But when no policeman's silhouette was visible on the horizon, as soon as he regained his breath, Friquet started to run again. He was out of every danger for the moment, but it was urgent that he warn Thérèse and Malabar. The Police had telephones.

"Hopefully I won't arrive too late!'

Fortunately, Friquet's run hadn't taken him too far away. But Thérèse's lodgings, situated not far from that of Van Vith, were in a particularly dangerous zone because of its proximity to the Ambassador. Some policeman was certainly guarding it. Finally! Friquet got there. C.25 immediately opened the door.

"Quick! Quick! Boss, let's get out of here!" Friquet, out of breath, gasped.

Two minutes later, abandoning everything, C.25 walked away rapidly with Friquet into the night. A taxi took them to Malabar's hideout. The Colossus was ready in a very short time. Just at the moment the three agents got to the door, three policemen were on duty. It was short work. His head lowered, Malabar butted into the stomach of the first one, while at the same time his two fists lashed out, hitting each of the other policemen.

"Let's go!" And the race started again in earnest. Without slowing down, C.25 told her auxiliaries: "If we're separated, let's rendezvous at the underground hanger. The plane will wait until we're all there…except as a last resort. In that case, it's every man for himself, provided Malabar is there! God help anyone who misses the flight!"

But, as successful as Malabar's offensive was, it secured the fugitives only a short delay. The policemen who had been struck down, got back up and resumed pursuit with renewed energy. Bullets soon whistled past the three Frenchmen's ears. At a crossroads, a sharp turn by the Deuxième Bureau agents put them face to face with two new policemen. Astounded by the burst of humanity, they were laid out by two magnificent blows before they knew what had happened. But the three French agents soon had five Holland policemen on their trail. More pistol shots, which the fugitives avoided with sharp detours. The French hadn't yet used their weapons. Behind C.25 and her agents there was the rumble of a motor. "Damn!" Friquet groaned, turning his head. He had hoped to see some vehicle that might be transformed, with some audacity, into a useful method of transportation. Alas! It aggravated the danger…policemen on motorcycles.

"Keep going! Keep going!" Malabar encouraged.

Another quick turn and C.25 verified that the pursuers, more or less bruised by their encounter with Malabar's fists, and seeing motorcycle reinforcements arrive, didn't pick up speed. One of them had even abandoned the chase.

"Stop! Put up your hands!" The motorcycle riders commanded without slowing down. The fugitives obeyed and went to stand in front of the two motorcycle policemen. One of the policemen, giving his motorcycle to his colleague, dismounted to place handcuffs on the docile fugitives. What happened? It was so fast nobody knew exactly. A few seconds later, Malabar, on one of the motorcycles, carrying C.25 on the luggage carrier, and Friquet on the other motorcycle, disappeared over the horizon while the real motorcyclists remained stretched out in the middle of the street. And further away, they could hear the rumbling of three new motorcycles in the chase. The three French agents' sighs of relief turned into an exclamation of disappointment.

"Still more," Thérèse groaned.

"They've mobilize all the flies in The Hague to chase us," Friquet complained.

Still more detour to throw them off the trail. But they couldn't return to the city where they would be immediately apprehended by superior forces. With a glance, C.25 estimated the distance which separated the two groups of motorcyclists.

"We're not far enough ahead to take out the aircraft and leave before having those fellows on our backs."

"We have to shoot some of them, two out of three," Friquet suggested.

The motorcycles raced along at full speed. Malabar and Friquet leaning over their handlebars tried in vain to get more than maximum speed from their vehicles.

"Be careful not to lead them toward the hanger if we're not enough ahead," C.25 recommended.

More useless feints and ruses to throw the Holland Police off the trail. They seemed to be gradually gaining ground. Suddenly Friquet's motorcycle began giving trouble. The motor sputtered several times. The speed decreased considerably; the trouble multiplied. There was no doubt that it would breakdown at any moment.

"Come on, jump! Don't wait!" Malabar shouted, slowing down.

Friquet jumped off his motorcycle. Then, slowly, C.25 helping, he climbed on Malabar's shoulders. Then the motor started again. But, bearing this new weight, it no longer kept up the former speed. And the pursuers were gaining.

"As soon as they're within firing range," Thérèse whispered.

One more minute, two minutes. Three successive shots rang out and a cry. The three pursuing motorcycles tumbled. One of C.25's shots had hit a tire. Running at full speed, the motorcycle had skidded, sowing disorder in the enemy army and as it crashed across the road, it brought the other two down with it.

"Keep going!" C.25 encouraged.

And Malabar, still leaning over his handlebars, was being careful not to upset the unstable equilibrium.

Friquet, seated on Malabar's shoulders as if on a horse, joked: "That's annoying. I'd really like to see them shoveled up."

Soon the Holland policemen and their vehicles were only an imperceptible speck on the horizon. Then the three French agents found themselves at the edge of the horizon.

"Finally alone!" the incorrigible Paris kid joked, as C.25 announced the followers had disappeared.

A quarter of an hour later, Malabar stopped, having again, picked up the road leading directly to the underground hanger. Friquet got down. C.25, followed by the Colossus rushed toward the hanger.

The three agents breathed a sigh of relief, finding nothing had been touched and that the aircraft was ready for flight. They all three had had the same fear: the discovery of the hanger or that some deterioration of the mechanism had occurred. Fortunately, nothing was wrong.

"No point in being stubborn about it. All our cover is blown in Holland," Thérèse Arnaud said.

Efforts by all three of the Deuxième Bureau managed to bring out the aircraft. The motor turned over. The roar kept the occupants from hearing the sounds of other motors on the road. And just as the plane took off, two motorcycle policemen arrived, watching that aircraft coming out of nowhere leave before their eyes.

"Goodbye, gentlemen," Friquet joked, thumbing his nose at the policemen.

After some time, the aircraft climbed and continued its flight, nearing the lines. Malabar began to show signs of worry. C.25 immediately noticed his strange attitude.

"What's wrong," she inquired anxiously.

"Gasoline has been leaking out of the tank since we left. The loss is progressively getting worse...so..."

Malabar didn't finish his sentence. Everyone knew the meaning of what Malabar wasn't saying. The lack of fuel meant a forced landing, having to descend over what could be enemy territory. It meant also coming within easier range of enemy fire, exposing them to chase, etc. A thousand dangers that not one of them didn't know. Fly over the sea? That was to lengthen the flight and risk falling into the waves. Besides, it was too late. The French soon saw the first shells exploding below them. A few minutes later, instead of exploding below them, the projectiles hit the aircraft. The noise of the motor stopped. Then suddenly, nothing. Nothing but great silence, and from time to time the noise of exploding shells. The aircraft began a descent, surrounded by firing.

Shortly thereafter a telegram arrived at the Deuxième Bureau.

"A French aircraft carrying a woman saying she was a member of the Deuxième Bureau, code name C.25, and her two aides, coming from Holland, landed at the French front lines due to shortage of gasoline. The occupants are under surveillance awaiting identification and instructions. The aircraft was destroyed."

The next day, after instructions from the Deuxième Bureau and intensive verification, C.25 and her two companions finishing their trip by rail, arrived in Paris. During the trip, Friquet gave C.25 the packet of documents that had caused all the trouble. The Secret Service agent smiled.

"You certainly know, my poor Friquet, that those documents were put there on purpose. That was the trap set for us after that meeting with Mata Hari."

"Fortunately, I have on me the photographs of the secret code used between Germany and Holland," smiled the Paris kid.

"Yes, that's even better. That will be a great deal more useful to us," C.25 answered.

As soon as they arrived in Paris, the three agents went to the office of Captain Ladoux.

"Oh! My poor children," he exclaimed. "What a story! A little longer and you'd have been taken for German spies."

Then he continued: "You were in Holland? I'm going to give you some news that will interest you." And he held out a translated message to C.25: *Saracco, Monte Carlo ballet director, well known in The Hague, going toward Basel, Switzerland. Mata Hari, dancer, left for Berlin after a visit to The Hague. Van Vith, Ambassador from Holland to Nice returned to his post.*

"Then nothing is lost," Thérèse Arnaud smiled. "We're going to meet again."

LES AVENTURES DE THÉRÈSE ARNAUD
ESPIONNE FRANÇAISE

N° 31

par Pierre YROND

La course à la mort

RACE TOWARD DEATH

I. A Tragic Argument

In the Paris summer, the Invalides Park, at the edge of the Boulevard des Invalides, offered relative coolness in its thin oasis of greenery. Outside, in the full sunlight, busy passers-by were going on about their business and casual on-lookers were strolling by. In the park, almost deserted at that time of the year when many children had deserted the greenery of the capital for the countryside, some urchins, less fortunate or less favored by fate, were playing their usual games. Here and there in the garden, some enthusiasts of calm were day-dreaming or reading their newspaper. A few women watching over their brats, were busy with needle work or crochet. A little to one side, two women on neighboring chairs were having a friendly chat, two women very different in appearance.

One of them, with a slender waist, thin, very tall, having a stylish look, a pleasant but pale face, was dressed with a somewhat affected elegance. The other, tubby, almost too much so for her short stature, her expression a little hard, brunette, dressed without the least affectation, seemed to have asked of her dress only that it be practical for use in all sports. In addition, the solid build, the strong muscles of that woman clearly indicated an athlete.

The conversation in a low voice between the two women went on a long time. But from the movement of their lips, it seemed apparent that the conversation was light-hearted. Perhaps, to pass the time, these two friends were exchanging trifling matters of current banalities or the usual gossip. Little by little, without the tone getting any louder, the conversation was accompanied by more jerky gestures. These new gestures seemed to indicate that each of the two speakers was supporting a different point of view and trying to convince the other one, not only using all her force of persuasion, but also giving weight to her argument. After a few minutes, still following the same rapid movement, the interview seemed to become even more animated. Their gestures became brus-quer. Were they menacing gestures, movements of denial, protestations of inno-cence, fierce accusations? And despite all the two speakers' desire to keep a completely friendly aspect to their conversation, the pitch heightened. Some-times a stronger word escaped. A few more minutes of this little game, and, despite all their checking themselves, the two former friends seemed fighting furies. In the short periods of calm which were soon submerged by a flow of tempestuous words, their throats, tight with anger, let out hoarse panting.

Suddenly, out of arguments, perhaps, one of the women got up. The bru-nette one! Probably her more nervous temperament was tired of that discussion.

But that was only a feint. She soon came back to her adversary without having gone away more than three feet. And dominating the blonde woman by her size, she let a new tide of arguments rain down on the blonde woman, punctuated by insults that the other woman tried to oppose. Shouts, the brouhaha of two furious voices each emitting crackling sounds at the same time, each trying to fill the vacuum left by the other.

Apparently abandoning the fight, the athletic woman went away yet again, but she soon came back. And the scene played out rapidly, stupefying by its simple brutality. The brunette woman approached the chair where the woman she had been talking to remained seated. She opened her purse. She put in her hand and before anyone understood, the hand, holding a little object shining in the sun, struck the breast of the elegant woman with one clean stroke. There was an immediate loud cry. A red stain mottled her bosom, a red stain getting bigger as it descended.

In the park, frightened shouts broke out, echoing the screams of the victim. Women fled, dragging their children away, as if they themselves were directly in danger. Passers-by stopped on the Boulevard des Invalides, surprised, trying to understand the reason for that flight. Others, who were beginning to understand, rushed forward to help the victim.

During this time, the murderer jumped over the low wrought iron fence which separated the park and the boulevard. Then she reached a motorcycle parked at the edge of the sidewalk. The noise of a motor, followed soon by a light cloud of black, nauseating smoke. And the outline of the motorcyclist rapidly blurred in the distance on the Boulevard des Invalides in the direction of the Boulevard Montparnasse.

Among those passing by who approached the elegant blonde woman, now motionless, were some soldiers from the 20th Recruitment Section of the État-Major. The circle of the curious moved aside for the uniforms. The wounded woman's eyes were closed. A reddish foam was forming at the edge of her lips. Her breathing was irregular, labored. And always, always, a slowly moving flow which grew and which nothing could curb, the brown stain on the breast grew. Little drops flowed together, forming a little rivulet flowing slowly to the ground.

"We must tell the Police," one of the soldiers, who seemed smarter and more accustomed to making a decision, said immediately. Some quickly left the group and went off in various directions. Someone brought information.

"There's usually a policeman at the corner of the Rue de Grenelle."

In several moments a policeman with an important and serious demeanor approached. Once more, the crowd where the circle had grown, moved aside to allow the representative of authority to pass through.

"She has to be taken to Necker," said the soldier who had before suggested going to look for the Police.

For an instant, with a suspicious eye, the policeman looked at the man who had dared to take the initiative. He growled:

"You, soldier, who asked your opinion? I know very well what I have to do."

Then after a silence to let the weight of his authority sink in, he concluded learnedly:

"It's obvious we have to take that woman to the hospital. See here, soldier, and your friend, you're going to carry the wounded woman to the edge of the sidewalk. While you're doing that, I'm going to look for a taxi."

With infinite precautions, the two soldiers lifted the elegant blonde. They had crossed the distance which separated the place of the drama and the sidewalk when the policeman appeared in an automobile.

"It's still lucky that he found a vehicle immediately, because, now, since the war, because almost all the taxis have been requisitioned, cars are rare…and in case of emergencies like this one…" said one of the curious.

After the two soldiers had placed the victim in the car, they exchanged a grimace which seemed to indicate that they thought the young woman's condition grave. The taxi drove off immediately toward Necker Hospital.

II. After the Drama

While the wounded woman was being transported to the hospital, the little group which had formed in the Invalides Park, dissolved, commenting on the events. Among the loiterers, a young man with a limp seemed to take a lively interest in the two women's discussion. It was certainly a rather incomprehensible interest, since no one could make out the reasons which thus pitted the two women against one other. Nobody could have understood the least word they had exchanged. When the crime was committed, the young lame man was one of those who had—despite his infirmity—approached the wounded woman the most rapidly. He had observed everything with curiosity, but without taking the least part in the action. Then, when the policeman had talked of transport to the hospital, the lame man had walked away in the direction of the quays. At the same time as he, another young man, with an innocent look and an intelligent expression, who had for some time immersed himself in the group, walked away. And in a few rapid steps he caught up with the lame man.

"The woman who gave her such a wound must have had some knife," he remarked.

The lame man gave the man who spoke to him a suspicious and not very friendly look. He agreed in an almost contemptuous tone:

"She lived her last hour! That happens one day to each of us."

Without staying any longer near this not very friendly witness, the young man went on his way. He disappeared near the quays at a normal pace, while, very far in the rear, the lame man, always with his limping walk, continued to walk in the same direction.

When he had gained 200 meters on the lame man, the young man suddenly stopped. He calmly lit a cigarette. He traversed the Quai d'Orsay. Then on the other sidewalk he reversed directions on the path he was following. When he crossed the lame man, he continued for a few steps. Then he made another about face. Then having thus begun his shadowing by this method he henceforth attached himself to the lame man's footsteps, following a short distance behind him. He walked across the Boulevard Saint-Germain, the Boulevard Raspail, the Boulevard Montparnasse and reached the Rue Delambre. The young man considered it useless to go any further. As the lame man turned into the sidewalk on the right, the man shadowing him stopped on the sidewalk on the left, content to follow his prey at a distance. The lame man soon disappeared under the coach way door of a building with the number 22.

"Well! There you are!" the man shadowing smiled. "The Boss was right!"

Whistling a song, he picked up his pace. Some minutes later the young man entered the home of Thérèse Arnaud. The famous secret agent was in her office. At the entrance of her colleague, she quickly questioned:

"So, Friquet?"

"So, he went into 22 Rue Delambre," the Paris kid answered.

"Consequently we won't see Languille this evening," C.25 concluded. "While waiting we're going to keep ourselves busy. Come."

"Where are we going, Boss?" Friquet asked.

"Well, to the Necker Hospital," C.25 answered.

"What's that, Boss, you knew?" the Paris kid said, astonished.

"If I hadn't known I couldn't have sent you to shadow the lame man!"

Just as he reached the threshold of the door with the Boss she stopped a moment.

"Let Marcel know that he's not to leave the laboratory. I will certainly need him when I return."

"All right, Boss," said Friquet, hurrying to obey.

From the first examination of the wounded woman, the intern left no hope. The knife thrust had been driven with a sure hand...with a hand that didn't tremble, with a hand that anger hadn't caused to go astray. The blade had gone through the lungs. The victim died shortly after her admission to the hospital without regaining consciousness, without having said a word. As the victim of that strange assassination was carried to the hospital morgue, the hospital administration began to inventory the objects found: clothing, undergarments, shoes, and handbag. During that operation, the Commissioner of Police arrived. A few instants later the Bursar was informed that a lady insisted on being seen without delay. "She had come, she said," reported the nurse who presented the request, "about the crime in the Invalides Park."

The Bursar looked at the Commissioner of Police. The two men winked at each other.

"She's right on time," murmured the Commissioner.

"Let her come in," the Bursar nodded.

Thérèse Arnaud entered. "Madame?" questioned the Bursar in the voice of a man bored with being interrupted in the course of important work.

C.25 held out an identity card. The attitude of the Bursar immediately changed. He put on a friendly smile.

"How may I be of service to you," he asked, and, while thinking C.25 did not see it, he surreptitiously pushed the card toward the Commissioner of Police.

"First of all," Thérèse Arnaud smiled, "give me back my official identity card from the Deuxième Bureau…"

"Oh! Pardon…the Bursar hurried to say.

"Next," she continued, "I would like to see the clothing of the victim of the crime in the Invalides Park…and particularly the hand bag."

"But," the Police Commissioner objected, "these objects must be used as the basis of the official inquiry."

"I know that perfectly well, Sir. I don't wish to encroach in any way on the prerogatives of the Police. On the contrary, I am completely willing to communicate to you any information which may be useful to you…but I am myself charged with a mission that I must fulfill."

"Charged with a mission? By whom?" inquired the Commissioner, unaware of the desperate looks the Bursar was sending him.

"By the Deuxième Bureau."

"Oh! Pardon! I didn't know…" the Commissioner apologized. "In that case…"

Shortly thereafter, the Police Commissioner made his official inquiry and C.25 fulfilled her secret mission, examining all the objects belonging to the dead woman. The Commissioner glanced briefly over the clothing. In short, he sized them up only in order to establish what social class the victim could have belonged to.

"Nothing interesting," he murmured.

"May I?" Thérèse Arnaud asked.

She carefully examined each of the items, scrutinized them, patted them, looking for some hiding place in the lining, some secret pocket. She went through that examination under the vaguely ironic eye of the Commissioner of Police. Suddenly C.25 smiled. She took out from a secret pocket hidden inside the belt of the skirt a small packet like those used by pharmacists. She opened it. She smelled the contents.

"Obviously!" she said.

"What is it?" the Commissioner of Police quickly asked.

Without answering directly, she asked the Bursar: "Would you be kind enough, Sir, to analyze the contents of this packet?"

"Gladly!" he quickly answered.

Thérèse Arnaud returned a part of the contents of the little packet of powder. The remainder she carefully wrapped up in paper. She put the new packet thus obtained in her purse.

"But..." the Commissioner began.

"I'm sharing, Sir. You'll have the powder after the analysis. About a gram! I'm keeping the other gram for my own examination."

During this short dialogue the Bursar had left the office. He returned and handed C.25 a paper and the little sachet of powder. She handed the packet as well as the piece of paper that she had briefly glanced at to the Commissioner of Police.

"Cocaine..." murmured the Commissioner. "So, the victim would be..."

"The victim's purse?" she asked. "And also, Bursar, the weapon of the crime..."

"Here it is..."

As the Commissioner came forward, C.25 opened the purse. She found there, as in the purse of every elegant woman, face powder, a fingernail file, a lipstick, some rouge, some eye shadow.

"Yes," the Commissioner stated, "the usual things."

Continuing her examination, in another pocket of the purse C.25 found a rather remarkable piece of stationary paper. It was a type of deluxe paper called "white sage" and a matching envelope.

"A letter...that's something interesting," the Commissioner said happily.

"Yes," C.25 agreed, passing the piece of paper and the envelope to the Commissioner. It was absolutely void of any writing and had no information.

"Is that all? No identification papers? No other letters? Nothing?" the Commissioner asked.

"Nothing, Sir."

"Ah!" he sighed, disappointed.

The crime weapon held Thérèse Arnaud's attention a long time. She examined it meticulously, looking at it in the daylight. She turned the blade over several times, taking the greatest care not to touch it except with great care.

"May I?" the Commissioner of Police asked.

"Of course...but I would prefer that you not touch it too much...because of the fingerprints. And the shoes?" she asked.

The Bursar hurried to do as the Deuxième Bureau agent asked. He handed her immediately a pair of elegant low-heeled shoes. She carefully examined the heels, trying to unscrew them. Somewhat disappointed in her turn, she murmured, "No...nevertheless..."

"All in all," the Commissioner summed up, "we haven't learned anything! A woman has been murdered. We have only a vague description of the murderer. Very vague! We don't know who the victim is! We know nothing at all about this mysterious affair..."

"Nothing!" Thérèse confirmed.

"I'm going to make my report. As for punishing the guilty person…" grimaced the Commissioner, who was about to leave.

"If you don't mind," C.25 said, "I have two things to ask you."

"What are they? Believe me, if it's in my power…" the Commissioner smiled amiably.

"Will you turn over to me, for a few hours, the weapon of the crime?"

"Agreed! Next?"

"I would also like to have for some time the sheet of paper and the envelope."

"The blank sheet of paper and the envelope without an address?" the Commissioner asked, astonished.

"Exactly!"

"Ah! Also granted!"

The Commissioner and C.25 exchanged a few banal sentences of politeness. Then, while the Magistrate was leaving the hospital, C.25 asked to see the corpse of the victim. She rapidly took down diverse facts. She kept the results to herself. Then she left in her turn, carrying very carefully the weapon of the crime and the white paper.

Passing through the lobby, near the office where there was an employee charged with giving information or guiding relatives of newly arrived accident victims, Thérèse Arnaud had a brief chat with Friquet whom she had left still on duty.

"Anyone?" she asked him.

"Nobody," answered the Paris street kid.

"Stay there. Same job: immediately follow anybody who enters and who attempts to obtain any kind of information about the Invalides Park crime…or who asks to see the victim…"

When she returned to her house, C.25 went straight to the laboratory.

"Take this, Marcel. Some work for you," she said, handing the Chemist the articles she had brought back from her visit to the hospital. "Start by working on the envelop and the piece of paper. We'll look at the knife later. This is urgent, Marcel. As soon as you discover the least thing, come tell me."

"Understood, Boss, I'll get to work on the job immediately."

On leaving the laboratory, C.25 returned to her office. She sat down in her chair, impatiently lighting a cigarette. After waiting five minutes she returned to the Chemist.

"Well, Marcel?"

"Nothing yet, Boss!"

"It's taking a long time!"

"It's been hardly five minutes," the Chemist explained. "I've already tried several chemicals…without the slightest result."

"Nevertheless, there must be something," said C.25. She promptly left the laboratory to return to her office.

"To find something, that's very nice, but still, there must be something...an address, some sort of text," remarked Marcel, doubly on edge as much by the failure of his chemicals as by the unusual impatience of the Boss. A few minutes later, a satisfied Marcel, a Marcel with a happy face entered Thérèse Arnaud's office.

"Here it is," he said, holding out the piece of paper.

"And the envelope?"

"There's nothing on the envelope," the Chemist answered.

"There is certainly something," she maintained. She glanced rapidly through the text which began to appear on the piece of paper.

My dear Lea
I would like to see you tomorrow at about 5 o'clock in the Invalides Park.
Bring you know what.
Georgette

Marcel, still smiling, was waiting for C.25's reaction. After reading it, the expression on the Boss's face again became sullen. She handed the paper back to the Chemist. In an irritated voice she exploded:

"That's not the text I want to know, my poor Marcel, it's the other one. I've known about this one a long time. I'm the one who wrote it! Don't be discouraged. This is only the beginning. This paper—which was absolutely blank—must tell us many things."

While the Chemist went back to his laboratory, C.25 sat down again in her chair. Then she immersed herself in deep thought. She pronounced in a low voice the bizarre sentence without any apparent connection which dominated her thoughts.

"The rendezvous...the argument...the *real* text of the letter...the lame man who went into the building with two entrances on the Rue Delambre...the heel that can't be unscrewed, the fingerprints which *must be* found on the dagger."

There was a heavy silence filled with multiple thoughts and studded with fragments of sentences. Then, suddenly, she reached a conclusion.

"All in all, everything is logical. *Too logical!* Everything is understandable. *Too understandable*! Let's not get all balled up!"

She tried again to return to her thoughts. She was very impatient with the results of the work given Marcel. She returned to the laboratory several times but each time to the question, "So, Marcel," the same disappointing answer, "Still nothing, Boss."

Finally a Marcel who, this time, couldn't contain his joy any longer came to the office.

"I've got it!" he exclaimed. "This will make you happy. I understand why the first text didn't satisfy you."

"Let me see!" C.25 cut him off sharply. And underneath the first text she read the following sentences:

"Don't stay in touch any longer with A.F.3, nor with H.806. Get back at any price the documents from A.F. take out H.806."

On the envelope in the same writing and with the same color of ink, the following superscription:

"H.42, Le Raincy. A.R. H.191." Then across the file : *"Urgent and Confidential."*

"Le Raincy," she murmured to herself. "That's just what I thought! That confirms everything! But, and there's the danger: everything is verified and confirmed too easily. And there's the mistake!"

Thérèse herself had scarcely finished reading when the text began to blur again, to disappear completely some instants afterward. And it was a piece of paper absolutely blank and an envelope absolutely void of an address that she returned to Marcel.

"How did you get at the second text underneath, Marcel?" the Boss inquired.

"A rather complicated chemical, with a basis of silver salts which required three successive baths in a well-defined order."

"Good!"

Again, some silent thoughts of Thérèse Arnaud. Then, little by little, her expression relaxed. Her eyes lit up. The wrinkle on her forehead disappeared. Her jaws relaxed. And she happily summed up:

"This time, Marcel, we're on the right track. Everything is clear! Even too clear! Pay attention!"

Then quickly changing subjects, or rather, continuing the logical process of her thoughts, C.25 reminded the Chemist:

"Don't forget, Marcel, the fingerprints on the knife."

"Immediately, Boss. I'll take care of it!"

Marcel left the office to take care of his task. C.25 rapidly took down on a piece of paper the text that had just been revealed. Then again, slowly, separating the words, she re-read: *Don't stay in touch any longer with A.F.3, nor with H.806. Get back, at any price, the documents from A.F.3. Take out H.806.*

A short silence, then: "Logically the victim in the Invalides Park, whose identity we don't know, and who is perhaps either the 'Chère Léa' or the 'Georgette' who signed the letter, must be known under the number H.806, controlled by Tiergarten Agents."

Then, still following her line of thought, C.25 continued: "Unless the victim is A.F.3 who had refused to give back the documents that it was necessary to *take back at any cost*," and she concluded: "To my way of thinking, this wasn't just a single crime committed between agents of the Tiergarten. Another is being prepared. Who was the first victim: A.F.3 or H.806? Let's not hurry to draw a conclusion. Besides, for us, that fact has no importance, whoever the victim, the case remains the same!"

The telephone rang. She picked up the receiver. Languille's voice came through. She listened to the communication and took down some notes on a piece of paper. Then she dictated new instructions.

"Very good, Languille, up to now. Continue to follow the man. I'll send you back-up. It must be understood that whatever happens, it's the man you're shadowing, even if he separates from the group."

As soon as she hung up, she stated firmly: "Decidedly, everything is confirmed."

She told Friquet to go immediately to find Malabar, who was resting in the garage. And while the Paris street kid was obeying in haste, C.25 went back over the first links of the chain which ought to give the solution to the Invalides Park crime.

Languille sent in a report via telephone: "The man entered No. 22 on the Rue Delambre."

C.25 didn't seem to let that fact preoccupy her. Languille told the Boss that after a long wait he had seen the man he was supposed to shadow leave by way of the door of building No. 90 on the Boulevard Montparnasse. Now, for C.25, this wasn't a mystery. The building on the Rue Delambre wasn't classified as one with two entrances. But for those who knew about it, it was easy to go from the building on the Rue Delambre into the courtyard of an organ factory, then after having gone through several courtyards, after having thrown the shadower off the track, to come out coolly on the Boulevard Montparnasse. As for Languille, he had been instructed at the same time to expect the exit of his "client" at the other exit. Up to this point, events had progressed exactly as C.25 had foreseen. Languille's telephone call had told of the outcome of the shadowing. After many twists and turns and some maneuvers to throw off possible followers, the man had reached Raincy. He had immediately gone toward a small café situated toward the end of Montfermeil. There he had met a couple who seemed to be impatiently waiting for him. No other suspicious fact.

What suspicions did C.25 have about the man she was having followed like this? No proofs existed. Only the fact of leaving through a hidden exit without being seen. But weren't there for this single fact many other explanations other than accusing right off, a man of espionage or murder? To go into a café on Raincy where a couple was waiting didn't constitute any more proof. Nevertheless, Thérèse Arnaud murmured:

"Everything is confirmed."

Just then Marcel returned. He held out to the Boss the proofs of two photographs he had taken—the fingerprints found on the dagger. At the first examination it could be seen clearly that two different people had handled that weapon the most often. In fact, among the many others, many series of fingerprints belonging to the same individuals were repeated.

"Collate those with the files of the Deuxième Bureau," was all C.25 said, and handed the two proofs back to Marcel.

Malabar and Friquet came in.

"Here's the sickliest of the troupe," said Friquet presenting Malabar. "Not surprising, he's still gaining weight. He was sleeping…"

Thérèse smiled. "He was right to sleep to gain strength. I'm very afraid that before long we're going to need him."

Then, speaking to the Alsatian, she ordered:

"You're going to take the car in the direction of Raincy. You'll find on the road near the end of Montfermeil a small café and in that café a man being shadowed by Languille—and a couple. You'll take charge of the couple. Now be careful. In case Languille's client has already left the place, look around. Try to find out what happened in the café."

"Understood, Boss!"

"And keep your eyes open…" Friquet recommended.

"Don't worry, wimp!" smiled the Colossus while rushing to carry out the orders received.

III. Race to Death

The summer night was clear. A light breeze nonchalantly pushed along a few fleecy clouds. The Montfermeil road spread out in the distance in front of the automobile's headlights, making the shadow of their lights triangular on the recent tarring, at times revealing a few villas. Suddenly Malabar slowed down.

"We're getting there," he murmured. "No use getting ourselves noticed. So let's try to find that famous café."

The automobile proceeded about 100 meters. The place was deserted, unpleasant, leaving a painful impression the onlooker would have difficulty in accounting for. A few trees in the fields seemed to be the phantom silhouettes of crouching monsters. Further away a little house could be seen at the edge of the road. An isolated little house, a kind of big, badly constructed cabin giving an impression of dirtiness and a lack of comfort. At the door, two iron tables and some chairs. On a kind of awning, its colors faded by the rain, was a pretentious sign: "Parrot Café." A kind of niggardly light filtered through the badly joined venetian blinds. An odor of rancid trash cans floated around the area, adding to the impression of poverty and dirtiness which emanated from the whole building.

The automobile stopped some meters beyond the café. Malabar retraced his steps. From a rapid glance through the openings in the venetian blinds, he could discern, in the badly lit room, the shadows of four drinkers. One of the clients was Languille. Malabar quickly deduced that he had arrived where he was supposed to. The four drinkers were seated like this: the Acrobat and the man he was shadowing, then the couple that Malabar was supposed to shadow. The Colossus didn't hesitate. He entered. Four pairs of eyes were automatically trained on him. Six eyes were filled with mistrust and Languille's apparently without expression.

The interior of the Parrot Café was not appealing. Wallpaper with faded colors covered the walls. In places, torn pieces of paper stained with mold revealed the plaster beneath. From the ceiling hung a light fitting where the fly-specks made a frosted shade, and which gave off a miserly amount of light falling mostly on the saucer serving as a reflector, leaving great holes of shadow in the room. The owner was sleeping behind the counter. He hadn't heard Malabar enter. Malabar's attention was suddenly attracted by a sharp noise from the corner of the room. In the obscurity he could see the shabby plumage of a green parrot that, bored, was trying to amuse himself by pecking on his dish.

"Nice, the Parrot Café," Malabar thought.

The atmosphere was thick with a floating sickly odor—spilled alcohol and wine, the smoke from cold cigarettes. Odors from bad cooking and burned grease covered everything, mingling with some cheap perfume forgotten by an elegant client who lost it there.

The owner finally shook off his torpor. Malabar, having reached a table, sat down. In order to avoid the trouble of getting up twice, the owner asked in a haughty voice, without budging from his counter:

"What'll you have, Sir?"

He took the order. With a resigned air he searched among the alignment of flasks of all shapes spread out in front of him. He chose two of them. He picked up a not-too-clean glass in which he poured a parsimonious amount of the aperitif ordered. Then, with a deep sigh, he left his counter and brought the drink to the table. Without looking at his client, his conscience clear with the accomplished chore, he returned to his place behind the counter. And soon, his head between his hands, he seemed to go into very profound meditation which was only a prelude to sleep.

Languille, a solitary drinker, was absorbed in reading a newspaper. The couple and the man who been shadowed continued to talk—an uninterrupted whisper, a sort of rapid buzzing. But no word, no sentence came distinctly either to Languille's ears or to those of the Alsatian. And from time to time, to add some liveliness or to put a nuance of local color into the café, the parrot rattled his chain or pecked on his dish.

Now the trio being watched consulted notes. One of them entered some information in his notebook. It appeared that they were summing up together the principal points of an important conversation. There was a short silence. The two men, aided by their notebooks, seemed to check the information exchanged. The woman silently approved with a slight nod of the head. Then she abruptly got up. She held out her hand to the two men who let her depart without the least reaction…as if it had always been agreed that she would leave first. The owner, still following a vague dream behind his counter, didn't even shake off his slumber. Malabar and Languille exchanged a rapid look. While the woman was walking toward the door, the two men she had just left started another conversation which Languille couldn't hear. The noise of a motor starting was heard, the sound of an impatient motor. Malabar threw a coin on the table. With a leap he was outside. The woman was already seated on a motorcycle, probably hidden behind the Parrot Café, and was leaving. A few seconds later, Malabar, at the wheel of his vehicle, began a pursuit of the fugitive. No doubt. No feint. For the woman the situation was clear. She was being followed. She had been found out. How? A mystery, but the fact was there. They were on her trail. And salvation, the only salvation possible, lay in the speed of the flight…or in a ruse throwing them off the track.

For Malabar the flight of the motorbike was a proof of guilt, a proof that he was on the right track. And in the middle of the night, under that too blue sky now totally cloudless where there floated a laughing moon, this was a truly deadly race. A car behind a motorcycle! The road to Paris! In the sleeping suburb it was a stampede out of control, careless of cross roads, of dangerous turns, roads in bad repair. The two vehicles rolled, jumped, bounded, vibrant. The woman and the Colossus, both bending over their respective steering mechanisms, both eyes fixed on the distance, looking for any way to gain a little ground, even at the cost of death. And the left turns, the streets crossed without warning. Roaring of the two motors. Triangular lights which lit the road. Trees, houses passed at a gallop. Soon that deadly race brought the two vehicles to the gates of Paris. There they would have to pay double attention.

Malabar made another effort to close the distance which separated him from the fugitive. He managed to gain several meters. But that wasn't enough. In the capital, the many opening avenues would allow the fugitive to make sudden turns more easily and she could disappear at once. Continuation of the ruse in the avenues in which the fugitive turned. Then with a sudden unexpected turn, she left the great arteries to enter the labyrinth of little streets, without, however, managing to throw off her attentive pursuer, able to foresee all the ruses, all the feints, skillfully managing his vehicle. Realizing the futility of her maneuver, she went back to the large avenues. And straight toward the center of Paris! Still at full speed! The quays opened their gloomy bluish street lights perspective. The Passy Quay! The Porte de Saint-Cloud! And it was again toward the suburbs. Again it was the continuation of that mad, deadly race in which the two adversaries were relentless. The two adversaries were strong! Neither gave up. Neither gave the least sign of fatigue. Two triangular lights still tracing their luminous field. Still the two drivers clenching their steering wheel. Still the harsh hum of two motors pushed to maximum output. Saint-Cloud, the S shaped climb which led to the station! The Ville d'Avray road with the dizzying passage across the dangerous Pont Noir. Then suddenly a sharp turn. And the deadly race went on in the direction of Marly-le-Roi, the situation almost unchanged since the departure from Raincy.

Neither of the two adversaries could gain a clear advantage. It was a kind of wearing-down war. Which one would tire first? Which one of the two drivers or of the two vehicles would tire the quickest? Again some turns. Again the countryside asleep under the Moon. The countryside lined with pleasant little houses with their windows blinded for the night. The Celle Saint-Cloud! Bougival! The rapid descent which ended at the bridge. The two motors clicking more furiously. For several instants the motorcycle seemed to gain a slight advantage over the heavy automobile, even though it was more powerful. Malabar was aware of that and pressed harder on the accelerator. All the pistons of the automobile vibrated. The motorbike had already reached the bridge. So, it was finished! The fugitive found herself in the automobile's headlights. The Colossus very clearly saw the motorcycle make a sudden swerve and drop over the parapet into the void and disappear. Several seconds later C.25's automobile stopped. With one jump, Malabar was at the spot of the accident. The parapet showed traces of the motorbike's passage. And below, the Seine! Tranquil water in which the Moon sparkled. A whirlpool…Circles in the water getting bigger and fading. The spot the vehicle and its rider had just fallen into. Malabar didn't hesitate. He dived from the top of the bridge. But the noise of the fall had alerted the sailors from two barges anchored near the bridge. Rescue was quickly organized. The barges rapidly reached the spot where the motorcycle and its rider had disappeared. Malabar dived several times. During this time the men on the barges explored the river bed with their grappling hooks. The search went on, still without the least result. Neither the motorbike nor the fugitive. Now doubt was no longer possible. All hope of finding the motorcycle rider alive had to be abandoned…if she hadn't been killed by the accident. Malabar still waited in hopes of seeing the sailors snatch a cadaver with their grappling hooks. Still nothing!

About an hour after the motorcycle rider fell into the Seine, Malabar decided to telephone Thérèse Arnaud to bring her up to date on what had happened at the Parrot Café and of the deadly race and its conclusion.

The Boss did nothing but dictate the following decision: "That's good! No reason to stay at Bougival! Go back to Languille."

IV. At the Parrot Café

The woman's departure hadn't caused any change in the position of the drinkers in the Parrot Café. The owner had scarcely half-opened an eye. The two men renewed their conversation which their comrade's departure had interrupted. Languille, seemingly indifferent, was trying in vain to hear a word of their interview which would orient him. Some moments passed, the tiresomely calm atmosphere still spreading. And from time to time, the sound made by the parrot jumping about on his perch.

Suddenly, before Languille had had time to set up any movement of effective defense, the two other drinkers, knocking their chairs over behind them, quickly jumped on the Acrobat. With a prompt return to consciousness, the owner of the café jumped over the counter with extraordinary agility for a man who seemed to be asleep. Faced with the brutality of the attack, Languille had fallen, despite his agility, despite his defiance, despite being accustomed to combat. Set upon by three men, surprised, he was vanquished. Reduced to helplessness, tied up, gagged, Languille was soon picked up by the three men, who carried him to the attic.

"And there's another one who won't bother us anymore," said one of them.

"What's to be done with him" asked the other.

"Let's leave him there and wait for instructions."

Languille silently blessed the spirit of discipline motivating the enemy agents. They had to wait for instructions. That was still a respite! It would have been so simple if personal initiative had been given to the two men to finish it once and for all! The cold barrel of a revolver placed on a temple…That's all! Or two hands squeezing a little strongly around a throat! And it was done! Or again, a raised hand showing the bright glitter of a knife…then the same hand brought down, like that at the argument between the two women in the Invalides Park. And everything was settled. But because they had to "wait for instruction"…

Nevertheless, the Acrobat's situation was far from ideal. The instructions awaited would probably only determine by what method and in what place the "prisoner" would be executed. The only thing Languille gained by his respite before execution was the ability to think. His destiny was the same, actually, as that of the man condemned to death who, certain of not being able to rely on any pardon, awaited the date of his execution. Heavy minutes! Long minutes! Interminable instants! What hope could be born in the mind of Thérèse Arnaud's assistant? What chance of salvation for him? What intervention could save him one more time from the vengeance of enemies?

Languille reflected. He had found himself in worse situations before. He had been captured before by German spies when the Boss didn't know where to find her assistant. While this time C.25 knew that Languille was at Raincy. Malabar had confirmed his friend's presence. When Malabar finished his mission, he would report to the Boss what had occurred right up to his departure. When C.25 became worried about the lack of news about her auxiliary, the place where he had last been seen would obviously be where she would try to find some clue allowing her to pick up the trail. Therefore she, or one of her collaborators, would necessarily return sooner or later to the Parrot Café.

However that hope wasn't worth very much. The instructions the enemy agents were waiting for might arrive from one minute to the next. Weren't the spies' hideouts marvelously organized? The telephone and the radio transmitter were working very well there...Consequently, the order to terminate the prisoner might come from one instant to the next...or even to transport him elsewhere. Because of that, Languille's head posed another problem. Obviously, if the orders came for execution on the spot, everything was useless. But, on the contrary, if the spies decided to transport Languille, how could C.25 be warned? How to let her know that her auxiliary had fallen into the hands of the enemy? How to leave a trace of the trail which wouldn't escape Thérèse Arnaud's investigating eye when she tried to pick up the trail? But what trace? And how?

The Acrobat had tried many times to see how solid his bonds were. If he had the smallest possibility of doing the least thing, if he could untie himself, his preoccupation then would not have been to alert C.25, but to escape, by his own means, from the hideout where he was a prisoner. The minutes dragged on. Long minutes! Slow minutes! Interminable moments! Interminable and where did they lead? Toward death? Toward salvation?

Following the instructions of the Boss, Malabar had left the sailors carrying on their futile search. Barges spangled with gold by the Moon on the Seine turned in a small circle around the point where the motorbike and its passenger had been swallowed up. Barges on which shadows raking the river were profiled. Tragic décor!

At full speed, Malabar had crossed the distance from Bougival to Raincy. Was the Parrot Café still open? Would the return of the Colossus raise suspicions? Besides, hadn't his departure following that of the woman warned the couple of enemy agents? Malabar didn't look for an answer to these questions. He mechanically bent his arms, flexing his biceps. And he murmured:

"Bah! I'll take care of that."

Despite the late hour, the same stingy light still flashed on and off through the blinds of the Parrot Café. Malabar parked his automobile several meters further off. He opened the door with a firm hand. He entered with a confident step, ready however for an attack. The décor was the same, still the same gloomy and dirty room, the same undefinable atmosphere. At the table where, shortly before, there was a trio of German agents, two young workers were talking in a low voice. Of the preceding couple, no trace. And Languille himself had disappeared. For the Colossus everything was normal. And the explanation was the following: having finished their conference with the woman motorbike rider, the two enemy agents had left. Languille had dashed out behind one of them, behind the man he had been especially told to shadow, and he followed the trail.

In those conditions, what could Malabar do? Wait for Languille's return? Nothing indicated that Languille would return to the Parrot Café. Very much to the contrary, his quite precise mission to follow the man who had gone into the building on the Rue Delambre seemed that it would keep him away from the café on Raincy for a long time. Malabar hesitated. C.25 on the telephone hadn't been precise. She hadn't even envisioned the hypothesis, although very normal, that returning to the Parrot Café Malabar wouldn't find his friend there any longer after an hour and a half absence. An hour and a half! It doesn't take that long not to find a man charged with shadowing at the same place! Two solutions for the Colossus: remain at the Parrot Café…waiting for what? Some problematic event? Or return to Paris and go to C.25's house. But in that case what was the use of this return to Raincy?

The two young workers continued their peaceful conversation, still without any word rising above a general whisper. The owner behind his counter was continuing his dream. Only the parrot, from time to time, gave some sign of activity. Noise of a chain rattled against his perch. A hard beak hitting the white iron of the feeding tray. Suddenly there was a long stretch of silence. The two young workers stopped talking. The owner's dream was transformed into sleep. No sound in the room. And the same stifling, sinister atmosphere seemed, because of this fact, to spread out and make it impossible to breathe.

Suddenly a voice…a strange voice, a voice which was at one and the same time laughing a laugh that cascaded into sobs…and sobbing sobs which ended in bursts of sinister joy. A laugh at the same time inhuman and Machiavellian! A voice giving an impression of suffering…A voice which resonated too high pitched for the deep silence of the room. A voice resembling the nasality of a reed pipe, falling suddenly into an indistinct, unintelligible crackling, resembling the shock of the broken bones of a skeleton rubbing against each other.

Surprised, the two young workers looked at each other. Malabar had a strange feeling and the owner seemed suddenly to arouse from his dream. Automatically, with the same intonations, with the same pauses, the same quaver, and the same indistinct ending, the voice took up the same refrain: "The guy…the guy is…in the att…"

And the parrot, satisfied, jumped about on his perch, ruffling his multicolored head plume… "The guy is in the att…"

The owner took out his watch. He yawned significantly. He intended to let his three clients know that it was closing time.

"The guy is in the att…"

Malabar had now made a decision. Obedience to the Boss's orders. It certainly wasn't without a motive that C.25 had sent Malabar on a second trip to Raincy. Therefore, since he was in the place, he would stay there!

Responding to the owner's yawn, the two young workers had thrown some change on the table.

"All right! We understand. You want to go to bed! Good night!"

"I want to go to bed…yes. But if I didn't want to go to bed it would be the same thing. The time is the time. And I have to close."

"Good evening, Patron. Sleep well!"

The two clients left. Malabar, motionless, remained alone.

"The guy is in the att…"

The owner advanced toward Malabar. With amiability at odds with his attitude and suddenly with the incomprehensible aim of not alienating a client, he said politely:

"Sir…It's closing time. Two minutes!"

Malabar took out his watch and continued: "It's only a quarter to twelve."

"But the time to clean up, to put things away…"

"I'm waiting for someone," the Colossus said.

The café owner smiled. "Someone? Here? Now?"

"Why not? We aren't in the middle of the Sahara. People can go to Raincy at midnight."

"Nobody ever comes," the owner growled. "Besides, we aren't in Raincy." And still grumbling, he began to put everything in order, without taking his eyes off his stubborn client.

"The guy is in the att…" the parrot squawked again.

Some minutes later the café owner tried again. "It's useless to wait any longer. I told you! Who do you expect to come here?"

"You never know," the Colossus replied evasively.

Then changing tone, the Parrot Café owner said: "If he's coming, you'll wait for him outside."

"Give me a Vermouth-Cassis," ordered Malabar, hoping in this way to obtain a new truce.

"Too late! At this hour I don't serve anymore."

The too sharp reply ruffled Malabar.

"Excuse me. You're still open. I asked you for a drink. You have to serve me."

"If I want to," objected the owner, phlegmatic.

"That remains to be seen!"

"It's already been settled!"

Their voices were now raised.

"What's been settled," the café owner said, suddenly menacing, "is that I'm telling you to pay me and leave. My house isn't a hotel. I'm not going to stay open for you. Besides, the Police regulations order me to close at midnight. It's midnight. Leave."

Malabar answered with a disconcerting calm: "And if I don't want to leave?"

"Well, look at this…"

With a quick movement the café owner had drawn a revolver, putting it under the Colossus's nose. But the half-completed gesture wasn't finished. A scream of pain rang out. A dull sound, the revolver falling to the floor. A new cry from the café owner who, his arm twisted by Malabar's powerful fist, moaned:

"Don't break it!"

"It's not your arm I'm going to break," Malabar said. "It's…" And putting advice into action: "no speeches, action," he immediately carried out his threat. There was a thud. The café owner, his arm unbroken, crumpled on the ground. "Yes!" was all Malabar said, looking down at the café owner, inert, on the floor.

"The guy is in the aataataa…" screeched the parrot, excited by the noise.

Malabar looked at the bird once again. He slowly repeated the mysterious incomplete sentence. Then he calmly picked up the café owner, carrying him under his arm. He balanced him for a moment over the counter so that the fall would be less far. He dropped the café owner behind the counter.

"You'll be alright there. Leave us in peace…" Malabar said encouragingly, without fearing the slightest contradiction from the café owner, knocked unconscious by the masterly blow of the fist he had received. Then Malabar walked toward the parrot's perch. Using his sweetest voice, he began:

"He's a pretty darling."

The parrot rolled his eyes.

"Pretty little dear," Malabar continued his flattery.

Glad to be the object of such attention, the feathered friend ruffled the plume on his head. Then, disguising his voice and trying to imitate as faithfully as possible the birds intonation, Malabar tried to encourage him:

"The guy…is in the aat…"

Happier and happier, the bird repeated: "The guy is in the att…"

Malabar renewed his trick. The bird repeated. And suddenly the word, the word Malabar had been so long searching for, the incomprehensible word that ended the sentence burst out:

"The guy is in the attic…" screeched the excited parrot.

"Thanks, old friend," Malabar said. "We're going up there to see."

A few minutes later, having taken every necessary precaution—locking the door leading to the road, having his revolver in his hand in case some unknown person came out of any of the rooms—Malabar began the climb. No obstacle opposed the Colossus, who was determined to go forward. He reached the attic. The locked door didn't resist a slight blow with his shoulders. Darkness. The faint light from Malabar's lantern brought out from the shadows old furniture, smashed straight chairs, broken armchairs. He saw a form on the floor. In one movement Malabar was kneeling near the bound man. The light threw its beam on his face.

"Oh, it's you, my poor Languille!" breathed Malabar.

"Yes, my big fellow! I was beginning to grow old, all alone, tied up, in this nest of spider webs. Yes," Languille sighed, stretching his stiff legs and flexing his arms.

Without wasting any time, C.25's auxiliaries had a rapid consultation. Languille told about the attack against him. Malabar recited why he had returned to Raincy. "The result," the Acrobat concluded, "is that my prey, the man who entered the building on the Rue Delambre and left by way of the Boulevard Montparnasse, slipped through my fingers."

"And me, the woman motorcycle rider rolled into the Seine."

"Empty-handed," Languille groaned.

"Not completely," Malabar corrected. "We still have the owner of this unusual café."

They made a quick decision and put it into immediate execution. The café owner was removed from behind the counter. Still carried by Malabar, he was thrown into the car.

"Let's go," Languille murmured. "We'll see what the Boss will say."

As Thérèse's two assistants were getting ready to take their places in the automobile, one at the steering wheel, the other beside the captive, two shots rang out. The purr of their motor suddenly stopped, sharply cut off.

V. A Missing Woman in Good Health

The owner of the Parrot Café had just been brought into Thérèse Arnaud's office. Marcel, Malabar and Languille were present near the Boss.

"So," C.25 started off, "are you ready to be more talkative today than last night?"

"I know nothing! I don't understand anything that's happened!" the man said stubbornly.

During the night, Thérèse Arnaud had seen her two aides Malabar and Languille arrive. The former still held a bound prisoner under his arm: the Raincy café owner. Languille had immediately recounted what had happened: his capture by the enemy agents, Malabar's arrival, put on the right path by the parrot's sentence, the decision to return to Paris with the captured man. Then, just as the vehicle was about to leave, the enemy agents began an offensive to thwart the transport of the captured man.

"Just as we were about to leave," Languille recounted, "two shots rang out. Before we were able to get into motion the vehicle was attacked. In the darkness on the other side of the road we saw a small group firing on us. Not knowing the number of our assailants and given the impossibility of our getting out of the line of fire by rapid flight, we had to use a ruse. We put our bound prisoner between us and those firing. And we did this while Malabar hurried to make a very temporary repair to the damage enemy fire caused to one of the tires. But one of the enemy agents had managed to break away from the group. By crawling, he had managed to get to the other side of the car. And suddenly standing up from his vantage point, he fired twice at Malabar, who miraculously had stooped down just at that moment to finish his repair. I immediately shot back. Hit, the man let out a cry of pain. Lacking all prudence, the group of our assailants went to help the wounded man, and while one part of the German agents picked up the wounded man, the other part attacked us head on and tried to grab our prisoner. Then after several skirmishes, when the wounded man was out of the line of fire, a voice rang out:

"Too bad! Retreat! We'll get him back soon!"

"The German agents fell back, not without trying again to hit us. However, the presence of their comrade hindered their fire. Finally, the tire repaired, here we are, Boss," the Acrobat concluded.

"Excellent!" Thérèse Arnaud approved.

She had at that point tried to interrogate the owner of the Parrot Café. The man claimed innocence. Brusquely interrupting her interrogation, C.25 ordered the man shut in the holding room, from which she had just had him removed.

"You know nothing," she repeated.

"Absolutely nothing," the man confirmed.

"That's all right," she concluded drily. "I know enough to send you to be shot."

The man turned pale. There was a long silence. C.25 surreptitiously observed her adversary's face. She examined it; she scrutinized it, while keeping an apparently indifferent faraway look. She casually lit a cigarette. Then, speaking to the Colossus, she said drily:

"Why are you waiting? Take him back to the holding room. He can stay there until we can have him put into the hands of the military authorities. It's over. That's all. His fate is sealed. No use wasting our time."

The man turned pale again. Malabar, carrying out the order received, approached the man. But just as the Colossus began moving, Thérèse Arnaud stopped him:

"Just a moment!"

The Alsatian didn't finish his approach.

Walking slowly toward the prisoner, C.25 asked:

"What do you think about freedom?"

The man's look was expressive. What he thought about it was clear. His opinion was that of a man who had just been confronted with the following tableau: a sinister morning, a pale early morning scarcely broken away from the night. A fog that envelopes the trees and cloaks the horizon. A naked space. A stake buried in the ground. A wagon comes. A man gets out and sees some meters from the stake a dozen soldiers ready to execute the order: "Fire!"

Ask such a man what he thinks about freedom, freedom which lets him taste the many pleasant things in life, to take advantage of the Sun and beautiful weather.

Thérèse Arnaud continued:

"I was probably wrong to ask you that question. Freedom isn't for you. You had to stay an honest owner of a café…"

"But I am an honest café owner," the man claimed.

"Of a café where strange things happen."

"It's not my fault," maintained the keeper. "I don't know anything. I'm not responsible for my clients. I don't know it if they commit reprehensible acts. Me, provided that they pay…"

Languille interrupted: "Then me, who hadn't done anything, why did you lend a hand to the two German agents who brought me down…"

"But, I didn't know they were German agents," the man answered.

"That's enough," C.25 broke in. "He'll explain somewhere else."

But at the moment Malabar was going to take charge of the prisoner again, Thérèse Arnaud, still very calm, without addressing the captive directly, remarked:

"After all, it's quite possible…maybe he didn't know."

The man breathed a sigh of relief and immediately defended himself.

"That's right," he said. "I didn't know and it would be unjust to hold me responsible."

"You'll explain that to the Military Authorities…" said C.25.

"Of course, but they could make a mistake."

"Then," Thérèse Arnaud consented, "explain to me how you could not have known."

"It's very simple. I saw clients come into my café. They were really free, right! Free enough to go somewhere else. They were talking. Me, I didn't hear what they were saying. I wasn't even paying attention!"

While continuing to pour out his story with volubility, the man was looking at C.25, trying to guess the impressions his claims made.

"After all, that's possible," C.25 added.

The prisoner's looks brightened.

"Only," the Secret Service agent went on, "after such business you'd have to change countries. You would abandon your café."

"Oh…yes! To live peacefully," the prisoner hurried to add.

"You would open a café somewhere else…"

"Yes…yes…"

"If you need, if you had to have a little money to buy the business, that could be found," C.25 continued.

"Oh!" the prisoner agreed, full of hope.

"That would be your dream, wouldn't it?"

"Exactly!"

"Well," broke in the Boss, "since you didn't know anything; since without doing it on purpose, you lent a hand to clients who started a fight in your café; since you furnished your attic to shut prisoners up there; since you use a revolver to throw clients out; since you have to have the place empty to allow clandestine meetings; since your friends tried to free you when you were captured; since, on the whole, as I've just clearly demonstrated to you, it seems you are completely innocent, you can say goodbye to your dream…to your future little café in a peaceful place where you'll lead a nice life without a past history. I can't do anything about it! You'll be shot. It's not my fault if you don't know the names of your clients and what they were doing in your café."

The man's face had gone through all phases of expression during Thérèse Arnaud's reply. Hope first of all, then doubt, then fear, then again terror! Certainly, now, once again, the man saw the last tableau of the drama dance before his eyes: bandaged eyes...the man placed against the stake and bound...and the crack of the shots.

"Since you don't know anything," C.25 continued, "I can't do anything for you! Absolutely nothing! You have less memory than your parrot. It's too bad you lost all memory of what happened in your café..."

The man hesitated. Very gently Thérèse Arnaud continued. "So, I'm going to help you. What happened to H.84?"

"H.84...I don't know," the man claimed.

"But, yes, you do," C.25 insisted. "H.84 who went to your café every evening to meet A.F.803 to receive stolen documents.

"I don't know," the prisoner maintained.

"I'm better informed than you are! Do you want me to show you H.84 and confront you with A.F.803? *They spoke to each other.* We aren't psychic, you understand. If we found the Raincy hideout, it was because H.83 and A.F.119 talked. We know a great deal too much about you. They told us everything."

"Oh, the betrayers!" the prisoner burst out.

"Take him to Captain Ladoux," Thérèse Arnaud decided. "If he doesn't know anything, we, on the contrary, know everything."

"All right, let's go!" Languille decided.

Malabar had already gone down to take the car out of the garage. The man was shocked. There was a last interior combat. He saw the little quiet café. The Caponnière at Vincennes. It aroused a desire for vengeance in him.

"Since they've betrayed, me, I'm going to tell everything."

Thérèse Arnaud's face suddenly lit up with a triumphant smile.

"Be careful," she threatened. "You've seen that I'm informed. I've proved it to you. I've told you that they have all talked. Therefore, I can immediately verify what you say. I warn you that at the first lie, at the first equivocation, at the least attempt to deceive me, I won't listen to another word from you. Not a single word! Languille is here. In two minutes the car will be downstairs. I will have you sent away immediately. Weigh your words very well."

"I'll talk," the man repeated.

"Good," she said in an expressionless voice, perfecting disguising the sensation of triumph.

Just at that moment the office door swung violently open. A Herculean form came in, a Herculean form who held another form a great deal smaller under his arm. It was fighting furiously. Suddenly turning loose of his prey, that fell on the floor, Malabar said only:

"Here you are, Boss."

Before the young woman, Malabar's prisoner, could rise, Languille had jumped forward and tied her up. Leaving the owner of the Parrot Café for a moment, Thérèse Arnaud went toward the new arrival and greeted her very courteously, saying:

"Good morning, H.191. I was expecting you, but I didn't think I would receive your visit so soon."

Then, going back to Malabar, she said:

"You were very kind, Malabar, to invite the lady to come upstairs to see me! But explain to me how you ran into her."

Malabar, very happy about his exploit, told C.25 how it happened. Carrying out the order to get the car to take away the Raincy prisoner, the Colossus went toward the garage. He suddenly saw a motorbike in the street coming toward him, a motorcycle driven by a woman. And he bounded forward. He had recognized his fugitive from the night before. The woman who had disappeared with her machine, fallen into the Seine from the Bougival Bridge. The Colossus didn't hesitate. At the risk of being crushed by the machine, he jumped on the motorcycle, seizing the woman riding it. And despite the kicks she was giving him, saying nothing more, he put her under his arm and brought her immediately to the Boss's house, which was close by.

The café owner and the new prisoner exchanged a rapid look.

"Be careful!" was all C.25 said to the strange café owner. "You know what you promised. We'll continue our conversation later."

In order to deal with the new prisoner, C.25 had the café owner taken to the holding room.

Now we're going to get comfortable," she said, approaching H.191. "But before conversing profitably, let us take care of formalities." C.25 gave instructions to Marcel, who immediately brought what was necessary to take the fingerprints of the German agent. The results were conclusive. The fingerprints were the same as one of the series of fingerprints on the knife found beside the victim of the assassination at the Invalides Park.

"There's the signature of the crime," said Thérèse Arnaud. "So then, you were the one ordered to take out that famous A.F.3, from whom documents were to be retrieved at any cost."

The prisoner shrugged her shoulders disdainfully.

"Afterward, as soon as you were in possession of the recovered documents by murdering one of your Tiergarten colleagues, you went to Raincy, where you met your accomplice H.42. You gave him the recovered documents. Not badly played! Too bad I'd been made aware of all that affair. Before! Except for that, you had every chance of success."

Taking advantage of the Boss's silence, Malabar, always slow to comprehend, asked:

"You knew about it before...? Then maybe you'll explain to me how that woman I followed yesterday evening from Raincy to Bougival, that I *saw with my own eyes* fall into the Seine with her motorcycle, is alive today! Because, even so, the Seine…my dives, the sailors' searches…"

"Child's play, my poor Malabar," said C.25. "Child's play for H.191, scarcely the risk of an accident crossing the parapet. Then a dive, the motorcycle abandoned. You didn't know that H.191 is a first rate athlete so she swam across. And my poor Malabar, while you were waiting for the sailors to pick up the victim's body, this woman came to ground on one of the banks on the other side of the river, and peacefully made off. However, Malabar, I must admit that my intuition was at fault. I thought that as soon as H.191 left the water she would rejoin, however she could, the espionage center at Raincy. That's why I ordered you to return there. Finally, this wasn't a useless race since it brought about Languille's safety and a German agent."

After that explanation to satisfy Malabar's curiosity, C.25 returned to H.191.

"Why don't we chat a little, dear Agent 191, about the murder of Agent H.806."

The prisoner responded with the same disdainful shrug of her shoulders.

This wasn't the first time C.25 had run up against such an attitude from her prisoners. So she didn't get upset. Hiding the disappointment she felt because of this muteness, she decided:

"My dear H.191, I'm sure you're still a little troubled about how we found out so rapidly. To put you back in a good mood, to cheer you up, I'm going to give you a few minutes of solitude to pull yourself together. After that I hope we'll be able to pick up again, fruitfully, our interesting conversation."

"You won't learn anything," screamed the German spy.

Nevertheless, Malabar and Languille rapidly carried out Thérèse Arnaud's orders. While the owner of the Parrot was again taken from the holding cell, H.191 took his place there. The operation was completed without the two prisoners being able to exchange a single word.

C.25 had the prisoner placed in front of her.

"Our turn," she said.

The man indicated by a sign that he was ready to answer. In order to avoid wasting time, and instead of leaving the café owner time to make up a story, Thérèse Arnaud conducted the interrogation, limiting herself to bringing out the points that especially interested her.

"I know you are French. I have your dossier. Your credentials are good. I'm not unaware that you currently have a son fighting at the front…"

"My son," the man murmured with deep emotion.

"Yes!" C.25 continued with more vehemence. "Your son! You should have thought about that before accepting the job you did. Don't you understand that, acting as you acted, you became the enemy of your son? You facilitated the task of those who, any minute, can send him a bullet, a piece of shrapnel…"

The café owner lowered his head. Changing her tone brusquely, C.25 asked:

"How did you become the aide of the German agents?"

"Just the way things worked out!"

"Oh! Just the way things worked out! That's very quickly said," Thérèse Arnaud answered sharply. The man quickly explained.

He bought the Parrot Café one year before the declaration of war. He had put in it everything he had. But the investment had been over estimated. In reality the Parrot Café, poorly situated, without a clientele, had been a deplorable business. The owner was very quickly at his wits' end. What he took in was hardly enough to pay general operating expenses. It was a niggardly life. Always the struggle to pay the rent, the expense of gas, of electricity, of the telephone. Then the very short sickness and death of his wife just before the declaration of war. His son left for the front almost immediately. Alone at Raincy, his situation worsened. The war had diminished the small number of clients. Entire days went by without any customers coming in. Suddenly, one evening, two men entered who examined the room with curiosity. They ordered many drinks and talked together for several hours. They came back the next day, bringing some friends. They rapidly became regular clients. Income grew. In a short time, they engaged the owner in conversation. They wanted—they said—a quiet place to get together and not be disturbed...even if the meetings took place at night. After some hesitation, pressed by the need for money, the man agreed, the clients having promised to pay for everything in case of a fine levied for breaking the closing laws. It was only later that the man became aware of the real work his clients exercised. But he was already caught in the gears. He couldn't get free. He feared reprisals...Then, also, he was beginning to get some profit. That let him send some packages to his son.

"But, there you have it," he concluded with a great gesture of resignation.

The story had been told with an undeniable accent of sincerity. C.25, accustomed to seeing comedies played out by German agents, wasn't mistaken this time. The man was telling the truth.

"The regular customers who frequented your café, were there many of them?" she asked.

"They were almost always the same ones who came back. They didn't always come together. They met sometimes with one, sometimes with another. They talked together; they left. That's all."

"Did you sometimes have the impression that they exchanged papers, packages?"

"Papers often, yes! Packages, no."

"How did you know that?" C.25 questioned.

"The easiest way in the world. After some time they no longer paid any attention to me. My clients always spoke in a low voice. I could never hear the exact sense of their conversations. But I often saw them take out their letter cases and remove some papers they exchanged," the man said.

"Papers...or envelopes?" C.25 asked.

"Both. Sometimes I noticed some envelopes carefully sealed. Besides, it was always the same client who received the envelopes. Other times it was a matter of papers. In that case, the man who received the document examined it and sometimes I heard exclamations such as: 'Oh, interesting!' and 'Oh, that's a good job,' or 'Compliments!' and so on," the café owner explained docilely.

"About how many of these special clients, in your estimation, frequented your café?"

The man thought several moments and then he answered precisely: "Between 15 and 20. Some came more often than others. Yes, 15...20...not more."

"Do you know their names?"

"I never heard them use names, not even first names."

"Numbers, then?" C.25 asked.

"No! They never asked anything. The first one to arrive sat down and waited."

"Did they never give you the smallest piece of paper to deliver to a designated person...Were you never given any kind of commission?" C 25 insisted.

"Never!"

Then, opening a drawer of her desk, Thérèse Arnaud took out a big album. She placed it in front of the man.

"Now, pay attention. Since there were scarcely about 20 of the special clients who frequented your establishment, you knew them. You would be able to recognize them. You must be able to recognize them. So, flip through this album of photographs and point out those you recognize."

C.25's voice had suddenly become more commanding. She dominated her vanquished adversary. The man felt the futility of any resistance, of any attempt at trickery. He hesitated one last time. Then he began to turn the pages of the album with a trembling hand. From time to time he stopped at a photograph. He raised his eyes toward C.25, who was attentively following each movement of the café owner. He didn't say a single word. He accused no one. But at each pause, at each look, C.25 understood that he had recognized one of his clients and she took down notes on a sheet of notepad.

When the man turned the last page of the album, he exhaled a heavy sigh and a cold sweat pearled his forehead.

"I'm a dead man!" he exclaimed. "They warned me!"

Thérèse Arnaud picked up the album. She leafed through it more rapidly than the man had, like someone who knew exactly what he was looking for.

Putting one photograph back in front of the man, she asked:

"The man who received *only* envelopes is this one, isn't it?"

The Parrot Café owner made a slight affirmative sign.

"Good," C.25 whispered.

There was a short silence. Soon the famous Secret Service agent spoke again.

"All these men, let's say all these enemy agents, certainly had a leader. Did it seem to you that one of them gave orders?"

The café owner hesitated a moment. With difficulty he explained.

"Yes and no."

"That means?"

"All those who came regularly seemed to have the same rank. They seemed to be only carrying out orders. People to whom you say: 'You'll do such and such a thing'…and who obey without taking their own initiative. Nevertheless…"

"Nevertheless?" Thérèse Arnaud asked, quickly interested.

"Nevertheless, they answered to a leader, a leader they never clearly identified, that I never saw…but who certainly came to Raincy."

"Explain yourself," C.25 insisted.

"Here's how it was. At three different times my clients rented a room for the night. However, only a very small number of those who came regularly came those times. But two automobiles were parked near my café."

"Would you recognize the occupants of these vehicles?"

"No! I didn't see them! On those nights I was specifically instructed not to appear. One of my regular clients took my place at the café at closing time. And me, I was supposed to disappear and not come back into the room under any pretext…" the man explained.

"Do you know the dates of these meetings?"

"Yes! That struck me. I remember very well. The night of 10-11 September, the night of 15-16 March, the night of 25-26 June…"

"Wouldn't that be instead the night of 24-25 June?" C.25 asked

The man searched his memory. "A Thursday to Friday night…"

C.25 passed him a calendar. The man looked at the French Secret Service agent admiringly.

"You're right," he stated.

Without acknowledging that praise, C.25 started again rapidly.

"You don't know anything about what happened at your café on those nights? You saw nothing, heard nothing? No particular detail struck your imagination? The slightest fact?"

"No…nothing…or very little…It was night. I was in my bedroom in my house. When I heard a car stop I was near the window. Through the cracks in the blinds I only saw…recognized very badly…silhouettes: two men and a woman.

"…that you couldn't recognize?"

"I saw only their backs, at night…from my second floor…so…" the man apologized.

"Think again…not the least fact, even in the case you're talking about?"

"Perhaps, but I wouldn't swear that one of the men was missing an arm, or had a wounded arm, because the arm of his overcoat seemed loose, floating."

"And it was during the night of 24-25 June that you noticed that?"

"Yes," the man confirmed.

Thérèse went to search through a drawer full of photograph packets. She placed on the desk in front of the café owner a photograph of a woman viewed from the back wearing an overcoat. The man's expression lit up a moment.

"A mistake is always possible in such situations," he murmured, "but that is exactly the impression the silhouette gave."

"Mademoiselle Doktor…" murmured C.25.

Thérèse Arnaud asked her prisoner some additional questions of detail. He answered in a satisfactory manner.

"Good," she said. "You are temporarily free. You're going to return to our café at Raincy, as if nothing had happened."

"But…the others…Those shooting yesterday…when I was captured…"

"After all that…yes…It's preferable."

She rapidly gave her auxiliaries instructions to set up a trap at the Parrot Café. Then she established a hideout for the café owner. There, in a safe place, he would await orders. Just as she was finishing, Friquet, out of breath, entered.

"Boss," he said, "someone came to the Necker Hospital to ask to see the victim from the Invalides Park."

"You followed him?"

"There was no need, Boss, I know him and you do too."

"Who?"

"Peter…the man from the Rue Madame case, the Luxembourg Pavilion."

"Good," said Thérèse. "That one isn't useful to us any longer now. We're going to put an end to his exploits."

While C.25's auxiliaries at Raincy were finishing the set up for the German agents frequenting the Parrot Café, Thérèse Arnaud took some rest.

The evening newspapers reported:

While train 457 was traveling toward Montereau, nearing the Melun station, the alarm sounded. The employees rushed toward the compartment from which the call originated. They found the cadaver of a man struck in the stomach by a dagger. The man had just died. Just as the train stopped, some persons saw a man flee from the compartment where the drama had taken place. Immediately chased, seeing himself surrounded, he killed himself with a bullet through the temple. The victim was the owner of a café at Raincy called the Parrot Café. As for the murderer, he could not be identified. However, it is thought that he was a suspect known under the name of Peter…who was under surveillance of the Police.

When she had read those lines, C.25 murmured: vengeance of the Tiergarten agents. Poor owner of the Parrot Café. There are certain mistakes that can't be atoned for…They have to be paid for."

In the evening after a new and fruitless attempt to question H.191, she was turned over to the military authorities. While Malabar and Languille had gone to collect the prisoner, the telephone rang. The voice of Captain Ladoux was at the other end of the line. A curt voice, shaken with gasps of emotion.

"C.25, would you come to my office immediately," said the Chief of the Deuxième Bureau. "Immediately," he insisted. "Drop every case…"

C.25 said only: "I'll be at your disposition in five minutes."

THE WOMAN WITH THE MUFF
(The Capture of Mata Hari)

I. Rue Pigalle, 5 p.m.

A fine, soaking rain fell relentlessly from a low sky. The winter night began to envelope Paris. Lights came on. The hustle and bustle of the pedestrians, the cars, in the fog, in the mud, intensified with the approach of evening. Activity around the cafés on the Pigalle square doubled. Then, in the Rue Pigalle, made slippery by the rain, electric signs of bars began to blink, throwing their multi-colored lights on the sides of houses.

On the sharp slope which connects the Pigalle square to the crossroads of the Rue Chaptal, Notre Dame de Lorette and Fontaine, a horse-drawn vehicle descended slowly. The coachman of the covered vehicle was holding back the animal whose hooves were sliding on the oily cobblestones. Near the driver, a man, impassive, lost in some faraway dream, was smoking short puffs on a pipe. With a competent hand, the coachman brought the vehicle to the sidewalk. Then he stopped. The wagon had halted in front of a rather nice looking furnished house. The ground floor and the second floor were occupied by a night club. A large electric sign, not yet lit, covered four floors of the façade, spreading out above the sidewalk the famous name of the night club, so that it was visible from a distance.

As soon as the vehicle stopped the two men jumped to the sidewalk. With mechanically professional movements, they unhooked a long sliding ladder fixed to the exterior of the vehicle. They carried it over to the house and placed it up against the wall near the sign. Their purpose, probably, was to test or clean it. While one of the men remained on the sidewalk, the other quickly climbed up. At the third story level, he appeared to examine the letter A with great interest. Then he suddenly put his hand into a big pocket of his shirt. He took out a medium-sized package that he slid into the interior of the sign, between the electric light bulbs which formed the letter A. With the same speed, the man came down immediately afterward. He whispered some words into his companion's ear. The two individuals folded their ladder and replaced it on the side of the vehicle. They climbed back on the seat. They glanced around briefly to be sure no one had seen what they had done. And the vehicle went away very slowly down the Rue Pigalle.

The wagon had scarcely disappeared when a woman pushing a bicycle with a packet of newspapers on its handlebars came out of the carriage entry of the adjacent house. After glancing around, the young woman pushed her bicycle to the street. Then she nimbly mounted the bicycle and started down the Rue

Pigalle, trying to narrow the distance that separated her from the wagon.

A few minutes afterward, in the window closest to the electric sign on the third floor of the house, a light turned on. The curtain drew back and revealed a human presence behind the window. The window slowly opened. And while the body of the room's occupant remained invisible, hidden behind the sides of the window, a feminine hand advanced toward the sign, very directly toward the letter A. Shortly thereafter, the same hand, which with remarkable agility had reached into the letter A, disappeared in the window, carrying the packet put there by the workers. The window closed again. The light behind the curtain was turned off.

Under the carriage door of the building situated across from the night club, a man of imposing stature, who seemed to have been taking shelter there from the soaking rain, murmured:

"Now's the time!"

Immediately leaving his refuge, he went across the street. With a firm step, he entered the furnished house. In a very short time, he came back out walking beside a young woman of middle height who seemed to be very frightened. The couple walked along a short distance silently. The man had passed his arm under that of his companion. A car with all its blinds down was parked at the corner of the Rue Rochefoucault. When he came to the car, the man opened the door. He gestured to tell his companion to get into the car, and he accompanied this gesture with a slight pressure as if he was afraid of a refusal. As soon as the young woman had disappeared inside the car, the door slammed shut. The man got behind the steering wheel. The motor roared; the car started off and was rapidly lost in the Rue Notre-Dame de Lorette. Driven with a sure hand by the man who knew Paris, the traffic jams that could slow his speed, the car stopped in front of Thérèse Arnaud's house. The driver got out. He opened the door. He helped the young woman to get out of the vehicle. And still holding her by her arm, probably to guide her more safely, he helped her go down the sidewalk.

As soon as the couple had reached the domicile of the famous French Secret Service agent, the man entered, having the young woman enter in front of him. He went across C.25's office. Still preceded by his companion, he conducted her into the corridor. He opened a door which was the only entry to the fortified room. With a light push he made the young woman enter. On the threshold she drew back somewhat. He closed the door, which locked automatically. Then with a clear conscience, probably satisfied with the result of his mission, he returned to Thérèse Arnaud's office. He settled himself comfortably into an arm chair. He took a pipe from his pocket. He lit it casually. And he lost himself in an endless dream, following with his eyes the rising blue curls of smoke.

Malabar was dreaming...

II. A Strange Vehicle

In a few minutes of pedaling, the cyclist caught up with the horse drawn wagon, which continued to descend the Rue Pigalle. At that point, the young woman adjusted her speed to that of the vehicle. She arranged it so that she always trailed just behind without letting herself be outdistanced by road jams or necessary stops caused by traffic.

Several times the wagon halted at the edge of the sidewalk. The two men immediately got out. While one seemed to oversee his companion's task, the latter carried out some rapid repairs, either to a sign, to some window pane, or to some safety rail. And always, as soon as he had reached the place where he had some work to do, he took a little packet out of his shirt pocket that he concealed in a hiding place chosen in advance. As soon as he had placed his mysterious package, he rapidly returned to the wagon that resumed its jolting progress without delay. The itinerary the vehicle followed seemed laid out by some eccentric person. In the trail of the vehicle, the cyclist rode across the Rue Pigalle, the Rue Saint-Lazare, the Boulevard Malesherbes, the Avenue de l'Opéra, the Rue Rivoli. Then in a sudden detour, the wagon reached the left bank. It stopped in the vicinity of the Jardin des Plantes. It parked again in the Rue des Écoles where the driver seemed to take care of a repair to the tile floor of a public urinal. Then after a new stop beside a garden fence on the Rue de Vaugirard, near the little pavilion in the Luxembourg Gardens, almost at the corner of the street with the same name, he started toward Montparnasse. Another stop took place on the Boulevard Edgar Quinet, in front of a building under construction. The coachman worked at pasting a poster on a sign board. But, once again, for anyone watching him, he hid a package in a kind of box fixed behind the signboard.

Then the vehicle came to the intersection of the Rue Vandamme and the Rue du Château. There the wagon entered a sort of shed. The cyclist stopped several meters from where the wagon had disappeared. And she waited. She waited until the coachman and his companion had left the shed. On foot, walking casually, they went toward a small rundown café. From the outside, the cyclist saw their two silhouettes in front of the counter. Still pushing her bicycle, she went away several meters. She was soon joined by two men to whom she said some words in a low voice. And accompanied by the two men, she went back to take her place near the little café where the other two men from the wagon were still at the bar. On a word from the cyclist, one of the men left the group and went in his turn into the café. He approached the two drinkers. A soon as the latter were ready to leave, the newcomer rapidly paid for his drink and left the establishment the same time as the strange drivers of the vehicle. Outside a scuffle rapidly broke out. As soon as the man who had plastered the sign and his companion set foot on the sidewalk, another man came forward quickly. From inside the café the client pushed the drinker who preceded him into the street. A commanding voice ordered:

"No use crying out. No point in making a scene!"

And in a few fast movements, the drivers of the strange vehicle, hand-cuffed, were pushed into a taxi parked some meters further away.

"Let's go!" the cyclist ordered, taking a seat near the two men with one of her aides, while the other was installed near the driver.

Malabar was still in C.25's office when she entered, following the two prisoners flanked by Friquet and Languille .

"Well, Malabar?" the Boss inquired.

"Well," the satisfied Colossus answered. "I operated as you instructed me...And 'the client' is waiting for you in the holding room."

"That's good! Go get her! We're going to question all three of them to-gether."

The two drivers of the wagon cast worried looks around them. During the trip from the place of their arrest to C.25's house they had protested, complaining of the fate reserved for them and demanding the reasons for their capture. C.25 had only answered all their complaints and demands for explanations with: "We'll see later!"

And Friquet had murmured, "They have some nerve, those two clients there! As if they don't know what they've done!"

Malabar, following C.25's orders, hurried to take the young girl he had captured in the furnished house on the Rue Pigalle out of the holding room, where he had locked her on his arrival. Entering C.25's office, the prisoner looked at the two men, handcuffed, guarded by Languille and Friquet, also waiting to be interrogated. However, Thérèse Arnaud could detect no sign of complicity, not the least indication in the rapid glance. The three prisoners looked at each other with astonishment. But nothing, absolutely nothing, indicated that they already knew each other. In any case, if they had already had any connection, their indifference was perfectly acted. And it seemed believable that they found themselves in each other's presence for the first time.

Thérèse began by interrogating the two men from the wagon. She asked them to explain their bizarre itinerary and the jobs carried out. The answer was disappointing. One of the men furnished the following information:

"I do what my boss tells me to do. I work, with my friend, at an advertising agency. Every morning I get a list of repairs to make. When I've finished, I take the horse and wagon to the shed on the Rue du Château. So you have no reason to hold me prisoner."

During that explanation the other captive, nodded, approved silently the details his colleague furnished.

"And the package? The packet that you regularly placed at each of your stops in the most diverse spots and in the strangest hiding places. These were very carefully pinpointed in advance," Thérèse Arnaud demanded. "Was that also part of your job?"

The two men exchanged a rapid surprised look. They seemed to be questioning each other and questioning themselves. The expression on their faces showed the most total lack of comprehension. The man being interrogated by Thérèse, asked his companion:

"Do you understand anything about that story?"

"Me? Nothing at all. What packages? What hiding places? What…"

"There is certainly a mistake!" the prisoner complained once again. "You've mistaken us for someone else…"

"But of course," Thérèse threw in ironically.

The two men exchanged a new surprised look, but that time a kind of silent worry seemed to be coming over them. Leaving the two men for a moment, Thérèse Arnaud addressed the woman prisoner.

"Do you want to tell me what they're refusing to enlighten me about?"

"How can I? I don't know these two men! I don't know anything about the story you're talking about!" protested the woman.

"And you also don't know anything about the packets, right?"

"What packets?" the young woman asked.

C.25 looked at the three prisoners for a moment. She often had to fight against the ill will, the bad faith of the German spies. She had never yet found agents of the Tiergarten likely to act out that comedy to her with that tranquil assurance, that confidence, and that perfect command.

"Truly, they're very strong," she murmured. "What perfect actors!"

During that silence, the three captives continued to look at each other, with looks empty of all expression. Going back to her interrogation, still addressing the female prisoner:

"What packet? That's easy. The packet one of these gentlemen put inside the letter A of the electric sign mounted along the front of the house you live in. To be even more precise, the bedroom you occupy where the window opens nearest to the letter A of the sign, that allows you to pick up the parcels placed in that spot."

"The parcel? The sign?" stammered the young woman.

"You don't know anything?" C.25, getting worked up, asked.

"Nothing at all," the captive replied with unshakeable calm. Then, changing tactics, she continued with volubility:

"If I knew something, I would immediately tell you so you would realize your error and turn me loose. I don't understand anything about your story of a sign. I have been living in a furnished house in the Rue Pigalle for the past two weeks. I don't do anything! I don't know the men or women neighbors! I'm a dancer. I get in very late at night. I sleep part of the day. I don't take any interest in what happens in the street. And besides, I had just got out of bed when someone broke into my bedroom to bring me here…So I can't give you any information about the little parcel you're asking me about…"

"Then how do you explain that this parcel was found in your possession?" Thérèse Arnaud asked calmly, waiting to see that argument trouble the captive.

Still with the same calm, the same expression of total ignorance, the young woman answered without the slightest hesitation.

"But what parcel, Madame?"

"Malabar?" C.25 called. "The parcel?'

The colossus looked astonished.

"The parcel?" he asked. "I don't have it!"

Thérèse Arnaud's eyes flashed. In a curt tone she questioned:

"How's that, Malabar. You don't have the parcel?"

"No, Boss, I didn't know!"

Thérèse Arnaud's shoulders shook in rage.

"All right. I'll speak to you about that later," she said curtly. She turned toward Languille. In a low voice she gave him some rapid instructions. The Acrobat immediately left the office murmuring: "O.K. Boss."

The three prisoners hadn't missed that short scene. Without the least change of expression on their passive faces, a furtive smile seemed apparent nevertheless. But so furtive!

Taking advantage of that incident, the female prisoner replied.

"There's certainly proof of the mistake! I don't know why, but you're searching for a woman who took a package from the electric sign. Now me, I don't have any parcel! It wasn't found in my bedroom!"

"I didn't search it! I didn't know…" Malabar interrupted.

"If you had searched it, you wouldn't have found it…because I didn't have it…" the woman continued. "I'm not the one…"

"That's enough!" Thérèse cut her off curtly. Leaving her three prisoners, she went to settle into her armchair. She lit a cigarette. She nervously took a few puffs. And still without paying attention to the occupants of the office, she raged in a low voice:

"This is really too stupid!"

When Languille returned, out of breath, he went straight to Thérèse Arnaud. "Well?" she asked.

In a low voice, the Acrobat told her the result of his mission. He had gone to the furnished house on the Rue Pigalle. He had gone into the prisoner's bedroom. He had carefully searched everywhere. And he had found nothing. Absolutely nothing! To have a clear conscience, he had also searched the hiding place in the sign. It was empty.

Thus the proof Thérèse Arnaud was looking for, the proof which would confound the stubborn prisoner, was escaping the agents of the Deuxième Bureau. And that, through Malabar's fault. Since Languille's departure, the three prisoners, even though they had never seemed very worried, seemed to be reassured. Their faces seemed to have a mocking expression. it was now certain that no one would find the physical proof in the bedroom on the Rue Pigalle which would serve as a basis for the accusation hovering over them.

A long silence followed Languille's report. Several times the Boss's eyes, still flashing, rested on the confused Malabar...then on the three prisoners seemingly impassive...but ironic. In a curt voice, Thérèse Arnaud ordered Friquet and Languille:

"Take the handcuffs off them."

The prisoners breathed an imperceptible sigh. C.25's aides obeyed, somewhat disappointed.

In an emotionless voice, mastering her anger, the French agent threw out:

"They can leave! They're free!"

The prisoners immediately took advantage of that authorization given them. And without a word, they left the office.

"Follow them?" questioned Friquet as soon as they had left.

"Oh! Now it's absolutely useless!" C.25 said irritably.

As soon as she was alone with Malabar, Thérèse Arnaud exploded:

"Really, Malabar, I wonder what you were thinking about!"

"But, Boss..." Malabar defended himself.

"There's no 'But Boss.' I sent you to the Rue Pigalle on surveillance. I pointed out to you in advance what might happen...because I knew what was going to happen. I was certain of it. I specifically said that when events came about as I had predicted, you had only to go up to the third floor, the last bedroom in the corridor and to seize, with the least possible noise, the woman who was occupying it! You see that woman taking out a packet...and you don't have the simple presence of mind to bring back the evidence! That was really too stupid!"

The Colossus was devastated. That was the first time he had received such a reprimand from C.25. Obviously he now understood the importance of his gaffe. But it was too late!

"Do you really think, Malabar, that the German agents were less stupid than you! As soon as the young woman was picked up, they rushed to make the evidence that we were missing disappear. And without physical proof I could not hold my prisoners! I had to release them. Nevertheless, I'm sure we had the three German spies...and not the least important!"

And then, leaving Malabar, distressed, standing in the middle of the office floor, C.25 went to sit in an armchair and remained silent a long time. The clumsiness of one of her agents had transformed the brilliant afternoon capture into a screwed up defeat. Now it was too late to expect to lay hands on the three spies again. The alarm had been given. No doubt was possible. The three Tiergarten agents who had succeeded in getting out of a bad situation, were going to be doubly cautious. And beginning the next day, their way of communicating among themselves would be changed. It was therefore an important lead that could have led to the capture of an important contingent of enemy agents which was canceled. It also meant many days of research before finding out what new method of communication the spies affiliated with the Nachtrichten Bureau were using to correspond and to send their documents and their reports. It also meant, until a new lead was found, that French secrets would cross the borders. That meant French lives cut down!

"Stupid! Absolutely stupid!" C.25 continued to rage.

III. An Interesting Invitation

Thérèse Arnaud hadn't yet managed to come to terms with the anger caused by Malabar's ineptitude, when the evening mail arrived. C.25 examined with a doleful glance the envelopes with her address handed to her by Friquet. She examined one among the stack more carefully. The expression on C.25's face changed. The frown creasing her forehead disappeared. C.25 opened the envelope promptly. She took out an elegant invitation card. She read it. And a smile again spread over the lips of the famous French agent.

Madame Maria Flamato begs Mademoiselle Janine Félerat to do her the honor of attending a soirée that she will give February 12, 1917, at her town-house. The dancer Mata Hari will perform her most recent creations.

RSVP

152 Rue St. Honoré

Thérèse Arnaud contemplated the invitation addressed to her a long time.

"Finally," she murmured, delighted, "We're going to get our revenge!" And C.25 immediately sent her acceptance.

During the next days which still separated the date of the famous evening reception, C.25 seemed to abandon all the leads she was following. To the great astonishment of her agents, she gave no orders to try to lay hands on the three enemy agents released for lack of proof. On the contrary, Thérèse Arnaud ordered them to cease all surveillance of the usual hideouts watched and to totally abandon the building on the Rue Pigalle. Several days in advance of Maria Flamato's soirée, she told her agents the reasons, indicating with a precision which left no place for any doubt the role they would have to play. Malabar was charged with preparing Thérèse Arnaud's new automobile, and to see that everything was ready, whatever service the car needed. Marcel, Languille and Friquet received orders to be part of either the personnel engaged for the evening or of the guests. In that way, the area around Maria Flamato's private residence, the cloakroom, the study, the reception rooms were under the direct surveillance of C.25 or her agents. Ingenious combinations had been given to each of the famous agent's aides to communicate with each other, discreetly and rapidly. The information thus gathered could reach the Boss immediately who, by the same means, could dictate what they should do.

Through an excess of caution, Friquet had been charged with obtaining the address of the hotel where the dancer was staying. His mission was to stay close to Mata Hari and to shadow her as soon as she left her hotel. Next, following the famous movie star, Friquet was to enter the reception rooms and act his role as a guest. Thus Thérèse Arnaud would immediately know in case the dancer had some suspicious meeting between the hotel on the Champs-Élysées where she lived and Maria Flamato's house.

On the other hand, in order to be able to use all her aides, C.25 had asked Captain Ladoux that some additional forces be put at her disposal that evening. But, to her great surprise, after having answered affirmatively to her demand, Captain Ladoux, in the afternoon told her that the reinforcement asked for would be supplied by the Police. The Head of the Deuxième Bureau couldn't, or wouldn't, explain the motives that had dictated that decision.

Thus, at about 9 p.m., the following dispositions were taken:

1. Foreseeing important events, Malabar would remain on guard at C.25's house, having the car ready at the door. Next, after midnight, if nothing had happened, the Colossus would rejoin the Boss in the reception rooms of Maria Flamato. 2. Friquet would shadow Mata Hari from the time she left the hotel on the Champs-Élysées. He would follow her to Maria Flamato's and throughout the entire evening he would most especially follow in the footsteps of the dancer, noting the individuals who approached her. 3. Marcel, acting as an invited guest, would circulate in the reception rooms and act as liaison between C.25's auxiliaries. 4. Languille, first of all, would organize the surveillance service furnished by the Police that would stay on the outside of Maria Flamato's townhouse. Next, he would enter the reception rooms and, according to the circumstances, be ready to play whatever role, transforming himself, if need be, into a waiter, a cloakroom boy, a guest. At 10 p.m., Thérèse Arnaud, known to Parisian society as Janine Félerat, would make her entry into Maria Flamato's reception rooms, followed at a little distance by Marcel.

For the occasion, Thérèse Arnaud had dressed in her most sumptuous evening attire. So dressed, the Boss had the appearance of the true and authentic woman of the world. Nothing was lacking, neither grace, nor the natural distinction of bearing, nor the ease of talking a great deal to say nothing…and to listen.

When C.25 arrived, Maria Flamato's reception rooms already presented a joyous animation which was perhaps more forced than sincere. While couples were dancing in the gallery, others were spread out through the reception rooms, in the winter garden. The conversations seemed to be gaining animation. The Parisian society brought together by Maria Flamato was composed of the most disparate elements. Business and major industry rubbed shoulders with the aristocracy and the military. While some exchanged words of no importance sprinkled with laughter, others carried on conversations about business. Deals were begun. Influence was peddled more or less openly. Flirtations developed. And over all these combinations, perfume floated, smiles were exchanged, masking by their apparent banality the more serious conversations exchanged.

Announcement of Mata Hari's appearance had assured Maria Flamato the greatest success. In fact, the dancer's fame was such that it was enough to arouse every kind of curiosity. And many of Maria Flamato's guests would not have responded affirmatively if they hadn't been drawn by the certainty of seeing Mata Hari and to feast their eyes on the spectacle of her dances.

Shortly after Thérèse Arnaud's departure, Malabar who, ruminating sadly on the fallout of his recent mistake, standing guard at C.25's house, received an urgent letter from the Deuxième Bureau. Leaving his post for several minutes, he carried the letter to Languille, who was just completing the arrangement of the Police reinforcements. Thérèse Arnaud was soon in possession of the message addressed to her. She went to one side for a few moments to read it. The envelope contained these single lines written in the hand of Captain Ladoux himself:

Do not touch Mata Hari for reasons
that I will explain to you later.

Glancing over this text, Thérèse Arnaud couldn't hold back a quick movement of irritation. These simple lines totally paralyzed her action. It meant just simply reducing to nothing all the precautions taken by the famous agent to unmask—finally—the dancer. Under these conditions, her presence and that of her agents in Maria Flamato's townhouse no longer had any reason for being, since, whatever happened, C.25 no longer had any freedom of action. For a long time she had been working in secret to carry out her plan. For a long time, despite everyone, despite the evident ill will of the Deuxième Bureau, in spite of the allegations C.25 brought up during preceding cases which had put her in opposition to the dancer, C.25's goal was to catch Mata Hari and to furnish positive proofs. Faced with these, the authorities would certainly be obliged to accept the dancer's guilt and acknowledge her constant rapport with German spies and the agents of the Tiergarten. And once again, just as C.25 was ready to take her revenge and triumph, formal orders from the Deuxième Bureau prohibited laying hands on the guilty woman. Cruel disappointment was written on C.25's face.

"That's fine!" she complained. "Under these conditions, it's useless to waste my time here!"

She was preparing to send orders to her auxiliaries to leave when she suddenly changed her mind.

"Perfect!" she decided. "Since I can't do anything against Mata Hari this evening, I won't touch her whatever the evidence! And whatever rancor I feel, I'll obey…like a soldier! But I'll stay here. I'll get the evidence I'm missing. Afterward we'll see!"

Then after an effort of will that brought back a smile of control to her face, she again strolled toward the reception rooms where the guests continued to flock. Since she had received instructions from the Deuxième Bureau, Thérèse Arnaud's plan had been changed. Not being able to move against Mata Hari, the famous agent had decided not to stop the surveillance of the dancer. If, by order of a superior, Mata Hari couldn't be touched, just by her presence, she could furnish some clues about certain people she approached. Their suspected activities would, by this fact, be confirmed.

At about 11 p.m. the dancer made her appearance in Maria Flamato's reception rooms amid flattering whispers and unanimous praise of her grace. Thérèse had placed herself in advance in the path the dancer must follow to greet the mistress of the house. Therefore she saw the dancer climb the stairs on the arm of an extremely chic man of aristocratic bearing. Behind this first couple, and without doubt getting out of the same vehicle, was a second couple of perfect elegance and distinction. Then slightly behind, as if he had just arrived some instants afterward, Friquet's silhouette stood out. Thus, Thérèse's instructions were punctually carried out.

For a second, extreme satisfaction was painted on C.25's face. It took just one look at the famous French agent's face to discover the following facts, which strangely clarified the situation: 1. The man whose arm Mata Hari was holding was, without a doubt (despite the make-up and the change of costumes), the driver of the strange covered vehicle parked in the Rue du Château...the man who, for some hours had been the prisoner of C.25...the man who, with rage in her heart, despite her personal conviction, she had been forced to release for lack of physical evidence. 2. The couple mounting the stairs immediately behind Mata Hari and her escort was no less bizarre. It was composed of the sign repairer, bill poster, and the female prisoner from the Rue Pigalle. So, while they were prisoners at C.25's holding cell, the three German agents were play-acting. They knew each other perfectly well.

Therefore, from the beginning of the evening, from the arrival of the dancer Mata Hari at Maria Flamato's townhouse, C.25 again found, in the train of the dancer, the trio of German agents who had escaped her a few days earlier. Through the intermediary of Marcel, she sent that information to Languille and Friquet. Constant surveillance must be exercised not only on Mata Hari, but also on the three suspects.

Mata Hari's arrival had brought the guests' curiosity to its height. Now, in every conversation, it could be heard repeated everywhere with respect and admiration these two words: Mata Hari, Mata Hari. And everyone was waiting for the moment the dancer would begin her number.

IV. Some Small Incidents at the Soirée

At the announcement that the famous dancer was soon going to appear before the public, the crowd of guests suddenly deserted the reception rooms and moved toward the winter garden transformed into a theater. An intense brouhaha rose from the mass of guests. Laughter! Comments running together! And always dominating the diffuse noise, these two words: Mata Hari! Mata Hari! The heat became stifling. Perfumes mingled. Evening gown colors made a hodge-podge sprinkled with the stains of men's black evening clothes. The lighting made jewelry sparkle. The orchestra was warming up, tuning the instruments. Suddenly the lights dimmed. Conversations hushed. There was suddenly a religious silence, a great empty gap into which bursts of laughter would have fallen. The first measures of the music opened. The curtain opened. Magnificent, unreal, Mata Hari stood in the middle of the stage, enveloped by the converging lights from the multicolored projectors. A great thrill gripped the most incredulous, the most skeptical, the most closed to all artistic appreciation. An almost religious murmur made from an imperceptible "Oh" of admiration rose secretly from each breast.

Now the immobile dancer began to move, always followed and surrounded by the lights of the projectors. The orchestra vigorously attacked the theme of the dance. Loose veils surrounded the dancer, colored by changing lights. And the spectacle continued. Magnificent. Pagan. Admirable. A veritable triumph greeted the end of the dance. Curtain calls! Enthusiastic shouts rang out from the delirious crowd. Flowers snatched from boutonnieres and corsages rained onto the stage. Somewhat breathless by the emotion caused by that spontaneous manifestation, the dancer bowed. After a short intermission, a new dance obtained the same success. At the end of the number there was a kind of apotheosis! Never before had Mata Hari, who, however, had known resounding triumphs in every country, achieved such a success.

Still moved by the dance and by the homage given to the dancer, the crowd flowed out, leaving with regret the theater of the spectacle. Marks of admiration continued to rain down. Admiring critiques were exchanged. The same enthusiasm united all the spectators. Abandoning the buffet, the crowd rushed toward the reception room serving as the dancer's dressing room. In the corridor leading to Mata Hari's dressing room, although large, the crowd of guests packed together, crushing each other, continuing to applaud. Soon, in Mata Hari's dressing room there was a string of many admirers. The dancer, who had again put on her evening dress, received the praises seated in an armchair. Her breast still rose with joyous emotion. She answered everyone with a friendly word, while in the dressing room the two men and the woman who had arrived at the same time as she were busy arranging costumes and various accessories for the scenes.

Thérèse Arnaud, one of the first, had gotten near the dancer, but she stood a little to one side, letting the flood of impatient guests pass in front of her. Snatches of conversation reached her.

"In Spain! Yes...perfect! Everything went very well..." Mata Hari stated to a man who had just bent double bowing in front of her.

"At the Elysée-Palace? Could I meet you there?" another one asked the dancer.

"Yes...very gladly! But telephone beforehand because I'm very busy...I'm only in Paris for a very short time," Mata Hari answered.

"How's that? Just arrived, you're already thinking of leaving us!" a third said, very sorry.

"I must. I have an engagement in Holland," Mata Hari informed him.

"Naturally in Holland," thought C.25. "In Holland now that Van Vith and Saracco are in no position to be of service to the Tiergarten."

The crowd of guests filed past for a long time before C.25 approached the dancer. However, the last spectators were arriving. Thérèse Arnaud took her place in the line. When the French agent was in front of the dancer, Maria Flamato introduced her:

"Mademoiselle Janine Félerat..."

An imperceptible shock...imperceptible for everyone but C.25. A slight shudder, only the length of a flash of lightning, had shook Mata Hari. But, as a perfect actor, the dancer very quickly dominated her emotion. She held out her hand to C.25 with a smile, exactly like those she had distributed to the string of admirers. She said something friendly, while C.25's compliments went to swell the flood of banalities already stacked up from the beginning of the procession.

In the corridor, on leaving Mata Hari's dressing room, C.25 was joined by Languille. For a few steps, the male guest in evening dress walked near the female guest in an evening gown. They probably also exchanged their impressions of the spectacle which had just been offered them. But very quickly Languille whispered in the Boss's ear:

"The two guys surrounding Mata Hari introduced themselves as Jean Saliès, an industrialist...He's the one who works as bodyguard to the dancer...and de Valbert Morat, a professor of philosophy...He's the escort of the woman from the Rue Pigalle."

After having presented their homages to the famous dancer, the crowd of guests made their way toward the buffet. Still surrounded by her friends, who had never left her except during her act, Mata Hari also made her appearance. As she approached, the groups opened to give her free passage. And the concert of praises was still mounting. At the abundant and richly garnished buffet the numerous waiters were busy trying to satisfy the number of guests and to avoid a bottleneck. Mata Hari and the trio of her friends had reached one end of the buffet. A maître d'hôtel seemed especially posted to their service.

Soon a plate of oysters was placed before the dancer. Not far from the group, C.25 and Languille, seeming very busy enjoying caviar tarts, were watching the least actions and gestures of the dancer and her friends. Now, the empty oyster shells were stacked up on the plate. Mata Hari, after a rapid glance at Valbert Morat, looked at the plate which remained in front of the group. The dancer's eyes had an unusual expression. And it seemed she was eyeing one particular oyster shell. Suddenly the maître d'hôtel, who had been busy some steps away, came back toward the group around the dancer. With a professional mechanical gesture he picked up the plate. At that moment a young employee helping the server came forward quickly and, having obligingly taken the plate from the maître d'hôtel, disappeared into the kitchen. This rapid maneuver, which hadn't escaped C.25 brought a quick smile of satisfaction to the Boss's cheeks.

Languille, who had immediately left Thérèse Arnaud, went, after a short absence, into the kitchen disguised as a maître d'hôtel. As soon as he entered, he saw one of his "colleagues," precisely the one who seemed especially posted to serve Mata Hari, rummaging through a pile of oyster shells. But before the Acrobat had time to do anything, the employee helper, passing by him, gave him a rapid look and murmured:

"Let him search…"

And Friquet passed an oyster shell wrapped in a napkin to Languille, who shoved it into a pocket…A few minutes later, Languille, again dressed in his tuxedo as a man of the world, approached the buffet where Mata Hari, her friends…and some steps further away, C.25, were standing. Coming near the Boss, the Acrobat discreetly passed her the oyster shell which Friquet had just put in his hands. Thérèse Arnaud only lowered her eyelids as a sign of perfect comprehension. Then, rapidly, in a low voice, she gave Languille some instructions. She was careful to raise her voice from time to time to let her neighbors hear perfectly banal sentences having to do with Mata Hari's dances.

Following C.25's instructions, Languille soon left the buffet. He left Maria Flamato's townhouse. He had a rapid chat with each of the inspectors furnished by the Police, who were continuing their surveillance of the outside. During this time an argument broke out between a waiter and a guest. The waiter was the one who was very specially assigned to serve Mata Hari and her friends. The guest was Jean Saliès himself. The reasons for the argument were vague. But instead of calming down, the irritation of the two men reached a pitch. The staff hired for the evening by Maria Flamato probably didn't have the usual tact, since it's the duty of every servant not to argue with a guest. On the other hand, Jean Saliès, as a guest of Maria Flamato, should have realized the incongruity of having dealings with a servant. The altercation was about to degenerate into a brawl when another servant arrived. Very serious. Very dignified. And of an imposing stature. He put an end to the situation in a few words, ordering the waiter to immediately leave his service.

While that incident was taking place behind the scenes of the buffet, Valbert Morat, professor of philosophy, had exchanged rapid opinions with his companion and with Mata Hari. The trio had looked several times toward the kitchen door, through which Jean Saliès had disappeared. After a new conference, Valbert Morat, in his turn, left the buffet and disappeared through the kitchen door. He saw no one. Still searching for his friend, he took several steps and opened a door. He rapidly jumped back. But immediately seized by two powerful arms, he was pulled toward the interior of the room where Languille already held Jean Saliès immobilized. Malabar shook Valbert Morat vigorously. Then when Morat was somewhat stunned, the Colossus commanded:

"Let's go! Don't act stupid! It's useless to resist! You're done for this time. Hold out your hands."

Languille quickly handcuffed the so-called professor of philosophy. The two prisoners didn't say a word of protest.

Malabar commanded: "Now, let's go! We're leaving the townhouse by the 'actor's exit'. My car is waiting for you in front of the door. No disturbance…Not a word!" and the Colossus took a revolver from his trouser's pocket, keeping it in his hand.

The two prisoners, well-guarded by Thérèse Arnaud's auxiliaries, went down the service stairs. They went down a long corridor. Malabar opened a little door. A gust of cold air came in. The two prisoners hesitated slightly.

"Let's go," Languille said.

C.25's car was parked at the edge of the sidewalk. Two Police agents were on guard, ready to intervene if needed. The prisoners realized the futility of any attempt to flee. Resigned, they crossed the sidewalk. One of the inspectors opened the door. Valbert Morat and Jean Saliès disappeared inside the vehicle. The door slammed and was locked.

"Automatic lock," smiled Languille.

Malabar took his place behind the steering wheel. The Colossus waved a friendly goodbye in the direction of the Acrobat and the automobile disappeared in the night.

During this time, the guests continued to flock around the buffet. Mata Hari, who had been left some minutes before by Valbert Morat's companion, began to show some signs of impatience. But still the object of flattering comments, she kept an air of composure. Some steps from the dancer, Thérèse Arnaud, also encircled, exchanged chit chat with guests. Taking advantage of a moment when the buffet had few guests around it, C.25 approached Mata Hari. And quickly taking out from a hidden pocket the oyster shell Languille had given her, she showed it to the dancer without saying a single word. Mata Hari trembled. In the space of a second, the dancer had become pale. A cold sweat pearled her forehead. Mata Hari looked around to find Jean Saliès and Valbert Morat at her side. Thérèse Arnaud smiled. Then in a low but very friendly voice, in the most exquisitely polite tone, she informed her:

"They have left. They're far away now. You'll certainly never see them again…at least this evening."

Pale, her throat tight, the dancer asked:

"And me? You're not arresting me?"

"I can't! I regret it!" Thérèse Arnaud spat out. Shortly thereafter she left

Maria Flamato's reception rooms. C.25's car was parked in front of the town-house door. The famous agent went toward her car.

"It's done," Malabar said. "I've made the delivery!"

"Good," she answered. "Let's go. I'll give you instructions through the intercom."

V. The Little Auteuil House

Guided by the Boss, Malabar at the wheel drove with his usual competence. On leaving Maria Flamato's townhouse, C.25's car reached the Champs-Élysées, the Place de l'Étoile, then it turned into the Avenue Kléber. Malabar didn't know the final destination. When the car reached the Trocadéro, Thérèse Arnaud gave the following instructions: Rue de Passy…Avenue Mozart, Rue Jasmin. Stop at the corner of the Rue Jasmin and the Rue Jaffet…And the automobile continued its race through the night. When the car stopped, Thérèse Arnaud got out quickly and commanded:

"Wait for me. Whatever happens, however long I'm gone, don't budge."

The winter night was cold and sinister. A heavy fog wept from a black velvet sky. Opaque clouds accumulated in a pitch black firmament which hid all its stars. In the Rue Jaffet, absolutely deserted at that time of night, small private houses had sprung up, modest constructions dating from the time when Auteuil was still a suburb of Paris. Gardens and empty land were between the houses. Some rare street lights far from each other, threw out gloomy light. Thérèse Arnaud's footsteps set a dog to barking. Arriving in front of a small iron fence, C.25 went in without hesitation. Without taking the least precaution to muffle the sound of her footsteps, she went across the little garden at the same pace. She went up the two steps to the entry. Then, without ringing, she turned the door knob, which opened with no difficulty. She found herself in a vestibule poorly lit by a frosted glass lightshade. A ray of light coming from under a door guided the famous French agent. In several strides she reached the door. She opened it. Sitting in an armchair in front of a flaming wood fire throwing out lively and gay lights, a woman was smoking a cigarette. At C.25's entry she abruptly stood up with a start.

"You!" she said.

C.25 answered only, "Me!"

There was a short silence during which the two women looked at one another. Always with the same calm, Thérèse Arnaud continued:

"I know I wasn't the one you were expecting."

"So?" C.25's questioner asked in a defiant tone.

"So…" C.25 continued with the same calmness, "so, Mademoiselle Doktor, I've come because of this."

With a quick gesture, she showed the oyster shell from the plate put on Maria Flamato's buffet in front of Mata Hari and stolen by Friquet. "Because of

262

this…" continued the French agent, "and because the person you were waiting for couldn't come herself."

"Arrested?" asked Mademoiselle Doktor in a strange intonation, an intonation in which could be sensed a sort of restrained joy.

"No! Not yet!"

"Why?" Mademoiselle Doktor inquired.

Thérèse Arnaud calmly explained:

"Officially, I don't know! But I guess French justice wants proof. If it were only up to me, I would have put an end to Mata Hari's operation a long time ago."

"So would I," murmured the Tiergarten agent.

But Thérèse Arnaud continued as if she hadn't heard the comment—really rather incomprehensible at first—"if Mademoiselle Doktor…"

"For me, and for a long time, there has been no doubt as to Mata Hari's guilt. The numerous cases in which I had to fight her were enough to clarify my opinion. Unfortunately, the authorities on whom I depend, refuse to believe in her guilt so long as it's not proved to them by physical facts. Me, I have only moral charges…"

"Yes," Mademoiselle Doktor threw in, "as long as Mata Hari was useful to me I was able to keep the proofs from falling into your hands…"

"I know," Thérèse Arnaud remarked.

"Then what have you come to do here?" demanded Mademoiselle Doktor. "You may perhaps imagine that you can capture Mademoiselle Doktor like this. You find me alone, in my house, in a deserted neighborhood…You think perhaps…"

"No!" C.25 interrupted. And clearly articulating her words, she hammered them in:

"If I had wanted to take you in, I wouldn't have done it like this. Believe me!"

Rendering homage to her adversary's valor, Mademoiselle Doktor stated:

"That's true."

After a short silence, she asked the same question again. "Since you haven't come to try to take me prisoner, why did you come here?"

Thérèse Arnaud didn't answer. There was a long silence broken only by the crackling of the wood fire. Thérèse Arnaud continued, very slowly.

"I told you that I came in place of the person you were waiting for. I know what would have happened between you if she had come."

"I don't believe it!" Mademoiselle Doktor threw out quickly.

"I'm certain of it," Thérèse Arnaud maintained calmly.

Mademoiselle Doktor looked at her implacable enemy with strange admiration. She was trying to guess what she knew, just to what point she had penetrated the secrets of the Tiergarten's major spy. After a short pause, she affirmed:

"That's impossible. You couldn't know. I'm the only one who knows the decisions to be carried out. There is only one person who knows."

"Let's agree that there are two of them: you and I," Thérèse Arnaud corrected her with the same composure.

Mademoiselle Doktor's eyes again scrutinized Thérèse Arnaud. If the French secret agent was telling the truth, C.25 knew the most secret decisions of the Tiergarten. What a woman to be feared Thérèse Arnaud was! For one second some slight fear appeared in Mademoiselle Doktor's face. Still smiling, C.25 continued.

"Don't think that I'm trying to bluff you. When I say I know, I'm in a position to prove it."

Short of breath, Mademoiselle Doktor said: "I'm listening to you."

"Here it is: For some time H.21 hasn't been a reliable agent for you. She, for a very long time, well before 1914, has provided you with very valuable services. And currently, for reasons you know as well as I, Mata Hari no longer wants to work for you. Now, when you're an agent for the Tiergarten, it's until death. It's not possible to resign. You have suspected Mata Hari for some time wanting to stop being agent H.21, and more or less found out by French authorities, you're afraid she may buy her freedom…with secrets…secrets that she must not pass on! You're afraid Mata Hari will become a double agent…Your agent's last trip to Spain caused you worry."

"Yes, so?" Mademoiselle Doktor questioned quickly.

"So…what I know," C.25 smiled, "is that however painful it was to give up an agent who, in the past, was very useful and for whom there has been indulgence as long as possible not given to the others, you have decided to do away with Mata Hari and you put yourself in charge of the execution."

Mademoiselle Doktor, very pale, rose. She stood up very straight in the middle of the room. Her silhouette cast Chinese shadows, profiling itself strongly on the pale wallpaper.

"Now I understand what you want," said Mademoiselle Doktor.

Thérèse Arnaud didn't answer. Mademoiselle Doktor continued.

"You aren't lacking in audacity. You don't realize that you've just shown yourself in my eyes more dangerous than I supposed, since you know the decisions that only I can make. You don't realize that my duty is to do away with you immediately, as one destroys his most implacable enemy, the one who, more powerful than we thought, has already held us in check many times…You don't realize that it would take only a shot from my revolver…"

"I've thought about all that, and even about other things," Thérèse Arnaud stated calmly. "I thought also that we would be woman against woman…if you want it that way…and I came."

There was a long silence which seemed interminable. The two adversaries observed each other, eyes shining. Finally, after one last hesitation, Mademoiselle Doktor said:

264

"You're right! The Tiergarten doesn't much like to execute its agents, most of all when it's a matter of former collaborators such as Mata Hari. She's lost to us! It would be better for us if you took charge of the task."

Saying this, Mademoiselle Doktor went to a panel in the wall. She pressed a spring in the molding. Slowly, smoothly, the panel moved back revealing a safe. The German spy manipulated some keys. A click could be heard. Mademoiselle Doktor took a file from a strong box. She closed the safe. Then, when the panel was put back in place, she brought the dossier, which she threw on the table in front of Thérèse Arnaud.

"Here are the proofs you're lacking, C.25. With these documents, as incredulous as they wish to show themselves, the Deuxième Bureau will be convinced. I deliver Mata Hari to you."

C.25 held out her hand to take the file.

"Just a minute!" Mademoiselle Doktor cut in. "A deal for a deal. You know too much Thérèse Arnaud! You know my hideout! You're abreast of the latest decisions of the Tiergarten…I'm giving you the file you need to win 24 hours of neutrality in exchange. A truce…to allow me to disappear. During these 24 hours you won't try anything against me and I swear not to attempt anything against you. At the expiration of that short truce, the battle will begin once more. More terrible now that I know you are more powerful than I thought!"

"Deal!" said C.25.

"Here you are, Thérèse Arnaud," ended Mademoiselle Doktor, holding out the file.

"Thank you!"

Some minutes later, Thérèse Arnaud's automobile rolled down the Rue Mozart.

VI. The Woman with the Muff

Valbert Morat's companion hadn't escaped the surveillance of C.25's agents. When she left Mata Hari at Maria Flamato's buffet, Marcel followed in her footsteps. The young woman, after having strolled through the reception rooms trying to find news of Valbert Morat and Jean Saliès, decided to leave Maria Flamato's reception. In the cloak room she picked up a heavy fur coat and a muff. Then, wrapping herself tightly in her cloak to escape the sharp North wind, her hands tucked into her muff, she took several steps down the avenue. A taxi which was circling around picked her up.

But, a car behind Marcel, requisitioned by one of the Police inspectors, had already arrived and dashed forward in pursuit of the woman with the muff. After having taken down the address of the young woman and having left an agent on surveillance, Marcel returned to Thérèse Arnaud's house. The Boss, very happy, put together the results of the evening. She gave the following instructions to Marcel: not to be in a hurry to arrest the woman with the muff, but to watch her.

Thus, without knowing it, the former renter in the Rue Pigalle house would put C.25's agents on the trail of new agents of the Tiergarten. Then, when the necessary information had been obtained from the woman with the muff, to act without her, she would be arrested.

The next morning the Chemist went to take up his guard duty at the house of the woman with the muff. Marcel's wait was of short duration. Although having spent a part of the night at Maria Flamato's reception, the woman with the muff left her lodgings about 10 p.m. She still wore her sumptuous fur coat and her inseparable muff, which she seemed to think a great deal of. Taking many precautions trying to throw off anyone curious, Valbert Morat's companion arrived at the shed on the Rue du Château where a short time before the two German spies had parked their vehicle.

While Marcel was watching like a hawk from the little neighboring café, Friquet, who had received special instructions and who had hidden in the shed where the wagon was still parked, saw the woman with the muff approach the wagon. Then she unscrewed a spoke of one of the wheels. The Paris street boy noticed that she removed from that strange hiding place, different rolled-up papers that she carefully shoved into her muff. Then she immediately left the shed and was immediately followed again by Languille. He, according to C.25's instructions, was waiting for Marcel to come take his place in the little café next to the hiding place. On leaving the Rue du Château, the woman with the muff had herself driven to the Champs Élysée Palace where Mata Hari lived. Malabar, who was on guard duty in front of the Champs Élysée Palace, noted the arrival of the woman with the muff, soon followed by Languille.

Without asking anything in the Champs Élysée Palace vestibule, the young woman got into the elevator. She indicated the floor where Mata Hari resided. Without halting on the landing, she rapidly went down the corridor which led to the dancer's apartment. On the way, she saw a maid coming toward her. The woman with the muff trembled. She suddenly turned around and in haste went down again in the elevator. Overcome by evident fright, she went across the vestibule. On the Avenue of the Champs Élysée she hesitated a second before turning in the direction of the Place de l'Étoile...still followed by Languille, who had remained on the lookout and had shown some surprise on seeing his prey stay so short a time in the hotel.

In the corridor which led to Mata Hari's apartment, the maid smiled when she saw the woman with the muff make an about face.

"Oh! It's useless to run after you," C.25 murmured. "We'll find you."

And calmly, appearing to be busy, Thérèse Arnaud continued to guard the corridor.

In the Place de l'Étoile, Mata Hari's strange friend called a taxi. And, still followed by Languille, she had herself taken to the corner of the Rue Jasmin and the Rue Jaffet. Then she hastily walked toward the little house where, the night before, Thérèse Arnaud had met Mademoiselle Doktor. While the Acrobat, after having seen the young woman disappear into the house was hesitating on what to do—wait or go himself also into the house, the woman with the muff, appearing disoriented, left Mademoiselle Doktor's hideout. Evidently, Valbert Morat's companion, recognizing Thérèse Arnaud under the maid's disguise in the corridor of the Élysée Palace, had recognized the danger Mata Hari was running. So she had rushed to warn Mademoiselle Doktor, in order for the latter to give her instructions for the dancer.

But the little house in Auteuil was empty. Entering the cottage, the strange renter of the furnished house on the Rue Pigalle had found the hideout abandoned. Certain signs even showed a rapid departure. On the other hand, Valbert Morat's companion knew that the famous German spy's general headquarters had been established at Auteuil for some time, and nothing had allowed such a rapid departure to be foreseen. Therefore a new fact had arisen that obliged Mademoiselle Doktor to leave her domicile, and to leave it quickly, as the armoires emptied of only the essentials testified.

That double circumstance, the presence of C.25 near the apartment of Mata Hari at the Élysée Palace and Mademoiselle Doktor's abandoning the Auteuil house, seemed to disorient the woman with the muff. She had the impression that imminent danger threatened the Tiergarten envoys. It was necessary at any price to give the alarm, to warn! The disappearance of Valbert Morat and Jean Saliès had already been cruel losses for German espionage. Perhaps these arrests would be followed by others if the Tiergarten envoys were not immediately warned that Thérèse Arnaud, their implacable enemy, was on their trail. At the corner of the Rue Mozart, another taxi picked up the woman with the muff. Shortly afterward, Languille, in a second taxi, continued the chase. Valbert Morat's companion was visibly terrified. She had herself driven to the Rue Bondy.

"Of course, she too must go there. It's lucky we know the hideout."

But the trip to the Rue Bondy was as short as that to the cottage occupied by Mademoiselle Doktor. There too the woman with the muff found the apartment which served as a hideout for the Tiergarten agents abandoned. There too remained the traces of a rapid decampment. The woman with the muff deduced from these facts that someone had given the alarm and all the German agents had left their hideouts. To make such a decision, from all the evidence, the danger was great. Still more worried, Valbert Morat's companion had herself driven to the Villette, still dragging the Acrobat in her wake. But the Villette hideout too was empty of all enemy agents.

Leaving the Villette, Mata Hari's friend, desperate to find some German agent who would take it upon himself to warn the dancer of the danger she ran, rushed into a post office and asked for the Élysée Palace telephone number. Languille, who was in the adjoining telephone booth, heard the telephone call. The woman with the muff asked the main hotel telephone number to connect her to the dancer's apartment. The Acrobat got ready to listen to the words exchanged. But he didn't hear anything, only a new request by Valbert Morat's companion, who hadn't been able to get the number she asked for the first time. Some moments later, the woman left the post office completely disoriented. She understood why the telephone calls had no answer. Either the telephone had been cut off or the Élysée Palace switchboard had been ordered not to allow any telephone communication between Mata Hari and the outside. So the danger was turning out to be even greater. A kind of panic overcame her.

About a half hour after the attempt to telephone, a small incident which passed almost unseen by most of the travelers took place at the Lyon Railway Station. Just as the express going to Switzerland by way of Pontarlier, was about to leave the station, a young woman traveler was bumped into by an unknown man as she was about to get into the railway car. Even though the traveler had not complained and seemed only concerned with going to take her seat, two men, soon joined by the man who had jostled her, approached her. And as the train left the station, the young traveler, surrounded by the three men, disappeared into the Office of the Police Superintendent.

Languille—understanding that the woman with the muff, sensing the danger closing around the German agents on whom she depended, had decided to flee—judged the time right to arrest Valbert Morat's companion. The woman, searched in the Office of the Police Superintendent, was found to be carrying a packet of documents (taken from the spoke of the wagon wheel in the hideout on the Rue du Château) and a sum of 16,000 francs. Questioned about the source of these documents and the money, she refused to furnish the least information. Obviously the contents of the muff were to be delivered to Mata Hari...perhaps the reason for a new mission for the dancer...and the price agreed on for a trip to Holland.

VII. Mademoiselle Doktor's Mission

Before going to take up her job as a maid in the Élysée Palace corridor, C.25 went, very early, to the Deuxième Bureau. She had been seen immediately by Captain Ladoux.

"You've probably come to learn the reasons behind my official note yesterday evening," the officer said.

Thérèse Arnaud's slight smile informed the Chief of the Information Services of her agreement.

"You must not touch Mata Hari!" He continued. "The last reports I received seemed to indicate that we were embarked on a false trail. I never wanted you, C.25, I told you so, to follow that path. Certainly, like you, I found in Mata Hari's actions some facts that could be interpreted in a strange way. But nothing proves that the interpretation you gave them is the right one. And given the dancer's reputation, given the numerous friends she has in the social and diplomatic worlds, an error in her case risked causing us the worst problems. The dancer's powerful supporters wouldn't fail to protest if without proof, with just the suspicions we have, we allowed ourselves to upset her..."

"Without proofs, yes," Thérèse Arnaud interrupted calmly. "But what if I furnished you the proofs of Mata Hari's real business and the true purpose of her trips...!"

The officer looked at C.25. Captain Ladoux knew that Thérèse Arnaud had for a long time been relentless in demonstrating Mata Hari's guilt. And despite the confidence the officer had in the famous French agent, he didn't share her opinion with regard to the dancer. With the pained look of a teacher who sees his best student make and perpetuate an error, the officer remarked:

"Moral proofs, yes, but you should beware of moral proofs. You can reason very correctly but still reach a false conclusion if the point of departure of the reasoning is not correct. C.25, you start with the principle that Mata Hari is attached to the Tiergarten. And you have brought forward all the facts observed to support and verify your reasoning. Now, if your reasoning is not correct..."

"Here are the physical proofs that will demonstrate its accuracy," Thérèse Arnaud smiled, holding out to the officer the file turned over to her by Mademoiselle Doktor.

Looking surprised, Captain Ladoux took the documents offered him. With a skeptical smile, he began to leaf through them. Soon the expression on his face began to change.

"Where did you get this?" murmured the officer, continuing to leaf through the documents just handed him.

After having examined the documents for several minutes, the Chief of the Deuxième Bureau said:

"Yes...this is sufficient! Too sufficient!"

"Wait...You haven't yet learned everything," Thérèse Arnaud remarked, smiling.

"Later!" concluded Captain Ladoux. "Right now we have to move without delay."

The officer picked up the telephone and asked for the emergency switchboard of the Police.

The next day, at about 11:00 a.m., Commissioner Priollet, accompanied by two inspectors, presented themselves at the Élysée Palace and asked for the dancer's apartment. It was immediately given to them. In the corridor the three men encountered a maid who seemed to be keeping watch. Paying no attention to the domestic, the commissioner knocked on Mata Hari's apartment door. The maid was interested in the three men's actions, watching them with curiosity. Commissioner Priollet showed some impatience at her presence.

"We don't need you. You can go on about your business..."

The maid didn't budge. Then, after having carefully studied her face, Commissioner Priollet made a gesture of excuse.

"Oh! Pardon, Madame, I didn't recognize you…And the only excuse for my error is the perfection of your disguise…"

Without replying to the compliment, Thérèse Arnaud asked: "So, Commissioner, you've come to arrest…?"

Suddenly very cold, Commissioner Priollet said simply:

"I received all the necessary instructions from my superiors and I've come to carry out the mandate I was given…"

"Good," Thérèse Arnaud said simply.

But changing tones, the commissioner immediately continued:

"I spoke to you as a magistrate. It didn't become him to congratulate you on the part you have in this arrest. But, as a civilian, the man I am can offer you the expression of his admiration for the useful work you've accomplished…"

Then standing to one side of the door and pointing out to Thérèse Arnaud the place he had occupied, he continued:

"If you want to make the arrest yourself, I will cede my place to you."

With a gesture of courteous refusal, she replied:

"Thank you. I did my duty. My job stops at the threshold of that door. The rest is up to you. My job is to put enemies beyond doing harm. To be part of their defeat when they are lost: no! After all, Mata Hari did what she believed to be her duty. She carried out the missions which were confided to her. She is defeated. I have no curiosity about the scene of her defeat. It would even be painful for me…"

"Then, under those conditions," said Commissioner Priollet, and he entered the apartment followed by his two aides. Thérèse Arnaud immediately left the Élysée Palace without waiting for the magistrate to accomplish his task. Only Friquet, who had been stationed at the hotel since the morning in case he was needed saw, sometime later, Mata Hari come down the steps of the hotel, go across the vestibule for the last time and get into a taxi parked in front of the Palace.

During the course of the afternoon, the news of Mata Hari's arrest spread throughout Paris. As soon as it was confirmed, the most diverse rumors circulated. The Deuxième Bureau was attacked at the same time. Thus, as Captain Ladoux had predicted, the arrest of the dancer (who had been the idol of Paris) raised the most fierce protests. Many well-known personalities—and those among the most influential—got busy trying to furnish proof of the dancer's innocence and called for her release. The Chief of the Deuxième Bureau had to give an account of the facts that had prompted his action. And the officer even had to give over certain of the secret documents given him by Thérèse Arnaud to avoid being censured by higher officials. During the whole time the directive continued, the dancer's many friends refused to be beaten. They used all their weight to avoid the dancer's appearance before the Counsel of War.

Nevertheless, despite the many efforts attempted, despite all the more or less official pressure which was applied, as much on the Police as on the

Deuxième Bureau, justice took its course. Right to the end Mata Hari hoped that her powerful protectors would succeed in getting her released from prison.

But despite the brilliant defense of the dancer's lawyer—who was numbered among her friends and had already represented her in many business lawsuits—the military judges, having seen the secret file and all the damning documents it contained, remained deaf to all the appeals for pity and rendered their verdict. Mata Hari, German spy, agent of the Tiergarten—where she was known under the Classification H.21—convicted of espionage and collaborating with the enemy was condemned to death.

Nothing more remained for the numerous friends of the dancer, except one hope, a Presidential pardon.

Thérèse Arnaud had not followed the session of the Counsel of War. As she had told Commissioner Priollet her job was finished the moment the German spy was no longer able to do harm. The news of the dancer's condemnation to death only accentuated C.25's moral uneasiness. For long months Thérèse Arnaud had stubbornly tried to prove Mata Hari's guilt, guilt which the Deuxième Bureau and the Police had refused to see. Therefore, Mata Hari's arrest and her condemnation to capital punishment represented for Captain Ladoux's collaborator a very clear victory. A victory dearly acquired by the previous battles on the Riviera and in Holland, as well as in certain Parisian drawing rooms which had pitted the dancer and the famous agent against each other. But the ultimate victory remained bitter to Thérèse Arnaud.

Generally, in fact, when she pitted her strength against enemy forces, against the cleverest agents of the Tiergarten, she herself fought. She herself put together the bundle of proofs, helped by her usual auxiliaries. And in the course of this work she put herself in danger, she fought with no armor. She played on a level field, risking each instant of the fight being beaten or taken prisoner. But in this case, the defeat of Mata Hari wasn't due just to her audacity, to her courage, to her attributes. In the final analysis, Mata Hari had been arrested only because the Tiergarten had decided on the fate of the dancer...Mata Hari had only put on the garb of the prisoners of St. Lazare because Mademoiselle Doktor, preferring to leave to the French authorities the burden of executing the dancer condemned by the Tiergarten, had furnished the documents which had dictated the conduct of the Deuxième Bureau and the Police. In reality she had not, by her own means, unmasked Mata Hari, had not brought together the physical proof of her guilt. In order to put an end to the German spy's dangerous activities she had concluded that bargain, that pact with Mademoiselle Doktor. And more than any other person, she felt the heavy weight of that bargain.

Perhaps, in her inmost being, C.25 hoped that the dancer would be spared...despite the number of French lives she had contributed to cutting down. And for the duration of the dancer's trial she had remained thoughtful, melancholy. It wasn't the Deuxième Bureau agent triumphing loyally over an enemy. It was in essence only thanks to Mademoiselle Doktor's betrayal of one of the oldest and the most esteemed collaborators of the Tiergarten that C.25 had brought down the dancer.

After the sentence, the same influences continued to work more or less secretly, even enlisting the diplomatic corps and powerful foreigners in order to spare Mata Hari the death to which she had been condemned. In all justice, could they execute at Vincennes that dancer who had been the idol of fashionable Paris, who counted among her friends innumerable members of the political, military, diplomatic and artistic world? Could they treat as a common spy the one before whom the most outstanding personalities of the century had bowed? Could they remain deaf to the appeal for clemency which rose everywhere, imploring forgiveness for the dancer?

And because the dossier on which the guilty verdict was based had never been made public, and because certain meetings of the War Counsel had taken place behind closed doors, there were still numerous partisans of the dancer who spoke of a judicial error.

Since it was not permitted to reveal on what flagrant evidence the condemnation was based, many were struck by the severity of the punishment given the publicized evidence, which did not clearly demonstrate culpability.

While outside the prison all influences were in play to arrive at a solution which would save the dancer, the one in her cell at St. Lazare was living apparently calm days. Regular visits by her lawyer probably allowed her to hope for the end of her detention soon. However, one by one, the hopes of Mata Hari's partisans faded. Despite all the resources used, the passing days confirmed that the pitiless judgment of the Counsel of War would be carried out in all its rigor.

One day Thérèse Arnaud had a long conference with the Chief of the Deuxième Bureau. Captain Ladoux had listened carefully to his collaborator. Several times he made vague gestures which seemed to indicate total inability to answer the request made of him. Then in his turn, the officer spoke. And he had probably set to rest the excessive scruples of his subordinate. He had demonstrated to her that she had done her duty. And he believed he had quelled C.25's remorse. Then C.25 related the following:

"This morning I had a visit from Mata Hari's lawyer. He showed me a letter coming from a furrier in Amsterdam demanding payment in the sum of 8,000 francs, the price of a fur bought two years ago. The lawyer asked me, 'Do you think that if Mata Hari had really betrayed, she wouldn't have had the necessary money to pay such bills, minimal given the style of life the dancer led? And, in fact, didn't the investigation reveal that Mata Hari possessed nothing?'"

Captain Ladoux looked at her a long time. Then, very calmly, very slowly, he answered:

"You yourself brought absolutely irrefutable evidence of Mata Hari's treason. Proof which had to be admitted. Proof which had convinced all those who had been known to be so skeptical and however prejudiced they might be in favor of the dancer. Proofs which couldn't give any idea of the number of human lives Mata Hari has cost France. So…"

After a silence, the officer continued:

"As for the rest of your request, C.25, do as you like. You're acting out of a charitable motive that I understand…but do not share. Mata Hari, for me, is a spy like any other. It isn't because she had powerful contacts that she should escape the punishment she merited. Your sensitivity wants to 'envelope' this punishment with veils of hope. So be it! You contributed too much to the arrest of the guilty one for me to refuse you what is in my power to do for you. As for the rest, I can do nothing."

And Thérèse Arnaud took leave of the officer. She went immediately to the dancer's lawyer. The last information gathered confirmed that every hope of sparing the dancer the supreme punishment was absolutely vain. Thus, C.25— and it was that authorization she had gone to ask of Captain Ladoux—had decided to soften Mata Hari's last moments. Thanks to the lawyer's complicity, Mata Hari had learned that it was necessary for her execution to take place to set an example. But it would be a fake execution. And after this mock execution, the dancer, who would have pretended to fall under the bullets of the execution squad, would be saved.

One morning, in the early hours, a wagon stopped at the Vincennes Prison. The dancer, elegantly dressed, came out. She looked around the sinister countryside, the stake driven into the ground. Then at the men who, some meters away, were getting ready to form a line. She fixed her regard for an instant at the end of the rifles, those rifles that in a little while would fire blanks and at the end of which was liberty for the dancer.

Then confident, docile, she let herself be led toward the stake in the ground. And smiling at the hope of her future liberty, she remained standing up straight, immobile, proud.

And it was like this that she died, retaining in death the supreme smile she presented to the future, that completely new future that she believed she saw opening up before her.

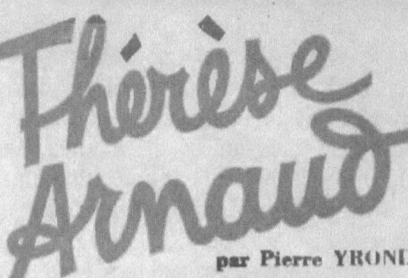

Thérèse Arnaud

par Pierre YRONDY

LA VENGEANCE
DE KARL HIMMELFELD

Récit de contre-espionnage

SF & FANTASY

Henri Allorge. *The Great Cataclysm*
Guy d'Armen. *Doc Ardan: The City of Gold and Lepers*
G.-J. Arnaud. *The Ice Company*
Charles Asselineau. *The Double Life*
Cyprien Bérard. *The Vampire Lord Ruthwen*
Aloysius Bertrand. *Gaspard de la Nuit*
Richard Bessière. *The Gardens of the Apocalypse*
Albert Bleunard. *Ever Smaller*
Félix Bodin. *The Novel of the Future*
Louis Boussenard. *Monsieur Synthesis*
Alphonse Brown. *City of Glass; The Conquest of the Air*
André Caroff. *The Terror of Madame Atomos; Miss Atomos; The Return of Madame Atomos; The Mistake of Madame Atomos; The Monsters of Madame Atomos; The Revenge of Madame Atomos; The Resurrection of Madame Atomos*
Félicien Champsaur. *The Human Arrow; Ouha, King of the Apes; Pharaoh's Wife*
Didier de Chousy. *Ignis*
Captain Danrit. *Undersea Odyssey*
C. I. Defontenay. *Star (Psi Cassiopeia)*
Charles Derennes. *The People of the Pole*
Georges Dodds (anthologist). *The Missing Link*
Harry Dickson. *The Heir of Dracula*
Jules Dornay. *Lord Ruthven Begins*
Alfred Driou. *The Adventures of a Parisian Aeronaut*
Sâr Dubnotal *vs. Jack the Ripper*
Alexandre Dumas. *The Return of Lord Ruthven*
Renée Dunan. *Baal*
J.-C. Dunyach. *The Night Orchid; The Thieves of Silence*
Henri Duvernois. *The Man Who Found Himself*
Achille Eyraud. *Voyage to Venus*
Henri Falk. *The Age of Lead*
Paul Féval. *Anne of the Isles; Knightshade; Revenants; Vampire City; The Vampire Countess; The Wandering Jew's Daughter*
Paul Féval, *fils. Felifax, the Tiger-Man*
Charles de Fieux. *Lamékis*
Arnould Galopin. *Doctor Omega; Doctor Omega and the Shadowmen* (anthology)
Judith Gautier. *Isoline and the Serpent-Flower*
Léon Gozlan. *The Vampire of the Val-de-Grâce*
G.L. Gick. *Harry Dickson and the Werewolf of Rutherford Grange*
Edmond Haraucourt. *Illusions of Immortality*
Nathalie Henneberg. *The Green Gods*
V. Hugo, P. Foucher & P. Meurice. *The Hunchback of Notre-Dame*
Romain d'Huissier. *Hexagon: Dark Matter*
Michel Jeury. *Chronolysis*
Gustave Kahn. *The Tale of Gold and Silence*
Gérard Klein. *The Mote in Time's Eye*

Fernand Kolney. *Love in 5000 Years*
Louis-Guillaume de La Follie. *The Unpretentious Philosopher*
Jean de La Hire. *Enter the Nyctalope; The Nyctalope on Mars; The Nyctalope vs. Lucifer; The Nyctalope Steps In; Night of the Nyctalope*
Etienne-Léon de Lamothe-Langon. *The Virgin Vampire*
André Laurie. *Spiridon*
Gabriel de Lautrec. *The Vengeance of the Oval Portrait*
Alain le Drimeur. *The Future City*
Georges Le Faure & Henri de Graffigny. *The Extraordinary Adventures of a Russian Scientist Across the Solar System* (2 vols.)
Gustave Le Rouge. *The Vampires of Mars; The Dominion of the World* (w/Gustave Guitton) (4 vols.)
Jules Lermina. *Mysteryville; Panic in Paris; To-Ho and the Gold Destroyers; The Secret of Zippelius*
Jean-Marc & Randy Lofficier. *Edgar Allan Poe on Mars; The Katrina Protocol; Pacifica; Robonocchio; Tales of the Shadowmen 1-9*
Xavier Mauméjean. *The League of Heroes*
Joseph Méry. *The Tower of Destiny*
Hippolyte Mettais. *The Year 5865*
Louise Michel. *The Human Microbes; The New World*
Tony Moilin. *Paris in the Year 2000*
José Moselli. *Illa's End*
John-Antoine Nau. *Enemy Force*
Marie Nizet. *Captain Vampire*
C. Nodier, A. Beraud & Toussaint-Merle. *Frankenstein*
Henri de Parville. *An Inhabitant of the Planet Mars*
Gaston de Pawlowski. *Journey to the Land of the 4th Dimension*
Georges Pellerin. *The World in 2000 Years*
Ernest Pérochon. *The Frenetic People*
Pierre Pelot. *The Child Who Walked on the Sky*
J. Polidori, C. Nodier, E. Scribe. *Lord Ruthven the Vampire*
P.-A. Ponson du Terrail. *The Vampire and the Devil's Son; The Immortal Woman*
Henri de Régnier. *A Surfeit of Mirrors*
Maurice Renard. *The Blue Peril; Doctor Lerne; The Doctored Man; A Man Among the Microbes; The Master of Light*
Jean Richepin. *The Wing; The Crazy Corner*
Albert Robida. *The Adventures of Saturnin Farandoul; The Clock of the Centuries; Chalet in the Sky; The Electric Life*
J.-H. Rosny Aîné. *Helgvor of the Blue River; The Givreuse Enigma; The Mysterious Force; The Navigators of Space; Vamireh; The World of the Variants; The Young Vampire*
Marcel Rouff. *Journey to the Inverted World*
Han Ryner. *The Superhumans*
Brian Stableford. *The New Faust at the Tragicomique; The Empire of the Necromancers (The Shadow of Frankenstein; Frankenstein and the Vampire Countess; Frankenstein in London); Sherlock Holmes & The Vampires of Eternity; The Stones of Camelot; The Wayward Muse.* (anthologist) *The Germans on Venus; News from the Moon; The Supreme Progress; The World Above the World; Nemoville; Investigations of the Future*

Jacques Spitz. *The Eye of Purgatory*
Kurt Steiner. *Ortog*
Eugène Thébault. *Radio-Terror*
C.-F. Tiphaigne de La Roche. *Amilec*
Théo Varlet. *The Golden Rock. The Xenobiotic Invasion; The Castaways of Eros; Timeslip Troopers* (w/André Blandin); *The Martian Epic* (w/Octave Joncquel)
Paul Vibert. *The Mysterious Fluid*
Villiers de l'Isle-Adam. *The Scaffold; The Vampire Soul*
Philippe Ward. *Artahe*
Philippe Ward & Sylvie Miller. *The Song of Montségur*

MYSTERIES & THRILLERS

M. Allain & P. Souvestre. *The Daughter of Fantômas*
A. Anicet-Bourgeois, Lucien Dabril. *Rocambole*
A. Bernède. *Belphegor*; *Judex* (w/Louis Feuillade); *The Return of Judex* (w/Louis Feuillade)
A. Bisson & G. Livet. *Nick Carter vs. Fantômas*
V. Darlay & H. de Gorsse. *Arsène Lupin vs. Sherlock Holmes: The Stage Play*
Séamas Duffy. *Sherlock Holmes in Paris*
Paul Féval. *Gentlemen of the Night; John Devil; The Black Coats ('Salem Street; The Invisible Weapon; The Parisian Jungle; The Companions of the Treasure; Heart of Steel; The Cadet Gang; The Sword-Swallower)*
Emile Gaboriau. *Monsieur Lecoq*
Goron & Emile Gautier. *Spawn of the Penitentiary*
Steve Leadley. *Sherlock Holmes: The Circle of Blood*
Maurice Leblanc. *Arsène Lupin vs. Countess Cagliostro; Arsène Lupin vs. Sherlock Holmes (The Blonde Phantom; The Hollow Needle); The Many Faces of Arsène Lupin*
Gaston Leroux. *Chéri-Bibi; The Phantom of the Opera; Rouletabille & the Mystery of the Yellow Room; Rouletabille at Krupp's*
Richard Marsh. *The Complete Adventures of Judith Lee*
William Patrick Maynard. *The Terror of Fu Manchu; The Destiny of Fu Manchu*
Frank J. Morlock. *Sherlock Holmes: The Grand Horizontals; Sherlock Holmes vs Jack the Ripper*
Antonin Reschal. *The Adventures of Miss Boston*
P. de Wattyne & Y. Walter. *Sherlock Holmes vs. Fantômas*
David White. *Fantômas in America*

SCREENPLAYS

Mike Baron. *The Iron Triangle*
Emma Bull & Will Shetterly. *Nightspeeder; War for the Oaks*
Gerry Conway & Roy Thomas. *Doc Dynamo*
Steve Englehart. *Majorca*
James Hudnall. *The Devastator*
Jean-Marc & Randy Lofficier. *Royal Flush*
J.-M. & R. Lofficier & Marc Agapit. *Despair*
J.-M. & R. Lofficier & Joël Houssin. *City*

Andrew Paquette. *Peripheral Vision*
Robert L. Robinson, Jr. *Judex*
R. Thomas, J. Hendler & L. Sprague de Camp. *Rivers of Time*

NON-FICTION

Stephen R. Bissette. *Blur 1-5. Green Mountain Cinema 1; Teen Angels*
Win Scott Eckert. *Crossovers* (2 vols.)
Jean-Marc & Randy Lofficier. *Shadowmen* (2 vols.)
Randy Lofficier. *Over Here*

ART BOOKS

Jean-Pierre Normand. *Science Fiction Illustrations*
Raven Okeefe. *Raven's L'il Critters; Rave's Faves*
Randy Lofficier & Raven Okeefe. *If Your Possum Go Daylight...*
Daniele Serra. *Illusions*

HEXAGON COMICS

Franco Frescura & Luciano Bernasconi. *Wampus*
Franco Frescura & Giorgio Trevisan. *CLASH*
L. Bernasconi, J.-M. Lofficier & Juan Roncagliolo Berger. *Phenix*
Claude Legrand, J.-M. Lofficier & L. Bernasconi. *Kabur*
Franco Oneta. *Zembla*
L. Buffolente, Lofficier & J.-J. Dzialowski. *Strangers: Homicron*
Danilo Grossi. *Strangers: Jaydee*
Claude Legrand & Luciano Bernasconi. *Strangers: Starlock*

www.ingramcontent.com/pod-product-compliance
Lightning Source LLC
Chambersburg PA
CBHW030356020726
47493CB00003B/844